"A Sparrow Alone"

~ a novel by Mim Eichmann

I am like a pelican of the wilderness:

I am like an owl of the desert.

I watch, and am as a sparrow alone

Upon the house top.

~ Psalm 102

Copyright 2019

Paperback ISBN: 978-0-9657113-9-5
eBook ISBN: 978-1-7344593-0-2

Library of Congress Control Number: 2019958020

Living Springs
Publishers

WWW.LivingSpringsPublishers.com

Cover model: Elizabeth Daniels
Cover photo: Stephen Charles Nicholson, SCN Photos, New York City – all rights reserved
Front cover design: Frank Wegloski, Maximum Printing, Downers Grove, IL
Map: US Geological Survey; Department of the Interior/USGS; public domain image

Dedicated to Alison, Brad and Todd

Author's Note

A stroll through a used bookstore one rainy afternoon many years ago led me to a journal written in 1890 by a divorcée named Emily French. Emily's detailed descriptions of her daily struggles enticed me into almost two decades of eagerly devouring women's journals, diaries and other writings of the late 19th Century. Set against the timeline of Cripple Creek, Colorado's gold mining bonanzas & busts, rampant prostitution of that era and the economic, social and political upheavals of that decade, the coming-of-age epic of my fictional heroine Hannah Owens began to slowly evolve, finally urging me to put pen to paper in 2017.

"A Sparrow Alone" revolves around the lives of Winfield Scott Stratton, multi-millionaire prospector, philanthropist and capitalist, and Pearl DeVere, madam of The Old Homestead brothel. As is often true with local characters, there is little verifiable accounting of either Pearl's or Stratton's personal lives. The best known biography of Stratton's life, *"Midas of the Rockies – biography of Winfield Scott Stratton, Croesus of Cripple Creek"* written by Frank Waters, was published in 1937, thirty-five years after Stratton's death. Mr. Waters acknowledged that his research, which was extremely thorough with regard to Stratton's progressive business dealings, was often forced to rely on popular hearsay regarding the man's personal habits. Like many brothel madams, practically all of Pearl DeVere's history is based on equally extravagant lore – not even a verifiable photo of the beautiful young woman remains. The combination of these two colorful characters gave me rather fertile ground upon which to sow my Hannah's story!

"A Sparrow Alone" is the first of two historical fiction novels

about Hannah Owens. An excerpt from the sequel, *"Muskrat Ramble,"* appears at the end of this book.

Acknowledgements

A huge round of applause to my publishers: Living Springs Publishers of Centennial, CO; my webmaster & administrative assistant, Todd Eichmann; cover photo model and one of my former Midwest Ballet Theatre soloists, Elizabeth Daniels; photographer Stephen Charles Nicholson, SCNPhotos, NYC; Frank Wegloski, Maximum Printing, Downers Grove, IL.

Many thanks to my diligent, supportive readers including: Kathy Carrus, Odette Cortopassi, Doug Lofstrom, Jan May, Eileen Morgan, Joyce Tumea, Diane Smith and Aileen Ziegler.

Additional thanks: Colorado Springs Pioneers Museum; Friends of the Colorado Springs Pioneers Museum; Richard White, longtime staff member at the Myron Stratton Home, Colorado Springs; Myron Stratton Home, Colorado Springs; "The Aunties": Rose Daniels, Nancy Milewski & Carol Raddatz; Bill White; Carol See; Mike Hurtt; Don Box along with many other friends and family members who have been encouraging throughout!

Contents

I. Hannah – 1890s Colorado
"Never lust after anything, Hannah, for it shall never come to be."

I sat quietly, staring at her face. Cold now. Immobile. But not much different from when it had seen life. Several faded brown tendrils curled against her weather-beaten cheek. Her cracked lips were a dark blue. She was lying on a sturdy wide plank bench that Jake, the Hughes' hired man, must have brought over in his wagon earlier this morning, for we had no chairs and only one rough-planked bench in our dugout.

Although the sun had been up for several hours, wisps of frosted steam still drifted through the poorly chinked walls. Mother had said that it would probably snow today. She said she could always feel it, way down deep in her bones. I knew that I should have started the fire while we waited for Father to return from the mill, but of course there was no dry wood in the box by the stove because Mother hadn't brought any in last night.

Thomas, Mary and I huddled together on the thin pallet of straw, stretched over the crude wood shelf we three shared as a bed. I thought of my mother hauling out our straw bedding last summer, pouring on the carbolic acid to rid the pallets of swarming carpets of black flies. Sometimes a tornado of flies would obliterate her gaunt, almost toothless face, enveloped by that large, faded sun bonnet she always wore. We would watch her long bony fingers shake the last acidic drops from a chipped milk bottle onto the ground in a methodic ritual. Motionless, she would stand watching, until the drowning flies' twitching had finally ceased. "Yer off ter a better place," she would mutter afterwards.

Father had insisted that we move out here three years ago,

saying we could live much cheaper deep in this canyon than out near the pass. He'd found an abandoned primitive sawmill alongside a rushing stream. Although he claimed to be a lumberman he didn't seem to know much Mother had snorted on more than one occasion. His squatter's claim included two starving oxen and a cow we'd found listlessly roaming the cabin site. Sometimes Mother sold milk, butter and her medicinal herb concoctions to families living in the canyon. This was usually our only money, for either the mill wheel would become unbalanced, or its gears would be in need of pitch, or the threadbare, patched harnesses would break yet again, or the oxen would simply have wandered off searching for better grazing possibilities whenever Father was ready to haul up the timber.

Near the cabin door oozed an oily pulp speckled with drowned black flies that Mother had emptied from the butter churn last night. She had put on a clean apron and her bonnet. Her clothes were twinkling with frost stars in the weak morning sun when I had discovered her. The hem of her thin, faded print dress had been tucked up into the waist, as though ready to begin the wash, her fingers still clenched around an empty, small dark-blue bottle. After savoring that last drop, she must have then relaxed against the cabin corner post, blank eyes looking peacefully up into that cold, clear night air. I could hear her voice: yer off ter a better place.

Last week our first snow had started falling as Mother was cooking supper. She was sitting on the rickety low stool, staring into the pan of blackening strips of venison. Smoke curls of the burning meat had swirled about her face, as her lips moved silently, almost like a prayer.

"Ma, you all right?" Thomas had whispered, but she had made no reply. Father, who had been sprawled asleep on the floor, suddenly jumped up and roughly grabbed her arm, shaking her so violently that she had fallen off of the stool onto her hands and knees. Slowly, while still on her knees, she had wadded a rag and pulled the charred skillet from the fire.

"Hannah, Mary, fetch some water," she murmured, and little Mary had run to fill the dipper. She rarely spoke any more. Sometimes she would nod or shake her head or just simply snort. Whether we were shoveling out the mud clods hailing from the cabin roof during unrelenting torrents of rain or sweeping up the ashes that spewed out from the gales that blustered down our chimney, making us all cough from another thick coating of the hideously sticky soot, Mother faced each harsh day with no emotion.

We heard Mrs. Hughes' wagon, undoubtedly driven by Jake, clamoring up through the uneven, rugged stone path. Abigail had said that her mother's back spasms kept her from handling any kind of reins, so she insisted upon always being driven in her wagon. Abigail pushed open the cabin door, while Jake looked to tie off the horse to anything reasonably sturdy so it wouldn't wander off through the scrub pines. Mrs. Hughes came in first, carrying a somewhat tattered piece of canvas, efficiently stamping dirty snow from her freshly blacked boots. I glanced down in shame at the pine-pitch encrusted rags wound up to our knees that served as Thomas' and my boots. At least Mary had on a small pair of dirty, torn moccasins. Jake pushed the ill-fitting log door closed as he and Abigail stepped inside.

Mrs. Hughes was a small, extremely prim woman, who seemed to be perpetually in mourning garb for one relative or another. She had a light sprinkling of freckles across her nose and a lovely porcelain complexion, both of which her daughter had most fortunately inherited, and a very slender physique, which rather unfortunately, she hadn't. Her thick brown hair, usually curled with expensive black lace or fake crushed violets was only slightly less perfect than usual despite the hazardous drive to our cabin.

"What happened?" she demanded loudly. Although she was looking directly at me I kept my eyes lowered.

Thomas glanced sideways and then shrugged. "Dunno," he replied. "She jes' dead, that's all me 'n Hannah an' Mary know."

"Where's your Pa?"

"He out makin' the box. He got some boards down at the mill. It was workin' last week. That grey mare, tho', she mostly lame missin' a nail, y'know. An' the harness, it broke agin."

"An' it's Sunday," I added quietly.

"Sunday?" Abigail broke in. "Yes, today *is* Sunday. Why's that make any difference, Hannah Owens?"

"Sundays 'er fer God," Thomas replied, unconsciously copying his father's singsong monotone. "Not fer workin'. No ma'am."

"Not fer workin', no ma'am," echoed Mary, shaking her head.

"But surely your Pa would go ahead an' bury your Ma on a Sunday! Jake says there's a blizzard just past the mountains! If you wait …" Abigail stammered, shuddering in horror.

She knew that the Owens were psalm-singers, and some kind of very strict crazy Puritans. Hannah's father had bragged that his grandfather's people were Scottish Covenanters to Abigail's mother one time. When Abigail had asked her mother later what that meant, Mrs. Hughes had snorted and said it wasn't the same as Catholics or Lutherans or Baptists or even godforsaken Presbyterians and had left it at that. But later when Abigail had asked me again, I had told her that early every morning we worshiped, read round a passage, and then Father wailed a hymn. And then we prayed some more. Before a fire could be lit or any food eaten or any other work commenced, we worshiped, read 'round a passage and Father wailed another hymn. And then we would pray. Every day. And all day on Sundays. *"None of the wicked shall understand; but the wise shall understand." – Daniel 12:10.*

Mrs. Hughes cut off two long locks of Mother's hair then quickly tucked the tattered canvas shroud around her.

"Here," she said, curling the hair up like a snake. "Hold onto this and put it somewhere safe, Hannah. I'll help you make it into a brooch for you and Mary."

I wound and unwound the long, brown curls on my finger, wondering what a brooch could possibly be but doubted that it would make my mother alive again. I thought back to a few months ago when Mother had wrapped the dead child she had just delivered in the tight cocoon of an old blanket that Mrs. Hughes had brought over. Mother had sat out in a nest of pine needles rocking that dead baby for hours, not even aware of the cold pelting rain. Father had wailed several psalms after digging the tiny grave. No one ever made a fire and we never ate that day. Or the next. And probably not the next.

There had been no money for a woman to come in and I was to help. But Mother's frantic shrieking had gone on for many days and my father had then just disappeared down to the mill to pray. Dr. Hughes, who had been out in Colorado Springs when Mother's pains had started, had told her to take a few drops from the blue bottle to help ease the pain if she needed it. He said he could tell that the baby was very big and she might have a rough time. But Father had spat out that the blue bottle was the devil's juice and that's what had actually killed the baby.

I wasn't sure how my mother had gotten the blue bottle for herself this time though. Maybe she'd stolen it when she had taken the butter down to the Hughes' home a few days ago. Dr. Hughes probably had tonics like that in a cupboard somewhere in their large house.

Looking up, I saw my father's long, dark frame in the doorway. He'd hauled the coffin on a makeshift sledge, the grey horse moving slowly with its loose shoe. Father brought the box

6

into the cabin and stated to no one in particular, "Have tuh bury 'er now. Snow comin' in o'er the mountain. Looks like a big 'un too." He shook his head in disbelief.

Dragging Mother from under her armpits off the bench, he pulled her into the wood box. Mrs. Hughes coughed and looked away, shielding Abigail's eyes as well. Then Thomas, Mary and I helped to lug the coffin, which bumped and scraped heavily, fastening it down on the sledge. It was only a short distance to the baby's grave, but I thought the sledge was going to be torn to splinters by the sharp rocks as the lank mare shuffled along. My father had simply carried the baby's small pine box to the site and none of us had realized that the trail's descent was so rough.

My father's wailings came from Psalm 69:

"Save me O God; for the waters are come in unto my soul.

I sink in deep mire, where there is no standing;

I am come into deep waters, where the floods overflow me.

I am weary of my crying: my throat is dried: mine eyes fail while I wait for my God.

They that hate me without a cause are more than the hairs of mine head:

they that would destroy me, being mine enemies wrongfully, are mighty:

then I restored that which I took not away.

O God, thou knowest my foolishness; and my sins are not hid from thee."

"Twenty-third would've been just fine," muttered Mrs. Hughes under her breath but almost certainly audible to my father. Abigail whispered that we should have gathered Queen Anne's lace along the way like they did in London. Her family had lived in London for two years which sounded to me like heaven. She went on to say that we could have each laid a stem in Mother's hands and said a silent prayer before the lid was nailed shut. I whispered back that it was winter and any wildflowers had been eaten by animals long ago. Oh, right, Abigail nodded. Thomas and Mary were breathing hard and I circled my arms around their waists as the hard clumps of dirt ricocheted hollowly on the coffin. As I watched it came to me that Mother would never again have to shovel the clods of dirt out of our cabin. That would now be my job alone I guessed since Mary was far too little. We quickly ringed the grave with the few flattened stones we could find, tamped sideways, and added a crude, whittled cross, same as the baby's, just as the winds from the incoming blizzard began to howl down throughout the canyon.

II. Colorado Springs

Within a few weeks Mrs. Hughes had convinced my father that he couldn't possibly look after all three of us. He was constantly praying and wailing out psalms but nothing much else seemed to be happening. There was never any food unless Jake, sometimes accompanied by Abigail, brought a few items out to us. The last of the straggling potatoes and onions from our meager garden went into my ever-thinning attempts at soup. The only dried beef slab hanging in our shed was green when we hacked into it and obviously poisonous. Winter's furious grip tightened each day; had we stayed in that dugout, we would all have either starved or frozen to death within another week.

The Hughes took me on to train "in service" as Mrs. Hughes claimed it was known in Europe. They had attempted to train a quadroon girl and then a Cajun girl, both of whom had run away when they had lived in New Orleans, and none of those gaudy London girls had been even remotely respectable, shivered Mrs. Hughes in detestable memory. She had some small hopes she remarked candidly that I might at least be of somewhat better caliber and learning a useful trade was the best I could hope for obviously. Abigail had told me that they had been in London because Dr. Hughes was trying to train other doctors to recognize the difference between yellow fever and malaria, and the treatment ascribed to each disease.

"A rising temperature means that it's yellow fever, and if it's malaria, there's no fever as such," she had informed me one afternoon. "Also, malaria should be treated with quinine – do you know what that is?" to which I had shaken my head. "Actually, I don't either," she admitted. "Anyway, so many doctors confuse the two," Abigail had said in amazement, "that they were actually killing their own patients all the time! My daddy told them what they were supposed to do," she had concluded with a smile. I had found her father's work truly fascinating especially when compared to my own father's meager industry that accomplished little except wailing psalms for hours on end.

However, after a violent cholera outbreak, the doctor's own health had begun to rapidly deteriorate, forcing the family to abandon London and seek the rarefied air and sulfur springs offered in the mountains of Colorado. Their house in Colorado Springs was almost finished and weather permitting, they would be moving there soon. Mrs. Hughes stated that the doctor would then be doing the mineral baths at Manitou Springs as well. The filthy air and tainted water in London had probably been making them all sick said Abigail echoing her mother.

My sister Mary was sent to live with my uncle's family out in Cleveland. They had six children of their own and were crowded into a tiny apartment over the small dry goods store that my mother's brother owned. In the letter answering Mrs. Hughes' query my uncle said they would take the youngest of us since that one would undoubtedly eat less. Jake, Abigail and I drove Mary in the wagon down to catch the stagecoach late in the afternoon, ice needles stinging the air around us. The coach driver, well warmed having consumed about two-thirds of his bottle of whiskey, assured us he would get her to the Denver & Rio Grande by the next morning. The last glimpse I ever had of my tiny sister, her dark eyes glistening with tears, she was seated between two evil-smelling old men inside the battered coach.

My father announced that he would now start prospecting for gold and silver once again. That was his real vocation he asserted, especially since his disparaging wife could no longer discourage him, he remarked. And, since Thomas was getting stronger, he would be able to work alongside as well. There were new rumors of sylvanite veins snaking thickly through Battle Mountain in Cripple Creek and possibly, a new area of claim sites, called Victor, just a couple miles from Cripple Creek. They could get work as muckers for other miners until they had enough money to try to grubstake out on their own.

When we arrived in Colorado Springs during a brief mid-January thaw, Mrs. Hughes found that their house was far from any remote state of completion. The workers and contractor had seemingly vanished along with the original architectural plans. This was not at all unusual according to gossip. We all lived in a cramped part of the kitchen while new plans were being drawn up by one of the Springs' best known architects, Winfield Scott Stratton. Apparently, Stratton was in the area only briefly while looking to refinance his grubstaking up near Cripple Creek. He had been working several claims for well over a decade, sinking one fortune after another into the ground, and talked about having had a dream of finding a veritable "bowl of gold" in Battle Mountain. Dr. Hughes said Mr. Stratton was way too brilliant a man to be so passionately foolish regarding such an absolutely worthless effort.

Dr. Hughes started helping at the sanitarium in Colorado Springs almost immediately, even though his wife admonished him that he was supposed to be curing himself, not continuing to squander his health for these worthless souls appearing in droves around them. But he did what he could to ease the final breath of hundreds of these long-suffering men, many of whom he shockingly discovered had been miners since as young as age eight.

Mrs. Hughes took it upon herself immediately to get her house completed even before Stratton's plans were finalized. The construction workers she hired were, "thankfully non-union supporting," she sighed, even though most of them were also consumptives trying to find any kind of work to extend their stay in the rarefied air. Nonetheless, the work went far too slowly for her. I can still see her tapping the toe of her perfectly blacked boot, arms tightly crossed, shaking her head while a foreman tried to reason with her regarding a latest setback. "I'm sorry, Mr. Jones (or Mr. Culver or Mr. Sully), that simply will not do," I heard her say time and again. At least the lumber mill on the outskirts of town was supplying her with excellent wood, quite inexpensively and on time. I couldn't begin to imagine my father trying to keep up with her incessant demands!

Also in Mrs. Hughes opinion, few of the wealthier families in the area were even remotely close to her station in life since almost all were brazenly new money, primarily resulting from mining speculations. The Palmers, Baxters, McAllisters and Wheldons, along with a handful of British families from the better areas of London, simply by their sheer scope of fortunes were at least tolerable. I learned from Abigail that Colorado Springs was often referred to as Little London with regard to its "cultural advantages" even though neither of us knew exactly what that meant.

Mrs. Hughes would mutter under her breath *ignis fatuus* when commenting on some foolish scheme, imprudent act or meaningless twaddle brought about by her neighbors or the ruefully inadequate shopkeepers in town. Her lengthy tirades about the proprietors or the contents of the dry goods stores, ("produced by decidedly inferior mills"), along with the furniture store which carried glassware, lamps, tin ware and wooden hollow-ware along with new stoves ("none of which were worth so much as a half penny"), the local apothecary stores ("thumb on the scale" or "those idiots can't read the simplest prescription") and the confectionery shop ("I can't believe they actually intend to sell this tasteless stuff as candy!") became quite well known throughout the town.

She railed at one of the blacksmiths for days when his repair of a nail for her horse's shoe was defective causing her horse to stumble almost tossing her. The blacksmith, not one to take abuse from any townswoman, claimed that if she had been a better horsewoman she wouldn't have suffered such panic. Then there was the small laundry that was owned by several Chinese families and used extensively by the three large hotels, the sanitarium, several boarding houses and many of the wealthier families in the area. At least they had the good fortune not to comprehend her habitual rants over blue bleach spots or scorched-in wrinkles.

Quite surprisingly, she hit it off instantly with one of the dressmakers in the area, a slender, attractive young woman named Mrs. DeVere, who seemed very eager to please the wealthier ladies of the town. No mention was ever made of a Mr. DeVere and more than likely he had actually never existed I concluded later. She lived alone in a small, rather airless, immaculate apartment over the druggist's shop. "At least someone understands quality," Mrs. Hughes would sigh as she examined the fine stitching along a gusset or a taut, perfectly turned and crisply pressed facing, or the intricate tatting at a sleeve or neckline. Remarkably, Mrs. DeVere could also stitch and trim hats, a service she continued to provide to her better patrons even after a milliner's shop ("did you see how unevenly that beading came together at the brim? And those ghastly women call themselves milliners!") had opened shortly after our arrival.

Once her home was almost finished Mrs. Hughes quickly set about getting her trunks and furniture delivered attempting to convey some fractional appearance of order to her household. Her day was always very organized, very exact and utterly systematic. Dusting the figurines on the mantle over the hearth in the sitting room for example was one of my many jobs to be done each Thursday. The sitting room fireplace, definitely the dirtiest one to maintain on the main floor, spewed an extraordinary amount of soot for a new fireplace. She would closely inspect all of her treasured statues to ascertain that I had delved into every tiny crevice on each ornate figurine as well as having thoroughly dusted the decidedly tawdry Minerva perched atop her beloved ormolu clock that chimed annoyingly every 15 minutes.

Her receiving day was Friday which explained why she wanted the sitting room cleaned on Thursday. She grumbled about it for months after we moved to Colorado Springs. Friday was the only day available that she might receive callers even though she detested most of the wives with whom she was forced to socialize. But she called on them, regardless, on Tuesdays. On alternating Wednesdays and Thursdays, there was either her Chautauqua Circle meeting or her garden club, and on Mondays she visited her dressmaker and attended to other small shopping needs.

So, that left Friday afternoons. Friday was also the only day the private teacher for Abigail's piano and singing lessons could be scheduled since he was already booked Monday through Thursday. This meant I had to sit in during her lessons since Mrs. Hughes was obviously occupied with her callers and it would not do for Abigail to be alone with Mr. Parker under any circumstances. Also, it meant that the girl was not available to receive guests alongside her mother, although they usually paid calls together when possible. Well, she would look fondly at Abigail, she would do her best to bring up her daughter as correctly as humanly possible, despite these pernicious, albeit unintentional breaches in etiquette.

Some of my other duties included helping the Hughes' cook, Zuma, a warm, dark-skinned woman whose infectious laugh absolutely boomed out all over the house. Zuma claimed to be of

African, French Creole or Digger Indian descent, or sometimes all three. Occasionally she would talk to herself in a language that no one understood and Jake claimed that she was just talking a bunch of nonsense to confuse the rest of us. I would shell peas or snap beans or stir a large kettle of soup while she tended to the more daunting task of accommodating Mrs. Hughes' capricious dietary expectations. Feeding two dozen brown chickens, hunting about the dark hutch to collect eggs, along with milking several sorry-looking spotted cows and churning the cream to butter were also part of my long day. Every few days when Zuma baked pies, she would roll the extra dough into what she called pie wheels, liberally sprinkled with brown sugar and cinnamon, adding a dash of ground nuts if they were on hand. "Shhhh," she'd murmur, quietly handing me two or three of the still-warm treats, her dark eyes twinkling. "Dis be fo' dat l'il chile who work so hard."

There was a new state mandate requiring that all children under the age of 14 attend school although it was only lightly reinforced. I had never had any actual schooling, although I did know my letters and could write my name at least. Abigail had always either attended school or worked with a tutor wherever her family had lived. She had already been attending the district school for several weeks while I was still working to get the household organized.

I arrived at the two room schoolhouse on the day of the monthly examinations and sat quietly looking through a sea of meaningless words on the well-worn pages of something called the McGuffy Reader. The teacher, Miss Weldon, a shoestring relative of the once-prominent Weldon family, had a nose like a pale old carrot, topped by a large, discolored pince-nez. Glaring over her pince-nez she gathered the examinations from all of the students, tut-tutting at my blank page in disgust. When the percentages for the exams were announced in the *Colorado*

Springs Gazette the following week, my score was obviously a "0," as I overheard Mrs. Hughes chuckle to Abigail over their tea. However, she was very alarmed that Abigail's percentage scores were quite low as well, although she had received an accolade for perfect deportment, along with being present every day. Unfortunately, so had the dreadful Baxter girls, along with no tardies. (Abigail had accumulated two tardies.) And even more vexing, Penelope Baxter had received the most credits in spelling that month as well. Mrs. Hughes felt that the Baxter girls were Abigail's biggest rivals in the district. Their father was a well-decorated, retired Union general and a managing partner of the Denver and Rio Grande railroad. The twins were most definitely serious competition from the standpoint of intelligence, felicity, affluence and certainly their exquisite looks. For despite her mother's best intentions, Abigail was indeed exceedingly dull company, not especially attractive and not at all quick-witted.

Miss Weldon started me in the easiest reader with the youngest children, two very fidgety seven-year-old boys, both named Evan. Embarrassed, I studied hard at home whenever possible and worked myself into the text just two levels below Abigail's by the end of the Spring term. When I had to sit in during Abigail's voice lessons I would memorize the words as I listened to her sing and would afterwards quietly peek into the songbooks to see how the more difficult words were spelled. Then I would quietly sing the tunes to myself when feeding the clucking chickens or churning the butter, occasionally taking a stolen moment to scratch out a difficult word or two in the dirt. Sometimes I would sing alongside Zuma, who also taught me some Creole songs while we were dusting or washing dishes.

On the last day of the term I learned that the Baxter girls had sent me an invitation to attend their birthday party. I was truly surprised and more than a little excited since I had never been to anyone's birthday party. Mrs. Hughes had opened the invitation while she and Abigail were having their tea and scoffed at those girls wanting to include a hired girl at their gathering. It certainly showed a lack of good breeding in her estimate. Abigail had carefully spoken up on my behalf saying that we all usually took our noon meal together in the schoolroom and were, well, sort of chums.

"Hmph," she said stiffly. "I suppose if Mrs. Baxter can overlook Hannah's mother."

"Hannah's mother?" whispered Abigail trying not to look in my direction, "she's dead, Mam, remember?"

"No, no, you foolish girl! And don't call me 'Mam,' I've told you again and again," Mrs. Hughes replied sternly, her voice rising. "I'm quite aware that her mother is dead you silly girl. It's how she passed that's relevant."

I felt my face beginning to burn as I closed the parlor tea caddy. With my eyes on the floor I started out of the room, fingers kneading my apron, not wanting to hear any more. Mrs. Hughes folded her arms, turning her head slightly towards me.

"Her mother obviously took her own life, my dear," stated Mrs. Hughes in her most clipped voice. "Supposedly she was so distraught after her baby died at birth, probably from taking an overdose of that laudanum, which she had been taking for months I might add. Mrs. Owens could no longer show her face among the living. I definitely saw her going down," she concluded with one of her stiff little shoulder shrugs I had already grown to detest.

I stumbled out of the parlor into the hallway, grabbing a small blanket. A stabbing pain arose deep in my chest. I felt Zuma's pie wheels rising in my throat and began to run, choking with hoarse convulsive sobs. Somehow I found my way outside into the deeply shadowed garden. She was right of course. I had tried not to think about those awful days when the baby was born. The blue bottle. My mother staring vacantly into the fire those last few weeks before she had died. She had been stealing the laudanum from Dr. Hughes all along. I knew what was said of nasty women who relied on chloral. They were considered worse than men who were alcoholics. The girls at school snickered about low women lying about in their drug fogs. I had always kept silent but now realized that they were undoubtedly laughing at me the entire time.

As I continued running I thought of little Mary, my father and my brother Thomas. Mrs. Hughes claimed that she had written them and that there had been no replies. I didn't really trust that she had even bothered. Dr. Hughes had mentioned reading in *The Courier* that there was another smallpox epidemic recently in Cleveland. Was Mary even still alive? And what about Thomas? Or my father? Were they both dead in some mine cave-in in Cripple Creek that I would never hear about? Or were they even in Cripple Creek? Maybe they had gone on to Leadville or Central City or Blackhawk or had given up on Colorado completely and had headed out to the San Juans. The Hughes' household staff talked nonstop about gold miners constantly migrating from district to district, going bust with disappointment after disappointment. My chest hurt so much from running and crying that I had to stop, bending over at my waist, certain I was going to retch.

The sickening plop that only a snake makes stifled my sobs. A black snake rippled only a few yards away, its darkly coiling body glistening in the dusky filtered light. Shaking, I wrapped the blanket tighter around my shoulders and quietly stepped backwards trying not to snap any twigs, away from the snake. Once I had backed up far enough I didn't have the strength to start running again. I had nowhere to run anyway. But I just couldn't return to the house and Mrs. Hughes' cruel tongue right now. I continued along the cold, dark streets, tripping several times in the deeper ruts. As I came closer to town I ducked behind a row of buildings along the boards, hoping not to meet up with any more snakes. Finally I stopped and sat down on an upturned crate.

Despite trying to push Mrs. Hughes from my thoughts she remained. I could envision visiting day conversations with the Baxters, Palmers or McAllisters:

"It's so good of you and your husband to have taken that poor little girl in and given her some kind of training, Margaret. Why, where on earth would the child be otherwise?"

"Well, yes. It was indeed a very tough decision you know. I'm sure you've heard all about her mother..." Mrs. Hughes would begin, then selecting a tiny, delicately sugared cake to complement her afternoon tea.

"No, actually I don't know anything. Just that she had died several months ago."

"Well ... yes," and then she would sigh, her eyes downcast, setting her cup firmly back upon the gold-rimmed saucer, her voice completely devoid of emotion. I put my fingers in my ears, scrunching my eyes tightly, but her image and irritating voice refused to evaporate. She's just like that snake, I thought. Cunning. Cold. Rabid. Vicious. Ready to strike even when not attacked, just randomly sinking her fangs into her victims. My mother had been a desolate, exhausted shell of a woman, who had absolutely nothing. Why should Mrs. Hughes have hated her?

I slowly let the pressure off of my ears only to hear voices. Quietly easing myself down from the crate I pulled further back into the deep shadows. The man's voice was Dr. Hughes'. The woman sounded quite familiar too, but I couldn't place her at first. Then it came to me. Of course. I was behind Mrs. Hughes' dressmaker's apartment. She must be ill. Selfishly I hoped she had not been so ill as to have been impeded from mending the heavy plaid cloak I was supposed to be picking up tomorrow. But as they moved slightly out of the doorway, still enveloped in semi darkness, I realized that his arms were around her. He stopped, lifting her chin and lightly kissed her mouth, then her forehead, tenderly brushing a long reddish curl from her cheek.

"Pearl, Pearl," he was saying gently. "This will be so easy for you. You'll be a rich woman within just a few months. Don't worry. Please my dear, don't worry." He took her hands and kissed both palms rubbing them in the cool evening air and then pressing them together to his chest. "Just think. No more hems. No more hat brims. No more having to alter last year's patterns to derive this year's. You could special order your own gowns from Paris. Anything you want. In any color. Silver, icy white, shimmering gold ... shell pink!"

"Albert my darling, you make this all sound so simple! I'm still rather concerned," she stammered, looking up at him. Her exquisitely pale face was surrounded by a cascade of thick sepia curls that danced in the fading light.

"Win Stratton is your architect. With all of this prospecting nonsense he's gotten himself into he's borrowed 'til doomsday and in hock to everybody – especially me. He's in debt to me practically a hundred percent to build your house! Even though you haven't seen the plans as yet, it's beautiful. Trust me. Win's a very good carpenter as well. Learned from his father. He built the magnificent McAllister house, you know. Best house around here without a doubt. He had to do some redesigning on my place when those fool builders pulled a bunk. Too bad my damned wife was too bullheaded to hire him in the first place. I'll talk to Win about getting in some of those marble fireplaces like he put in the McAllister place, by the way. I know you really love those," he added.

"That's very unkind about your wife," replied Mrs. DeVere, gently removing her hands from his. "You shouldn't say such vile things about her. She can be quite obstinate I'll agree, but she strikes me as a reasonably well-informed woman. Not all the women in this place are you know."

"Hah!" he laughed. "Reasonable? Hardly! And I'm sure you're going to tell me that the two of you are bosom buddies, sharing the latest mince pie recipes you found in Godey's."

"Godey's?" she laughed with a charming lilt. "Albert, Godey's hasn't been published since 1878! Although I still use some of their dress patterns occasionally, I confess. Some basic styles never change..."

"Oh, stop teasing me, Pearl!" he hugged her tightly, smiling. "Just listen. You can have two no, how about, *three* lavish crystal chandeliers. I know of a shop back in London. Extraordinary workmanship. Make all of those miners' wives pea green jealous lighting those smoky coal oil lamps each night trying to brighten up their dark little cabins and dugouts. And we'll build a dining hall better than any restaurant in New York City, London and Paris combined. The best cuisine anywhere. Elegant furnishings and quality, luxuriously thick Persian rugs your guests will absolutely sink into. A piano in the parlor as well as a baby grand in the dining hall. The best entertainment nightly. None of that tawdry gilded cage crap. And imported wallpaper from Europe. Handpainted wallpaper, Pearl!"

She shook her head gently, her loosened hair falling further down the back of her heavy woven shawl, and looked up at him. He kissed her gently on the top of her head. I noticed that they were almost exactly the same height; she had to tilt her head forward very slightly to receive his kiss.

"I should go my dearest. You know that I'm right. You know it's what's right for us both. You will only hire the most beautiful, intelligent, but very experienced young women. No whores. Courtesans, well-read, delightfully capable ladies, just like the mistresses of old for the nobility in Europe. You'll have the most exclusive parlor anywhere in Colorado. Hell, anywhere in the world! And in Cripple Creek, no one is going to order the place closed down on some ridiculous temperance whim like that nonsense out in Kansas. There are other places of course, all along Myers Avenue as you know, but yours is without a doubt going to be absolutely exclusive in reputation. I think we should call it The Old Homestead – do you like that name? We'll make a fortune together. And then sell it for a fortune and move on. We'll be together for the rest of our lives whether she's willing to give me a divorce or not. We'll head south. Back down to New Orleans or wherever you wish. As long as we can live as we choose and have the wealth we both desire."

He kissed her again then pulled slightly away.

"Sleep sweetly, my beautiful one," he said quietly, with his hands on her shoulders.

"Yes, my darling Albert," she replied, almost dreamily. "Yes."

III. Pearl De Vere

The next morning was grey with a cold, driving rain. Jake brought round the carriage early and helped the three of us over large, dimpling puddles as we stepped up into it. Abigail tripped over her sodden skirt and landed on her hands and knees on the carriage floor. Mrs. Hughes muttered something about her being hopelessly clumsy as Jake and I tried to help her regain her footing. Since it was discovered that none of Abigail's good dresses fit any longer and she needed one immediately for the Baxter girls' party next week, we were all headed to DeVere Gowns that dreary morning.

As we emerged from the carriage, Jake handed Mrs. Hughes and Abigail umbrellas, but with the slanting torrent, we all became quite equally soaked. Mrs. DeVere answered the door, her coppery brown hair pinned back quite severely in its usual prim bun, obviously surprised to see all of us profusely dripping on her doorstep.

"Come in, come in," she said hastily. "You're all soaked through! My goodness!"

"Yes," replied Mrs. Hughes, marching past her, vigorously shaking out the rain from her umbrella on the worn, entry rag rug. "I know we are only scheduled for a picking up today, but Abigail needs a new dress immediately. I'm sure as one of your best customers you can oblige me this," she finished briskly.

"Oh yes, well of course!" replied the dressmaker. "If you'll only just warm yourselves in front of the parlor fire while I finish another fitting. We were almost finished actually," she stammered. "And I was just about to put on some tea. I have some very good Darjeeling."

"Tea sounds just delightful," sighed Mrs. Hughes. "Try not to be too long about it."

As Mrs. DeVere returned to her other customer, Mrs. Hughes removed her soggy gloves and she and Abigail warmed their hands above the iron grating. On my knees, I tried in vain to work some of the mud from the hem of Abigail's hopelessly soiled, torn dress. As I moved around her, I saw something glinting, almost completely hidden beneath the fringe of the parlor rug near my right knee. Mrs. Hughes commenced loudly berating the lack of warmth from Mrs. DeVere's hearth as I quietly picked up a gold pocket watch.

It was Dr. Hughes'. I recognized the scrawled insignia on the cover immediately. My heart racing, I quickly slipped it into my sodden apron pocket hoping it wouldn't become tarnished or the works ruined by the dampness.

"She certainly has a lot of pretty figurines," remarked Abigail looking at two highly polished round tables near the window. "That one looks a lot like the one Father got for you, doesn't it? The one he brought you from Germany?"

"I'm certain that a dressmaker wouldn't presume to have anything quite that expensive. You must be wary of glittery appearances. These are undoubtedly just some cheap, imitative trinkets she can afford or perhaps things of her mother's or some other long departed relative," Mrs. Hughes remarked glibly. "I do wish she would hurry up with that tea. I'm quite uncomfortably chilled yet."

I stood up. The pocket watch weighed like an anvil in my apron.

"I'm sorry, ma'am. That's the best I can do with the mud," I stammered. "It's …very ground in."

"Um, yes, quite," Mrs. Hughes sighed through pursed lips, raising a disapproving eyebrow as she glanced down at my paltry cleaning attempt. "You can attend to it in earnest as soon as we return home. Since it's getting a bit tight on Abigail you would probably be getting it soon anyway. So if it's somewhat soiled..." her voice trailed off with a shrug.

Mrs. DeVere moved into the front entry with her other client, the short, rather buxom, newly remarried Mrs. Speyer. Mrs. Speyer had not spent nearly the requisite period of time in mourning the sudden death of Mr. Culver last year before she had married Mr. Speyer, in Mrs. Hughes' considered opinion. Worse still, the late Mr. Culver and Mr. Speyer had been business partners and very successful entrepreneurs in their banking establishments. It seemed like just one more well-timed business deal in Mrs. Hughes' mind even though Dr. Hughes had scoffed at her attitude telling her she was being just an old-fashioned busybody. Even worse, Mrs. Hughes' had concluded, Mr. Speyer was actually eight years younger than his new wife, an unheard of circumstance.

"Ah, my very dearest Margaret!" exclaimed the bouncy Mrs. Speyer. "Such a delight to see you! Horrid weather out today though don't you agree? I'm still shaking through with cold but I haven't time to stay for Mrs. DeVere's lovely offer of Darjeeling."

"Pity to be sure," Mrs. Hughes smiled thinly, giving one of her small, irritating shrugs.

"Well, perhaps we shall be able to talk another time," she bubbled as she wrapped her heavy shawl about herself, then winding several long colorful scarves around her neck and over her hair and hat. "You know I'm most interested in your Chautauqua's discussions to raise monies for adding onto the library. We, that is, Mr. Speyer and myself, might have some good ideas for you."

"Yes, well, you know when our meetings are, Elizabeth. Please feel free to join us at any time," Mrs. Hughes replied with a placid smile seemingly frozen on her face.

As Mrs. Speyer left a wild gust of wind swept into the small entry. Mrs. DeVere quickly shut the door and brought the tea tray into the parlor. After setting it on the small tea trolley she hurriedly began to arrange cups in saucers, setting spoons into sugar and milk. I noticed that one long curl had escaped its tight coif and trailed unnoticed almost halfway down her back, a beautiful copper wire dazzling in the firelight. She seemed very nervous, slightly spilling Abigail's tea after pouring it, and somewhat flushed.

The dress agreed upon was only slightly different from what might have been a school uniform and I truly felt sorry for Abigail. Mrs. Hughes wanted a high-necked, white Holland shirtwaist with a long dark grey silk skirt and whale-boned corseting. Abigail had detested this style since her inevitable graduation from the youthful freedom of shorter skirts and loosened hair within the last year. Mrs. Hughes also desired an additional puff over sleeve, scrunched ruffles or larger flounces over the bodice similar to the style typically worn by the Baxter girls. I sensed that Abigail cringed at the thought of such additions, but of course would wear anything her mother thought appropriate with little complaint. Mrs. Hughes had also become recently enamored with a tight top knot in a magazine picture which she insisted her daughter begin to emulate every day, thinking the style would make her thin straight hair look fuller around her plump face. Laura and Carrie, the other two Hughes' maids, thought it looked as though she had a broomstick poking out of her head and snickered that the hairdo had gone out of style at least a decade ago.

As measurement, tailoring variations and embellishments were being discussed I lightly fingered the pocket watch, my mind racing back to the scene from the previous evening. Did Dr. Hughes really intend to abandon Mrs. Hughes? I had never seen him gently caressing her shoulders or touching her face like he had Mrs. DeVere's last night. And what of Mrs. DeVere's husband? Of course, there was always the possibility that he was dead. Or that Mrs. DeVere was already divorced and had simply moved here with very good references and no mention of a divorce since a divorced woman would never obtain the patronage of wealthy married women. Better to have a husband about whom little or nothing was ever mentioned, dead or alive!

I was certain that Mrs. Hughes felt completely secure within her marriage. That whatever dalliances her husband might engage in could never possibly upend the sanctity of her role as a gentleman's wife and the mother of his only child. Any time her small sleek barouche chanced upon the carriages of the several divorced women who lived boldly in the town she would avert her eyes and order Abigail to do the same. Such women should not be allowed on the streets at the same time as decent ones, regardless of the circumstances provoking their current station in Mrs. Hughes' considered opinion. A divorced woman was still a notch above a prostitute, to be sure, but not a particularly large notch. The other wealthy women in her society's set completely agreed with her.

While Mrs. DeVere was refilling Abigail's cup I glanced at the figurines behind her on the table. They did look very much like the one Dr. Hughes had brought back from his trip to Germany. A series of boring lectures discussing possible treatments and also preventions for smallpox, influenza and diphtheria he had convinced his wife. Certainly he couldn't presume to drag her along on such a boring trek with absolutely zero time for sightseeing or socializing. Mrs. Hughes had readily agreed. He could easily have given the statues to both women so that was one possibility. Or had Mrs. DeVere traveled with him? I remembered that her shop had been closed for several weeks a few months ago while she had supposedly been visiting relatives out East but I had no idea if the times lined up.

"Hannah, you're being very rude staring at Mrs. De Vere," Mrs. Hughes scolded.

"I'm so sorry, ma'am," I faltered.

Mrs. DeVere smiled easily at me, offering advice on the cleaning of Abigail's soiled garment. Her reddish-brown hair framed her porcelain features. I suddenly realized that I thought she was truly the most beautiful woman I had ever seen in my life. One of the gas lamps then sputtered in obvious need of attention.

"Well, we have yet another errand to attend to and the rain seems to have let up slightly," said Mrs. Hughes, standing abruptly, leaving the requisite half inch of tea in her cup. "You are certain that you will be finished by next weekend?"

"Yes, ma'am," replied Mrs. DeVere. "I can begin the pattern alterations by tomorrow I'm quite certain."

"Very good, very good. Hannah, go see that Jake is ready with the rig."

IV. Quarantine

The incessant, cold driving rain continued for the next several days. All of the roads became mired with mud and were almost completely impassable. Only those who absolutely needed to travel did so and were thwarted by breaking axles or their horses' unsure footing if they attempted any mode of carriage conveyance. Riding on horseback was only a very slightly improved alternative.

Since errands, outdoor activities and any other planned excursions were not feasible, my ability to return the watch to Dr. Hughes' jewelry cache met with several abandoned attempts simply because everyone was at home. Neither his nor Mrs. Hughes' bedrooms were normally entrusted to my flimsy cleaning efforts. Their living quarters were in an upstairs wing quite removed from Abigail's rooms offering me no ordinary reason to enter them. Occasionally Mrs. Hughes would summon me to her writing desk to post a letter or various other small demands. But no one was expecting to send or receive any messages at present. Even after the rain would cease, it would be at least two or three days before any reasonable travel might resume.

Finally one evening while the two upstairs servants were in the kitchen, Mrs. Hughes and Abigail were looking over some old letters in the parlor and Dr. Hughes was in the drawing room, I crept quietly up the dark back stairs. Afraid that someone would discover the watch in my possession, I had hidden it behind a small loosened piece of molding just above the fifth step. Since only the house staff used these back steps the carpentry was not to Mrs. Hughes exacting standards, hence the ragged bit of wood.

I knew that Dr. Hughes' bedroom was the farthest from either set of stairs and moved slowly down the deserted hallway. A locked dark-tooled leather cache sat atop his burled walnut chest of drawers. I looked around wildly for some place to leave the watch as though it were forgotten or dropped, an attempt at feigning hurried forgetfulness on the doctor's part. Suddenly I realized that he was standing in the dark doorway quietly watching me.

"You know, this doesn't look very good, Hannah," he said, moving into the light of my candle. He grasped the watch by the chain flipping it into his hand. "Where did you find this?"

"In the...in the upstairs parlor, sir," I stammered. "When I was dusting the mantle today I found it next to the clock, sir."

A slow, but curiously sweet half smile crept over his face and he lightly scratched his mustache. "Hmm, I see," he replied, nodding his head very slowly. "If so then why didn't you just return it to me earlier this evening?"

"I thought it might look as though I had stolen it."

"And of course now, it doesn't look like that at all, does it?" he said rather humorously. "Odd too, you know. I don't believe I've even had cause to be in that parlor for at least the last week or so. And the watch disappeared even a bit before that. In fact, I'm quite certain it must have fallen out when I had removed my coat while treating one of my patients somewhere during that time."

I continued to stare at the glinting watch in his hands to avoid looking up at his face.

"There must be some better explanation," he ventured. "Were you planning on selling it and thought better of the idea?"

I shook my head quickly, looking up at him. "Oh, no sir!" I replied, horrified. "I ... I found it in ... Mrs. DeVere's parlor, in the fringe of her rug, sir."

"And I had to attend to Mrs. DeVere a little over a week ago. She was having some trouble with her back as I recall. But why would you not simply have returned it? Come now girl, that makes utterly no sense whatsoever."

I swallowed. No words began to form that might possibly help me and I just stared dumbly at his hands. He snapped open the case, then rather absentmindedly wound the watch for a few seconds, and then shut it once again, nestling it deep in his vest pocket. He then turned his gaze at me again.

"I won't mention this occurrence to Mrs. Hughes," he continued, "but I suggest you return items to their rightful owners more quickly to avoid any suspicion. You may go."

"Thank you, sir, thank you. I don't know what I was thinking," I somehow stammered, briskly trying to move past him into the hall.

"Hannah," he called softly after I had taken several steps. I turned slowly to face him, sweat trickling down my back. His face was almost in complete shadow.

"Whatever it is that you know, or let us say, that you think you know, you would be best to forget right now," he said quietly. "Am I making myself clear?"

"Yes sir," I stammered, looking at my flickering candle. "Perfectly, sir."

He turned up the Carcel lamp on the hall table and carried it into his bedroom, quietly shutting the door.

Over the next several days a violent outbreak of diphtheria struck the town. Rumor said it was brought in by an infected miner who had died in one of the squalid hotels on the city's outskirts. Quarantine signs appeared immediately on the doors of almost every house in the poorer sections of the district. The Baxter household was the first of the wealthier families to be hit, Penelope Baxter the first fatality. She died early on the morning of her fourteenth birthday and her twin sister Ella died that evening. They were laid out in the Baxter parlor in their identical creamy white dresses that had been intended for their birthday party. The undertaker's pictures of the girls were all any of us ever saw. In a surprising gesture of good faith, Mrs. Hughes had requested that Zuma bake a small mince pie with strict instructions to Carrie that she deliver it to the Baxter household but leave it on the outside table without directly interacting with anyone.

Abigail's dress at DeVere Gowns was never even begun most likely. Those long days and nights of howling rain and now the epidemic had found Mrs. Hughes reading Old Testament passages to Abigail, both of them shivering in front of the small downstairs parlor's fire. Zuma, Carrie, Laura and I silently crept about our duties speaking only in brief, terse whispers. Each day produced doors with new quarantine signs. Almost always by the next day those signs were shrouded in black crepe. Two apothecaries remained open but virtually all other businesses, saloons and hotels included, were closed. Roads deserted because of the rain remained deserted now due to the epidemic.

It was not at all unusual for Dr. Hughes to vanish from the house during these health crises, although, as even he ascertained, very little could be done until this dreaded illness simply spent itself. The restlessness, confusion and weakened pulse along with a distorted, swollen, bull neck were the usual symptoms one discovered in horror on a loved one. Within hours that loved one had almost always passed away.

A few days into the epidemic Mrs. Hughes started into a frenzy of spring cleaning, almost as though the disease wouldn't be able to penetrate her walls if we scrubbed our knuckles until raw. We heated tub after tub of scalding water, scouring the heavy draperies, double comforters, small rugs and overcoats, since Mrs. Hughes had long ago abandoned any dealings with the Chinese laundry.

Carrie, Laura and I cleaned several carpets with benzene which gave us all blinding headaches, oiled all the floors with linseed and thoroughly scrubbed the sooty coal film which inevitably formed on wainscoting, walls and windows. The benzene fumes were so strong that Mrs. Hughes became dizzy and retired to her bedroom after a few hours. Abigail sat upstairs in the semi-darkened room with her mother talking or reading softly. Later that evening Carrie, Laura and I were ironing shirts and mending collars while Zuma prepared Mrs. Hughes' favorite supper with fried apples and biscuits.

"Now, she don't have it, do she?" asked Carrie, a little nervously.

"Naw," replied Laura, as she dropped the iron firmly on a sleeve, water droplets and starch hissing. "She just poorly from the benzene. When they sick, they don't eat, I don't think. Ain't that so, Hannah?"

"I don't know," I shrugged. "I guess probably Dr. Hughes will know. He should get home soon when things ease up, I hope."

"Oh yes, when he git home," snickered Carrie, looking slyly over to Laura.

"Yeah, maybe he got to take a pulse," said Laura, "Or put on a new mustard plaster or splint..."

"Sure, or maybe rub on some more of dat sweet butterfly lin'ment," Carrie snorted, laughing convulsively, but quietly, wiping her eyes with her apron.

"Or, maybe, he's deliverin' the laudanum hisself again these days since the druggist, he might be pretty busy!" Laura added, elbowing me.

I stared at the frayed collar I was trying to mend, only glancing up at her momentarily, my needle working tightly. If Mrs. Hughes had an opinion about my mother that meant everybody was aware of it, of course, I thought dully.

"Well, all I kin say," blurted Carrie, "is I don't think Miss Abigail evuh gonna see that dress gittin' sewed, you know? With all respect to the Baxters, of course," she added.

I looked up suddenly.

"Oh, no! Did Mrs. DeVere..." I cried out.

"Die? Nah, course not! She left last Tuesday fer Cripple Creek. At least that's where my Tom drove the team hitched up to the big wagon. She stayin' at that Continental Hotel, right up there for all to see on Myers Avenue, he says, 'til her house finished gettin' built. She kin jes sashay right down the block to see it."

"What's the house look like?" whispered Carrie eagerly. "Come on, what did Tom tell ya?"

"Well," began Laura, glancing around, setting her iron back on the stove to reheat, "I heard it's all wired for electricity, has a gamin' room, expensive Persian carpets, runnin' water an', can you believe this -- two bathtubs!"

"Two bathtubs? Oh Laura, get on!" said Carrie in shock.

"Nope. That's what Tom's friend who works for Mr. Stratton said. Mr. Stratton, he's that architect, remember? But he jes struck it rich hisself with his Independence gold mine up there, so dat's his last buildin' project you kin be mighty sure uh dat!"

"Oh my," said Carrie, fanning herself with a large, worn potholder. "What else? Come on, come on! What else did Tom tell you 'bout the house?"

"Chandeliers. Two big ones. From some place in London or Paris maybe. And also, there's a telephone comin' soon! And mirrors, lots 'n lots of fancy mirrors. Oh, and Tom said there's supposed to be a great piano or something coming out by train this week. All the way from New York. They supposed to have some big lady opera singer comin' out too by the end of the summer. Oh, and then, there's some kind of peepin' room or something, smack dab in the middle of downstairs, but Tom wouldn't tell me 'bout dat! In fact, I'm thinkin' he maybe makin' dat part up!" Laura continued, shaking her head in disbelief.

"Oh, how awful!" Carrie giggled, covering her gaping mouth with her hand, her eyes bulging. "Can you imagine? Do ya think a peepin' room is worse than at them cribs?"

"When you seen them cribs, Miss Carrie Jones?" Laura demanded, a horrified expression on her face.

Carrie shrugged. "When I worked for the Perkins up in Leadville, I had to walk their girl Rebecca to school every day which was right past them cribs 'til the town made 'em move those eyesores. Them unfortunates would have the blinds up and be struttin' back 'n forth, back 'n forth, day and night, sashayin' just as nervy as you please, smokin' them smelly little black cigarettes, and only the smallest stitch of any clothes on. My, oh my, oh heavenly my! Sometimes just sittin' in the windows callin' out. Had the names they go by scrawled over the door – like Peek-a-Boo or Good Time Kate or Dirty Alice! It was somethin' else! "Specially for a little child like Rebecca Perkins to see every day. But I don't think Mrs. DeVere is gonna have to do like them sort," she shook her head. "She just too plain beautiful an' classy like, y'know?"

"Say, Laura," she continued, after sprinkling water on another shirt in preparation for ironing, "Do you know what happened to Mr. DeVere? How'd she get the money for this plum fancy house anyways?"

"I heard he was some kind of French Count. Not much family or money or nothin', but very weird. And Mrs. DeVere? She come from a wealthy family in Indianapolis but her husband took all her money and jes' gambled away ev'ry cent. He was real mean to her too so she moved away in a big scandal with some other man. Least, that's the story according to my Tom."

"Well, dat makes a good story, I s'pose. But I doubt there ever was a Mr. DeVere, French count or nothin'. I heard she was a workin' fancy lady down in New Orleans and went by the name of Mrs. Martin. And there weren't no 'mister' Martin anywheres down there neither! She sure can put together a fine dress ensemble though! That sure don't explain where the money comin' from."

"Hmm," said Laura, suddenly very quiet. "Well, whatever the story, but my Tom says that Dr. Hughes is her finance man now. He puttin' a lot of money up, he says. An' he says he heard it's actually Mrs. Hughes' money," she added, snickering the last phrase under her breath.

Suddenly I stabbed my thumb with the needle. Three huge drops of blood splashed onto the collar before I could react. "Here, I …I need to find the bluing," I said as evenly as possible, nursing my punctured flesh as I hurriedly left the room.

A few months back Abigail had begged me to help her read a partially finished letter that Mrs. Hughes had been writing to her father down in New Orleans who had passed away suddenly very shortly thereafter. In it Mrs. Hughes urgently had asked him for a substantial increase in her subsistence allowance. She said that some of Dr. Hughes' financial speculations had not played out very well and that they were stretched to the limit and that they might lose their house without an immediate increase. Neither of us understood what any of this letter meant, but Abigail was terrified and pushed me to ask Miss Weldon because she said that if she herself asked, Miss Weldon would be suspicious. No one ever wanted to let on to others in the town that there might be some kind of money problem or illness in one's family. I had cautiously asked Miss Weldon about it after school a few days later saying that I had overheard some of the other town girls just idly talking.

"When a woman of property is married," Miss Weldon had said briefly, "often a subsistence allowance is paid by her father so that a certain, well, level of prosperity can be maintained by the family."

"For how long?" I had questioned.

She cleared her throat and folded her hands in front of her waist, resting her elbows on her thin wide hipbones. "Well, it could extend for as long as her parents are alive, actually," she shrugged.

"What happens then when both parents die?"

"What an odd question! Did you read all of this in some cheap novel?" she sniffed, looking down sternly at me through her pince-nez. "Your reading skills should be applied to better literature if that's the case."

"Uh, no ma'am," I answered. "I was just wondering, that's all."

"Well, then the rest of the estate would go to her brothers and her husband," she replied, "for them to invest and keep for her. That's how it's always done, you see."

"What if she has no brothers or sisters, just a husband," I continued.

"You certainly are a girl full of questions today, Hannah Owens," Miss Weldon retorted. "Then obviously her husband is in charge of her inheritance for safekeeping."

"Is it possible for her husband to steal all of her money and then just up and leave her?" I blurted out.

Miss Weldon scrutinized me for almost a full minute before she answered.

"Well, yes, sometimes a solicitor would need to be hired in that kind of situation. But usually there's nothing that can be done unless the woman agrees to a divorce and then she's entitled to, I think in the State of Colorado, a third of her husband's earnings for the rest of his life. Anyway, it's certainly nothing that you will ever have to deal with, I'm quite sure."

On the day just before the diphtheria epidemic had hit in full force, Mr. Speyer, husband of the bubbly new Mrs. Speyer, and

Mr. Culver's replacement at the bank, one of the young Wentworths, had stopped by, looking for Dr. Hughes, who was nowhere to be found. Mrs. Hughes had seemed flushed and unusually agitated after their meeting, staring into the parlor fire for hours afterwards.

Mrs. Hughes' father's money was undoubtedly long gone, I shuddered. You could just hear the wealthy tongues wagging in disbelief. If Dr. Hughes money had indeed gone to Pearl DeVere's fancy house then the only way Mrs. Hughes could regain any of what was rightfully her own inheritance was to divorce him. And that was one course of action she would never accept. Suddenly Carrie came into the room.

"Hannah," she cried shrilly. "What in heaven's name are you doin' out here? And you've done absolutely nothin' about that shirt! It'll be a ruin fer sure! Here, give it to me. Zuma needs you in the kitchen anyways. Hurry or you'll see that strap fer sure, girl!"

V. Pike Street

A few days later Dr. Hughes appeared after yet a second far less congenial visit from the Speyer and Wentworth bankers. Rumblings of the Hughes' financial demise had spread through the entire town. When Mrs. Hughes had stopped at the dry goods store she was told stiffly by "that dreadful wretch" Mrs. Tollbert she would have to pay for her order in full. No further credit would be available for her the proprietress had relayed with a full smirk. She had stormed out of the establishment slamming down the items on the counter just in time to see Mrs. Speyer, the bustling banker's wife herself, swathed in her newest DeVere light green silk gown, look away and briskly cross the street to avoid Mrs. Hughes' path.

"You cannot imagine the humiliation I am suffering with this outrage, Albert," she railed, louder than any of us had ever heard her, the sitting room doors surprisingly flung wide open thus allowing the staff full access to their heated conversation. "Have you placed my entire inheritance in these gambling schemes...these absurd nonsense speculations? I believe I had requested that you invest in land. Land! Not these ... these fairy tales!" We all sensed her tiny black taffeta clad figure shaking with rage. "I demand that you sell out on these idiotic ventures immediately," she continued. "Surely there must be other fools willing to get in on such ridiculous tripe. You are embarrassing me beyond belief!"

Dr. Hughes' reply was muffled and I caught nothing other than a reference to Abigail.

"Don't you drag her name into this! She's all I've put myself towards all these years dealing with you!"

"Hah!" Dr. Hughes mocked, his voice now raised as well. "You mean when you weren't criticizing the poor thing for biting her nails to the quick or for low marks in arithmetic or deportment or for myopically tripping over rugs and furniture or for not being able to conform to your antiquated concept of a fashion statement."

"How dare you!" she growled. "Here I am raising our only child ..."

"Yes indeed!" he interrupted. "But I might point out that it would be rather difficult for us to have another under the circumstances don't you think?"

"Oh, as though you would have time to fit me in, between all of your disgusting clandestine...nocturnal activities! How very nice!" she spat out. "Must I be disgraced in every single town we live in?"

"It's your tongue wherein lies the disgrace my dear, far beyond any actions of mine," he replied with light sarcasm.

"And I suppose it is my tongue which has brought upon us this monumental debt? We have two immense notes now unpaid and no hope of any funds I am told at the bank with which to secure payments. Mr. Wentworth said that you have multiple loans out to speculators that have not paid back so much as a nickel, even in interest! Can you not get back something? We are desperate, Albert!" she wailed.

"So, let's see, what do I do," he replied coolly. "Collect my miners' picks, shovels and sluice boxes? Dismantle all the machinery and leave it to rust? Take the feed from their jacks and burros and pack mules or just turn them loose? Tell everyone to just leave and hope that they, or anyone else for that matter, don't simply jump any of my claims?"

"Albert," Mrs. Hughes said as though she were addressing an obstinate child, "just how do you propose we shall continue to live? Just tell me. That's all I want to know. There seems no hope to hold on to this house and my few shreds of anything resembling a decent life unless you sell these worthless claims to some other fool."

"Ah yes, well, maybe then you've quite hit upon it," he brightened. "We do have better than half interest in the house, of course. If we sell it we won't lose it in mortgage notes."

"What!" she exclaimed. "You're not serious!"

"Absolutely my dear. Something small should suffice, a bit farther out of town – this keeping up with the whole Columbia Street thing here is terribly expensive you know. Minimize the house staff, fewer rooms to heat, fewer animals on the grounds, less land for upkeep and so forth."

"I refuse to do this," she snorted. "You cannot expect me, Margaret Katherine Claytor to do this."

"Well, I'm afraid you have no choice, Margaret," he sighed. "In fact, I actually have just sold the house this afternoon. That's really why I'm in town you see. You will need to vacate within the next five days."

Several blistering seconds of silence ticked by.

"I see. And just exactly where are we moving, my dearest husband," her voice barely suppressing her rage.

"Pike Street," he said pleasantly. "I have rented a house temporarily for you and Abigail."

"You mean you won't be there."

"I'm joining in on the excavations myself I've decided. At least through the summer," he said merrily. "Did you know that Win Stratton's just made good on his Independence Mine? His wild 'bowl of gold' theory on Battle Mountain actually proved to be a reality after seventeen years! Completely took us all by surprise!"

"You're crazy! You're absolutely crazy, Albert! With your fragile health you'll never pull through!"

"Well, interesting as that might be I feel stronger than I have for many years. Seems this rarefied air has indeed been helping clear my lungs. And I'm not at all convinced that many a gentleman's ills aren't brought about by this more sedentary lifestyle we all now seem to adhere to, or for that matter, the marriages we must often endure. So my dear, that's it then," he concluded simply.

We heard his footsteps move out into the hall followed by the abrupt slamming of the sitting room doors by Mrs. Hughes. I was reworking the damaged threads of a tattered antimacassar while Laura was mending the torn tatting on a lace pillow. Frowning, she looked up from her work at me but neither of us spoke for several minutes. Laura placed the pillow in the mending basket and then stood, smoothing her wrinkled brown skirt. She looked into the hallway to see if anyone was near before she spoke.

"So what d'you think is going tuh happen now?" she whispered hoarsely, turning back towards me. "Should we all try to get in over at McAllisters? With Mrs. McAllister's parents and her invalid sister now livin' with all the others already in that great big white house, they might be needin' more help maybe."

I had stopped working as well and just looked at Laura unable to think at first. "I kind of doubt they would take all of us, Laura, but ..." I finally stammered and my voice just trailed off as I shook my head.

"I'll talk to Carrie an' Tom an' Jake," she continued. "If we git there first, jes maybe, there's a chance. But of course, it ain't much use talkin' with Zuma. She'll wanna stay wherever Dr. Hughes is gonna be so's to keep track of her payments."

"What payments?" I whispered, putting the antimacassar back in the mending basket.

"I dunno if Zuma knows that we all know about her payments exactly, but her brother down in New Orleans is in jail for killin' a white man. This all happened when they all lived down there. Dr. Hughes kept him from gettin' lynched on the spot an' Zuma's payin' t'get a good lawyer an' a honest trial so's he kin be freed, 'cause there ain't no way he did it. He was workin' his boat that night, even his white boss said he was workin' that boat, an' that boat was miles an' miles away from where that foolish old man got hisself robbed 'n knifed."

"So he's still in jail?"

Laura nodded her head. "S'far as I know. Zuma has some kind of account at this fancy lawyer's office down there. Through Dr. Hughes, of course. She makes them payments ev'ry month to him to put on her account. When she has enough they say she kin git her brother's fair trial. So, she gonna work an' work, that much I do know. An' wherever Dr. Hughes wants her to work, too. So if he wants her to stay on, she'll be stayin' on. Or if he's gonna take her with him, she goes. You kin pretty much count on that, oh yeah."

"Well," I replied slowly, "you should tell her anyway that the rest of us are trying to get in at McAllister's I think. She should know that's what you're planning."

"I'm gonna find my Tom now. I bet he kin get over to McAllisters somehow today, maybe talk to Mrs. McAllister. She's a good person, I think. An' if she can't pay us much, me, you an' Carrie, we kin take in washin' each week. It don't make a lot extra, but it'd give us somethin' more, fer sure."

Mrs. Hughes bitterly resigned herself to the move. She pawned several pieces of her mother's jewelry, sold three complete rooms of furniture including her exquisite two-month-old dark mahogany dining room set to, of all people, Mrs. Wentworth. She also sold Abigail's baby grand piano and an unusually ornate, hand-carved chiffonier to Mrs. Speyer. An extra set of coffee cups and saucers, sauce plates, a sugar bowl and cream set from her wedding trousseau, a rarely used sauce boat and ladle and various gold-rimmed goblets and pitchers were sold outright to Hamilton's department store. A Kodak camera, never used, some sort of prize from her Chautauqua group, was quickly sold to the photography studio in town. Abigail alternated between noisy gulps while sobbing and ferociously biting her nails punctuated by her mother's stern admonishments to "just hush up! Mercy!"

There was no confusion however, of callers being turned away; the news had seemingly been telegraphed throughout the town for everyone knew immediately. Everyone that is except poor Mr. Parker, Abigail's piano and voice teacher, who arrived punctual as usual on Friday for her lesson. I met him at the door relaying the changes as briefly as possible.

"Oh dear, oh my, I had absolutely no idea," he lamented, shaking his head, mopping his high forehead with a rather grimy-looking handkerchief. "And the Schumann book and that lovely new song book I had ordered for her have finally arrived. I was so looking forward to beginning work on them. I thought maybe they might pique her interest a bit since she, er, doesn't always seem ... oh my, I don't mean to sound rude, please don't misunderstand me... terribly involved in her music studies," he sighed. "Well, they're paid for, so let me leave them with you to give to her. I will wait to hear from Mrs. Hughes when she wishes to recommence Miss Abigail's lessons."

"I'll be sure to give them to her," I promised, taking the small package from him.

"Well, thank you, Hannah," he said. "I certainly am very sad to hear of Dr. Hughes' new financial problems. You know something like this happened just a few months or so ago with the Weldons. I was teaching their children also. Mr. Weldon was quite overextended with his creditors as I was told. Very unfortunate. I've heard from Mrs. McAllister that it will take years before they can possibly recover. Well, I prattle on. Forgive me. Such very dark news. Please give my best to Miss Abigail and Mrs. Hughes," he concluded, his Adam's apple making one last bobble as he departed.

Abigail had never been at all comfortable in the social expectations of her mother, but this abrupt ostracism was decidedly worse. She clung to me desperately as we packed her things for the move, sorting through clothing and other personal belongings which "if not absolutely necessary" should just be tossed according to her mother. And, although Mrs. Hughes had to constantly remind her to practice her music, having the lessons taken from her so brutally brought on yet more scalding tears. Somehow I felt that giving her the new music books now that her piano had been sold would only upset her further. I placed the books at the bottom of my own small battered trunk intending to deliver them to her sometime after the move.

The small, low-ceilinged cottage on Pike Street boasted two smoldering, soot-belching stoves, walls that were stubbornly blackened from years of neglect and floors notoriously battle-scarred beyond salvation. There were two holes in the roof which Mrs. Hughes ordered be fixed by her new landlord but they were still fist-sized openings weeks later. The cottage was located quite far outside town.

Carrie, Laura and Tom were offered employment at McAllisters which they eagerly accepted despite the fact that the wages were even lower than the lowest they had anticipated. Zuma, Jake, a housemaid named Katie, and another hired man and myself stayed on, although we were none of us certain how long we might actually be retained. Terrified of her mother's wrath, Abigail clung to me, tearing at her nails and sniveling about everything from the perpetual stench of the aging water closet to the reddish-brown dust raining from the ceiling onto her pillow each night. For Abigail's sake I was especially grateful that school was out for the summer. Her school chums would definitely have excluded her from their presence and if they hadn't, their mothers would certainly have seen to it.

For our first supper in the house Zuma fried up two small rabbits that Jake had shot and cleaned. A slightly damp but serviceable sack of flour yielded a mound of her delicious saleratus biscuits, along with molasses beans, newly churned butter, canned raspberries and tea. So our first meal was at least a good one. Mrs. Hughes refused to eat with the rest of us however, determined to maintain that proprietary distinction. We ate after she and Abigail had finished even though we all shared the same rough hewn kitchen table. We were finishing the last of our tea one evening when we heard a buggy stop outside the door.

"It's your solicitor, ma'am," called out Katie.

"Show him in," replied Mrs. Hughes from the sitting room. I wondered if she had contacted him or if he had been sent by Dr. Hughes. Dr. Hughes had thus far made no visits to the Pike Street house. Zuma motioned for all of us to follow her outside. Zuma wanted to continue working the badly overgrown garden in hope of planting a late crop of beans.

"What do you think Mr. Evans wants, Hannah?" Abigail asked, poking idly at a muddy hole in the ground with a large stick. "Do you think my daddy is going to come see me finally?"

"I don't know but let's hope for some good news," I smiled at her.

Late that night I was suddenly awakened by a gentle, but firm hand shaking me. I sat up with a start to see Zuma, her large frame backlit in the bright moonlight, finger to her lips. Wrapping my blanket around myself I followed her out into the kitchen.

"Sweet l'il chile, you need to find out what's in dat documen' dat lawyer bring here tonight," she said in a hoarse whisper. Her jaw was squarely set and her usually merry black eyes were pinched dark pits in a haggard face. "Dat woman, she ain' gonna tell me nothin' an' I needs to know when da doctuh gonna be here agin. It's real important."

"I know that," I said slowly, looking up at her. "Laura told me about your brother."

"What she know?" Zuma frowned.

"That you're trying to get him a fair trial. That you have an account for it," I continued quietly.

"So she knows 'bout my paymens, too? She say how she found dat out?"

"No, she didn't tell me. She just said you were paying Dr. Hughes so your brother could get a fair trial in New Orleans."

"Hmmph," Zuma muttered. "Person sure can't keep no secrets 'roun this town, dat's fer sure."

I shook my head slightly and smiled at her in agreement.

"So I needs you to ask Miss Abigail what her mama toll her 'bout Dr. Hughes' comin' round," she continued, putting both of her hands on my shoulders.

"There's a good chance she won't tell her anything, Zuma. You know that."

"Why not? He her father ain' he?" she said indignantly. "He comin' home sometime see dat poor girl. He da only one care 'cause dat woman sure don' an' he knows dat!"

"I just don't think Mrs. Hughes will speak to anyone except her solicitor about it. I'm sure it's all in those papers. I know where she keeps her strong box and she probably locked the papers in there already. If I can find the key," stopping myself mid-sentence wondering what was I even thinking. "But I don't think it will really do much good. It may not say anything anyway and then the writing is so hard…"

"Why not? You read mighty good fer not much schoolin'."

"Writing like that is just really…different," I explained, looking up at her drawn face, chiseled in the semi darkness.

"I unnerstan' but you gotta help me with dis child. I know dey gots big money troubles," she held up her broad black arms gesturing up to the ceiling, "an' I don' wan' dat witch to fin' out dat da doctuh, he gots ma money, 'cause she such a witch, she'll take it fer own own, I jes' know it, an' not believe dat it really mine he savin' on my account!"

Or worse. Maybe there was no account for her brother at all. Would Dr. Hughes have stolen Zuma's money? Impossible, I thought. But then maybe not. I remembered my father saying that a little information was dang more dangerous than none at all. I thought back on Dr. Hughes' stern warning to forget anything that I might know or thought I knew. Where did Zuma fit into any of this? Actually, if her money had been placed in Mrs. DeVere's new parlor trade, much as I hated to admit, that would most likely prove to be a very profitable investment. Certainly in Cripple Creek where several thousand miners were working at productive claims in the last two or three years, and both gold and silver extractions were flowing like fountains I had heard. The town was truly booming everyone said. And the fancy lady business, as one of my school friends had giggled as she whispered the words to me once, was booming right along with it. I wondered if Dr. Hughes had actually put any money at all in mining. Somehow though, I was sure that he wouldn't do anything to hurt Zuma's brother's chances of a fair trial.

"I'll try to find the lawyer's letter and do my best to read it, Zuma," I promised.

As she hugged me, I realized that her face was wet. A large tear splashed on my cheek. I was struck with a fierce desire to help her, a kind of love that I had never felt for my mother and certainly not for Mrs. Hughes either.

"I'll nevuh fergit this, sweet l'il child, nevuh," she said hoarsely, kissing me on the top of my head.

I found the slightly dented strong box hidden beneath a

board under Mrs. Hughes' bed that Sunday, just after she and Abigail had left for church. Although it was padlocked, the pin hadn't been pushed in completely and the small lock fell open easily when I moved it. On the top lay two stock certificates for a railroad somewhere in Virginia, a fragile-looking copy of her father's will, a very old opera program written in Italian or French or something, a tiny pair of opera binoculars and a beautifully tooled leather purse containing several large gold coins. I carefully pulled out a set of rolled, bound papers from underneath.

Dr. Hughes was indeed requesting a divorce based on desertion of services and loss of something called conjugal rights. Although he was currently unable to provide her with any monies if she were to agree to the divorce he would give her one third of his income for the rest of his life and fully pay for Abigail's finishing school education out East. If she refused to divorce him he would pay her nothing.

I rolled the papers back into shape and mindlessly retied the brown string. I knew that Mrs. Hughes would never agree to a divorce. If Zuma wanted to continue with her payments to the doctor she would want to leave immediately. And I realized that I wanted to go with her. She was the only person who had ever cared about me, that I trusted throughout all of this chaos.

Returning the strong box to its hiding place proved to be more difficult than its extraction. I couldn't remember exactly which direction it faced under the panel and didn't want the box to come crashing through the flimsy ceiling below. As I felt along the boards I became aware of Mrs. Hughes' voice in the hall. I panicked. Had the church service ended early today? Or had I been up here far longer than I realized? Zuma was supposed to let me know when their wagon returned. I curled up on my side under the bed trying to breathe as quietly as possible. The corner of the coverlet was slightly pushed up however and as she bent down she spotted me instantly. With a hysterical shriek she grabbed my leg, pulling me out with amazing strength. Twisting my hair tightly around her fist she yanked me to my feet. As one section of hair pulled out she seized another large fistful, slapping my face with her other hand.

"You filthy thief! You dirty, lying little thief!" she shouted. "I should have known you would rob me!" Mindless of my screams begging her to stop she grabbed yet another handful of my hair. "You're just a cunning little slut like all of the others!"

I could taste blood running from my scalp and my hands went to my head trying to massage the searing pain. But she had only momentarily stopped pulling out my hair in order to grab a belt off the back of a chair. She slashed it across my bare shoulders. I doubled over as she continued with a relentless, rhythmic flogging across my back, my screams getting louder and louder.

"If I could kill you, I would!" she ranted hysterically, the belt's sting punctuating every other word. "You have no idea what I've been through with your kind. As a favor to your stupid drug-fogged mother I took you in. And now ... my small scrimpings! All I've kept from that hideous man with his filthy grotesque habits! You have no soul!"

The belt had brutally slashed the back of my thin cotton dress into tattered strips. Clumps of bloody hair and fabric were everywhere and blood flowed freely down my face. I had curled into a tight ball in the corner, my hand grasping the chair leg. My cries were now more like whimpers as the strap sliced at random, opening agonizing cuts on my calves then again on my shoulders and back. For some reason I glanced up at the chair seat and saw her Bible. She had forgotten to take her Bible with her to church. That was why she had come home. To get her Bible. Why couldn't I have noticed that when I had come into her room?

"You have no right, no right whatsoever to traipse round like you do. You with your perfect skin and your graceful knack! You're nothing but a common trollop! I'm sick to death of hearing about your long, golden hair from everyone. 'You know, Margaret, that girl Hannah on your staff has the most beautiful huge grey eyes. And such a lovely voice! Why it's like the voice of an angel.' An angel! Bah! While my poor child just struggles. With absolutely nothing," she spat out accompanying the belt's rhythmic slashing.

Suddenly she gasped, stepping away from me, the blows ceasing. After a moment I cautiously looked away from the blood-flecked wall. Zuma's tall dark shape blocked the entire doorway. She had a large pistol aimed directly at Mrs. Hughes.

"Now you jes' hand me dat strap, Miz Hughes," she said coolly, her eyes practically black slits. "An' don' you think fer a minute dat I dunno how ta use dis gun here. Or dat I won' use it. Y'see, my brother, well, he a mighty good shot an' he done train' me. Real good I might add."

Never taking her eyes off Zuma, Mrs. Hughes backed away from me and flung the bloodied belt to the floor.

"Take her and get out," she snarled through clenched teeth. "I never want to see either of you troublemaking whores again."

VI. The Old Homestead

*"Fearfullness and trembling are come upon me,
and horror hath overwhelmed me. And I said, Oh
that I had wings like a dove! For then would I fly
away, and be at rest." Psalm 55*

A fresh warm breeze caressed my torn matted scalp. I was
lying in a nest of cotton ticking and straw tucked up next to the
buckboard. Zuma sat next to me. She and Jake were talking but
their words drifted away from me over the wagon. My body and
mind were thoroughly dazed. A pungent vapor of herbs tinged
with liniment hung in the air. I thought that I heard my father
wailing a psalm way off in the distance, one that I remembered
was my mother's favorite. Something about having wings like a
dove and flying away. After the horror. And then there would be
rest.

I now remembered Zuma gently carrying me outside the
cottage and going to fetch Jake. Lying weakly against a front post,
I remembered telling Abigail that I had fallen into the creek,
churning over the stones until I grabbed a branch and pulled
myself out.

"Oh no, how awful!" she had remarked, her eyes wide.
"Mother came home for her Bible. I waited for her outside the
church but when she didn't come back I knew something terrible
must have happened. So I guess she found you like that?"

"Yes," I managed to reply, trying to keep my voice from
wavering. "She...did."

Mrs. Hughes must have called her inside then. I had dim
recollections of Zuma peeling off my ruined dress and gently

washing me with soap that both soothed and burned. Jake had brought round Ole Bess and cautiously settled me into the wagon. I fell asleep shortly after we left.

Hours later I awoke, sniffing the fresh scents of pine and sagebrush and becoming gradually aware of loud men's voices.

"We gonna stop here, jes' fer a bit," Zuma said quietly to me. "Jes git you some warm soup, go with dem biscuits I got fer us here. Dat ol' witch ain' nevuh gonna git any mo' my good biscuits. I hope dem bedbugs git in dat yeast starter agin! Serve dat ol' witch right! Here chil', you try tuh sit up jes' a bit now."

She carefully pulled me up to a sitting position as Jake appeared with a bowl of soup. We had stopped at some kind of halfway house, a tar-papered shack set back in a widening of the road. A huge Concord coach, like those in Abigail's fairy tale books outfitted with a three-span of massive black horses, stood several yards away. As I sipped the delicious steamy broth a large man in badly stained corduroys ambled towards our small wagon.

"Kind of a tired, timid-lookin' animal ya got there, you know?" he said, clenching a pipe on the side of his mouth. "Think she gonna make that climb?" he gestured with the pipe stem to the steep mountain pass jutting out high above our heads.

Jake shrugged. "Don' got much of a choice ways I see it," he replied.

"Well," the man continued, spitting sideways before returning the pipe to his mouth, "you gonna have to take the new Shelf road through Phantom Canyon y'know."

Jake frowned. "I went de old route jes' two, mebbe three weeks ago. An' dat wuz after duh rain I might add. A long trek but not too much of any problems that I saw."

The man shook his head. "Nope. Cain't get through on the ol' road right now. Trees down blockin' every which way. Boulders movin' 'cross with all those flash floods after the streams swellin' up from the rain. That new Shelf road dug right outta the cliffs, 'cept, of course, for that stretch over at Eight Mile Crick. Lotta folks have trouble keepin' their wagons in check up yonder. And with that wind it's a mighty treacherous climb I kin tell you," he shook his head gravely. "Some mighty rugged hairpin turns, switchbacks, y'know? Just outside Limekiln one bend's so sharp, jes' before you git to Cripple Creek I gotta unhitch my lead team. A fellow down in Florence jes' last week tellin' me 'bout another stagecoach went rollin' backwards down that mountain an' straight down over the cliff. Wham." He shook his head again looking down at the ground. "Nary a soul made it, they say."

Jake scuffed one boot against the other glancing over at Zuma and then looking up sideways at the man. "Dunno why anybody would build a road dat was more dangerous den the one it replaced," he muttered to himself.

"I kin take the girl and her maid," the driver continued, nodding at us. "But that's all the room I gots. Law sez I kin only carry fourteen an' I got twelve set. An' I wouldn't have that 'cept one lady had to git off last stop cuz her baby wuz comin' an' I sure as heck couldn't hold up everythin' fer that!" he chuckled wiping his mouth across his sleeve. "Tell ye what. I won' charge ya fer the girl. She's jes' a l'il bit of a thing. But I'm fixin' to leave on the half hour so suit yerself."

As he walked away Zuma looked at me and then back at Jake. The warm breezes I had felt while still in Colorado Springs were long gone. A chilly mist laced the high mountain air. I shivered and curled farther down into the tick.

"Ya think dat he be tellin' da truth? Or he jes' tryin' to git one more fare outta us?" urged Zuma.

"Dunno," Jake sighed, scratching his thinning scalp. "I hate tuh admit it, but stands tuh reason dat he's right an' dat duh ol' road is closed 'til it gits cleared. Der were some trees down when

54

I went befo' but a wagon could still git by. But it was rough in places I sure have tuh admit," he continued as they watched the driver disappear into the shack.

They were both silent for several minutes. Then Jake said, "Zuma, wot you gonna do wid dis chil' when you git to Cripple Creek, anyways? Don' you go takin' her tuh work at dat bawdy house of Miz DeVere's. Even if she only cleanin' an' workin' in duh kitchen her name be sullied. You know dat. Not fer you neither. It ain' right. I don' need tuh be tellin' ya dat."

"Ovuh ma dead body dis chil' workin' in duh bawdy house! We kin' set up feedin' an' washin' fer duh miners. An' you know me. If I kin git me a lean-to built an' a fire goin' an' git me an advance on some flour, I kin sell bread an' biscuits tuh those hungry minin' folks real easy. You know dat! Jes' real easy. An' I kin do a soup soon as I have a few mo' dollars. Dats 'spectable. But da doctuh, he gotta help dis chil' an' me both now dat's all I kin say. So we gotta find him."

We arrived in Cripple Creek just before midnight. Jake had told Zuma to go to the Continental Hotel and ask for a Tom Winchester who managed the saloon in the hotel. Winchester owed him several favors and would put us up free for a couple of nights according to Jake. Sharp pistol shots and smoke filled the cold night air. Throngs of glassy-eyed men clad in heavy wool shirts or patched, faded corduroy coats milled aimlessly through the streets. Garish-looking women, many with shockingly red hair, brightly painted lips and coal-rimmed eyelids sauntered about, their open fur coats revealing bright-colored, skimpy silk wrappers beneath.

"Nothin' to be alarmed by," chuckled the driver, noticing Zuma's reaction as he helped ease me out of the coach. "Usual Sunday night's goin's on. Git out all that nonsense so's they can be back workin' before sunrise tomorrow! Actually, it's a tad quieter than usual. Hotel's right over there," he nodded. "Your stuff kin stay here 'til you git the girl in. I don' charge no extra for waitin' long as it's under ten."

"Lemme git her inside an' I be back right quick," Zuma replied.

Cradling me closely she began elbowing her way through the crowd trying to keep anyone from bumping into my raw back and shoulders. I whimpered in pain with each renewed jostling. Tom Winchester was good for his owed favors although he was concerned at first that I might be sick with the typhoid and didn't want to let us stay. The rank stench of whiskey mixed with vomit followed us upstairs to our room where the fetid mattress proved to be crawling with bedbugs. After piling our few battered wicker possessions in the corner Zuma quickly built up a small palette for us on the floor, sprinkling a barrier of quicksilver around it to keep the bugs away. The wheezing and snoring from the adjoining rooms, only slightly muffled through the thin, muslin-covered walls, along with the shuffling of heavy boots out in the hallways, soon blurred into an exhausted veil of sleep.

There were bloody feathers everywhere -- a red carpet randomly strewn over the bottom of a dank rust-pitted cage. A cool darkness beyond the cage beckoned. I tried to drag myself towards the door, towards the darkness.

"Where you goin," Hannah?" asked Mary, her thin little face obscured in the swilling murkiness outside the cage. "Mother said tuh milk them cows now 'fore it gits colder. I got the water all warmed fer strokin' the bag jes' right like you said. If it gits colder, they won't let you touch 'em at all, y'know."

"I'm trying," I mumbled. "But I'm hurt, Mary. I can't go so fast today."

"I know you is hurt," she replied softly. "But you'll get another skunnin' if you don' git up an' milk them cows, Hannah. Did I tell you that Thomas, he done caught two fish? They kinda small, but real nice. He so proud. Caught 'em this afternoon, down by the mill. All by hisself, too! Mother says you got to helps me clean 'em after we done the milkin' 'cause she thinks I'm too little to do it myself. I'm bigger now but she don' believe me that I kin do it myself. She don' ever believe me. Please Hannah. You tell her. Please? You gotta try an' move now. You gotta try an' sit up, chil'."

I realized that it was Zuma's voice nudging me from my dream. Zuma and Dr. Hughes were sitting next to me. I was still lying on my side in exactly the same position Zuma had placed me last night.

"Hannah?" said the doctor gently, "looks like you're a little more awake."

I squinted up at him. At the end of the room pale sunshine filtered through a small, dirt-encrusted window. "I'm very tired," I replied slowly.

"Zuma says you have some very bad cuts. She's worried about you. And what happened to your hair right here? That looks absolutely awful."

"I ... fell," I said my voice wavering. "Into the creek behind the house. Trying to keep a cloth ... from going," I managed to whisper, looking at Zuma.

She frowned, avoiding my eyes, and pursing her lips looked down at the floor. A siren's blast ricocheted very close by.

"Wot's dat fer? I heard dat a coupla times dis mawnin' already," asked Zuma.

"It's just a mine warning siren," said Dr. Hughes. "Probably from the Alhambra or El Dorado claims or maybe the Old Mortality since they're the closest to town. They always signal three minutes before dynamiting so anyone in the vicinity can move away."

"Hmmph," replied Zuma, shaking her head. "Guess dat's right nice of 'em. A big blast befo' duh big blast."

Dr. Hughes moved around behind me and gently pulled

away some of the wrappings from my back. After several moments he pulled the wrap back up and faced me again.

"Hannah, you didn't fall," he stated, clearing his throat. "Who did this to you? A boyfriend? He should face charges for this brutal an attack. You will undoubtedly have many of these deeper scars on your lower back for the rest of your life."

"No sir," I swallowed weakly. "I fell. Like I said."

He looked down at me frowning slightly and brushed his blonde mustache with his forefinger. After a moment he crossed his arms and cleared his throat again. "You know, you're not a very good liar."

I knew he was thinking of the pocket watch incident and closed my eyes trying in vain not to relive the humiliation of that day. Puzzled, Zuma looked at the doctor then back at me.

"You're not doing any good at all letting the scoundrel get away with this atrocity, Hannah. Did you promise him your favors and then have a change of heart?" he pressed.

"Doctuh Hughes!" exclaimed Zuma, in a loud, indignant voice. "Don' you go accusin' this chil' wid sumpin' like dat! She a good girl! She ain' no tramp! An' glory be she sure ain' no tramp like dey gots aroun' dis place! Goodness me, I ain' nevuh seen nothin' like it in all mah days."

"I was … caught stealing," I stated flatly. "Bit down the road from Mrs. Hughes' place."

"Well you must have been stealing the Queen's dowry for a beating like this."

Suddenly Zuma banged the floor with her boot. "Mis'ble varmits," she hissed crushing a fat, black insect. "We needs tuh git outta this here bug holler, doctuh. I kin take care of dis chil' jes' fine, but it cain't do her much good tuh be in dis nasty place full uh duh bedbug! I think dem critters been here fo' 'bout fifty years, deys so many of 'em!"

Several explosions resounded in the distance as the

dynamite blasts filled the air. The doctor had moved behind me again. After dipping his handkerchief into a small brownish bottle he held it under my nose for a moment. The room began swirling about me, an odd dark green. Dimly lit stars and a thumbnail moon began circling my head and continued for several minutes. I was aware that he had completely removed all of the bandaging from my back and shoulders and was washing me with something very cold, but I felt no pain. While he was working he kept talking.

"Actually, the town wasn't even here until a few years ago, Zuma. It was just a cow pasture that had changed hands plenty of times. A guy named Bennett owned it. He let old Crazy Bob Womack keep digging holes looking for assay, long as he kept covering them up so that Bennett's cows wouldn't fall into the holes. Curious, Bennett even took a sample to several Denver assayists wondering if Crazy Bob might actually be on to something. But he was told that, true to his name, Old Crazy Bob Womack was just burrowing in another one of his crazy schemes."

After rinsing away the strong-smelling soap and applying some other cold salve and a pungent disinfectant that burned slightly even through my haze, the doctor started unrolling layers of cotton gauze and began to wrap it around me.

"Old Crazy Bob just kept sinking shafts and pluggin' 'em back up. Actually, he moved his claim about a half dozen times without telling anybody and nobody even questioned it. And then," he tightened a section of bandaging, "here, take a deep breath, Hannah. This may hurt for several seconds. That's it. Good, good. And then, Crazy Bob struck real ore, Sylvanite to be exact. That's gold and silver mixed together. He quickly recorded that deed and a couple of other fellas did the same on adjoining property. As word spread hundreds of prospectors appeared here practically overnight. They bought cabin sites from Mr.

Bennett who was only too glad to have some temporary worth come from his property since his cows kept breaking through the fences and getting lost. He only asked that when folks left that they use the timbers they had felled for their cabins to patch the fencing around his cow pasture. He never really thought anybody would actually find any gold up here.

"Then, just a couple of months later, my friend Win Stratton had a vision of sorts. Win had been prospecting in Cripple Creek as well as a lot of other possible sites. Hidden among a tangled briar patch that he had probably ridden past hundreds of times was a kind of pink-hued granite outcropping on Battle Mountain. Win dreamed about a bowl of gold up there and, can you believe it? He struck into one of the richest veins ever found last summer on July 4th. In fact, he named it the Independence."

"So you banked in Mistuh Stratton's 'pendence mine, doctuh?" questioned Zuma. "Kin I jes' ask, if Mistuh Stratton made dis big gol' strike, how come rumor has it dat you is bankrupt if I may be so bold tuh inquire?"

"Here, Hannah," he said to me. "Turn your head just a bit -- that's it -- so I can get some of this on your scalp before the ether wears off. That's a big part of the problem with grubstaking that's never really taken into consideration by some folks unfortunately."

Zuma looked at him with a puzzled expression. "Wot's dis grubstakin' stuff mean?"

"Grubstaking is kind of like gambling even though it's supposed to be a loan. I give someone money betting that they will be successful in mining, rendering much more than the amount I lent them obviously, and assume I'll make a lot of money once the ore is extracted. But just like gambling, sometimes the house beats your hand out cold. One of the problems with gold is that it's worth a heck of a lot more in the ground than out of it. That's one of Win Stratton's favorite expressions actually."

"I don' git it. Gold's gold, ain' it, suh?"

"Not exactly. Getting the supplies up here to build the shafts, blasting the tunnels, building all of the framework and supports, hauling the ore in wagons out of the mine and getting it down the mountain to the smelters and assayers offices costs a real fortune all by itself. You may be into a part of the vein with rich yield – say $400 to the ton. Or you may have just a lot of scrap. Win Stratton has sold more speculations on his 14th level crosscut, because he's sure that's where the richest yield lies, than he's actually hauled out of the ground. So basically, we don't know what we've got until we've got it."

Neither Zuma or I could really understand much of what Dr. Hughes had just said.

"Hmmph. Sounds a lot more risky den I could evuh put ma hard earned cash down on, dat's fer sure!" Zuma snorted, shaking her head in utter disbelief. "An' I even a gamblin' woman, Doctuh Hughes."

Dr. Hughes chuckled and then added, "sometimes you can go week after week dumping a small fortune into prospecting and not clear so much as a penny. And then, when you get a couple of union organizers working along with your free miners putting crazy ideas into the free miners' heads like they've had in California recently, things can get really dicey for everyone involved."

"So doctuh, you into this 14th level crossaway thing too? An' dat's why you ain' got no money?"

Dr. Hughes had started putting his things carefully back into his bag. He didn't speak for several seconds and then said simply, "well, that's probably about the easiest way to look at it right now, yes."

"Well, Miss Hannah an' me, we gots no money an' no gol' mine friends neithuh," stated Zuma, crossing her arms. "An' no jobs an' no food an' no place tuh live."

"So you were both let go at Pike Street?" Dr. Hughes sighed.

"Well, yessuh..." Zuma replied, glancing uneasily over at me. "Miz Hughes jes' wantin' to keep Katie now an' I guess mebbe Jake. Anyway, if you kin jes' lend me a few dolluhs tuh git a set up, I kin git me a fire goin' and sell bread to these miners and take in washin', too. I heard of a woman dat made 'nuf dat way tuh keep herself an' her sick husband and kids from starvin' way up in that minin' camp at Altman. Dey had a good life in fact! I kin make enuf tuh keep me an' Hannah jes fine 'til she's able to work agin, but I needs yer help tuh start. Ain' nobody gonna give a color'd woman even two nickels, you know dat, doctuh."

Dr. Hughes let out a slow breath looking at me and then back at Zuma. He bit the edge of his mustache for a moment before speaking. "You would make a lot more money if you could work helping with the cooking at the Old Homestead, Zuma."

"Wot's dat?" asked Zuma suspiciously.

"Pearl DeVere's new... parlor establishment."

"Ma body be ten times dead an' ma flesh eatin' by a den of coyotes befuh I workin' at any bawdy house, doctuh! An' draggin' dis chil' dere? No suh. No way, suh!"

"Well, this isn't that kind of establishment exactly," he countered.

"Kinda like a gold mine ain' a gold mine? Hmmph! I don' think you kin convince me 'bout dat, suh! I admit I don' know nothin' 'bout gold minin' but these ole ears done hear plenny 'bout da bawdy bizness an' I ain' workin' in one up here I kin tell you dat!" she retorted.

"Well, you would be that much farther along towards finishing your payments to Monsieur Beaulieu. You can't expect the Louisiana courts to wait forever to review the records and convene a trial for Paul," he said quietly.

Zuma took a deep breath and muttered something in her Creole patois that made the doctor smile. She glowered under her thick dark eyebrows at him. "All right, so jes' how is it not 'dat kind' of 'stablishment 'xactly? Min' you, I ain' agreed tuh go, I is jes' askin'."

"Well for starters, it's much more high class," replied Dr. Hughes.

No whores. You will have the most exclusive parlor in Colorado, I remembered him reassuring Mrs. DeVere.

"Hmmph. Ain' nothin' high class 'bout takin' money fer it anyways I kin sees," Zuma grunted. "Dey take 'em down tuh dat 14th crossaway or sumpin' and roll 'em aroun' in a horse trough full uh gold dust?" she continued sarcastically.

Dr. Hughes laughed heartily. "Now actually, that's a really good idea! I hadn't ever thought of speculations along those lines!"

Zuma shook her head in utter disbelief. "You'll forgive me fer sayin' doctuh, but I always put you a mighty smart man. An' dis, well, it jes' don' seem too smart, I'm very sorry tuh tell ya."

"Well, we all gamble in different ways it seems," he replied, smiling. "The Old Homestead is due to open in the next couple of weeks. In addition to offering the best food and liquor anywhere this side of Pike's Peak, there's a fairly complete library, gaming table rooms, conference rooms, breakfast café area, music room – a singer from one of Covent Garden's famed opera houses is to open here in a couple of weeks – all on the main floor. You would never even have to set foot into the upstairs part of the house, which is really expensively decora…"

"I don' wanna hear nothin' 'bout dat," Zuma interrupted, covering her ears as she vigorously shook her head.

"You and Hannah would live in one of the frame buildings on the adjoining property, not in the house itself," the doctor continued. "And you would only be helping the chef that we've employed. Very rarely would you have any contact with anyone else in the household itself. And the money will be excellent, I can assure you. You'll have your savings in no time both for Paul's trial and then for yourselves as well. After that you can go wherever you want."

Zuma still looked anything but convinced.

"These clients will be the wealthy men of this area and there are hundreds of them I might add. After a hard day they just wish to relax a bit. They'll engage a very lovely, reasonably bright young woman for an entire evening or most of an evening's enjoyment, not just a few bored minutes of her time."

"An' den dey go back tuh their wives an' chillun back home," she concluded icily. "Don' seem right tuh me. Now I'll admit, Miz Hughes? She a real plum nut case. But Miz Palmer? She real nice. An' Miz Weldon. Miz McAllister as well, come tuh think of it. In mah simple headed opinion, suh, it jes' ain' right."

"Well," he sighed, "such are the many inequities of this life as I'm sure you're well aware by now."

"An jes' how all you fixin' tuh git evrythin' back 'an forth from Coloraduh Springs, suh? Wid da ol' road all tossed up all da time an' dat stage kin only hol' fourteen on dat worthless new Shelf road. An' lemme tell you, dat ain' no junket up dere! No suh! I ain' no smart woman, but even I knows dat jes' plum ain' gonna work out."

"Actually, there's a narrow gauge railroad being built which will connect the Denver and Rio Grande in the Arkansas Valley. When that goes through in the next few weeks it will pull right up to the back door here at Raven Hill. It'll bring thousands of newcomers, wealthy and otherwise, up to the camp from Colorado Springs and elsewhere, making the place much more respectable with better stores, nicer homes and such. The town has already built a new school building expecting a lot of new students to start this fall."

"First I evuh heard a town buildin' itself aroun' a brothel," muttered Zuma in disgust.

"Trains will soon be running a dozen or more times every day, eventually with cheaper fares. The mining district will be able to haul lower grade as well as high grade ores down to the mills and make a much better profit also. That'll make Cripple Creek the richest district in the state without question," he added.

Zuma sat quietly for a moment then looked over at me. I was lying on my side again listening to their conversation, tired, but in very little pain. The stars swirling around my head had finally disappeared. Although for the most part the conversation made sense, I really didn't know what a fancy lady parlor was all about. I could picture the beautiful Mrs. DeVere in long white silk gloves, applauding the opera singer or offering a cigar from a gold-embossed humidor to men reading in her library or gently reminding the cooking staff that the Swedish brown bean soup needed to simmer longer so that it was quite thick enough when served.

"I dunno, I jes' dunno," Zuma sighed. "You talk duh good talk, but you sure ain' convincin' me as yet. If it weren' fer mah po' brothuh's legal mess..." she started, her voice trailing off.

The doctor stood up, stretching his legs. "Let's plan on getting you both moved out there tomorrow afternoon." He held up his hand to ward off Zuma's expected protests. "Hannah should be ready to make the trip by then. I have business to attend to back in Denver over the next several days so I'll send over a wagon. And also, watch that quicksilver, Zuma. It's powdered mercury which is extremely poisonous."

"Hmmm," Zuma uttered loudly as the doctor left. "Tell dem nasty bugs dat so as dey don' come back!"

***

Although tiny, the wood frame building we moved into was solidly built with a surprisingly well-shingled roof. An old but recently overhauled cook stove in reasonably decent working condition warranted Zuma's approval immediately. She somehow managed to get a number of small loaves of bread and biscuits baked and sold to miners who came to our doorstep every day before she went out to work in the Old Homestead's kitchen. She gave me strict orders however, that even if there were additional loaves to sell, I was never to open the door to any of the miners.

"Jes' preten' nobody home an' they'll go away real quick," she told me firmly. Some of the men also dropped off mending or laundry which brought in more money. Zuma adamantly refused to accept any mending from the Old Homestead, however.

After a couple of months the pain from my beating eased quite a lot. Only if I carelessly twisted through my lower back was I reminded of just how deeply the belt had chewed into my muscles. My hair itched along my scalp where it had started to grow back in strange clumps. If I parted my hair along the opposite side and pinned it down along the torn side, it almost looked normal. The deep bruising on my face was slowly fading from its purple, green and yellow hues.

Although I cautiously asked Zuma about Mrs. DeVere, she refused to give in to my youthful curiosity and simply grunted in response. My first glimpse of the former dressmaker came many weeks later after a brief trip one afternoon to purchase a set of additional bread loaf pans at Lampman's Emporium.

Three men stood just within earshot and I overhead one exclaim to his companions: "Wait, wait! Just lookit over there, Frank! There she is!" Just then an exquisite black phaeton with shiny red wheels drawn by a matched pair of high-stepping, sleek black horses trotted down Third St. Sitting regally, looking straight ahead was Mrs. DeVere, holding the reins firmly on the single-seated carriage. She wore a dark green taffeta dress with shimmering puffs on the leg-o-mutton sleeves – a dress almost identical to those she had sewn for the wealthy Colorado Springs women. Shiny well-blacked leather boots peeked out from under the full skirt. A tiny black cape trimmed in jet beads was thrown over her shoulders, creatively allowing a full view of the rather shockingly low-cut bodice. A wide dark green velvet hat with a red plume was delicately poised on her dazzlingly upswept copper-colored hair. I thought I had never seen anything so incredibly breathtaking in my entire life. Speechless, I held on to a wooden pole as she passed by. She looked completely different from that meek woman who had always worn a high-necked collar and severe coiffure in Colorado Springs.

The men, dressed in denim overalls tucked into large, filthy boots and ragged corduroy coats, continued to gawk even after her rig had turned down Myers.

"Kin you imagine?" spat out the youngest man, "if I kin make $3 a day, that's a might good wage, y'know? I hear they chargin' $250 a night at Pearl's place!"

"Naw," chimed in one of the other two, "dat's jes' a rumor. Ain' no man kin throw away that kind of change! Even a rich man!"

"Nope, Frank he's right," countered the third man, shaking his head. "I heard that too. An' I also heard that Pearl herself cain't be bought at no price, haha!

"Hah!" guffawed the youngest man. "Now that'll be the day! A whore with no price tag! Slap me another good un!"

"Whar she come from, anyways? An' how's she able to build that huge place?" said the one named Frank.

"Dunno," answered the youngest man. "Somebody said she's from London or Paris. Mr. Stratton, you know, who owns the Independence? He's her architect put up that fancy parlor, they say. I hear he's a regular too! Don' surprise me none about that!"

"Oh yeah, an' they say that ole Blanche Barton is really hoppin' mad to have this uppity bitch in town takin' all of her big money customers right out from under her nose, too! Didn't Stratton used to go over tuh Blanche's place, the Mikado?"

"Well, that's the bawdy business fer ya! One dog chasin' out the other! Sit back an' enjoy the show fellas!" He slapped his friends on the back as they all roared with laughter and disappeared into Crapper Jack's Saloon across the street.

I edged out into the street, scuffing my toe along in the dust as I walked back.

VII. Cripple Creek

With the pure thou wilt shew thyself pure; and
with the forward thou wilt shew thyself forward.
For thou wilt save the afflicted people; but wilt
bring down high looks – Psalm 18.

Dr. Hughes stopped by every week or so to collect Zuma's payments towards Paul's trial. Eager for any news from the lawyer, she would pry him for information, but rarely did he have much other than a brief telegram verifying receipt of her last installment.

"By dis Fall, we kin head south, chil'," she often repeated to me, while counting and recounting the silver and gold coins she had carefully hidden just under the large water reservoir in her stove. "Git outta dis camp fo' good! Git my brothuh outta dat pokey and git you tuh finish schoolin' and git a teachin' certificate. Dey board duh teachers roun' wid duh fam'lies, same as aroun' here, so you won' have tuh be payin' out no rent. You a smart girl, Hannah. Den you find yusself a nice, fine man an' git yusself married nice like, an' have a nice fam'ly. You deserve dat!"

"Zuma," I finally asked her one day while she was busy daydreaming about our respective futures, "Laura told me that you once had a husband and a little girl down in New Orleans." We were sitting across from one other, each kneading a large round of dough.

"Yez, yeah I did," she replied after a moment, clearing her throat. "Dey both died with duh typhoid. Mah baby wuz only 'bout two years ol'. She died in her daddy's arms in duh afternoon. Den he died dat same night. It wuz jes' awful, chil'. I don' know how I got through dem dark hours. Dat's how I come tuh meet duh doctuh, y'know. He come tuh our cabin. An' a lotta white doctuhs, dey won' mess wid duh colored sick, y'know, not down South. But ma two loves, both too far gone by den. He stay wid me awhile, 'til Paul git dere tuh help me. Which wuz might nice of him. Den when Miz Hughes fire her cook, the doctuh ask me to come work fer dem an' I sed yes."

I reached over and touched her arm gently, leaving a trace of flour. "What was your little girl's name?"

"Amiette," she said wistfully. "It means little love. She wuz name aftuh my mama, Amiette Marceline. A very proud Creole lady in her day."

"What a beautiful name," I said, smiling at her. "Do you think you would ever want to be married again?"

She sighed and rhythmically slapped the dough on the breadboard. "Mebbe I fin' someone down in New Orleans. But I kin say dat I ain' foun' nothin' much I int'rest in anywheres up aroun' here. Dat's fer sure. But I dunno. Mah husband, may his soul res' in peace, he wuz a wonnerful man an' father tuh hiz l'il baby girl an' me both. Don' know if duh Lord got any mo' like him aroun' anywheres, chil'."

After a few moments I said, "Abigail mentioned that it was really hot all the time in New Orleans. Is that true?"

"Oh, my, yes! It hotter 'n blazes mos' duh time. She right 'bout dat!"

"I wonder how she's doing. Abigail, I mean," I said quietly.

"Well, all I kin say," Zuma retorted, pounding down into her section of the dough, "is dat I'm sure dat Katie gots her hands full wid dat po'fumblin' chil' an' dat witch she got fer a mother!"

"I think Abigail always meant well," I said. "But I don't think Mrs. Hughes really liked her very much. Maybe that's something that kind of pulled us together. I don't think my mother liked me very much either. Do you think my mother killed herself?" I suddenly just blurted out.

"I cain' say, chil'," Zuma replied. "She was a Godfearin' woman, so I sure don' think so."

"But do you think that my father knew that she was taking that medicine?" I continued. "He always said that God would take care of us in illness and that using medicine was against the Lord's order of things."

Zuma shrugged. "Well, dat I dunno. But yo' papa? He wuz real good at duh prayin' stuff but, 'scuse me fer sayin' it 'bout a white man, not good at a whole lot else, chil'. I nevuh in all mah days seen such a sorry mess of a house or a lumber mill from an able body man. It was might strange."

"I wonder if I'll ever see my family again. Or Abigail. Or Carrie and Laura."

"Well, jes' so's you an' me don' never see dat Miz Hughes agin," retorted Zuma, with one final ringing slap of her dough. "Dat's duh mos' importan' thing, y'know? Now git dose loaf pans grease up agin, honey so we kin git this here dough movin' along."

A few days later, I was headed out to the Bailey's place to help with their washday as a special favor for Dr. Hughes. Their regular woman was helping her own daughter who had just gone into confinement and had three other very young children. Mr. Bailey was also one of Zuma's regular bread customers. The father of seven, he occasionally dropped off some laundry and had asked if I might also be able to help out for a day if the family ever found itself in a pinch, which it now did. The four-room house sat level in the front, but was stilted up against the slope in the back and was one of the farthest from town, well past the Pisgah Cemetery. After a stop at Fairley's Emporium to purchase soap, I started through town. Suddenly I thought I heard someone calling out to me.

I turned and saw a beautifully attired young woman sitting on a rough bench just past the apothecary's shop. She appeared to be close to my age and wore a large matching sun bonnet of light crème, banded with a light brown trim, the veil drawn down tightly around her face. I glanced down self-consciously at my own repeatedly mended, coarsely woven and stained grey skirt.

"Excuse me, miss. Could you do me a favor?" the girl asked, keeping her head down.

"Well yes, I suppose so," I answered, curious.

Without looking up she extracted a scrap of paper from a small beaded reticule. I noticed that she wore very expensive ivory kid gloves which buttoned with a pearl at her tiny wrists.

"I need this prescription filled, please" she said handing it to me, her eyes still lowered beneath her veiled bonnet. I'll gladly pay you well over the amount owed so that you may keep something for your kindness."

"Please don't think me rude," I replied cautiously, "but why can't you have this filled yourself? If the information is false I will get in trouble as well you know."

"Oh no," she said, glancing up at me momentarily. "It's definitely written out for me. But I might get arrested if I enter the store and I can't risk that."

I stared at her. Then I realized that she must be a prostitute. There was a town ordinance that restricted prostitutes to shopping only on Tuesdays in the main part of town so that decent women would not have to be in stores with them simultaneously. Prostitutes could roam about freely over on the Myers Avenue end of town, but they had to be registered with the city officials. No decent woman ever set foot out in the street, much less in a store, on a Tuesday. They stayed home, kept their brood of children indoors and firmly fastened down the curtains.

But this young woman seemed quite pretty and was definitely expensively dressed. Not at all like the crude, hard-faced women in their flapping bright wrappers that I had seen when Zuma and I had arrived several months ago.

"Please, miss. I'm truly in a lot of pain. I need this to be filled. Please help me," she said again, still keeping her face averted.

"Yes, alright," I stammered after a moment, taking the prescription.

"Thank you so much," she answered graciously. "Here are several silver dollars with another two for your trouble. If possible you should try to get your change in gold coins though."

I glanced at the prescription. It was for a Miss Jenny Hays signed by Dr. Hughes. A prescription for laudanum. My breath caught.

"It's for my leg," the girl continued. "I had a terrible fall from my horse last year and broke my ankle. It wasn't set quite right and still causes me a great deal of pain much of the time."

"You should be very careful with this," I warned, biting my lip nervously. "Don't ever take any more than it says. Not even the least tiny bit extra. It's very dangerous."

"Oh yes, I know," she replied softly, almost laughing. "It makes things a bit queer at first, but then when the pain releases completely, it's like ... drifting along on rippling sunshine."

Drifting along on rippling sunshine I thought. I really couldn't quite imagine that.

The druggist glanced at the prescription then at me and muttered something before measuring the drops into the dark blue bottle. He started to hand out the change in silver coins when I remembered the woman's request that I ask for gold. His look narrowed considerably. After slowly depositing the coins back in the cash register, he lifted out the drawer to obtain gold coins from underneath. He very reluctantly counted out the correct change and handed it over to me. I could feel his eyes blistering into my back as I left the store.

The young woman graciously thanked me when I handed

her the medicine and her change.

"Could I just ask you one question," I asked. "I mean, just about the gold."

"Do you have savings in silver coin or paper?" she queried.

"Well yes, of course, a little. Not much. Everyone has silver and no one wants to accept paper," I answered, picturing Zuma counting out her silver coins on the previous morning.

"Don't let the banks give you anything in silver or paper anymore," she affirmed quietly.

"Why not?" I asked, frowning. Very few people wanted to accept paper money simply because it did not have a very good reputation of keeping its value from one year to the next. But gold and silver had both always been acceptable. In fact I had heard that almost all businesses conducted themselves in silver.

"Because I heard from ... well let's say, from a very reliable source ... that President Cleveland has just secretly called for a special session of Congress to meet immediately to repeal the Sherman Act in the next few days."

"I'm sorry," I replied, shaking my head and feeling very young, foolish and uninformed. "I guess that I don't know anything about a Sherman Act."

"Three years ago the government was forced to start buying thousands upon thousands of ounces of silver every month," she continued, glancing sideways to verify that no one was within earshot. "But former President Harrison did it because there was actually too much silver being mined, especially right out here. And since there was too much silver, it really wasn't worth anything. What makes something worth anything is because it's scarce, you know."

I had never even thought about what actually made anything valuable. A cold shiver worked down my spine.

"Now that Grover Cleveland is president he is urging that silver no longer be considered a monetary standard. According to my source, all of the banks in Denver, in fact almost all of them in the entire state, are absolutely on the brink of bankruptcy."

"But what does this mean exactly? How on earth could possessing lots of silver imply bankruptcy?"

"Virtually all of the banks in Colorado, railroads, and major businesses rely heavily on investments backed by the silver dollar, don't you see? When silver is no longer accepted they will all go under. Something like pulling the supporting timbers out from inside a mine shaft. Everything collapses on top of itself into a heap of rubble. A lot of people will be out of work because there won't be any way to pay them."

She continued to stare at the ground so that anyone passing by would not think that she was speaking with me. I was truly baffled that any young woman could know so much about politics and money.

"I need to get back," she said quite abruptly. "And I don't want you getting in trouble being seen with me. Thank you again for your kindness in getting the prescription. And just be sure that you exchange your silver coins for gold in the next few days. It won't be worth as much as a buffalo chip out on the open prairie...and at least you can burn those for warmth!" she laughed. I caught a brief glimpse of her face and realized that she indeed appeared to be shockingly close to my age.

"Couldn't I talk with you again sometime?" I suddenly asked, not wanting the conversation to end.

"Oh no. I don't think so," she replied quickly, starting to walk way. And then over her shoulder she added quietly, "well, maybe sometime. My name is Jenny. I'm at the Old Homestead. It's probably best if you let me find you, however."

"I'm Hannah."

"Yes, I know."

I told Zuma that I had overheard a rumor about the necessity of exchanging silver for gold at the bank. She shook her head in reply saying she had heard from some of the other kitchen staff that all the banks were telling everybody from the mayor on down that they were temporarily out of gold coins and everybody just had silver right now. But not to worry. After all, silver was king in Colorado. Just ask anyone. The huge silver mines at Silverton, Aspen and Leadville were pulling the stuff out of the ground by the ton around the clock. For those who were still suspicious and really wanted gold they had been assured that a shipment of gold coin from Denver was expected within the next week or so.

But that shipment never materialized. *The Crusher*, Cripple Creek's most reliable newspaper was out on the streets with a special edition after receiving the shocking telegram that President Cleveland had indeed repealed the Silver Act. According to the article, this was to prevent the depletion of the government's gold reserves as a result of an investment panic. Thousands upon thousands of out of work silver miners flocked to Denver the next day. In an effort to rid the city of its horrendous jobless population, the railroads were now providing free passage to anywhere. And the rails had just been completed through Phantom Canyon, bringing several thousand men right up to the town of Cripple Creek. They reasoned that since Cripple Creek was a gold mining camp that everything would still be running in full force and that they would be able to find work.

But, as *The Crusher* went on to explain, most of Cripple Creek's mining investments were also backed by silver and not by gold. Although initially I didn't understand how this could happen, after hearing it discussed constantly by everyone it all became clearer. Jobs for the original miners were becoming very scarce as their mines also shut down operations simply from lack of company funds to continue. Many of the incoming miners were foreigners willing to work for less than the established wage of $3 per day and longer than an eight-hour shift. The Cripple

Creek men had fought viciously with their employers to obtain those rights without resorting to the formation of a miner's union. In less than a week, the mining operations had come to a terrifyingly abrupt standstill. No smoke billowed out of the mine stacks. No whistles blew signaling shift changes. No rock slag spilled over the rockslides on the mountainsides. No screeching brakes from the big hauling freighters echoed in the canyons. But the eerie equipment silence meant that hoards of hungry, jobless, homeless and very angry men were lining the streets. What few nickels they did have at the bottom of their pockets typically found a way into the saloons, fueling hot tempers.

The camp's miners banded together, determined to run the newcomers out of town, so that whatever free bread and other rations that found its way to the town – most of which was personally distributed by Win Stratton – would not be squandered among the poaching ingrates. City officials were unable to bring the flagrant lawlessness under control and *The Crusher's* two daily editions were filled with detailed horror stories. Scores of unscrupulous townsmen were deputized to help move the non-residents out of town. But frequently their presence only served to cultivate an even deadlier climate. Angry shouts and gunshots filled the hot August skies both day and night. A typical morning revealed scores of corpses, blood pooling around them, strewn haphazardly along the raised wooden sidewalks immediately in front of the saloons. Women and children were urged to stay indoors unless accompanied by their men and several were injured or killed anyway when bullets pierced through the thin walls of their wooden homes. Unless you were on the prowl for trouble, you refrained from venturing out at night.

According to Zuma most of the big money men were surprisingly still arriving at the Old Homestead's doors. Usually tight-lipped about anything she overheard of those conversations she surprised me by grumbling that the gambling tables were actually running feverishly all night long. The hottest speculation commodity was the area's gold mines; perhaps Cripple Creek's return to solvency lay in the snap of a pair of winner-take-all deuces, one client had laughed.

78

VIII. Winfield Scott Stratton

*My heart is smitten, and withered like grass; so
that I forget to eat my bread. By reason of the voice
of my groaning my bones cleave to my skin. I am
like a pelican of the wilderness; I am like an owl of
the desert. I watch, and am as a sparrow alone
upon the house top. – Psalm 102*

Outside the parlor's well-protected grounds however, swarms of angry men continued to invade the town. Despite the fact that Zuma kept her pistol cleaned and loaded just next to our door, she begrudgingly insisted that I now accompany her each day to work at the parlor. And even more surprising, to keep traffic away from our own cabin's door, she insisted I now only take in clean mending from "the house" as she referred to it.

Zuma's greatest concern was the status of her account for her brother of course. If Monsieur Beaulieu had kept her account at the bank in either paper money or silver dollars was anything actually saved at all? She had bombarded Dr. Hughes with all of these and many more questions on the two occasions she had confronted him at the parlor. He replied that he had heard nothing, but was attempting to get the answers she so desperately sought. In the meantime, I had firmly stitched all of her gold coins into a false peplum which she wore beneath her skirt.

Mrs. DeVere's parlor was indeed an extraordinary place. I worked on the mending in the small winter storeroom just off the kitchen. Outside the window a tall intricately-laced black wrought iron fence was visible which completely surrounded the property. A gentleman apparently could leave his carriage or horse right at the gate with one of the attendants who would see that the animals and rig were immediately taken to the nearby stable to be rested, curried and well fed. Rigs were also cleaned at no extra cost. Inside the house I glimpsed russet, ochre and maroon-painted walls and dark-stained chair rails, wainscoting and heavy moldings. Beautiful damask draperies with gold cording and thick Persian carpets reaffirmed affluence. Several small settees with deep velvet cushions, variously-sized hand carved wood tables and paraffin lamps with hunting scenes painted on the glass globes lined the receiving room and library, which were the only two rooms other than the kitchen rooms that I saw.

Laura had been wrong about any electrical wiring in her information about the house, however. Several businesses back in Colorado Springs had been wired for electricity over the last several years, according to Dr. Hughes when I asked him, but he had never heard of anyone considering putting electricity in one's home yet. Although in his opinion he thought it was inevitable in the future. If there was electricity available in Cripple Creek, I wasn't sure if the Old Homestead would be considered a home or a business exactly.

I had been working on the mending in the storeroom for a few weeks when Dr. Hughes stopped by one afternoon. There was some faint music playing and he asked me if I would like to see the gramophone in the front receiving room. On a window table, perched like a giant metal ibis, was an enormous machine with a whirling wax cylinder, huge flared horn and flailing mechanical arm. Dr. Hughes deposited two nickels in a slot and I heard a band playing a march that he said was the U.S. Marine Band and then some ballads.

As I listened, something about one of the ballads suddenly seemed quite familiar. Then I realized that it was a Stephen Foster song that Abigail had just begun working on during the last few weeks of her lessons with Mr. Parker.

"Dr. Hughes," I said, reddening, my hand covering my mouth. "I just remembered that Mr. Parker brought two new music catalogues over for Abigail that last day before we moved to Pike Street. I hadn't thought about them until just now. They might still be in my trunk. At least I think that's where I put them. I can't say for certain. I can bring them tomorrow so that you can get them to Abigail. I'm really sorry but I had forgotten completely!"

"Ah, yes," he mused. "Yet another of my deluded wife's ideas. Piano and voice lessons for a tone-deaf daughter who couldn't replicate even one correct note if her life had depended upon it."

"It's not for me to say, of course, sir," I replied, glancing down, "but I don't think that's quite fair of you to say. Abigail practiced very hard, you know. And Mr. Parker was hoping…"

"Yes, yes," Dr. Hughes interjected, waving his hand abstractly, "I'm sure you're quite right about all of that. She worked hard at everything her mother told her to work hard at, of course. Poor kid."

"If you'll please excuse me sir, thank you so much for showing me the gramophone. You've been very kind. But Zuma expects me to finish the pile of mending today so I need to get back to work. There's some kind of conference going on this weekend so everyone's working even harder than usual."

As I turned to leave, he caught my arm lightly, just above the elbow. "My daughter may have not been able to replicate a correct note but I know for a fact that you can, Hannah. How many of those songs do you remember?"

"I don't know," I shrugged, wondering why on earth he could possibly want to know. "I haven't thought about them for a long while."

"Do you think you could sing for this special party this weekend? For maybe, say an hour, perhaps a little longer as the men are arriving?" he questioned.

"Oh no, sir," I stammered. "I couldn't possibly."

"So you mean, that you don't remember any of the songs after all."

"I probably do, but I have nothing to wear!" I blurted out. The moment the words tumbled out of my mouth I wondered at the complete lunacy on my part. I had never sung in front of any audience except a flock of chickens and a few scrawny cows.

Dr. Hughes laughed, shaking his head. "I'm sure Pearl can conjure up something around here for you to wear," he mused. "You'll be paid handsomely, Hannah. A hundred dollars in gold coin. It would take you more than four months to earn that amount with just mending. The singer we'd engaged had to cancel. Her manager said that she was ill but I think he's afraid to have her make the trip and perhaps not be paid given Colorado's current financial fiasco. Can't say as I blame him actually."

"But sir," I swallowed, fully aware that his expectations far exceeded my extremely limited capabilities, "I don't have copies of the music I used to sing. These are all new songs in these books, I'm sure."

Suddenly I also remembered hearing the hurdy gurdy girls as I walked past Crapper Jack's saloon, when I was helping out at Mrs. Bailey's house. Their low, raspy voices and raucous songs weren't anything that I would ever have wanted to duplicate! Not for all the gold in Colorado!

"And, I'm sorry, sir, but I don't know any of those …kinds of songs that are done in saloons."

"No, no," he frowned. "We don't want any of that low, cheap stuff. More of some of the lighter classics, you know. The kind of music one might hear in a salon in London or Paris, for example, or just plain English folk songs. You know songs like "Sweet Rosie O'Grady," "Get Up and Bar the Door," "Lily of the West," "Barbara Allen," "In the Gloaming" – that kind of thing. The accompanist will be here day after tomorrow. I'm told he's the best in the business or at least best in the business in this part of the world. He undoubtedly has copies of anything you know or more than likely he can figure it out. And dig out those new books. See if you can learn some of those as well with him. This is quite an opportunity for you," he added.

When I told Zuma later than evening about Dr. Hughes' request her first reaction was understandably quite negative.

"Wot else yuh gotta do fer dat one hun'red dollahs?" she glowered suspiciously, her black eyes narrowing with distrust. "You ain' goin' upstairs for no reason, is you?"

"No," I replied. "Just singing in the front room, where the piano is, while the men are arriving at the house for the gold conference."

"An' you sure dat's it, right?"

"Well, I do have to practice, of course," I replied lightly, knowing that's not what she meant.

"Don' you be sassy wid me, chil'. You know what I means -- ovuh an' 'bove dat, chil'," she asserted, heaving a worried sigh. "Duh doctuh, he knows dat I gots too much silvuh dollahs in mah savin's. I dunno how you an' me gonna finish payin' dat accoun' an' git ourselves on duh train outta here by the end of da year. Dis would help, chil'. I cain' lie tuh ya. But you a good chil'. He maybe fergettin' dat, but don' you ever forgit dat!"

"He said that the accompanist would be coming in day after tomorrow. If he thinks I'm able to do this, then I want to at least try. If I'm not any good, well then, that's that," I shrugged.

"Oh, you good, honey, you mighty good," replied Zuma, shaking her head. "An dat might jes' be the jump onto duh bad path, y'know?"

That morning was gloomy with sheets of cold, grey rain relentlessly pelting us. As we picked our way through the expansive puddles to the back entrance of the iron gating Zuma spotted a thick chain, secured by a padlock, wrapped around the gate. "Fine time tuh beef up duh secur'ty," she muttered and we had to continue all the way around to the front gate, becoming completely soaked.

"Wot's duh padlock fo' on duh back gate?" she fumed, wringing the water from her overskirts as Maggie, another of the kitchen workers, opened the door.

"I dunno," replied Maggie. "I hear that our miners are tryin' to form some kind of union, force this riff raff outta here. An' I think with this meetin' here this weekend, with all these big name political and money types, maybe they're afraid of somebody tryin' to sneak in an', well, you know. Make trouble like," she continued. "Oh, and Hannah, with all of this rain, they don't think that piano professor is gonna make it 'til pretty late today, 'cause he's gonna have to come on horseback with Mr. Barrington. So you're supposed to just work yourself for a time, accordin' to Miz Pearl. Oh, and if you can get to those shirts I've got sprinkled back there ironed up today that would make me most happy. I dunno when I'm gonna have time for ironin' with all this extra kitchen work!"

I had wrapped the two music books tightly in thickly waxed canvas sheeting hoping to protect them from the downpour. I carefully unrolled them as Maggie showed me through what seemed like a labyrinth of russet-hued hallways to the music room. Various tri-colored and hand tinted chromos graced the muted walls along the way. She unlocked the room, which seemed damp and rather cheerless until we had lit both a small fire in the grate as well as a couple of Carcel lamps to dispel the gloom. An upright piano stood in the corner.

Just as Maggie was about to leave, Mrs. DeVere walked in. I

hadn't seen her since that day I had observed her driving her carriage in town. She smiled warmly at me, touching me lightly on the shoulder. Her bright copper hair tumbled over her shoulders in long loosely pinned curls. Although I thought she looked a bit tired, she was as beautiful as ever.

"How good to see you again, Hannah," she said graciously, smiling at me. "And how good of you to agree to help us out with this program!"

"It's good to see you too, Mrs. DeVere," I replied, trying to keep the low comments of the three men I had heard that day from dampening my better impressions of her.

"Please call me Pearl, Hannah," she laughed, adding only slightly more solemnly, "let's hope I never have to align myself with those dreadful DeVere's back in England again!"

"Well, ma'am, I hope that I can help with your program," I stammered, becoming less sure with each passing moment. "I mean, I told Dr. Hughes that I've never really sung for an audience before. Just um..." I laughed nervously, "just the chickens and cows. Oh and possibly a few geese. I forgot about them."

"Well, Albert says that you have a very lovely salon type voice," she replied smoothly. "And goodness knows we both have certainly heard enough European salon music over the years so I absolutely trust his judgment! And who knows, you may find that your ability to tame livestock may come in very useful around this place!" she laughed gaily.

There was a soft knock and the door opened again.

"Jenny," said Mrs. DeVere, "here, I would like to you meet Hannah. She's going to be singing for the gold conference this weekend, we hope."

"Hello again," she replied kindly, as she extended her hand to me. Although not quite as attractive as Mrs. DeVere, she was still an extraordinary looking young woman. "Actually Pearl,

Hannah and I have met before. She helped me get a prescription filled one day when I was caught short."

Pearl frowned slightly. "You know that I don't like any slight measure of impropriety, Jenny. You need to be more careful. There can't be anything common or a misstep about our appearances in this camp."

"Yes, ma'am, I'm quite aware of that," she replied, nodding her head. "And I assure you that it won't occur again. I came in to tell you though that Mr. Barrington and Mr. St. George have just arrived from Denver. They are getting dried off and asked that you join them for tea. Actually," she winked, "Mr. Barrington asked if he could have his tea with a few drops of brandy. I told him that house rules are no liquor until after 3 o'clock on weekdays. He wasn't too happy about that!"

"Well, this is indeed propitious," said Mrs. DeVere. "Ask Maggie to bring the men up here and serve tea, please."

The accompanist, Mr. St. George, reminded me almost immediately of Mr. Parker, which put me ironically at some kind of ease. His traveling companion, John Barrington, was a rather handsome young man, who had arranged to meet with Mr. Stratton regarding Stratton's desire to purchase the Boston-Colorado Smelter business, which Mr. Barrington's uncle had recently patented in Denver. After tea and what I recognized gratefully as Zuma's delicious cinnamon and walnut pie wheels, Mrs. DeVere hooked her arm through Mr. Barrington's and they left to await the arrival of Mr. Stratton. Sitting at the piano, Mr. St. George blew his nose and cleared his throat several times, cursing the beastly weather in this part of the country as we started working through several songs.

"Here, Hannah, you should probably hold words ending in 'er' open a bit longer," he suggested. "You don't need to get to that consonant quite so fast. Yes, yes, that's much better."

Although at first I found myself holding back, I felt

surprisingly comfortable within a very short period of time. His corrections were sometimes stinging, but were always very helpful.

"And also, you need to smile when you are singing," he stated. "No one knows why, but you can actually hear it in a voice. Did you know that? Also, watch your breathing right in through here my dear in this passage. I would just go through that phrase so that you have room to take a larger breath immediately before that ascending scale. Well, that's sort of the idea, but even larger so that the note at the end of the phrase is sustained. Yes, yes, that's a bit better."

He suddenly stopped abruptly and rewrote a small section of the music accompaniment. "Whoever thought that chord was correct had soup for brains. What nonsense. Now, let's approach this line with more crescendo right up to here and then pull away a bit more quickly. It really gives the lyrics more punch, you know …a more lasting effect."

Two hours seemed to slip past in a blink. I couldn't think of any two hours in my entire life that had been so completely enjoyable. The door opened after a brief knock and Maggie entered.

"Excuse me, Mr. St. George," she said, "but Mr. Barrington and Mr. Stratton were wonderin' if you were plannin' to join them in the gaming room later."

"Oh my, good heavens, absolutely not!" Mr. St. George sputtered, as he hurriedly began repacking his music in a large leather bag. "I wouldn't know a royal flush from a full house! John Barrington is quite aware of my gambling distaste. I'm quite surprised that he asked. Well, maybe just a note of politeness on this part, I suppose. No, never. Not for this old dog. After a hearty meal, the site for which is yet to be determined, I'm just getting these old bones down to the National Hotel for a hot soak, a large brandy and a good cigar. Dr. Hughes has rented a suite of rooms near his own for most of those attending the conference, I believe. But please, er...Maggie, was it?" to which she nodded affirmatively, "please, Maggie, thank them both for the offer and tell them I will talk with them in the morning."

As Maggie left he turned to me, "well, not too bad, young lady. Maybe we'll try for a bit of that Debussy stuff in French tomorrow."

The following day seemed much more grueling and often incredibly beyond my small capability, although I was very much enjoying learning the music. Mrs. DeVere listened to a small part of our rehearsal and was most complimentary abating my fears at least slightly. She had brought a couple of Jenny's dresses for me to try on since she thought we were approximately the same size.

"I designed these for her before I left Colorado Springs," said the former dressmaker. "She hasn't even worn this pale green silk yet. This color will look quite stunning on you, I'm sure. Actually, you two girls have very similar coloring."

I noticed that the back of the dress was scooped out into something of a low teardrop effect.

"Um, Mrs. DeVere..." I began.

"Pearl, please, Hannah," she smiled back.

"I can't wear anything that's cut down quite this low in the back, ma'am. I have these red scars ..."

"Oh yes, yes, how foolish of me! Albert told me about your having all those horrible belt marks! He said that he couldn't imagine what you might have stolen to have provoked so severe a beating! Well, I can easily add some lace along the inset in the back. Or the lace and a Spanish lace shawl as well. Yes, that will be quite perfect, I think," she decided.

The dress indeed fit almost perfectly. When I looked at myself in the long cheval glass I couldn't believe that it was my own reflection staring back at me. The stiff lace covered almost all of the marks except for two red stripes along my left shoulder. By adding a flouncing of tulle, which she wound into a rosette pattern, these blotches also disappeared under the magic of Mrs. DeVere's creativity.

"There," she said, walking to the other end of the room, a pin still in her mouth just like the old days. "Now that should do quite nicely! What do you think, Hannah?"

"It's very beautiful, ma'am. Thank you," I replied quietly.

"You know, if you were to bring some of this tulle into your hair," she said as she experimented with a small ribbon, "maybe something like this perhaps. You really have absolutely gorgeous hair, Hannah. You should try to do more with it. Here, sort of how you have it now, but with even more hair, more curls piling up in the spot where the hair is starting to grow back. What do you think?" We both looked in the mirror.

I was grateful that she was pulling more hair over the tender new growth. In addition to better hiding the raw scalp, the effect certainly made me look older than my fifteen years. After a moment's hesitation, I said: "Doesn't Jenny mind that I'm borrowing her dress, however?"

"She's actually not that fond of it. I think the color is quite becoming on her but like so many of the young girls, she seems to be into this new all-white craziness that is just coming out of Paris and New York these days. Here, let me help you take this off without sticking yourself raw with pins."

"She seems extremely smart. About politics and money and everything," I said, pulling back on my own colorless cotton shirtwaist and skirt.

"Well, yes," replied Mrs. DeVere, taking a few moments to firmly reposition several pins in the new dress. "All of these young women who work for me are quite brilliant actually. Most of them never had a chance to do anything for themselves. They lost out on money, inheritances, land, any hope of family prestige due to their fathers' remarrying or older brothers' brutality or greedy husbands or the like. So they are here working for their own money, just not using their own name for the time being. Then, they can leave, marry well and respectably, and live elsewhere. It's done all the time you know. Of course, then there are the poor souls like Blanche Barton. Do you know who she is?"

"Well, sort of," I answered uneasily.

"Hmm," Mrs. DeVere smiled, not sure she should continue as she glanced at me. "She owns the Mikado. Which is a far cry from the striped tent she started out in a couple of years ago, let me tell you."

I felt myself blushing.

"You know who Win Stratton is, right?

I nodded my head. "I've never met Mr. Stratton, but I know about him."

"Win said," she chuckled, "that poor old Blanche had amassed a bunch of IOUs from this one crafty prospector who was always a little short on cash. She took her IOUs to Win asking him to decipher them because she figured it was time to collect the debt and he told her that she now owned 27 one-eighth interests in the same claim," Mrs. DeVere laughed.

I felt my blush deepening even farther. "Oh that's terrible!"

"No, no, Hannah," the former dressmaker continued, still laughing, "what's so funny is that old Blanche still didn't realize that she had been taken – twice if you think about it!"

My face was now undoubtedly completely crimson red.

"I'm so sorry," Mrs. DeVere apologized. "I've obviously offended you. I forget that your young ears are still quite so tender." She suddenly became quite serious. "I wanted to mention before you go however, that I was also whipped. By my husband, actually, many years ago. He had gone completely berserk. Except, unlike you, I ran. I ran as far away as I possibly could run." She looked at me levelly, her voice having taken on a rather odd tone. "And I'll never let any man own me like that again."

I regarded her quietly not knowing what, if anything, I should say.

"Rest assured though, my dear little one," she continued, gathering up her sewing kit, "that your marks will almost completely disappear. At least on the outside."

The weather cleared in time for the reasonably dry arrival of the men attending the gold conference. By Friday afternoon, carriages, stagecoaches, as well as a few men on horseback, were convening at the Old Homestead. Disgruntled miners camped outside the wrought iron fence watched the goings on while scores of vigilantes, hired by Mr. Stratton, kept a shrewd eye on the miners. When Horace Tabor, owner of the Matchless Mine, the largest silver mine in Colorado arrived, the miners' utterances of "take yer bloody swine home wid ya" and "ain't no room here fer yer greedy carcasses, ya bastard" brought immediate reinforcements from the camp sheriff, officials and deputies. Word had it that Tabor, even though he was selling all of his holdings in Leadville, including his famous opera house, numerous hotels, a spa, several apartment buildings and private residences and countless saloons, couldn't even begin to pull out of his bottomless quagmire of debt. He had also lost huge amounts of money in speculations in Mexico and South America. By attending the conference, Tabor hoped to find backers such as Stratton and Blair, a railroad magnate, to somehow ease out of the doom of the completely irreversible, financial disaster surrounding his empire.

After helping iron some of the women's dresses I had gotten dressed in the winter storeroom where I had been doing the mending. Rather oddly, Zuma was not in the kitchen and no one had seen her for the better part of the afternoon, making me extremely uneasy. I had never known her behavior to be unpredictable and now was certainly not the time to suddenly become unreliable in her work. Mr. St. George had arrived slightly later than expected and his cold had gotten far worse despite his hot soaks and large brandy remedies. Quite tired and miserable, he rushed rather mechanically through our warm up preparations. My uninspired attempts to work the tulle ribbon through my hair as Mrs. DeVere had suggested ended in abysmal failure.

Despite all of this, effervescence oddly buoyed my spirits. The cheval mirror had once again revealed an attractive young woman with a somewhat untamable mass of tumbling honey brown curls and large grey eyes set in a small, rather pale oval face, which I was discovering to be my own. On my way to the performance I met up with Dr. Hughes who had assured me that he and Mrs. DeVere would be seated to the left of the small stage. Next I encountered Jenny who introduced me to Win Stratton, Horace (or HAW as he loudly averred that everyone called him) Tabor and Alex Blair, who was the only truly solvent railroad magnate in attendance, he readily bragged to me. A lock of silver hair fell over one eye as Mr. Stratton clicked his heels in mock European fashion and kissed the back of my hand, his intense blue eyes looking directly into mine.

"Ah, at last I meet the lovely chanteuse about whom Albert and Pearl have spoken so highly! Indeed, you know I'm most interested in supporting new talent, young lady. Just ask anyone. Why just a couple of months ago I sent a very promising young violinist name of Aaron Gimbel to the Paris Conservatory to study for a year – all expenses paid by yours truly. He's one of the best in the program, I'm told. Certainly a credit to our country, without question. So, my dear, keep that in mind yes?" he winked slyly.

I nodded my head and smiled after also exchanging greetings with Mr. Tabor and Mr. Blair.

Mr. Barrington cornered me for a moment in the hallway just outside the salon. His dark wavy hair and deeply set hazel eyes gave him a somewhat exotic, almost gypsy-like appearance, although I had been told that he disclaimed so much as even the tiniest drop of any Bohemian blood adrift in his ancestry. "I was privileged to listen to a portion of your rehearsal a couple of days ago, Hannah," he said with a warm smile, taking my hand for a moment. "You definitely have a unique talent. How fortunate for us all to enjoy your premiere so to speak!"

"Thank you, Mr. Barrington," I replied carefully. "You're most kind."

"Please call me John, Hannah. Mr. Barrington is my father!"

"Well, thank you then, John," I smiled, with a slight curtsy which I hope didn't seem irreverent. "Let's hope my premiere, as you call it, goes without mishap."

For the first couple of songs I felt as though Mr. St. George was playing the correct notes and I was certainly singing my part, but we weren't really working particularly well together. Rather a bit like a running hem stitch, I suppose, when one's looping over is too broad or lean and the effect is withered or cockeyed. The stitch will hold, but it's none too even much less pleasing. By about the third song however, an odd sense of relaxation came over me. The room dimmed into a bluish haze of cigar smoke. That smoke, blended with the light fragrances of the girls' expensive perfumes and the intermingled scents of whiskeys, brandies and beers, settled into a delicious, almost mindless atmosphere. Several of the women, including Mrs. DeVere, had removed their long gloves I noticed. Their bared white arms adorned with diamond bracelets and glistening gold rings, shimmered in the gaslight.

Just towards the end of a very simple Mozart tune that Dr. Hughes had specifically requested, a messenger appeared through the door and handed the doctor an envelope. There was a long piano passage that ended the song allowing me to easily become drawn into them. Dr. Hughes read the message, asked the messenger a question, and abruptly left with him. After just a few seconds, Mr. Stratton, who had been standing against the wall, sat down in the doctor's vacated chair, which was positioned quite close to Mrs. DeVere. As the audience broke into applause he lifted her hand to his lips and flicked his tongue lightly across her wrist, looking deeply into her eyes. Her gaze was intent on him also. She kissed each of his fingers slowly and then released his hand, looking back towards the stage, folding her hands back into her lap.

Luckily, we were on our final song, "Guten Abend, Guten Nacht," a lullaby that Mr. St. George had determined would end the program. In my head I heard Dr. Hughes words to Mrs. DeVere outside her shop in Colorado Springs that they would be together always. I also heard the three men ogling the former dressmaker as she drove her spirited team of horses with their dancing plumes, stating that every whore had her price tag. And then, there was Mrs. DeVere's assertion to me as she was fitting Jenny's dress that no man would ever be able to own her again. Fortunately my concentration on the guttural German lyrics to finish the song kept me from mentally replaying the scene any further between Mrs. DeVere and Mr. Stratton.

After bows and congratulations the various groups began to move towards the gaming rooms or other pursuits. A lapse into business conversation brought an almost childlike chiding from Mrs. DeVere that the meetings would be continued tomorrow and the men were intended to relax and enjoy themselves this evening. Mr. St. George was fairly complimentary considering his illness about the outcome of the concert and insisted I get in touch with the new owner of the Tabor Opera House in Leadville.

"Give him my name as a reference," he said, loudly blowing his nose into what appeared to be his last even remotely clean handkerchief. "You'll have to provide an audition of course, but you should have no problem securing some kind of employment once all of this silver coin nonsense is resolved. Oh, and another thing. You should write the opera houses out in Clear Creek and Black Hawk. They are quite impressive venues and always looking for some new people for their choruses. I actually have two almost identical books of some of the music we did so I'm giving you this one. Here's my address in Denver if you need to contact me for any reason," he concluded with one final honk into his handkerchief as he walked off in his odd stiff-legged gait.

The performance over I drifted back towards what I assumed was the general direction of the winter storeroom to change back into my regular working clothes. I smiled to myself comparing this to Abigail's fairy tale book of "Cinderella." I hadn't exactly danced at a ball or met the prince of my dreams but getting back to the washing and mending chores was the end of this Cinderella's tale I was quite certain. I was also wearing a pair of Jenny's velvet slippers, which unfortunately didn't fit nearly as well as her dress, since my feet were decidedly wider than hers.

I realized that I had turned down a completely wrong set of hallways. I started up a rather dimly lit set of stairs that I assumed would take me back towards the kitchen. Servants' back stairs typically were unadorned and very sparsely lit. Although I was still troubled by Mr. Stratton's and Mrs. DeVere's interaction, I kept them from my thoughts and began pulling out some of the pins which were pinching my still somewhat-tender scalp as I continued walking down the dark hallway. All these young women who work here are quite brilliant actually, Mrs. DeVere had said to me. Most of them never had a chance to do anything for themselves. So they are here working for their own money for a time. Then they can leave, marry well and respectably, and live elsewhere. It's done all the time you know.

It's done all the time you know. The words echoed inside my

head yet again. Then I heard Zuma's voice. You a good girl, Hannah. Mebbe the doctuh don' be rememberin' it, but you gots tuh remember it. She was right of course. Where was Zuma anyway I suddenly wondered, rather irritated. What seemed at first like an irrational disappearance now seemed alarming if she wanted to stay employed at the Old Homestead. If Mrs. DeVere became upset over Zuma's work there were certainly hundreds of newly out-of-work folks in the camp who easily could fill in, at least on a temporary basis. What on earth was she thinking neglecting her responsibilities during such a critical time as this gold conference?

The hallway stretched along and became even darker. I turned a dark corner and spotted a very softly lit window that seemed to be looking into the center of the house. After a moment I realized that Mr. Stratton was standing just a few feet away from me. He turned slightly, beckoning for me to join him.

"Ah hah! Come here my sweet little sparrow! Such an extraordinary treat!" he continued, his voice more than slightly slurred from too much of Mrs. DeVere's excellent brandy, placing his arm firmly around my shoulders. "Wouldn't you like to up the ante to two Jennys for the evening?"

Frowning, I stared at him, having absolutely no idea what he meant. He ran his fingers lightly through the curls that I had just unpinned then turned me to face the window which had brightened slightly.

The window looked into an ornate bedroom. Jenny sat on a low-backed velvet settee, her long golden hair loosely draped over the back of the sofa. Her bare legs were curled over a white cushion. She fanned herself very slowly with a large white ostrich feather fan which she held in front of herself, gradually dropping it lower and lower, dragging the feathers over her breasts until she sat completely nude. She looked over her shoulder out the window, then lowering her gaze, carefully folded the fan shut and placed it on the settee. With a slow shake of her hair, arching her back slightly, she wrapped a white-fringed Spanish shawl about her shoulders. Then, tilting her head sideways for just a moment, she smiled, blew out the lamp and disappeared into the darkness.

Mr. Stratton now seemed to have his arms almost locked around my shoulders. As I struggled slightly to move away he whispered in my ear, "Now Hannah, just what were you paid for your excellent performance tonight? Seventy-five? A hundred? Multiply that times five for a delicious evening spent with your twin Jenny in there and myself. A secret among the three of us, yes? And, you can also count on my financing your singing career as well, my dear! Not too many girls, even with a fair amount of talent, can get anywhere without good money behind their career. Almost always they need some help from someone who appreciates them… from a man like me."

My blood seemed to be roaring in my ears as he turned me towards him. His other hand again caressed my curls and then my neck, and then he pulled my face firmly towards his, his lips a mix of whiskey and brandy. Suddenly I heard Mrs. DeVere's voice in the distance and Stratton stepped away. She was moving quickly down the hallway holding a spirit lamp.

"Oh, Hannah! I'm so glad Win was able to locate you! Albert has been frantic looking for you since the end of the program. Zuma's been arrested!"

Still in shock from Stratton's kiss, it took a few seconds for me to comprehend what she had said.

"Arrested?" I finally uttered. "What on earth has she done?"

"Her brother Paul masterminded a prison break with about a half dozen other inmates a day ago. They killed their guards and several other men in the process. It's a horribly ugly situation. There's a federal warrant for their arrest to shoot them on sight and they're certain that the men are headed here to connect with Zuma. They think she's planning to put them into hiding."

"But why was Zuma arrested? She's done nothing except send money in order for him to get a fair trial!" I replied, totally confused. "She's been sending the money to somebody named ... Beaulieu, I think the lawyer's name is ... through Dr. Hughes."

"Well, apparently this fellow Beaulieu bought the guns for their escape using Zuma's money. The authorities in New Orleans telegraphed Albert that they were urging for Zuma's immediate arrest and blaming the whole escape as her scheme since she knew there was no way her brother would ever get a trial. His telegram states that these men are extremely dangerous."

I swallowed hard and took a couple of steps backwards numbly feeling my way along the wall away from both Stratton and Mrs. DeVere. She took a step towards me, reaching out for my arm, but I continued to slowly back away.

"Hannah, Albert and I think that you should stay here at the parlor right now. It's too dangerous for you to go back to your own cabin. If her brother or the other inmates come looking for her ... you shouldn't be there by yourself..."

I shook my head in disbelief and stared hard at her, continuing to back up.

"No, I can't," I finally uttered, looking from one to the other of them.

"Hannah, please...stop," she said, handing the spirit lamp to Stratton and walking after me. "Please my dear, stop," she called after me. "You shouldn't stay by yourself. It's not at all a good idea! Please listen to reason! Hannah you need to..."

But I didn't hear the end of her sentence. I started running down the hallway, which to my relief, actually connected with the front entry. I raced out the front door into the night air, stopping momentarily to throw off the shoes which had gotten so painful I could scarcely walk another step. Several groups of miners still surrounded the property although it appeared that the crowd had thinned considerably. As I rushed out of the front gate I was aware of two men walking briskly towards me. I turned away from them and started running in the opposite direction.

"Hannah! Hannah Owens! You stop right there, right now!" yelled a familiar voice.

I stopped quickly, my chest screaming in pain and turned. And there stood my father and my brother Thomas.

IX. Jared Grady

In the Lord put I my trust: how say ye to my soul,
Flee as a bird to your mountain? For, lo, the
wicked bend their bow, they make ready their
arrow upon the string, that they may privily shoot
at the upright in heart." - Psalm 11

Like most men in the area, my father was out of work, having been laid off from a mining operation in Leadville almost immediately following the Sherman Act's repeal. Along with a smalltime grubstaker named Jared Grady, he had registered a tiny claim just slightly south of Stratton's Portland Mine on Battle Mountain in Cripple Creek. Because the site undoubtedly only contained placer gold, the two were certain that no one would have bothered to seed the claim, an increasingly insidious practice that had become rampant over the last several months. But so far, the mine, which they dubbed The Little Firecracker, had yet to yield up anything much even in the way of placer gold. Winter was soon to set in and their bellies already were growling with hunger.

Even more dispiriting, they had heard that Dr. Hughes' gold mine, The Argonaut, located adjacent to Stratton's Independence, had been developed to just beyond the second level and sold to Robinson Consolidated Mining. Hughes had retained a lucrative 20% share out of that transaction even though he had only owned it for six weeks before selling to Robinson. Robinson mining had been Stratton's biggest rival prior to the silver crash. Concerned that Stratton's non-union workers, now receiving a whopping $3.25 per nine-hour day, would tunnel through to the thickly laden veins that actually ran beneath their own claim, the Robinson enterprise now urged their shareholders and miners to accept the Colorado Mining Union's demands. They claimed that this would be their only hope to defend themselves against Stratton's ruthless onslaught as a monopoly. Robinson Consolidated was the only mining corporation in the district that encouraged its employees to join the union. Stratton was absolutely anti-union but wanted to meet the miners' work and safety demands which he felt definitely needed to be upheld. This put Dr. Hughes and Stratton on opposite sides of what was becoming an increasingly explosive situation in Cripple Creek.

Desperate for any quick money, my father, Grady and my brother Thomas had decided to locate me, assuming they would be able to cash in on whatever small familial prosperity I might possess. Family was family and money was money after all and I was still underage so technically required to obey my father's demands. After obtaining lurid details regarding my disastrous termination from the Hughes' employ, however, my father had apparently apologized profusely and inquired if Mrs. Hughes might have any knowledge regarding my current whereabouts. From Jake he learned that Zuma and I had headed out to Cripple Creek to find Dr. Hughes. Tracing the rest of it was child's play, of course.

Before we had left the Old Homestead that night, my father had demanded payment of my wages from one of Mrs. DeVere's hired men, as Thomas and I had waited outside the wrought iron fence. My father had also stripped Jenny's dress off me to sell back to them as well, even though I tried to explain to him, while wrapped only in a thin blanket, that it wasn't mine anyway. My brother now resembled my father. Although not yet quite as tall, his dark, gaunt body and removed, sour disposition kept me silent. I knew there was no possible explanation about my work that they would find believable so I simply remained quiet.

Grady, who was probably only a few years younger than my father, possessed two moth-eaten looking mules, rusted picks, jagged shovels and a cheap, probably illegal, line for additional supplies, as well as a crude lean-to far out of town that fitted up under a flimsy rock outcropping where they had all been living. A roughly cut sod roof, poorly mud-chinked timbers, no windows and an ill-fitting door, attempted to insulate the structure from what was undoubtedly going to be a vicious winter.

Grady claimed to have been married twice and said that both his wives had died in childbirth leaving him some money which he had invested in The Little Firecracker, pulling my father and brother into the deal since they were desperate for work. I felt certain that he was lying about his wives as well as those women being the source of his investments. Nothing about him struck me as truthful. He was a brooding, distant, skeletal but very strong man, with only a handful of black, decaying teeth remaining in a shriveled pinched-looking mouth. He could easily have passed for my father's brother. Unlike my father, however, he frequented saloons and his exploits were apparently well known all over town. His love affair with the bottle and cheap women, typically engaged at the Bon Ton or Laura-Belle's Golden Peacock, usually drained his last dollar, and for some reason was tolerated most of the time by those who knew him. After only a few hours of sleep following a lengthy binge, he would be setting out for the mine to put in a full day Thomas informed me. Most of the money as well as all of the provisions for the mining claim had come from Grady also, according to my brother, so they had no choice but to put up with the man.

In less than a week, my expected role in this operation became apparent. In addition to cooking, constantly foraging for reasonably priced food (I had actually seen a fresh chicken egg selling for 30 cents – for one little egg!) and cleaning for these men, it quickly became evident that I was part of the payback for my father's share to Grady. He suggestively brushed up against me, grinning with his blackened mouth and freely nuzzling my neck with his cold, disgusting, wet lips every chance available. All of this took place in full view of my father whose reaction to Grady's antics just seemed to be one of total amusement. One night, after only a few days had elapsed, Grady moved over from what I had been told by my father would be the "men's side" of a blanket that hung from the soddy's one reinforcing timber, and attacked me. With a knife point tickling behind my ear and his huge filthy hand clamped firmly over my mouth, he forced himself on me again and again that night. My eyes hard closed, my bottom lip clenched between my teeth, my body rigid to the relentless pounding, my soul seethed with a hatred unlike anything that I had ever endured as I lay there under that vile animal. I couldn't imagine giving myself up to men like this constantly, like any common prostitute must have to deal with, day after day, man after man after man, year after year after year. I would starve before I would willingly submit to this. Whoever Hannah Owens had been, whatever prior pain and disillusionment she had ever encountered, whatever fantasies or illusions of a meaningful future she might ever have dreamt about, all of that died on that disgusting night when I was sold to Grady's lust.

The following morning, there were pools of drying blood surrounding the two of us. Grady assumed my monthly had begun (and maybe it had … I really had no way of knowing) and after pouring water over himself and wiping himself down, he disgustedly threw the sopping wet rag at me to clean up the area. In agony, practically doubled over in pain, I somehow managed to cook their breakfasts of boiled meat, oatmeal, and tea (while listening to my father wail several psalms, of course), and put together their lunch pails. They left without a word to me. I sat down on a stool, a cup of stark coffee scalding my shaking hands, and wept. My body, completely raw and battered, reeked of Grady's filth. My bruised, slimy legs were unable to move more than a few steps in any direction without buckling under.

As I continued cooking and washing for the men over the next several days, fiercely willing myself to recover, my mind raced erratically, grasping for any rational solution of escape. I knew of course that Grady would strike again in a few days. That was a given. I had to get strong enough. And I had to somehow completely disappear from their lives without a trace.

I was cutting out biscuits for our supper when Thomas suddenly appeared by himself a few days later, at least two hours before I was expecting any of them. I now felt like a small rabbit cowering under a ragged leaf regarding my own brother. He was no longer someone I could trust and I was certain that he had to have known about the deal with Grady. My eyes felt hollowed out looking at him. I had no idea if he actually believed that my rape had been justified. The years that we had spent apart had obviously left us complete strangers.

"Supper's not yet ready," I said flatly. "You all back here this early? Finished up at the mine?"

"No," said Thomas quietly. "I'm suppos'd to be pickin' up some feed fer the burros. We're mostly out an' there's mebbe bad weather movin' in, but I…"

"Well, then," I replied, curtly, "you better go and see to it. Don't seem like a very good idea to be annoying them about animal feed."

Thomas swallowed and moved towards me, giving me an extremely awkward, one-armed hug.

"Hannah, I know you ain't no whore," he said softly, looking down as I pulled roughly away from him. "An' I honestly think that Pa knows it deep down, too. It's like this, though. He jes' owes a lotta money to Brady an' this was the only way he could figure tuh pay summit back 'fore Brady gets real hoppin' mad. He's gotta bad temper an' kin be meaner 'n a snake at times. We really didn' know jes' how mean he was when we took up with him. And then, well, you know, then there's Pa's honor an' ...well, all of that kinda...stuff."

I stared at him, stunned in disbelief. His honor. And all of that kinda stuff. The words cratered low in my still-raw belly. His honor. His honor! My father's goddamned honor! And my honor? But what honor, what rights did any stupid, completely destitute, totally unwanted, scarcely educated young woman have, when she had a father who could just shrug off those rights without any concern, I laughed at myself bitterly. As long as he just kept wailing his psalms to preserve his perception of God, he was saved. Hallelujah, praise be to Jesus! And if I was damned? Well, so be it. Nothing he could do about that. A sense of complete defeat and absolute loathing suddenly overwhelmed me.

"But, it's gonna get worse," Thomas stammered, suddenly whispering, looking around as though to make sure no one could hear him. "That's why I'm here talkin' to ya right now, Hannah."

"What could be any worse?" I asked dully, shaking my head, barely glancing at Thomas in disgust.

"Grady's been down at the Mikado gamblin' agin all afternoon, an' that's kinda high stakes type place so they say," said Thomas. "An' I guess he already owes a lotta men a whole lotta money. Pa an' me, we thought he had put up the money fer the grubstake fer the mine? But, seems he done borrowed most of that. An', Grady? He ain' too good a card player, they say."

I concentrated my focus on reforming and rolling the remaining dough scraps to cut out another couple of biscuits and finally looked up at my brother.

"And?" I replied. Somehow Mr. Grady's card playing foibles really weren't my concern.

"An' these men, they wantin' Grady tuh be payin' out. They's tired of waitin'."

"Well, they're probably right," I replied wearily, picking up the biscuit tin once again. If that despicable animal ended up getting lynched by a mob of drunks I sure wouldn't shed a tear.

"He's bringing a bunch of those men here tonight to work off summa that debt...with you," he swallowed.

I stopped cutting the dough. The small round tin dropped from my hand onto the packed dirt floor. I looked down at it rolling along in the dust and then in horror, totally speechless, slowly stared up at my brother.

"You know them two women Grady claims was his wives that died in childbirth? Coupla' other miners said they'd heard those women died 'cause he forced 'em to constantly whore fer 'im to pay off his gamblin' debts last year an' it killed 'em. Law can't touch him 'cause he claims them women were prostitutes anyway an' there ain' no law protectin' loose women like that, ya know."

"How could ..." I stammered, my body starting to shake now that the reality of my brother's words struck me full force.

"That's why I came back here now," Thomas continued, tears springing into his eyes as he put his hands firmly on my shoulders. "You gotta leave, right now, Hannah. I'll help ya git to wherever you kin' git, but you gotta git out now."

The only escape was to go back to the small cabin that Zuma and I had lived in behind the Old Homestead and see if someone could possibly help me move from there into hiding somewhere. It was almost dusk as we arrived on the grounds. Thankfully the back gate was now unlocked since the gold conference attendees were long gone, but the cabin door itself was firmly bolted with a padlock. I hid in a bush next to the cabin, sending Thomas to the kitchen's back entrance and told him to ask for Jenny. I prayed that she would not remember my horrified reaction on seeing her in the viewing room and that she would be willing to help me. I realized numbly that I was counting on a friendship which really had never existed. If someone had ever told me that the only people I might be able to depend upon were prostitutes, I would have laughed hysterically a few months ago. It was no longer amusing, however. It seemed like hours before Thomas finally reappeared at the kitchen door, Jenny walking quickly ahead of him.

When she spotted me she broke into a run, greeting me with a light, reassuring hug. After unlocking the cabin she lit the spirit lamp on the table just inside the doorway. A very cursory look around gave me a small hope that Zuma's and my belongings, what little there were, had not been disturbed. Our three shadows were elongated and very ghostly in the surrounding gloom.

"Have either of you had anything to eat?" Jenny asked. "I can probably bring out some food from the kitchen first if you want. Then we can talk for a few minutes."

Thomas shook his head.

"I needs to git back now," he stammered. "I told ya what happened, an', worse, what was gonna happen, Miz Hays. I'm jes' gonna tell 'em that Hannah was gone when I came back from the mine this afternoon. That I dunno where she is. You know they'll come here lookin' fer her agin' like before, but mebbe that Miz DeVere kin find a place fer her somewheres..." his voice trailed off.

"Don't worry," Jenny replied curtly, her eyes narrowing, visible even in the gloom. "I'll make certain that bastard Grady won't ever touch your sister again, Thomas."

Thomas nodded slightly to us both, then quickly ducked out the door into the darkening evening.

Thoroughly frightened, I suddenly began crying. Jenny pulled me into her arms and just let me cry without saying another word. Finally I pulled away from her and stepped towards the stove in the middle of the cabin, gulping between sobs to calm down.

"How can you stand these men ..." I blurted out. "The pain, so degrading ... oh God!"

Jenny walked very slowly over to a chair and then sat, looking down at the floor and then up at me. After a few moments of silence she finally spoke.

"My first experiences were very much like what you just encountered, Hannah," she said quietly. "And so were Pearl's, actually. Only I was raped by my uncle back East and Pearl was raped by her own father. Repeatedly. In the backwoods. In Indiana."

I stared at Jenny, unsure that I had actually heard her correctly. What could have possibly possessed these two beautiful women to continue their lives as prostitutes after being tortured like that? Somehow I had always assumed that soiled doves, as my school chums had jokingly referred to them, were just horribly lazy, terribly wicked, not particularly attractive girls who were looking for lots of easy money, fancy clothes and lots of cheap thrills. I was truly horrified.

"But why would you ..." I began, groping for the best way to ask that question.

"Both men claimed that we led them on. 'Harlots who led them into the vile act', so to speak," she shrugged. "With our ... let's see, what was it that Pearl told me that her father said? Oh yes, she looked so much like her mother, who had died a year earlier, that he mistakenly thought he was ravaging his wife when he was drunk, day in and day out. Supposedly he had no idea that it was his own daughter he was in bed with until she became visibly pregnant and then he threw her out. Pearl had a child by her own father, Hannah. A little girl. She's about seven now. A family back in Kentucky is raising her. The child doesn't know that Pearl is actually her mother, however…thinks she's just a family friend who visits every once in a while."

I swallowed. "Oh God. I … I can't imagine. Oh my God." I sat down heavily in the chair opposite Jenny. My legs were suddenly made of rubber and no longer seemed able to hold me. "And you?" I finally whispered.

"Ah, yes, well, my story is also pretty ugly," she sighed. "My mother's brother-in-law actually locked me in his cellar night after night. My mother had just simply abandoned us. And I never even knew who my father was, actually. I doubt that my mother even knew, to tell you the truth. My two little sisters, scarcely out of nappies, my mother and I lived in this absolutely deplorable shanty on the outskirts of town. One day we woke up and she had just vanished in the middle of the night. No food, no money, no idea where she had lit out to. Nothing whatsoever of any value left in that shack. No one had any idea where she had gone and no one really cared anyway. Officials in the town -- this was out in southern Virginia -- forced my aunt and uncle to take us in because they were fairly wealthy. My aunt pleaded with the authorities that she didn't want to have anything to do with such nasty relatives as the three of us, but apparently my uncle finally convinced her otherwise. I was the oldest, almost 11 at the time. My aunt was supposedly an invalid in the house and restricted to her several rooms on the main floor. Even though she could hear my shrieks when her husband was abusing me at night, she told none of her frequent tea time visitors, of course. In her eyes, I'm sure, given the scandalous history of my mother, I deserved it. I finally became pregnant as well. That's actually how I originally met Albert Hughes. Luckily I miscarried in about my fourth month and Albert attended to me. I almost died from a fever I contracted which had probably caused the miscarriage. And according to Albert, I'll never be able to have any more children, so that's certainly a relief. He introduced me to Pearl a couple of years ago. They had met down in New Orleans."

A long silence played out, our shadows dancing bizarrely in the light of the spirit lamp. "So that's why you've chosen the lives that you have," I said bitterly. "Just because these two vile men just…just put you out there like that…"

"You have to understand, Hannah," Jenny replied softly, with something of a lopsided smile, "it's your word against the rest of what is referred to as 'polite society.' Do you really think that either Pearl or I could ever go back to being considered sweet young debutantes, lovingly awaiting our Romeos' first kiss and subsequent deflowering on our wedding nights? Some of our frail sisters do eventually get married to decent men and actually are able to leave their sordid pasts behind. But trust me, they are a very small band in our number. And which of those seemingly decent men do you truly know to trust? And which ones are really just planning to be pimps even though you're their own wife? Oh yes, I see you're shaking your head in horror, but there's a lot of that out there, too, my dear Hannah."

"Pearl…was known as an extraordinarily gifted dressmaker in Colorado Springs," I countered. "That's where I met her, as you probably know. It seems like she could have continued with her business and not have had to work in …" my voice trailed off.

"In a brothel?" Jenny almost jauntily finished my sentence. "Yes, Pearl's dressmaking skills are truly exceptional. You're so right. In another time, in another world, her amazing creativity and sense of style would have easily rivaled anything out of Paris, I'm more than certain. She's that good, make no mistake. And she's completely self-taught I'll have you know. And her money to originally open that shop in Colorado Springs was from one of her 'benefactors' you should also know."

Although I didn't say it aloud I was fairly certain she was referring to Dr. Hughes.

"But her reputation was fast following her out here, Hannah. She probably couldn't have managed to continue in her dressmaking business for more than another month, if that, before her past had been exposed, and at that point, no decent woman who had the money to contract her services would dare. She started all of those rumors about having left some nasty European Count she claimed to be married to hoping women would be empathetic to her plight. Some were, but many others were becoming suspicious about that story. Her father did beat her when she tried to escape on several occasions, so that part of her story was actually true. But once your name and reputation are sullied, you're almost always damned for the rest of your life, Hannah. If Pearl and I can keep that from happening to you, we want to help. I think we both see a bit of our earlier selves in you. And I know that's what Zuma desperately wanted for you."

I sat quietly for a few moments, looking down at my hands, knowing that more than likely it was already too late to salvage my shredded reputation. Instead I asked, "Jenny, do you know if Zuma's been released yet?"

"Albert's been trying to learn more about her arrest, but so far, things look very bleak. The last he'd heard she's going to be sent down to New Orleans to answer to charges that she put up the money, knives and guns to that fraud of a lawyer she hired that led to her brother's attempted escape. You did know that all of those men were found and killed a couple of days after that escape, didn't you? Albert thinks that the whole thing was a vile trap just for the money and he feels responsible because he had put Zuma in touch with that Beaulieu shyster in the first place."

I shook my head. I hadn't known, of course. Everything Zuma had been hoping for had now vanished. Paul. Her only remaining relative. Gone. Would she now take Paul's place rotting out the rest of her days in a rancid jail cell down in Louisiana and that lawyer just trot off without facing any consequences? My own problems dimmed in comparison to the atrocities that Zuma, Jenny and Pearl had been forced to endure. Jenny stood up and walked over to the stove. "You really can't stay here, Hannah. Even tonight, I'm afraid," she said softly, facing me. "Grady and who knows what other half-crazed drunken bastards will come looking for you here, probably tonight, I should imagine. Pearl's hired men can keep them out of the parlor, but she would be very upset if all of this caused a huge disturbance on the property and she was shut down by the sheriff, even temporarily. That's why she handed you over to your father when he showed up in the first place. Unfortunately, the law is the law. Very bad for business when your clientele is the crème de la crème, you have to understand. In fact she had to insist that even some of those crème de la crème move their shouting matches about the mining union flare-ups outside her place just the other day."

I nodded.

"But I actually have a possible solution for you, I think. Do you remember John Barrington from the gold conference?"

"Yes, I think so," I replied. "He came in from Denver with Mr. St. George, that piano accompanist I worked with."

"John just inherited a house of sorts, really just sort of valuable land, from some distant cousin or other a few weeks ago. It's reasonably out of the way, but accessible to everything, which is actually a good thing. Just one fair-sized room, but a decently solid place for that flimsy part of town. Easy to duck about to various markets and saloons and such to obtain food and supplies with limited visibility actually. It's in an alley behind Third Street, back behind the butcher's place, off Bennett Avenue. He asked if I knew anyone who might want to rent it temporarily until he has a chance to make a lot of improvements and put it up for sale. I think he wants to unload it by early Spring. I'm assuming that you're still willing to take in our laundry and mending to help towards expenses?"

I nodded my head. "Of course."

"Are you willing to work with another girl? Someone you know, but probably doesn't have too much ... um, laundry type ... or probably any kind of work experience actually?"

I nodded again wondering who she might possibly have in mind. I could scarcely imagine any of the Old Homestead girls suddenly pining to work as a laundress! Jenny paced a few more steps and then faced me again.

"You remember Albert's daughter, Abigail?" asked Jenny.

"Yes, of course."

"We had to move her yesterday out of Albert's rooms at the National Hotel and took her over to this place of John's. She's scared witless since she's there all by herself. If you're able to help out with her both Pearl and I would be extremely grateful. I'm not sure how we ended up in the middle of this mess exactly."

I didn't ask why Abigail was in Cripple Creek living with her father; I assumed that I would find out in due time and the arrangements sounded miraculous given my current dire circumstances. Jenny and I quickly gathered up most of Zuma's and my things including Zuma's gun, which Jenny checked and assured me wasn't loaded, and we walked quickly through the brisk evening air. Every time I heard shouting or gunfire I panicked worrying that Grady was on our trail. I didn't know if it was just my imagination, but it seemed as though the noise level had increased tenfold since Zuma and I had lived in the town. It was only about a ten-minute walk to John Barrington's place, but somehow it seemed much longer, the dusty, badly rutted streets thickly roiling with filthy, very foul-mouthed men.

Mr. Barrington's shack, for indeed the structure wasn't much other than a shack, was set way back in an alley and could practically have just been a tall fence, it was so well disguised. We walked towards the side and Jenny rapped quickly five times, calling out Abigail's name softly.

The bar was somewhat clumsily released from the inside and then Abigail opened the door, excitedly hugging both of us simultaneously and sniffling. Jenny was finally able to pull away from Abigail's embrace and the three of us brought in my few things, placing them just inside the door. It was almost completely dark in the shack despite the meager attempts of a very dim spirit lamp.

"Pearl's going to be anxious for me to get back, and I'm not even dressed for this evening yet," Jenny said to us both. "There's just a lot going on right now. Things are really sort of difficult and ... well, no need to go into that mess with you. Abigail, do you have any of that food left I brought over this morning?"

Abigail nodded and replied with a little shrug, picking at a loose thread on her sleeve, "well, yes, most of it ... some of it ... well, maybe a little of it anyway."

"Well, it will have to do until sometime tomorrow," said Jenny firmly. "With any luck, your father will be at Pearl's tonight or tomorrow night. No one really seems to know when he's returning from Denver. If he gets in tonight I'll try to get him over here first thing in the morning if at all possible. Then we'll try to get everything else sorted out. That's all I can do for right now. I hope you both understand."

She hugged us both quickly, Abigail still sniffling somewhat, and stepped out of the shack. I pulled the heavy bar down on the door; I could see why Abigail had so much difficulty raising it since the bar was quite warped and a very tight fit which was probably all to the good actually.

"When did you come to Cripple Creek? I assumed that you were still in Colorado Springs with your mother," I said, walking over to the table and easing myself down in the chair. I was completely exhausted.

"I'm living with Papa now," she sniffled, wiping her eyes

along her sleeve. "Or, at least, I thought I was going to be living with him." She blew her nose loudly on a handkerchief she had extracted.

"Mother threw me out," she stammered. "I don't know where to begin," she whimpered. "Do you want some tea? Do you mind fixing it for us? I really don't know how to do it very properly," she suddenly blurted out.

"Sure. I think we both need some tea. Do you think you have some Darjeeling? Or chamomile maybe?"

"Not chamomile, please," Abigail replied, still sniffling audibly. "It gives me the loose stomach. And I don't have any sugar or lemon or cream."

"Does anyone these days?" I answered. I rooted through the shelves near the stove, locating a small bag of nondescript and undoubtedly very old, tea leaves.

Abigail's face was quite red and puffy from crying and she had very noticeably gained even more weight unfortunately.

Our tea finally brewing in chipped mugs, we both sat at the small table.

"So, your mother threw you out," I said gently. She had begun to gnaw on her right thumb in between noisily slurping the steaming tea.

"This is good tea, Hannah," Abigail said. "I remember you said that Zuma showed you how to make it so good. That it was all in the steeping more than the actual tea."

I frowned very slightly. Actually, I didn't remember Zuma ever making tea. But Mrs. Hughes' tea was quite delicious I recalled although I declined from mentioning this to Abigail at the moment. And our current mugs of the beverage were definitely left wanting. There was a long pause.

"Well, yes. So," Abigail finally nodded. "Mother threw me out. She had to start taking in boarders, did you know that? We didn't have enough money. And the court said that Papa didn't have to pay her anything more. She refused to sign for a divorce, you see. Even though Papa said he was the party at fault, whatever that means exactly. So that Mother wouldn't have the stagnant ... I don't remember what it's called ..."

"Stigma?" I offered.

"Yes, right," she nodded. "Stigma. The stigma of being divorced. So she could still be in society and go to her church and attend her Chautauqua meetings and shop in good stores and such. Or at least that's what Papa said -- that she'd be accepted by society and everything."

I shook my head slowly. Other than a few idle thoughts I realized that I had quite comprehensively blocked anything regarding Mrs. Hughes from surfacing for a very long time. And much as I hated to admit it to myself, I hadn't given any thought to Abigail at all.

"No, I didn't know any of that. Did she actually open a boarding establishment or were you still living on Pike Street and she took in boarders?" I marveled that the meticulous Mrs. Hughes could withstand anyone sitting in her grandfather's hand-carved late 18th Century oak chair, reading a book borrowed from her private library, even though she absolutely despised the Pike Street house.

"Yes, we were still at Pike Street," Abigail said, sipping her tea absentmindedly. "At first, there were just these two lady boarders. I think they were cousins or something. They both stank terribly of garlic though. Anyway they were both really old and I don't think they ever washed. Well, the one was real old anyway. The other one I guess, really wasn't all that old. But neither of them ever washed I don't think. Anyway, Mother claimed the one that wasn't so old was having men up in her room on Sundays while Mother and I were out to church and that's how they were paying part of their rent. Can you imagine? So she gave them some of their money back and forced them to leave that very day."

She looked back down at her cup again and became very silent.

"And then," I prodded.

"And then," Abigail continued, with something of a sigh, "two men moved in. Again, one was really, really old. I mean, he was positively ancient! And he was badly consumptive. He would cough and cough all night long and kept everyone awake it was so maddeningly loud. There were several times when Mother thought he might have died in his bed because she didn't hear him coughing or stirring about or anything for several hours and he failed to make an appearance for a couple meals.

"But the other man, he was a much younger fella and very nice looking, too. With very nice manners and he even had clean fingernails! He would always say please to you, miss, and thank you, ma'am and please, ma'am, if you could kindly pass the butter dish. And we sometimes even saw him coming from that Methodist church on the corner on Sundays. His name was Jim. Jim Lawson from Denver."

I frowned very slightly. Unless he was a laborer for the family she really shouldn't have called him just by his Christian name, I thought. But life seemed to be changing everywhere. She continued to bite the skin around her thumb. Lank strands of her brown hair had pulled away from an untidy bun which had been systematically unraveling low on her neck.

"Go on," I replied, taking another sip of my tea. "Please."

"Jim was always so nice to me. So different from how everyone else has always treated me. Well, not you!" she gushed quickly, looking at me earnestly. "You were always nice to me, of course. And Zuma and Jake always were too, of course. But with Mama and Papa, I always felt like I was never pretty enough or clever enough or talented enough or any of those important things. But Jim was just so wonderful to me. He told me he liked girls who were a little more plump like me. And that he thought my hair was pretty. He said it shone like a bright new penny. And he even laughed at my jokes and thought me clever at times. I showed him some of my poems, too, and he said that he really liked them. Did I ever tell you that I wrote some poems, Hannah?"

I shook my head.

"He even gave me some deep purple velvet ribbons for my hair with matching neck ribbons for my birthday. Since Mother completely forgot my birthday again and Papa never would remember anyway, of course, it was my only gift. Do you remember that purple is my very, very favorite color?"

"Sure, I remember, Abigail. That sounds quite lovely," I said. Actually I hadn't a clue that her favorite color was purple, but I was happy that someone in her life had taken notice of her. "Where did he work?"

"Actually, he was looking for work in Colorado Springs," Abigail shrugged. "He had worked at a lot of really different jobs, mostly selling things, books and pictures and the like, back in Denver. But after the silver crash he said there were no more jobs. Anywhere. That everybody was leaving."

"Yes," I nodded. "I heard that as well."

"So, he was looking and looking. I told him that Papa had given me a little bit of money so we used that to buy food for our picnics. Oh, I didn't tell you about that part. About the picnics, I mean." She looked sideways at me, swallowing hard. "Please don't hate me, Hannah."

"Why on earth should I hate you for buying food for a picnic?" I replied, pouring more hot water into my mug in an attempt to both revive my tea and to stay interested in Abigail's story.

She put her mug back on the table and started twisting her hands. "I loved Jim very, very, very much, you see. Do you understand what I mean? He would read poetry out loud. Oh my, he had the most wonderful voice to read poetry! Very deep and just pulled you along. Kind of like that minister we used to have. Do you remember? You just knew that everything that he said was exactly as God meant it in the Bible," she sighed with a faraway look.

"Well, anyway, that's kind of how Jim was too, except he wasn't reading verses from the Bible. They were Persian poetry, actually. I didn't always understand it. Actually, I really didn't understand it at all. But it always sounded so beautiful when he read it. And he knew where to buy these wonderful rounds of cheese and delicious long loaves of fresh-baked breads – the kind with the salty tops that I love so much. Oh, and also this dark red wine in these fancy little wicker baskets. Everything was just like in a dream. Do you remember that story of Cinderella? Well, that's just how he made me feel on those warm sunny afternoons. It was so very dreamy, just like a fairy tale. He would count the kisses on the tip of my nose and then my shoulder. Then he would kiss every one of my fingers again and again until he made me giggle. We had so much fun."

She stopped for a moment, and then continued. "So much fun, you know?" she sighed, looking past me to the door. Then she looked back at me and with a shrug of her shoulders finished abruptly with: "and, well ... I'm gonna have a baby, probably in about three months. That's why Mother threw me out."

"Oh, Abigail!" I replied, trying not to let the shock register in my voice and find the best words to comfort her. "I'm sure your Mother will see things differently once you and Jim are married. Many girls have found themselves in rather a family way more than a bit before their weddings," I tried to smile encouragingly, thinking how different Abigail's experience to mine. "It happens far more often than we might expect, actually."

"Well, not exactly," she replied, twisting her hands. "When I told Jim about the baby, he seemed very, um distant, I guess is the best word for it. And then, he left town I think. At least, he came to get his things out of his room on Pike Street while Mother and I were at church the next day and I haven't heard from him since," she finished tearfully.

"He just left me. I waited for awhile before I told Mother, thinking that maybe he would feel bad about everything and come back. But I guess I was a complete idiot, just as Mother said. She said that I was completely hopeless. And that what on earth possessed me to think that any man would ever want someone as stupid as me for a wife. Someone as ugly and dull and clumsy as I am. Then she started beating me with this horrible belt, and shrieking and shrieking! I've never been so frightened of her in all my life! I ran to the train depot and luckily had enough money to get up here to find Papa."

She had started crying again and I pulled her head to my shoulder, even though I was at least as weary as she.

"Oh, Abigail," I said softly, "I'm truly sorry about all of this for you. Maybe something happened to your Jim and he's trying to get back to you. What does your father have to say? Surely he must be more understanding. I mean, since he's a doctor, he's had to deal with so many problems."

"I haven't yet told him," she gulped. "He hasn't been back to his hotel yet. He's been so terribly busy and, drinking a lot everyone's told me, and that's probably why he hasn't been home yet. And anyway, I'm so afraid maybe that he'll throw me out too. Do you think he'll throw me out too, Hannah? I have no money and nowhere else to go. He wasn't in his rooms when I got to his hotel a few days ago and that man who runs that place wouldn't let me stay there. He said that Dr. Hughes had never mentioned anything about having any daughter or that she might be coming out to stay with him so he wouldn't allow it. Said that he ran a 'respectable establishment' or some such nonsense."

She took another bite of her thumb. "He rattled off a lot of names of people who I might recognize of Papa's friends and I recognized Mrs. DeVere's name of course. The man laughed a lot and had one of his clerks take me over there. I really didn't understand why he thought that was so funny. But I must say the house she lives in now is so much nicer than her store in Colorado Springs, don't you think? Anyway, Mrs. DeVere was really surprised to see me, and I mean really surprised! And she had that woman Jenny and some other girl bring me here and said they would find Papa. Oh, and I almost forgot. While I was at Mrs. DeVere's house there were all of these very well-dressed men there in her parlor screaming at each other about some kind of miners' strike that was going to happen and that only Mr. Stratton's mines were going to be staying open because he paid so much more than any of the other mine owners. Or something like that. These men had very nasty names for Mr. Stratton! Papa and Mr. Stratton used to be good friends but it sounds like now maybe they aren't any more."

Our tea was now stone cold and I suggested we were both very badly in need of some sleep. The noise barely subsided outside our hiding place; sleep was a long time in coming, even though I was exhausted.

X. The A & H Laundry

Early the following afternoon Jenny appeared with Dr. Hughes, along with a large basket of food, all of the clotheslines that we had forgotten the previous evening from Zuma's and my cabin, and a 'bottle of the doctor's favorite brandy' Jenny winked to me. She had apparently told him about the fact that I was living in the shack giving only a scant explanation. She set about pouring a large glass of the brandy for him, gave him a tiny kiss on his cheek and left saying she would try to come back to check on Abigail and me that evening and that she would see Dr. Hughes back at the Old Homestead later.

Dark crescents pooled under Dr. Hughes' eyes, which seemed very recessed into his skull. He was obviously quite weary and I suspected would be extremely short-tempered when confronted with the reason behind his daughter's sudden, totally unexpected appearance.

Abigail explained her desperate situation to her father, wisely leaving out the parts about the Persian poetry and picnics. At first, he simply said nothing, staring dully at her as though the words she had just uttered were in some unrecognizable tongue. Then he closed his eyes for a moment and sat back in the chair, shaking his head and interlacing his fingers in an almost painfully slow, deliberate design. He took a deep breath, expelling the air gradually, and then reached for another healthy gulp of his brandy. Something in his overall reserved manner rather frightened me, however.

"Are you quite certain about this?" he finally uttered, taking another large mouthful. "There's no possibility of a mistaken diagnosis here?"

"Eh, diagnosis? You mean am I sure that I'm really with child?" she questioned.

"Yes, Abigail, that's exactly what I mean," he replied rather loudly, his face like granite.

"Well, yes ... yes, I'm sure, Papa. I can even feel the baby kicking. A lot these days, in fact," she replied, visibly shaken, and began to gnaw loudly on her thumb again.

"Godammit girl! Stop biting your nails for Christ's sake!" he suddenly exploded, abruptly standing once again. He raised his hand as though to strike her and Abigail shrank back, cowering in her chair. "You're going to be a mother and you're still acting like a three-year-old yourself!"

Abigail started sobbing. "I'm so sorry, Papa," she wailed, covering her face with both hands. "Mother never told me anything at all about how you get babies, you know! She never told me that babies could come that way! How should I have known?"

"Well what in the hell do you think's going on when you see dogs or rabbits or horses or any other animal for that matter going at it hammer and tongs in the barnyard for Christ's sake? Huh? Were you too dense to figure that out for yourself? No wonder your mother threw you out!" he barked. "What was she supposed to do? Tell you that everything was just fine? Oh how wonderful, Abby my dearest," he cooed, imitating his wife's shrill voice with frightening ability. "Why let's sit down to some tea this afternoon and start knitting some little booties and nightgowns together. I just happened to purchase some delightful soft white wool over at the dry goods store last week."

Abigail's crying grew even louder. "I'm sorry, Papa! I'm so sorry," gulping for air. "It'll never happen again!"

"No, I seriously doubt that. And just where is this gallant Romeo these days? Do you have any idea?"

"Maybe in Denver?" she sniffled, wiping her nose on her sleeve. "I'm really not completely sure. I think he might have been planning to go back there, but maybe I have that wrong."

"Yes you seem to have a lot of things wrong, that's for certain."

"He said," she gulped for more air, "he said once that you had treated him for a horse bite. On his leg. He showed me...the scar. Out in Denver."

"Too bad the damned horse didn't bite him any higher," snorted her father.

"Papa!"

Dr. Hughes rubbed his hand over his face.

"Do you think that maybe you remember him, Papa? In Denver?" she sobbed.

"What the hell's his name again?" he demanded.

"Jim. James Albert Lawson. He has the same middle name as you!" she added with a slight attempt at a teary smile.

"Never heard of him," he retorted. "I suppose I might have treated him and forgotten his name if he paid on the spot. That my own flesh and blood would be so stupid as to be taken advantage of by some drifter, some worthless bounder, is utterly incomprehensible!" He downed the last of the brandy from his glass and immediately poured another large drink for himself.

Bleakly, Abigail looked down at her hands, which she had locked together tightly in her lap to keep from gnawing at her thumbs. "You hate me! I knew you would! I just knew it! Jim told me that he loved me and I believed him! And why shouldn't I?" she suddenly blurted out defiantly. "You just left me, Papa! Just upped and left me. Without so much as one teensy little glance back. I missed you so much! I wanted so terribly to have someone love me after you left us in Colorado Springs."

"Don't you dare turn this around and try to blame any of it on me, you foolish girl! I absolutely will not have it," he exclaimed, his face now crimson.

"Yes, Papa," she replied quickly, "I didn't mean to ... I'm sorry..."

"What is it with you women these days anyway?" he continued angrily, pacing the small room in heavy strides. Suddenly he whirled to face me.

"You," he grunted, "get yourself practically beaten to death by some irate boyfriend you've obviously more leniently bestowed your maidenly charms upon! And my own daughter doesn't even seem to display the sense of a half-witted mule! You've brought this upon yourself, Abigail. You can just figure out how to deal with the situation without me. You're over eighteen now. A full grown woman as far as I'm concerned. Don't expect my help in any of this."

For a moment there was almost no sound except a loud argument going on among several men out in the alley.

"Actually, I'll only be seventeen in August next year," she muttered, almost inaudibly. Then in a slightly louder voice she added, "I can understand why you would hate me about all of this, Papa. But there's something you should know."

"And just what pray tell might that be?" he sighed heavily.

"Actually it's about Hannah, not me. And Mother. It's Mama who beat her that day, Papa," she continued. "With this horrible belt. I heard her screaming when I came back from church and I hid outside because I was so frightened. She accused her of trying to steal the money she had in the lock box under the bed."

We both stared at her. I had no idea Abigail had witnessed any of that incident. Dr. Hughes turned toward me.

"I was looking in the lock box, sir, that's correct," I explained, even though he hadn't actually addressed me directly. I felt hot under his unwavering scrutiny as I stood up, bracing myself behind Abigail's chair. "But not for any money."

"Well then for what, in heaven's name? Looking for my

wife's love letters? I daresay *that* was a fruitless search."

"I was looking for the papers from your lawyer about your divorce proceedings, sir. For Zuma. She was worried about finding you to continue making payments on her account for Paul. And with the silver crash and everything she knew that no one would care about a fair trial for a black man in Louisiana. Also, she had no idea if any of the money she'd paid you towards her account for him was even any good anymore. Now that Paul's dead that part doesn't really matter, but I'm hoping that you can still help Zuma with the charges against her now. And I … I know I was terribly in the wrong … I shouldn't have tried to look in the box…" my voice trailed off since I didn't really know what else I could possibly say.

Dr. Hughes suddenly closed his eyes and sat back down heavily.

"Oh my God," he groaned, leaning his elbows on the table. "Margaret the Malevolent Mauler strikes yet again. She beat an eight-year-old mulatto girl in New Orleans once that she swore up and down had stolen her grandmother's 18th Century silver urn. The poor little tyke couldn't even have lifted the damn thing. For a woman who is too timid to control a horse worth a damn she's…." He broke off mid-sentence with a deep sigh and shook his head, taking another gulp of brandy. "Look, I'll make arrangements for the little bastard after it's born, Abigail, and pay the rent for this house of John's for the next few months. After that, you're both on your own. That's really all that I'm willing to do."

"Papa, can I ask one more thing?" Abigail said timidly.

"Of course," he sighed.

"Can you … I mean, will you that is," she began haltingly, trying to gather her courage to continue. "Will you help me when it's time, you know, with the baby and everything? Since you're a doctor?" She started to chew on her thumb again and then hastily rammed her fists back down in her lap.

"You'll be fine, I'm sure. You're young. It's unusual that you find a healthy first time mare with difficulty delivering its foal," he replied briskly.

I closed my eyes afraid that my expression might convey the rage I felt lurking just beneath the surface. How could he compare his own daughter to a horse? True, he was giving her a temporary place to live, but that appeared to be the extent of his commitment. And I thoroughly doubted that he would make even the slightest attempt to place the child with a family. More than likely he would choose the largest city orphanage he could find to dump off the infant as soon as possible without a moment's thought.

"I see," Abigail replied in something of an odd voice, rapidly unraveling a very loose thread on her sleeve. And then she added in a low, almost lifeless voice, "I won't ever trouble you about it again. Thank you. For everything you've done, Papa."

Dr. Hughes finished off the last of his glass of brandy and left with only the briefest of a goodbye. We sat for several minutes in the dim room after I had barred the door once again. The group of men who had been arguing in the alley had dispersed. Even though it was afternoon almost no light filtered into the place. I dipped a section of twisted rag into a tin of fat and lit it from the stove, which had almost died out during our conversation. The makeshift lamp cast eerie shadows that danced grotesquely along the rough wooden walls of the shack. There were some fried potatoes and biscuits that I had set back in the warmer and we ate them in silence. I didn't want to unpack the basket that Jenny had brought over just yet.

"Oh Hannah, maybe Jim *is* trying to look for me," Abigail suddenly blurted out. "I always feel like there's this, well, very slight chance, you know? I shouldn't be thinking of letting Papa take our baby to be adopted by somebody else after she's born.

And, I'm sure it's a girl. Did I mention that? In fact, I already have a name for her: Alice Elizabeth Hughes. Don't you think that's pretty? Alice is my aunt's name. She's the one down in New Orleans if you remember my telling you about her."

I nodded. "Yes, it's a pretty name," I said softly, looking at her. "But you do know that she won't go anywhere with any name at all, don't you?"

"Well," Abigail sighed, staring at her plate, "to me, she will always be Alice Elizabeth Hughes. And I'm certain that it's a she. Alice Elizabeth Lawson is nice too ... don't you think that's even better?"

Actually, I thought it better to just change the subject altogether.

Jenny didn't appear again for another couple of days. When she did, she and another girl she introduced as Sadie, who had a large black and white magpie perched on her shoulder, hauled a small cart with another basket of food, a large tub filled with items to be washed, an overstuffed canvas bag of items needing to be mended and two new fresh straw pallets since the ones in the shack were pathetically thin. Abigail looked out at the piles of laundry and then from one to the other of us as if we'd just given birth to chickens. I explained to her about my arrangement with Mrs. DeVere to do much of their laundry each week and cautiously added that I hoped she was willing to help me now. Before she could reply the magpie suddenly began madly flapping its wings and shrieking "Hello sucker! Go to hell! Buy me a drink, cowboy? Only eight bucks a go!" The bird continued to squawk obnoxiously in what may have been French, then tilted its head and began whistling what sounded like strains of "Dixie," regarding Abigail and me with a beady black eye.

"Stupid bird," said Sadie, with a mock swipe at its tail feathers. "One of the girls took it in trade thinking it would be a fun novelty or something silly like that. We've tried to get it to at least learn the right price! Go away you miserable bandit!" she laughed, brushing the bird off her shoulder. It flew up into the crossbeams of the shack and began a kind of prancing cakewalk, his long tail dragging along the beam, still tilting its sleek head regarding us with its beady eye.

While Sadie tried to coax the entertaining bird back to her shoulder, which certainly helped to distract Abigail, Jenny and I quickly discussed how best I should get the laundry back and forth. We decided that I would make two deliveries each week, around 4:30 a.m. before the first mining whistles started to blow but well after last call at any of the bars, since few people would be out then. Also, we agreed that Abigail and I would only take what was referred to as small laundry. The heavier laundry, sheets, towels, bedspreads, and rugs would still be sent to a Chinese laundry on Bennett Ave. There was no way that I would be able to handle all of it without Zuma's relentless energy. One of the maids at the Old Homestead was always up working very early and would let me in the back kitchen entrance of the parlor. I was to itemize everything that had been done within each delivery and would be paid only in gold coin, of course, and would find our payments for the previous delivery inside Pearl's large wooden darning egg. When the egg's top was twisted slightly to the left it revealed a small hidden compartment, Jenny explained. The egg sat inconspicuously on a shelf with dozens of other sewing notions which no one ever really noticed in the back hallway. She also said that she had arranged for someone not connected with the parlor to bring loads of wood and water out to us a couple of times each week, thank goodness.

It was far too dangerous for Jenny to make any additional trips out to the shack since Grady or my father could easily follow her and irrationally attack any of us. She encouraged us to make the most of the food in the new basket; from here on we were really on our own. Sadie finally got control of the prancing bird which squawked a final chorus of "So long sucker! Sweet dreams!" several times as they left.

Without waiting for Abigail to begin complaining I said, "I need you to help me with this wash starting right away, Abigail. If we can get these things in to soak now, I can scrub when the water's hot enough in the boiler in a couple of hours. I brought along Zuma's washboard and I still have lots of excellent clear soap and sand from before. We can string the clothesline over back and forth along the walls and center beam over the stove. And I also have Zuma's terrific sturdy iron...which remarkably doesn't have a speck of rust. What do you think of calling ourselves the A & H laundry?" I said, with a small smile.

Abigail gave me a very odd look. "All of this stuff really smells very queer, Hannah." She picked up a very lacy silk undergarment. "And is this some kind of new fancy French nightgown? It's certainly made of very thin material...and, whew! It's really stinks!" she exclaimed, holding it at arm's length. "There's lots of perfume on it, but it still really stinks."

I then had to explain to her the nature of Pearl DeVere's establishment in Cripple Creek. And, although I had serious reservations about it, I also mentioned what I had overhead her father and Mrs. DeVere discussing back in Colorado Springs that evening. She remained very quiet and asked no questions. Finally, she dropped the silk garment into the soaking tub and continued with helping me load the tub with other garments.

"You know, Hannah," she said slowly, "I really used to love my Papa. When I was growing up I always thought he was the smartest, kindest, most handsomest man anywhere in the whole world. When he would come back after several days of being gone taking care of patients, I would run out to him and just hug him and hug him and didn't want to let him out of my sight. He knew everything about everything under the sun I thought. And I would just beg him to tell me stories about his travels and he usually would laugh and hoist me up on his knee for 'another chapter of Uncle Albert's Tall Tales' as he would call them. Of course," she shrugged, "I haven't been able to fit on his knee for a long time. But, anyway, I sure don't feel that way about him now." She paused for a few seconds. "And I guess I really haven't for ages."

Long after Abigail had fallen asleep that night, I finished with a final rinsing and pegged up the last of the items on the dizzy patchwork of crisscrossed lines we had strung over the stove and all around the shack. I tumbled down into an exhausted heap on my new pallet and fell immediately into a deep, absolutely dreamless sleep.

XI. After the Ball

Not unto us, O Lord, not unto us, but unto thy
name give glory, for thy mercy and for thy truth's
sake. Wherefore should the heathen say, Where is
now their God? But our God is in the heavens: he
hath done whatsoever he hath pleased. Their idols
are silver and gold, the work of men's hands. –
Psalm 115

Despite her expanding frame, frequent complaints and usual aversion to anything even remotely resembling hard work, Abigail became surprisingly adept, albeit slow, as a laundress in a short period of time. Over the next couple of months we worked as a good team changing off the scrubbing or bleaching, along with ironing, folding and packing duties. She had helped me build a medium weight sledge to haul the laundry back and forth as well. The long hours of work were exhausting, however, and resulted in painfully raw, cracked flesh on our hands much of the time, as well as numb, aching arms and shoulders and occasionally blinding headaches as a result of bleaching fumes.

Without any kind of garden, food was extraordinarily expensive and supplies of anything fresh extremely sparse. And Abigail was very hungry most of the time. I was grateful that Dr. Hughes was paying for our rent since our earnings from our laundry services barely provided for the most meager of meals. On two different occasions on my way back from a laundry delivery, I grabbed a plump chicken that had undoubtedly escaped from the butcher's cages. Without a second thought I quickly snapped its neck and stowed it under the dirty laundry after verifying that my actions weren't being observed other than by the numerous sprawling drunks littering the road, sleeping off last night's whiskey.

I was still extremely cautious, however, quite terrified that Grady or my father might yet discover my whereabouts, even though more than two months had now elapsed. Other than my nighttime deliveries to the Old Homestead, I always used charcoal to darken deep circles under my eyes and hollow out my cheekbones, as well as rubbing a little white ash and mud paste on my face and streaks in my hair which completely altered my looks. Occasionally Abigail and I froze in place, especially at night, when there were abrupt changes in the noise levels surrounding us. Sometimes it was a menacingly flapping side board in the wind, a band of coyotes, wild dogs or wolves howling close by or pistol shots fired close together. Six pistol shots in succession was the camp's signal for fire. Like all hastily built mining towns, the entire town was built almost exclusively of wood, and fire was always a very real threat. We had placed Zuma's gun in a small canvas sack, mixed in with several clothes pegs, and suspended it from the clothesline. Although not loaded, it might at least serve as a deterrent, I hoped, should Grady find us.

On my next delivery to the Old Homestead I was surprised when Jenny opened the kitchen door. It was raining fairly hard, so I had covered everything on the sledge with rubber sheeting to keep it from getting ruined and had to dodge numerous large puddles during the short walk. Jenny and the usual maid helped me get the sledge into the back kitchen and we loosened the lines I had tied over the sheeting. The maid began taking the clean laundry up the back stairs, returning with soiled items after each trip and packing them on the sledge.

"It's so wonderful to see you!" Jenny said with tired smile, giving me a small hug. I realized that she had probably been up all night. "I have some hot tea made and some warmed biscuits for you to take back for your breakfasts. They're not nearly as good as Zuma's pie wheels, but a close second!"

"Ah, well, nothing can ever touch those pie wheels as you well know," I replied, shaking out the rain-soaked covering. "I don't suppose anyone's heard anything about her?"

"Unfortunately, no, although I know both Albert and Win keep writing the courts down there," she admitted. "Sit down for just a minute and have some tea – you'll forgive me if I don't drink any ... I'm still planning to head up to get a bit of sleep when we're done talking."

The tea was absolutely delicious; I had forgotten just how good real tea made with sugar and cream tasted. I felt it only polite to ask how things had been going at the parlor as I savored every drop of the tea, guiltily agreeing to a second cup.

"Lots of absolutely crazed, insanely wealthy men here these days, especially from Denver. And then the usual Colorado Springs crowd, of course. I think they've managed to get past the miners' unionizing threats finally and are now crimson-faced debating whether the cyanide being dumped in our streams from the new smelters is poisoning everyone and everything. There's some kind of expensive plan to move the contaminated materials from the mills to the flag station and then out by train to be disposed of out in the desert and that this should solve the problem. But, of course, as you can imagine, none of the mine owners want to pay for that additional expense, especially now that they've just met the $3 per day, eight hour day demands of the miners in agreement that the miners not unionize. The mine owners blame all these interfering preservationists from Denver for this constant barrage of expenses. I'm so tired of these nightly arguments after they've had their dinner and brandy. It's become very tedious, I must say," she sighed. "And Pearl's upset because all of this nonsense has kept her from getting to visit with her

little girl out in Kentucky. She absolutely lives for those visits,
Hannah. More and more, it seems. I'm not so sure that's wise, but
she really does.

"Anyway, that's part of why I wanted to talk with you," she
continued. "Win Stratton is sponsoring a huge ball this Saturday
night in an attempt to alleviate some of the tensions among these
corporate mine owners – throw down their spears so to speak!
It's so rare that Win gets involved in any kind of social interests,
we were all quite shocked, I must say. He contacted Jonathan St.
George to just play up in the front parlor this time and hired a
small orchestra from Denver to play in the main ballroom. You
know, cakewalks, schottisches, two-steps, that kind of thing, for
dancing. Different entertainments, different rooms, is his idea
apparently. Anyway, Win has gone all out for this party. He's
ordered several cases of French champagne, caviar from Russia
and, if you can imagine it, crates of wild turkeys from Alabama
to be sent by express rail. He's also bringing in two of Denver's
best chefs. Pearl wants to have some kind of tropical garden
decorations or something as well. Apparently some kind of huge
exotic flowers brought up from Mexico."

"Jonathan St. George suggested that you sing again. There's
no time for any type of rehearsal, unfortunately, but since you
would be just a sort of greeting ensemble, St. George thought that
would go fine since it's only been a few months since your other
concert. But, most importantly, it pays another hundred dollars,
Hannah," Jenny said. "Money your deranged father can't steal
from you this time," she added shrewdly.

"So, Mr. Stratton himself didn't actually ask for me to sing
again?" I asked. I wasn't sure if I was relieved that he didn't
remember my reaction to his shocking proposals at the other
concert or if I was disappointed that he didn't remember
anything about my music.

"Um, sorry, not that I know of," Jenny replied. "Win's a

rather strange guy, Hannah. You just really have to play along with his whims I find. If he's in a temper, I just leave him be until he's settled down ... kind of like that goofy magpie of Sadie's. Anyway, how much do you know about him?"

"Really nothing except that I heard Mrs. DeVere ... uh, Pearl, refer to him once as a 'capricious Croesus'," I said with a smile.

Jenny laughed loudly. "Indeed! Pearl definitely called it! He's really ordinarily very shy, you'd be most surprised. He drinks a lot of whiskey, way too much at times, to try to overcome being so shy. It's like he's two different men, quite honestly. There are times that he can be positively brutal, especially to women. Did you know he was actually married once when he was much younger, for all of about twenty-four hours? But he found out that the woman, whose name was Zeurah, was already pregnant, so he threw her out and divorced her. Turns out though, she was actually pregnant with his child and he even knew that at the time! But apparently, he had decided that he just didn't want to be married to her." Jenny stopped and shook her head asking me if I wanted any more tea.

"No, thanks," I replied, thinking that I really should get started on my trek back as soon as I found out a few more details about the ball as Jenny continued talking. Abigail would be awake soon and undoubtedly hungry for something resembling breakfast.

"Anyway, Henry, Win's son, who is now in his 20s, and the spitting image of Win, by the way, had his education and lots of other expenses paid for by his dad. Very strange arrangement to be sure. But Win's always helping subsidize people down on their luck you'll find and then doing other quirky things as well. Recently, he built this massive, ridiculously ostentatious mansion down in Colorado Springs, which of course, is where all of the other wealthy mine owners reside from Cripple Creek as I'm sure you know. None of them would actually lower themselves to live in Cripple Creek itself, naturally! But Win has never stayed at this 'Monolithic Monstrosity', as he calls it, and doesn't ever plan to either. He has some snooty women's group give expensive tours of the place and contributes all the earnings to several orphanages. He still lives in this rambling, non-descript house that he built right in front of his Independence Mine up on Battle Mountain. There are a few crude outbuildings, but nothing about that place, inside or out, other than his Impressionist art collection, is even remotely opulent.

"Anyway, very sorry I'm rambling so much. I guess I'm more tired than I realized. I know you need to get back before it gets any lighter outside. If you can be here around 6 or so on Saturday night, that should be perfect. If you still like that green silk dress of mine, you're more than welcome to wear it again. Although, you'll probably want to iron it that evening since I'm sure it will be a wrinkled horror just from hanging in my wardrobe."

"I don't have copies of any of that music anymore, though," I said. "I hope Mr. St. George is able to bring all of that with him."

"I'll definitely mention that to Win, don't worry," Jenny replied.

When I arrived at the Old Homestead that following Saturday I was surprised someone had already ironed Jenny's green silk dress as well as the ribbons. Two young girls were trying to coax stubbornly resistant long-stemmed fresh flowers, which had been brought in from Mexico on express trains, to twine on a series of white trellises. The girls were more than happy to take a break from their exasperating labors for a few minutes to help me into the dress and pin up my hair in the back storeroom. They even added a couple of the flowers to my hair, which helped us all out.

Preparations were well underway for the sumptuous feast and various entertainments. The two cooks, hired from the

Buffalo Park Hotel, an expensive, very popular resort just outside of Denver, already had a chicken medley, many pounds of roast beef, veal cutlets, two variations of garlic and cheese potatoes, pickled beets, and creamed corn in various stages of completion. A tray laden with huge loaves of rising bread, lightly covered with creamy white towels embroidered with 'BP Hotel', filled one long counter. One of the regular kitchen staff grappled with a cranky ice cream maker while another worked shelling peas. The aromas of blackberry and currant pies hung deliciously in the air. Problems with shipping the wild turkeys from Alabama had cancelled that portion of the preparations several days prior, much to Mr. Stratton's disapproval. But the promised cases of French champagne and rare Russian caviar were cooling next to several huge blocks of ice outside, protected by a half dozen of Pearl's hired men.

The walnut table in the front parlor upon which the gramophone had been originally placed had been moved elsewhere to accommodate an upright piano. I thought the larger instrument looked more than slightly cramped in the window niche. I wondered if Mr. Stratton would receive his guests from this front room or if our music would be too much of a noisy distraction. I overheard Sadie, the girl with the magpie, and another girl, complaining that Stratton hadn't offered all of them a substantial house or flat fee for the evening. Apparently when an entire evening had been bought out like this a house fee was expected in addition to the regular customer charges by the girls. I felt my face warm ever so slightly hearing their conversation, but, quite truthfully, I was no longer shocked by anything that occurred in this place.

Mr. St. George arrived once again stricken with a slight cold, but somehow we managed a cursory attempt at rehearsing a few tunes. There were countless interruptions of more food, beverages and flower deliveries or a few early arrivals looking for directions to the National Hotel, the El Paso Club or the prearranged tour of the Independence and Portland mines. I had been singing quite a bit these last few days while Abigail and I had been working. She was a little put out that I could remember all of those songs when, even though she had tried so hard back in Colorado Springs to memorize them, she could hardly remember how any of the notes and words fit together. But she was definitely happy about the extra money coming in.

The small orchestra arrived from Denver and allowed everyone to drift in and out of their rehearsal in the ballroom. I recognized several delightful tunes from performances that I had heard with Mrs. Hughes and Abigail at Colorado Springs heritage programs. My feet seemed to start tapping completely on their own as the group warmed up on a repertoire of polkas, two-steps and sprinkling of charming reels. Mr. St. George introduced me to one of the violinists, Charles Schmidt, one of his longtime friends.

The parlor girls started to filter down from upstairs and naturally gravitated to the ballroom to take in the wonderful orchestra music. The young women were beautifully attired in glistening, tight gowns, some with full skirts and others seemingly molded onto the girls hips, as well as perfectly curled hairstyles cascading over their bare shoulders. Some wore jewels, others did not. One of the girls had on a stunning dark green brocade gown trimmed with black velvet and some kind of fur, probably mink, I thought. Sadie the magpie girl and another girl also named Sadie wore very revealingly low-cut cream-colored silk gowns, which although not nearly as sumptuous in design as the brocade, were every bit as elegant. With a bit more modest cut, one would marvel at these gowns on any debutante in Old New York I reasoned. I was quite certain that Mrs. DeVere had undoubtedly designed the dresses for the girls, and more than likely had sewn them all as well.

The orchestra broke into a waltz just as Win Stratton appeared. He was grumbling irritably about the razor-sharp creases which his new maid (predictably fired the same day as hired) had firmly pressed into his trousers. Everyone knew that he never wore creases in his pants he fumed, and his housekeeper had even expressly outlined this at least three times to the foolish girl! As I looked at him I realized that Stratton was one of the most unspectacular millionaires one might ever encounter in Cripple Creek. He was actually quite good looking with a slim build, rather thick silvery hair and startlingly bright blue eyes. His dress habits rarely deviated from the white shirt with moderately starched collar, sack coat of a never-changing cut and a light-colored Stetson or Columbia make hat, which was exactly how he was attired tonight, even though most of the other men in attendance were either in black or white tie. Stratton's only luxury consisted of multiple pairs of handmade, shiny, high-heeled riding boots, which, of course, he also sported this evening. His boots were made by an old Swiss German shoe-cobbler whom he had brought over from Europe, to both manufacture as well as maintain his boots exclusively.

Stratton's ranting about his ill-fitting trousers came to an abrupt halt when Pearl DeVere suddenly drifted into the ballroom, eliciting rousing applause from all of us. She wore a creamy pink chiffon gown which clung perfectly to her every curve, scalloped so low in the front the puffs of chiffon scarcely covered her breasts, and dipping even lower to her tiny waist in the back. Combs and pins of the seed pearls and sequins which embellished the bodice were affixed to her many layers of curls which were piled high on her head, leaving her neck and shoulders completely bare of any ornament. Her long pink silk gloves and a plush white ostrich feather fan completed her costume.

Mr. St. George coughed slightly and indicated that we

should get to our places in the front parlor to begin our program. As though there were some mine whistle going off, now that the madam and soiree's patron were both in attendance, the bulk of the party began filtering in the front entry. Conversations surrounded us as we performed, and to my relief, no one was really listening to anything I was singing. At that point, I simply relaxed and just concentrated on being inside the music, which was a wonderful experience for me again. Men continued to arrive, sometimes singularly, but more often in small groups, for the first hour or so.

Different girls were stationed at the door to receive them, offering the men drinks, food and whatever roaming desires of entertainment they had in mind. By invitation only and with a hefty $650 entrance fee for the evening, the party was bound to be a rousing success for the elite in attendance. It was assumed that for a party of this kind, even if you had a regular girl, more than likely you would be with someone else for the evening. None of the men seemed to be distraught with the newer arrangements, however. And it was obviously common knowledge that no one would have any one girl for an extended evening as was the usual custom at Pearl's parlor. But as yet a third Sadie mentioned (it was a very popular pseudonym), the opportunity to switch everything up with some new men made it a lot more fun for everyone … kind of like being in a lower class brothel for a lovely, exhilarating change. Sadie had gone on to say that so many of these wealthy married men who were so bored with their wives were just as boring themselves to all of the girls. But she had then laughed wickedly and said she would never tell, of course!

As our concert progressed, Mr. St. George glanced at his pocket watch numerous times since things were waning considerably in the front parlor. In the ballroom, however, the orchestra had really kicked things up a notch, and loud music, shrieks and laughter as well as lots of waiters carrying in heaping trays of lavish appetizers and countless bottles of liquor flowed through the doors. After we repeated a set of Schumann pieces, which definitely went much smoother the second time, he heaved a sigh and closed the music. He took off his glasses and began meticulously polishing them with his handkerchief.

"Well," he said, clearing his throat, barely stifling a yawn, "let's wait just the wee bit and see if we will actually be needed to continue. If all expected are in attendance, I'll see if I can catch the band on its next break so I have a few minutes to talk with Charles."

"I don't believe Dr. Hughes has arrived yet," I said. "Do you think we should leave before that?" And, awkward as it seemed, I prayed that I might manage to talk with Mr. Stratton before he had been drinking too heavily. The slender hope prevailed within me that he might consider sponsoring me, as he had many others I had learned, to apprentice at a small opera house somewhere. Even small towns now were building opera houses these days. They had become as important a monument to art and culture as a church was a monument to piety. Once Abigail had her baby I had no idea where either of us would be headed. And nightmares of Grady's possible resurfacing festered dangerously close to the surface constantly.

"Hmmm," Mr. St. George sighed, his thin shoulders drooping. "Yes, you're absolutely right, I must concur. We should indeed await the doctor's arrival. Well, no matter what, we're due a break at this point. Let's find some food and a glass of that splendid French champagne that everyone's been thoroughly raving about."

I nodded in agreement. I realized that I was famished. There were lavish buffets set up in both the large and small dining rooms where we filled our crystal plates with perfectly roasted beef, mounds of garlic mashed potatoes, creamy corn, and some kind of strange tiny grilled beet slightly drizzled in light vinegar. Everything was delicious although my very small taste of the Russian caviar was more than adequate. A glass of the champagne seemed to fizz directly to my head, I felt so buoyant. After eating, I had started to move carefully towards the gaming room, hoping perhaps to find Mr. Stratton plying a winning poker hand, when Mr. St. George reappeared at my side.

"I've spoken with 'the ownership'," he said, lifting his expressive eyebrow. "Another twenty-five minutes and we can then collect and go home. Mr. Stratton told me where we would be able to find him."

"That sounds excellent," I nodded, smiling warmly as we walked back towards the front parlor.

Two old men were sitting in the front parlor as we returned and began clapping. They each took a sip from their heavy cut glasses of brandy, and nodded at us from under shaggy grey eyebrows as we performed a couple of songs. An audience is an audience, of course.

At that moment the front door pushed open and Dr. Hughes practically crashed in. He looked extremely pale, his face quite strained and very bloated somehow. Rather like the pallor of a dead fish belly, it came to me. He acknowledged both of us with a small nod and was absolutely reeking of whiskey.

"We were just going to do a few more songs before we ended for the night," I began, "if you'd like to listen for a bit..."

Dr. Hughes stared at me mutely for several moments as though trying to comprehend what I had just said. "No, no," he replied brusquely, waving me off. "Where's Pearl? Did she get that telegram?"

"I believe she's still in the ballroom, Dr. Hughes. Do you want me to help find ..."

He shook his head vigorously and was already stepping out into the hallway towards the ballroom.

"Telegrams rarely mean good news," I swallowed, looking at Mr. St. George.

"Don't be silly, you little goose!" he retorted. "That gown of hers came from Worth in Paris and cost over $800 I'm told! What kind of problems could a young, beautiful, wealthy whore possibly have? You know, maybe in a few years when she's hideously obese and has lost her looks and her fortune ..."

Although difficult to keep silent, I knew I needed to refrain from replying to his crude remark. The orchestra's music in the adjacent ballroom continued to swell, filling the Old Homestead with even livelier tempos. Now that a male singer had joined the ensemble the songs had definitely become bawdier, sounding like the raucous renditions at the Bon Ton or Mikado.

"Here then," Mr. St. George continued, as he once again closed his book of music and stood. "I suggest that we look for Mr. Stratton and collect our due. Rich people never understand that we working poor are quite eager for our compensation, you know. They assume that we guppies can all wait at leisure for the big fish to scrape along at the lining of their deep pockets and toss us a few stale breadcrumbs."

I smiled at his amusing mix of references thinking that maybe he had possibly enjoyed one glass too many of that magnificent French champagne.

"We'll head up the servant's staircase to Mr. Stratton's rooms," he began. "He said to knock and he would definitely hear me."

"Mr. Stratton lives here now?" I asked, wide-eyed, stopping in my tracks.

"Well, yes. Well no. Not exactly either, of course, Hannah! You know how these people are! He has quarters which he's paid for here or some such arrangement. Rooms in which only he is allowed for whatever ... uh, purpose. Surely I don't need to spell this out for you, my dear girl, do I? It's said he's quite smitten with that woman Jenny. Although, truth to tell you, I haven't seen hide nor hair of her this evening, and she's usually quite the standout." He mopped his brow with his handkerchief as if to underscore the remark.

He was right, I suddenly realized. I hadn't seen Jenny all evening either. And now that I thought about it, when we had glanced in the ballroom after our meal, I actually hadn't seen Pearl either. And, unlike her girls, she would never leave during an important party like this with any gentleman, even Mr. Stratton or Dr. Hughes; as the hostess she needed to be accessible to all her guests for the entire evening.

I followed Mr. St. George up the servant's staircase and we made a couple of turns down a series of very dimly lit hallways. As we turned down yet another hallway, I realized that we were looking straight into the lowly lit viewing room. Mr. St. George muttered something about "well wouldn't you know Stratton would be right in line of sight with that...." But then we both stopped as we realized who was in that room.

Pearl DeVere lay stretched out on the white sofa, completely nude, her pink gossamer gown tossed lightly over a footstool. Her coppery curls dangled over the sofa's arm onto the floor, her arms folded behind her head. One of her legs was stretched over a plump white silk pillow, the other thrown over the back of the sofa. Her skin seemed almost translucent and gleamed like a marble statue. Ashamed, I looked quickly away, too embarrassed to see her like that. My gaze was pulled back to her almost as fast, however. She was much too still I realized. Her lips remained slightly parted and her clear blue eyes were staring out into the blackness of the hallway.

I gasped, then grabbing Mr. St. George's arm, stopped him mid-sentence, one hand covering my mouth.

"Oh, my God!" he stammered loudly. "No, this must be some kind of bizarre folderol. Sometimes these people go so overboard with their mischief making...." He stopped again. I knew that he didn't actually believe she was enacting some outrageous artistic tableau.

Suddenly there seemed to be people everywhere. Shouting erupted in all parts of the house calling for Dr. Hughes. I caught a glimpse of Jenny and Mr. Stratton trying to break into the viewing room, which appeared to have been partially blocked by the sofa. As they finally pushed into the room, the door cracked violently into the back of the couch. I watched in horror as Mrs. DeVere rolled over and fell face down with a sickening thud onto the wood floor against the viewing window.

"I'm going to be sick," I whispered suddenly, turning away as the bile rose unrestrained in my throat. Frantically, I began retracing my steps down the hallway maze hoping to find my way outside. As the news rapidly spread throughout the house, more people pushed past me. Then I heard a gunshot overhead. Then another. Screams followed, but not as though someone had been shot. Screams about the discovery of the beautiful madam's final repose. I realized that Mr. St. George was only a few steps behind me. He grabbed my arm and led me out a side door to a small patio, both of us trying to breathe in the cold night air. Stumbling, I knelt down in the dirt and vomited, vaguely realizing that I had just undoubtedly ruined Jenny's dress. My head in my hands, I rolled onto the ground, sobbing. After awhile, I felt Mr. St. George's hands on my back. He carefully helped me stand, kindly keeping his arm as a strong support to my uncontrollable shaking, and gently suggested we go back in the house out of the cold.

After several minutes we moved slowly into the kitchen where there was already a sheriff's deputy talking with some of the staff. The dining rooms, library and front rooms were filled with people. The two girls who had been fixing the flower trellises when I had arrived were sitting on a bench, sobbing loudly as more people began funneling into the front rooms.

Suddenly another gunshot filled the room. A small piece of plaster tore loose from the ornate cornice over the door and landed soundlessly on the thick rug. Pearl DeVere had never allowed guns to be fired in her house, I remembered Zuma telling me. It was her first and absolutely firm rule. No exceptions. But already broken multiple times within this last half hour alone.

"All right, now then," said the deputy. "I need everyone to quiet down. We need to get everyone's names before they can leave the premises tonight."

"Do they think Pearl might have been murdered?" asked a few of the guests, obviously uncertain that they wanted to be included on this attendees' list.

"Couldn't tell ya," replied the deputy. "Sure looks like a simple case of suicide to me. Or maybe just an accidental overdose. You know as well as I do that all of these prostitutes are opium fiends. Practically sprinkle the stuff in their soup and all over themselves like talcum powder, too! She coulda jes' done a little too much tonight. Or maybe up-di-dooed her painkillers – they're all hooked on laudanum or morphine you know. Some folks thought she looked a little odd all day today. But the sheriff needs just a brief statement filed from anyone who spoke with her in the last hour or so before they leave tonight. A Miss Hays gave us the name of some older married sister and we've just sent word back East. The sheriff thinks maybe she comes from some money out in Philadelphia. If this sister wants to investigate Pearl's death, well, then I guess the sheriff will have to comply."

"Why wouldn't her sister want to investigate her death?" I interrupted.

"Lady, Pearl DeVere was just a whore. Ain' nobody's really gonna care how she died! Except if her family has money and wants to pay us to pursue it, then that's an entirely different matter. That's why we had to question people tonight. You know, just in case this here sister expresses some kinda concern. I mean, nobody else is gonna come forward to pay for any kind of investigation or anything. If someone knows who to blame then they'll take to settlin' matters in their own way, if you know what I mean. Not much I kin' do 'bout that. And, chances are, when this here sister arrives and finds out that ol' Pearl was making her booty in the trade, well, she'll be out on that next train back to Philly faster than you kin say President Grover Cleveland!" he laughed.

"I see," I replied slowly, feeling incredibly limp. "Have your men finished questioning Miss Hays yet? I would really like to talk with her if I could."

I turned to Mr. St. George. "There must have been something in that telegram that Dr. Hughes asked us about. I'm going to try to find her."

He nodded and then yawned, excusing himself. "Hannah, I'm going to go. They've put me up at the National again for tonight. When things have settled down a bit and I can locate Mr. Stratton, I'll manage to get our payments for this evening and send that to you … where? I don't know where you're living these days actually."

"Just leave it here in care of Jenny, please," I replied. "I'm sure she'll get it out to me."

To my surprise, he gave me a very long, warm hug. "Take care, little songbird. Let's hope better times lie ahead for us all."

I waited around in the kitchen for at least another hour, hoping that Jenny would finally make an appearance but she never did. Finally one of the Sadies showed up and told us what had happened. Pearl had received a telegram that evening – from Kentucky. Her little daughter Katie had died earlier that day. While astride her new skittish little pony, which Pearl had just bought for her, she had placed the pony's reins around her neck and then leaned down to fix her stirrup over her boot. It was thought that a snake had spooked the pony and it started galloping uncontrollably. Katie had fallen off and had been dragged by her neck for almost a mile. She was dead when they had finally gotten the horse to stop.

I felt completely numb. Without her daughter in her life, Pearl DeVere undoubtedly felt she had no reason to continue living either. I completely understood her tableau in the viewing room. She had staged her suicide so everyone would know: she was just a whore. After all, who could possibly care? Despite all of her creativity, her brilliant mind, her endless love for her little girl, her empathy for all those suffering around her and her extraordinary talent … despite all that, because of her father's abuse resulting in her out-of-wedlock pregnancy, she was indeed, just…a…whore.

When Pearl's sister arrived from Philadelphia several days later, she took one look at her younger sibling's copper hair (which apparently the mortuary had ruinously attempted to bleach back to its original dark brown) and declared on the spot that this harlot was certainly no sister of hers. In a statement that appeared in *The Cripple Creek Times* she avowed that "Cripple Creek could bury its own dead!" and caught the first available train back East. On a bitingly cold day with low grey clouds scudding across the horizon, Pearl wore her beautiful pink gown one last time, her lavish funeral paid for by two anonymous donors, which everyone assumed were Dr. Hughes and Mr. Stratton.

XII. The Flame Burned Up the Wicked

*The earth opened and swallowed up Da'than, and
covered the company of A-bi-ram. And a fire was
kindled in their company; the flame burned up the
wicked.* - Psalm 106 17-18

It was well after midnight that night when I finally left the Old Homestead. Rain had been thundering on the parlor's metal roof for many hours by then and the streets and sagging boardwalks were nothing but a disgusting quagmire of thick mud, studded with countless drunken bodies. Jenny's sopping wet, vomit-stained dress, was tightly wrapped around my legs, making walking very difficult. Somehow I still hoped to salvage the gown if possible. Usually my knocking was loud enough to awaken Abigail and I prayed that she would hear me tonight; even a few extra minutes of time trying to rouse her seemed more than I could face right now. To my surprise, when I arrived, the door was already pushed slightly open with an enormous puddle slopping up in waves against it. The puddle then stretched almost to the center pole. Since there was no way that I could shut the door completely, I closed it as far as possible and cautiously waded into the dark room.

In the swirling gloom I managed to find the spirit lamp on the table, luckily next to a small box of dry matches. Once I lit it and my eyes adjusted to the darkness, I realized that Abigail was rocking back and forth, sitting on the chair next to the stove, making very strange keening sounds.

"Abigail?" I asked quietly. "Are you alright?"

She didn't answer.

As the lamp sputtered into a stronger light, I noticed a brownish rivulet, which seemed to be seeping out from under her chair. After a moment's confusion, I realized that it could only be blood.

"Abigail! The baby!" I gasped. "It's coming!"

She shook her head slowly and then looked sideways at me. "No. No," she answered without emotion. "The baby's not coming."

"But, you're bleeding!" I stammered as I raced over to her, but then stopped short.

Jared Grady was slumped just beyond the stove. He lay in a huge brown pool of blood on the floor, a gaping hole in his neck where a bullet had torn completely through.

"Looks like your friend Jenny was wrong about that gun not being loaded," Abigail said flatly, still rocking, looking down at Grady. "It was."

For several moments I couldn't speak. I just stared at Grady lying on the floor. The rain had intensified and the puddle under the door made slapping and grotesque sucking sounds as it enlarged its perimeter.

"Where's ... where did you put the gun?" I finally managed to say.

"I put it, uh, back," Abigail shrugged, gesturing over her shoulder.

"Back where?" I had closed my eyes, but the sight of Grady's mutilated body refused to disappear.

"Back in the little blue and white cloth bag with the clothes pegs, Hannah," she answered, finally stopping the rocking motion and looking up at me. "That door wouldn't close all the way so I couldn't get the bar down after you left tonight. That's how he got in. I didn't know it was Mr. Grady at first, but then there was all this stuff he was ranting about. He was stinking drunk, Hannah. Stinking, stinking, drunk! He thought I was you, and he started screaming and screaming about gold I owed him and how he was taking me down to Mexico to work for him and how dare I run out on him when my father had sworn me to work for him or he was going to kill me right then and there! Then he started tearing at my clothes ... it was like being attacked by a totally insane black bear! No, no, even worse! I was so scared, Hannah! You just don't know!" she went on. "Somehow I got over to the clothesline to get the gun like you told me and scare him away, but it went off instead. I didn't know that I had actually hit him until he fell on top of me and then went crashing down on the floor. Then I sat down and just waited. But I have to admit, if he'd tried to get up? I was gonna just shoot 'im again."

I knelt down and put my arms around her, both of us shaking. "He was not a good person, Hannah," Abigail stated bluntly. "And I am not sorry he is dead. Not even one little bit. Not one."

"No, I'm not sorry either, Abigail," I agreed quietly. "But we have to get him out of here. Now, while it's still dark."

The rain continued to drum loudly overhead as I stood up and rubbed my throbbing head trying to devise some kind of plan. No one would care about looking into the death of a common prostitute like Pearl DeVere, of course, but a white man shot in the middle of the night? Well, that of course was a different story altogether, I thought bitterly, even if that man was a notorious drunk, habitual cheat, brutal womanizer and probable murderer.

"If we can curl him over, I think we can load him on the sledge, Abigail," I said clearing my throat. "Tie him down with the laundry lines and tie the rubber sheeting over him. We'll take him out to that dugout he had way out past Poverty Gulch. If anyone is out there we'll just push him down into the bramble, down that steep hill. Maybe it will look like someone shot him trespassing. I have no idea really. But that's enough out of the way … maybe animals …" I stopped myself mid-sentence. But I realized that neither of us was even remotely appalled about how I had intended to finish that sentence.

"When we get back I'll soak up all of this. Then bleach out all the rags and rubber sheeting. Tomorrow's Sunday so we should be able to get it done without anyone bothering us."

"What if someone stops us while we're out," asked Abigail nervously, biting her thumb. "You know, like the sheriff or somebody else."

As we continued talking I quickly changed out of Jenny's dress into my woolen one, laying the sopping garment over the table. I had foolishly left my only other day dress at the Old Homestead earlier this evening I realized.

"We just tell them we're delivering laundry," I replied. "I'm always out delivering laundry in the middle of the night, remember?" And the sheriff 's probably still busy anyway, I thought sadly. I'd had no time yet to tell Abigail anything that had happened at the Old Homestead tonight.

"But, is that going the same direction, Hannah? Same as the Old Homestead?" she frowned, fairly certain that it wasn't.

"No. Poverty Gulch is the opposite way but, we could say that we picked up some extra work … from down at the cribs," I said.

"You mean we have to go past those nasty places to get …" she started, then looked at me and reversed her statement quickly with: "Right. Good plan. Very good plan. Let's get going."

Dragging Grady up onto the sledge, we somehow managed to fasten him down. Despite his gaunt frame, he was a lot heavier for the two of us to move than I would have imagined. An early rigor had already set in making it very difficult for us to bend him onto the sledge's frame. Abigail said she needed to rest for a few minutes after wrestling to tie Grady down. I used that time to soak up the puddle of blood behind the stove with rags, wringing them into a slop bucket, which I then emptied at various places outside. Might as well let the rain dilute as much of it as possible, I reasoned.

We started pulling the sledge along the muddy streets, and, realizing that there was already the faintest hint of dawn visible despite the continuing needles of rain, we pushed ourselves to move even faster. Walking in complete silence, we were sweating hideously within a few minutes both from the strain of Grady's weight as well as the fear of discovery. As we passed the long line of cribs only one woman was sitting up in her window. Barely covered by her filthy yellow kimono, she appeared glassy-eyed, just staring out into the rain, probably from some substance that numbed her from the cold as well as from life itself. We certainly didn't need to be worried about anything she might observe I thought wearily.

When we got out to Grady's place, it appeared to be deserted, and even more in our favor, part of the soddy had actually collapsed in on itself. Abigail and I dragged him off the sledge, pulling him part way under the collapsed section as best we could. We could only hope that the rain would continue for at least another hour or so to completely erase the drag marks the sledge had made coming up the steep hill.

We managed to get back home unobserved – even the woman in the crib had given up looking for any last-minute trade and turned down her lamp. I worked to tie down the door as best I could and planned to deal with the huge rain puddle later. We both threw all our garments, rags, towels and the rubber sheeting into the two zinc soaking tubs and then fell down on our pallets, asleep within a matter of a few seconds.

Sunday and Monday were a blur to us both. We got up late, continued with additional soaking and bleaching of clothing and other laundry, ate some stale hunks of bread, oatmeal and bland tea, and fell back asleep. The rain had finally ended sometime mid-morning on Sunday and by that afternoon I was finally able to get the door shut and barred once again. Over the course of the two days I told Abigail about all that had happened at the Old Homestead on Saturday night.

Late Tuesday afternoon there were five knocks on the door. Jenny stood there looking very limp, completely exhausted, with a small basket that I sincerely hoped contained food, I'm ashamed to say. It was doubtful she had slept at all since I had last seen her. Her heavy black woolen shawl and large plain brown bonnet actually made her look matronly. She said she had just come from Pearl's funeral.

"Of course, Pearl had to be buried on a Tuesday, so that all of us girls could attend," she shrugged as she came in.

I asked if she would like some tea and she shook her head saying that she could only stay for a few minutes, but did willingly take a seat, still wrapped in the shawl. Abigail had been sleeping and woke up just as Jenny sat down.

"I brought your money from Win, Hannah," she said, handing over a small silk drawstring purse. "I'm sorry that I didn't get to hear any of your program the other night, but I heard that it was quite nice. The money from the last laundry you delivered is also in there." She sat back farther into the chair.

"A woman named Hazel Vernon from San Francisco is buying out the parlor and making a lot of changes to the place. She won't be continuing to have you and Abigail do their small laundry. So, what's in that pouch will be our last payment, I'm afraid." She looked down at her lap and then continued. "I don't care to stay there to be a part of her new establishment and none of the other girls want to either. So, I'm heading out. Thinking maybe about Arizona. Several of the girls are planning to head up to the Yukon, though, so maybe I'll go up that way instead. There's a lot of booming mining going on out there now I hear. And I'm sure those men will be ready for a little female entertainment, just like men anywhere else," she smirked.

Wouldn't she miss Mr. Stratton, I wondered? I really didn't know how to ask her that question, however, and of course, it really wasn't any of my business.

"Can you write me?" I blurted out. "Let me know where you are and how you're doing?"

Jenny laughed very slightly and tilted her head, her expression looking momentarily so much like Pearl it caught deep in my chest. "Can't think of any young women ever asking me to keep up a correspondence," she remarked. "Maybe I shall use a, what do they call it, *nom de plume*? We'll see. But, what I really wanted to let you know is that Win finally heard from the courts down in Louisiana about Zuma's trial. It took place last week."

I swallowed. Let it be good news, I prayed. Please, just this one time, let it be good news.

She gave a very tired smile. "Zuma will only have to serve an 18-month sentence for whatever may have been her role in her brother's attempted escape. Win has paid in advance for her to have a private cell. He also paid for outside help to make certain that she gets meals twice a day, clean clothing daily, and a bath and clean linens once a week. Not even many white men get that kind of treatment while in prison, as you might guess. As I told you, Win's wonderful about getting involved with situations like this."

"Thank God. I've been so worried about her!" I cried out, a huge lump in my throat, throwing my arms around her and fiercely hugging her. "Please tell Mr. Stratton thank you! None of this could have happened without his help, I'm positive! And I honestly don't know what I would have done without Zuma's help last year when ..." I stopped short not knowing what I should say in front of Abigail.

"...don't know what I would have done without Zuma's

help last year when my mother beat you half to death because she thought you were trying to steal her stupid opera glasses or something," Abigail volunteered, finishing the sentence. "The woman's an absolute lunatic, Jenny. No wonder my father left her for Mrs. DeVere. And I'm so sorry to hear about her death. She was a very good lady I always thought and very kind to me."

"Thanks, Abigail," Jenny replied, smiling sadly. "I know she would have appreciated that."

Jenny was silent for a moment and then looked at me curiously. "And, I heard through the town grapevine that Jared Grady was found dead last night, up at that place he'd been living a while back. Shot through the neck. Probably been dead for a day or two already they said."

I looked over at Abigail and then at Jenny. "Well, I can't say that I'm exactly sorry ..." I began, "but ..."

Jenny broke in with a snort. "Like anyone would care when that piece of filth stopped breathing! He pimped two poor unsuspecting young women to their deaths, that cunning son of a bitch. Whoever did in that bastard deserves a trophy made of 24-karat gold."

Then, calmed down somewhat she added, "the sheriff knows though that he must have been killed somewhere else and dragged there."

"How would they possibly know that?" I asked, as evenly as I could muster.

"Simple. No blood anywhere. And that soddy has been collapsed in on itself for well over a month they said. It would have been impossible for him to have been shot and fallen underneath that complete a cave-in," she replied, looking a bit past us.

Trying to keep my breathing steady, I looked over at Abigail. But she appeared oblivious to our conversation, engrossed in working an imaginary splinter from her index finger.

"Just remember that you heard all about it from me," Jenny said with a small wink, then adding, clearing her throat, "and just to be safe, you might want to keep Zuma's gun hidden as well. Just as a, um, precaution."

Looking for some attempt to change the subject I said, "Oh, by the way, I've washed out your dress and ironed it. But I'm afraid it's permanently stained, very slightly, but all along and somewhat above the hem in front. In strong light it's definitely visible."

"Do you still like the dress?" asked Jenny, gently, touching my sleeve.

"Oh course!" I replied. "I think it's absolutely beautiful! I'm so sorry that I couldn't do a better job cleaning it."

"I know Pearl would have wanted for you to have it, Hannah. Please. Take it. And please be sure to get in touch with Win when you can about singing again. Don't lose sight of that. Promise me. And maybe think of Pearl and me whenever you wear that dress for a performance, yes?"

Jenny stood up and then handed over the basket. "Your woolen dress is in here, Hannah – not cleaned or ironed or anything else, I'm afraid to admit, but I knew you would need it back. Also, I packed some of the roast beef and those amazing garlic potatoes and breads left over from the party. I had set them back on ice afterwards where no one else could find them. Think of it as our secret bounty!"

She quickly hugged both of us and then left; there were tears in her eyes and mine as well. I knew of course that she would never write me -- that I would never hear from her again.

Abigail looked at my concert earnings as a huge windfall, but I had to remind her that until I could find other laundry work, we were now without any income whatsoever. And with her baby due any day now, we needed to be very frugal in our purchases. I did buy several yards of unbleached cotton flannel to cut into squares for diapers, splurged on safety pins and three pairs of knitted wool soakers and a special kind of soap that was supposed to be better for getting that disgusting sulfur smell out of diapers without bleach (which was a waste of money I discovered at a much later date – only bleach was effective). I also purchased two glass baby bottles with the most horrible-smelling rubber nipples, which Abigail insisted she would need if we had to feed the baby cow's milk at any time. We didn't own a cow, of course, but we both knew that I would have no problem in siphoning off some milk from someone else's cow in the middle of the night if necessary. We also cut out and stitched together several infant sleeping bags of thermal cotton, lining a couple of them with bits of wool for extra warmth when needed.

All of the hotels had their laundry done by the Chinese laundries, of course. And none of the housewives in Cripple Creek needed any such services either. Or even if they did, their husbands refused to allow such ridiculous extravagances. Where did their wives think they lived, Colorado Springs? I started making the rounds looking for small laundry and mending type of work from the countless brothels along Myers Avenue, which was definitely nasty work, but all things considered, far easier than the backbreaking loads from the hotels.

I tried first at the Mikado and the Bon Ton and continued working my way down Myers Avenue. One of the girls at the Mikado said they already had a small laundry service but that she was sure those horrible women at the end of Poverty Gulch in the cribs would love to have their stuff washed and made better smelling … but you sure wouldn't catch her touching any of their disgusting under things! "D'know them crib whores jes' keep a piece of oil cloth at the foot of their bed 'cause their customers don't take nothin' off but their hats," the girl informed me. "Can you imagine that! And the girls don' want their bedspreads muddied by them men's boots! Git right up to business! Don' even think tuh git in line 'less you is ready to perform, haha! Now don't that jes' beat all?"

By the time I rang the bell at Laura-Belle's Golden Peacock, the possibility of finding any laundering work was looking extremely bleak.

"Whaddya want? We ain't open 'til five today," a nasal voice shouted out the back door of Laura-Belle's. The parade of golden peacocks, some in very imaginatively seductive poses for a bird I thought, charmingly embraced the front entrance.

"I wanted to speak to someone about possibly washing and mending," I shouted back.

"Oh, yeah, really?" the door opened with a loud creak. "How much are ya askin' fer it, anyways?"

The girl who stood in the doorway looked to be scarcely older than fourteen. Her dark thickly matted hair obscured most of her face and hung like seaweed in a densely tangled mass down to her waist. She wore a badly torn, ill-smelling peacock-colored silk wrapper that hung open revealing her very scant, horribly dingy undergarments beneath and I found myself looking away very self-consciously.

"Yeah, we ain' like them high payin' snooty places up the way," she snorted, pulling me into the dark entry and closing the door. "We don' got no regular washin' an' ironin' girls. Well, I guess they did try it once. But them girls was in the trade fer themselves on the side! Takin' our customers, an' not payin' back to the house! No, ho ho ho! Nobody cuts in when ya ain' payin' yer share in! I mean, there's rules!"

"No, that certainly makes sense," I replied evenly, realizing that I was totally exhausted, and that it was an effort to continue to just look at this unattractive girl.

"Yeah, so how much did ya say it was? Or did ya say yet?"

"Well, it would depend on how many items each time, actually," I answered, attempting to sound at least somewhat businesslike. "And then if they need extra bleaching, or starch for ironing or a lot of fine mending, it would be a bit more, obviously."

"Oh," she frowned slightly, scratching a large open blister on her thigh which made me wince. "Sounds like it might be too much fer us."

"But, not a lot more," I added quickly, realizing that this might be my only hope for any work. "We could do 75¢ per dozen and then no more than say, 10¢ per item if it needed any kind of extra work like mending. Our mending work is excellent, I should let you know."

"Yeah? Well, haha to that! Don't think any of them jokers would even notice a shredded chemise in this joint." Suddenly she pulled off all of her garments and piled them in my arms with absolute ease, standing stark naked in front of me. Her body definitely looked older than fourteen, I now realized, but not by much. She seemed to have a lot of discolored greenish areas around her left breast and arm I noticed uneasily. She motioned for me to wait as she walked down the dark hallway and returned with a fairly large bundle tied in a soiled, tattered blanket, which was long past attempting to proclaim any specific color.

She laughed heartily. "Here ya go! Hey, am I embarrassin' ya? Ain' no time fer a lot of priggish nonsense aroun' here, I gotta tell ya. Jes' how it is. Lemme talk with the other girls at supper. You come back tomorrow afternoon, with all those things clean an' prettied up, okay? An' then we kin' make a final deal, y'know? Real good doin' business with ya!" she grinned. "Hey, I'm Sadie Jane, by the way. There's already a regular Sadie."

Two Sadies. No surprise there.

Abigail seemed frantic, pacing relentlessly, when I got back to her. It was so dark already that she had wanted to light the lamp, but she couldn't find any matches and somehow she couldn't tip the wick enough to light it from the stove. I managed to get the lamp lit and we ravenously dished up the last food Jenny had brought over. Then Abigail stood up and started pacing again while I tried to feed more dry kindling into the stove. Now that we wouldn't be working for the Old Homestead any longer, the deliveries of wood and water would also cease. I would have to start pricing out both and hoped that I would be able to haul everything on my own. Or at least I would be hauling everything on my own while we had a place to live, I thought. I should be grateful for that obviously. I resolved to keep focused on each day, one at a time.

"I'm just feeling very queer, Hannah," Abigail said slowly, bringing my thoughts back to the present. "Like when we were in the steamer when we went over to London. Things are just kind of rolling around inside me with nothing staying still."

Abigail's knees suddenly gave out and she sat down hard on the chair, her eyes large with pain.

"It's all of a sudden starting to push up ... like a huge, hard mountain," she gasped. "It takes your very breath away!"

I tried to ease her down onto her back on her straw pallet.

"No, no!" she cried out after a moment. "Please, please, Hannah! Help me roll on my side! The pain is like a knife cutting through me if I'm on my back!"

I helped her to curl up sideways as best I could.

"Yes. This is much ... better," she said, still breathless, her hands rubbing over her belly.

I was grateful that the smoldering fire had finally caught and was sending out more heat. I added even more wood to bring it up and hurriedly filled the boiler with water from our rain barrel. My only experience with childbirth had been with my mother and that seemed so many years ago now. A cold knot formed high in my stomach and I mentally worked to push that away.

Abigail was moaning. Or chanting. Or praying. At first I couldn't understand anything she was saying, but then I caught snatches of a childhood prayer that I remembered Mrs. Hughes had taught us.

"I can get through this hour, I can get through this day, with your help O Lord, please show me the way," Abigail repeated. Sometimes several words would almost be shouted out as a pain hit intensely, followed by sobs and loud shrieks, after which she would continue with the chanting. Then she started into a pattern of falling asleep for a minute or so and then awakening with anguished cries, sometimes still chanting a part of the prayer and massaging the top of her huge stomach.

After several hours I became frantic. This couldn't be normal. Had my mother's labor been like this? I couldn't remember anything other than her begging me to find the blue bottle for her to cut the pain. The laudanum. Which my father had claimed had killed the baby. And which ultimately had killed my mother. And Pearl DeVere. There was no blue bottle but the possibility of death during childbirth was every pregnant woman's greatest fear, whether it was the birth of her first child or her last. There's nothing to bringing a baby that wants to be brought. Dr. Hughes' words hung in the air paralyzing me. Well, little Alice, if that's who you are, I said to myself, let's pray that you want to be brought. I carefully began ripping up the two large flour sack dresses that I had made for Abigail during her pregnancy; they would be useful for additional rags.

Then I realized that her water had broken and she was completely soaked lying on the bare pallet. She moaned as I pulled off as much of the wet clothing as I could manage, wrapping her mummy-fashion as best as possible in some of the cotton flannel we hadn't yet cut into diapers. She was still shaking but breathlessly asked for a drink of water.

After a long stretch of silence she suddenly started to chant the little prayer again. Then she screamed that she needed to stand. I grabbed her as she tried to push herself up alone, helping her limp over to the center post in the cabin.

"I don't think this will…" I started to say as she groaned, one fist shoved in her mouth, her other arm wrapped tightly around the post, one thigh pushing against it. I knelt and tried to mop the blood now running freely between her legs. Suddenly a large dark patch became visible through the blood.

"Abigail! I think maybe I see the baby's head!" I brought my hands close in to her, as warm blood coursed down my arms.

Abigail's face looked almost black in the shadowy light as she started grimacing, pushing hard, almost banging her head against the post.

"Yes!" I cried. "It's … it's," I broke off as the child slid out effortlessly in what seemed like a greasy white cocoon into my arms. The umbilical cord and membranes thumped out over her tiny belly, making her cry out with a lusty yelp. Abigail had her little girl. I somehow managed to cut and then tie off the cord, grateful of my rural childhood, and wrapped the baby in a towel, placing her for a moment on the floor behind me.

Exhausted, Abigail had crumbled into a limp heap still holding onto the center pole. I sponged her off with warm water, then pried her fingers loose and carefully eased her back to her pallet. She was shaking violently, saying she was freezing cold even though I had covered her with every warm blanket and shawl we had. I couldn't trust her to hold her daughter while she was shaking even though she kept asking. I gently washed the effects of the birth from the baby's silky skin and thick shock of dark blond hair. Her bright little eyes, like a pair of dark steely marbles, stared up at me, a slight pout on her tiny bow-shaped mouth causing a little scowl across her pink forehead. She was absolutely beautiful. Welcome to the world, baby Alice, I whispered to her, swaddling her in another section of the cotton flannel, as well as one of the boiled flour sacks I had torn apart from her mother's dress an hour ago.

XIII. Six Pistol Shots
*Psalm 119-83: For I am become like a bottle in the
smoke; yet do I not forget thy statutes.*

It was several hours until Abigail's spasmodic shaking
finally ended. Then she wanted to hold Alice, who had fallen
asleep just after birth and had no interest in attempting to nurse.
Abigail fell asleep shortly afterwards, the sleeping Alice nestled
in the crook of her arm. A long lock of Abigail's hair encircled the
two of them as they slept peacefully. She was a beautiful, healthy
baby. I shuddered wondering if Dr. Hughes could really just
dump his beautiful granddaughter in some rancid infant asylum
for illegitimate offspring, hoping it would die before becoming
old enough to get transferred to an orphanage -- like dumping
slag down the ravine.

While they slept I made an attempt to wash out the horrible
laundry from Laura-Belle's. Even using the strongest soaps, the
animal smell of the garments permeated the air far worse than
anything I had ever washed coming from the Old Homestead.
Fortunately, there wasn't a lot, but even so, my arms ached after
all the scrubbing, double and triple rinsing, and running
everything through the wringer, which had been extremely hard
to crank over the last couple weeks and needed repair. After I had
pegged everything up on the line I left a short note next to Abigail
that I was going to try to find us some kind of food from one of
the saloons. This was far more expensive than shopping at one of
the markets, but we had eaten absolutely nothing since I had
spent the entire day looking for laundry work. I was desperate to
find something quickly.

An eerie dry wind had picked up and now howled around the entire town. Boards heaved and rumbled loudly in our shack. Though wrapped tightly around me, my shawl served a meager buffer as it flapped in the blinding swirls of dust. The wind was so strong it had surprisingly dried up all the standing rainwater in a matter of a couple of days. A thick carpet of broken glass surrounded the pine doors at Crapper Jack's so I picked my way around the carnage to its nearest rival, the Heritage Saloon. Several men were slumped over tables, probably after a long night of gambling and drinking. The bartender would more than likely give them another hour to wake up and start drinking again or just have them thrown out back in the drunk room as soon as business started to pick up. A fairly nice-looking, clean shaven man, he looked up from drying a collection of sturdy glassware.

"Help ya miss?" he called out. "If ya tell me jes' who yer lokin' fer, I might be able to tell ya if they was here or not. Or still is," he added with a low chuckle, nodding at the sleeping men.

"Actually," I replied quickly, almost tripping over a pair of badly scuffed boots that had dislodged themselves from their snoring owner's large feet, "I'm looking to buy any scraps you might have."

"Well, I don' usually sell scraps to nobody but my regulars," he said. "Or if they ain' my regulars, then the price is pert nigh steep, y'know, miss? So, not sure I kin help ya." He finished drying a glass and set it on the bar. "But, y'know, now that I'm lookin' a little closer at ya, you actually look a mite familiar. I deliver extra liquor up to the Old Homestead sometimes. Didn' I see you workin' there fer Pearl's party jes' a few weeks back?"

"Yes, but not working ... like that," I replied, feeling my face redden. "I sang there a couple times for two of her parties. Mr. Stratton hired me in fact."

"Oh yeah, of course, now I remember," he chuckled, patting

my hand. "I remember old Stratton saying that you had the bes' voice of any whore he'd ever met! Of course, he was probably drunk out of his mind when he said that, so maybe he was jes' lyin' 'bout your voice like he exaggerates everythin'! What I wouldn' do if I had that man's millions! Jesus! Well, all I kin say is that it's lucky fer you, my own girls are still upstairs sleepin' off last night. They might not take too kindly to you bargin' in on their territory, y'know? We have mighty nice shows here at the Heritage, too, ev'ry night, y'know? Don' need no scrawny songbirds to pull any payin' custom in either," he sniffed, looking me up and down.

"Look, please," I took a deep breath, trying to keep the desperation out of my voice. "Is there any chance you have anything left from yesterday you could sell me?"

He eyed me for a moment and then spat into a corner under the large red-lettered sign which boldly stated 'Absolutely no spitting tolerated on these here premises.' I was ready to just leave and try my luck elsewhere when he yelled over his shoulder. "Hey, Pete! We got us a songbird out here needs to take some grub worms back to her momma. Ya got anythin' left?"

A large flushed man stepped out from an adjoining room, glaring at me. "Yeah," he grunted. "Gimme a minute."

I raced home with a far larger bag of food than I could possibly have hoped. Abigail was just stirring as I arrived with our incredible windfall.

"I'll have to feed Alice first," she murmured, as though she had been doing this for months already. She pulled Alice over to her, stroking the baby's cheek. The infant greedily rooted onto her mother's breast, a movement already familiar to them both, I realized with a sad smile. We would probably still have a few weeks before her father or John Barrington would come back to see if she had given birth. Maybe by then, we would have some kind of plan in place. But I had no clue what that plan could possibly be. I pulled various small pieces of raw meat, potato peels, onion and carrot tops from the jumble of contents, leaving a mound of vegetables to cook for tomorrow's dinner. Adding water to them in the skillet, a delicious aroma quickly enveloped us, finally helping dispel the laundry stench which had prevailed until then. We ravenously devoured two huge portions and I set about cooking the vegetables to put back for tomorrow. The hot winds continued to drift about us, moaning even after the sun had set which seemed ominous to both Abigail and me. Alice would slightly whimper to announce her hunger, but quieted easily once fed. We seemed to already be in some kind of easy routine. I had realized quickly, however, that I would need to find more cotton flannel to cut into diapers!

Early the following afternoon, I walked over to Laura-Belle's with their laundry. Sadie Jane was able to produce less than half of what was owed, saying that the girls had decided that they really weren't interested in a small laundry expense. But thanks all the same. If they wanted to wash their stuff they could just do it themselves. As I began to walk slowly back towards our place, the hot winds continuing to increase in intensity from prior days, I mentally tried to work through our expenses against the money that remained, balancing out just how long we might be able to manage. Whenever I had tried to gently nudge Abigail into talking about contacting Dr. Hughes, she either abruptly changed the subject or started quietly crying, her tears splashing on her sleeping daughter's tiny face.

Suddenly, the sound of a pistol shot, followed rapidly by a series of five more shots startled me out of my dissonant thoughts. Looking out past the direction of the Old Homestead, I saw a narrow, but concentrated, thick black plume of smoke snaking into the sky. The pistol's signal was repeated yet again and the sounds of rapidly tramping feet, galloping horses and shouts erupted all around me, the sounds surging immediately into chaos. Shrieks of "fire!" began filling the air as I broke into a desperate run back towards our shack. Whipped by the wind, huge columns of heavy, black smoke, streaked with purplish-red fiery tongues, now filled the sky from Myers, snaking along the way towards Bennett. I could see great tongues of fire lapping down, beginning to crisscross from one roof to another with an almost deafening, snapping roar as the inferno rapidly intensified.

Someone shoved me out of the way as the camp's bright new fire engine, bravely clanging its bell, rushed past, pulled by two enormous grey work horses. I prayed that the reservoir was more than its usual half full since we'd had those torrential rains so recently. Even though our drinking water was brought in by carts, to help keep the reservoir as full as possible in the event of a fire, it was common knowledge despite assurances by authorities that even a small conflagration would most likely be deadly. The streets were alive with confusion, people pushing in all directions, some shrieking offers of outlandish sums of money for anything with wheels, although everyone was too busy already trying to move some of their own treasured possessions to pay any heed.

"Hello, Sucker! Go to hell! Buy me a drink, cowboy? Only eight bucks a go!" The Old Homestead's magpie landed on my shoulder, then quickly took off again. If all of the girls had indeed left when Mrs. Vernon had taken over, then Sadie must have left her bird behind. In spite of the dire situation, I smiled to myself. The bird still hasn't learned the right price, Jenny, I thought.

As I opened the door, Abigail was up, pacing slowly, cradling a whimpering Alice. "How bad is it?" she asked, her voice quaking.

"I saw the fire truck go by, but ..." I stammered. "From where I was standing I could see the winds blowing the flames over half of the city. I don't know how much good the fire truck will be even if the reservoir is full to the brim. We've had so much rain! Surely that will help slow down the fire..." my voice trailed off.

"I've dragged some things onto the sledge. If you can help me strap it. Also, here's the money pouch," interrupted Abigail, handing me the purse quickly.

"It's a stampede out there," I shook my head. "If we can just make it to Freeman's Placer! I think that's where a lot of people are trying to get over to. Just leave everything, Abigail. We'll never make it otherwise. I hope you can walk that far!" I said, tucking the pouch into my shift. I grabbed the small top bundle off the sledge and hastily buried Zuma's gun in it as well.

"I'm fine, Hannah," she replied firmly.

I threw both of our shawls into the soaking tub, which luckily was filled only with water, and then quickly wrung them out. We moved out into the smoke-filled street. "Put your shawl around yours and Alice's face," I yelled, doing the same, as we were buffeted along by frightened people and animals streaming away from the flames. Suddenly a series of loud explosions rocked behind us.

"Idiots!" I heard one man bellow. "Damned drunken lunatics are dynamitin' jes' fer the hell of it! No way kin they be tryin' to dynamite a fire break with this kind o' wind!"

"D'ya know how it started?" coughed a woman between the man and us, pushing along with two young boys riding astride each hip.

"Maybe at Central or Topics. One of them raunchy places. Somebody said some whore and her john was fightin' and they pushed over a coal oil stove. Place went up like a matchstick. Golden Peacock, Crapper Jack's, the Mikado. They're gone. Old Homestead just exploded I heard into a million pieces," said the man.

"Well, good riddance to that," the woman snorted, jostling

the larger boy up to a new position higher on her hip.

"Yeah, well you'll see, lady. They'll git them places up an' runnin' first!" laughed the man heartily.

We kept our wrapped faces down, moving slowly since Abigail was still not able to walk very fast, but managed to work ourselves steadily out to the streambed at Freeman's outside of town. Several overturned carts and wagons, along with frantic runaway horses and burros added to the confusion. Once the men had their families safely removed most of them struggled against the tide to return and help fight the conflagration as best as possible.

But nothing anyone could attempt helped, however. Until the wind abated very late in the afternoon and the flames died out seemingly by themselves all at once, the fire held free reign. The sun finally appeared as the smoke began to clear, and, almost like somnambulists, we slowly worked our way back towards town, where we discovered that the entire east portion of the camp was burned down completely to cinders, including our place. Everything on Carr Avenue, which included many of the rooming houses and most of Eaton Avenue's better homes, lay in an indistinguishable charred pile of rubble. Poverty gulch and almost all of Myers Avenue was reduced to a smoldering incinerator.

Dazed, looking out over the destruction of our homes, rumor flowed quickly among us that Mr. Stratton was sending up food, supplies and tents, both from Victor, our closest neighbor and mining camp, and Colorado Springs, by railroad later that evening. A desperate telephone call from Cripple Creek's mayor to Colorado Springs before the lines were silenced by the conflagration had initiated Stratton's immediate action. We moved towards the Midland Rail Terminal hoping that the rumor was indeed true and shortly after nightfall, the first of Mr. Stratton's two trains arrived with abundant supplies. While awaiting the trains, we had all listened to our mayor's platform stating that the fire was actually a blessing in disguise. That from now on, all of the buildings would have to meet much stricter specifications, for "as everybody knows, gold is refined by fire and we here are a city built of that very gold!"

Abigail, Alice and I moved into one of the huge tents, sharing the space with at least six other large families, but had abundant food and blankets, even an abundant supply of diapers for baby Alice. Prior to daybreak some of the men began starting to rebuild their homes before the ashes had completely cooled. Eerily, however, the hot winds' low, sustained moans continued to surround us.

Three days later, the fervor motivating the town's reconstruction was completely paralyzed, however. At almost the exact same hour, six rapid pistol shots once again crackled through the air. Anyone who thought this a gruesome practical joke was quickly jolted to reality, as within seconds, those same dry winds blew showers of sparks over whatever structures remained standing in its path on the west end of the town. Unlike the first fire, which boasted a series of dancing vertical flames, this renewed one voraciously rolled over the entire town within mere minutes. No one tried to salvage any belongings, praying silently as we were pushed to the outskirts of town that our families would just be able to survive. Stratton's tents and supplies were engulfed as well. Huge explosions from the El Paso Livery Stable as it blasted into two sections were punctuated by horses' screams as they burned in agony.

The throng had been cut off from retreating to Freeman's Placer this time because of the intense heat and moved out the other direction to the Mount Pisgah cemetery. Abigail sat down on a low tombstone and nursed Alice, facing away from the fire, its own hunger finally abating once all was consumed within its path. The flames ceased as night fell, but this time, no train from

Stratton or Colorado Springs was announced to help out with
provisions. There were no blankets, no pillows, no water, and not
a crumb of food. Exhausted, everyone curled up and slept as best
as possible, heads cradled by various gravestones, grateful that
they had escaped and worrying about friends and neighbors who
may not have been so fortunate.

Within two days, trainload after puffing trainload of food
staples and construction supplies, sent again by Stratton, were
being unloaded at the dock where the Midland Terminal, also
burned to the ground, had once stood. The eccentric millionaire
didn't wait for any kind of promised financial backing from the
Colorado Springs Bank, Mr. Speyer, Mr. Wentworth or anybody
else. Word came to the stranded town that Stratton himself, his
shirtsleeves rolled up, was working a hoist to load bricks and 2 x
4s onto pallets destined for the charred city which housed his
mining interests. Overnight the eccentric millionaire's reputation
changed from one of dubious suspicion to that of an out-and-out
hero.

The only building left intact was the Town Hall which now
housed all the women and children. The men folk, even the
husbands, were restricted to outside quarters. Many of the
prostitutes tried to pitch makeshift tents behind the Town Hall
building. But the mayor, rallying to staunch protests, almost
immediately forced them all to take their temporary shelters back
down to the smoldering ashes where Poverty Gulch had once
stood. Children seemed to be milling about everywhere and no
one knew who belonged to what child. We knew that either
Abigail's father or John Barrington would show up but in the
meantime, both mother and daughter grew stronger each day.
Abigail's quick energetic return and rapid weight loss took me
quite by surprise.

In less than a week, about eight blocks along Bennett
adjacent to the Town Hall was already under construction. The

rhythms of hundreds of hammers and saws filled the air which was brisk with the pleasant smell of the new wood. I noticed larger buildings under rapid construction on Myers Avenue also. No one was wasting any time getting the Old Homestead and the Bon Ton back on the map, it seemed. Like all the respectable women, Abigail and I mended smashed thumbs, helped with cooking huge vats of stew, baking bread, roasting undersized pigs over spits and making fruit compotes and stewed root vegetables sent up by Stratton. We rigged up an old caldron with hot coffee and lashed a tin can to a small metal rod to use as a ladle. Even though Stratton was of course providing the coffee beans, people were willing to pay a few cents for a hot cup of coffee offered in the middle of their day we discovered very early on.

Not surprisingly, John Barrington showed up one afternoon about a week or so after the fires, while Abigail and I were buried up to our elbows punching down dough. Alice lay next to me, loosely bundled on a board, sucking her thumb and sleeping quietly. Abigail scarcely looked up as her rolling pin stretched out another square of dough on a floured piece of tarp and methodically started cutting biscuits with a sharp tin.

Mr. Barrington sat down next to me, curling a tiny lock of Alice's soft hair off her forehead. "It's good to see that everything is going well. I just came to check on you girls. Your father was very concerned with the fire and everything, Abigail."

"Hah!" snorted Abigail, "Concerned. My father. Right." She pounded another round of dough into submission. "You tell my father, that I'm just dead, all right? There's a list on that wall right outside of the Town Hall, did you know that? You can see it from here, in fact," she continued, gesturing in that direction. "You go over there and put my name on it, you hear? You put my name on it as missing. You tell him that I'm missing, presumed dead and everything will be settled between that man who calls himself my father, me, and my baby."

"I'll need to tell Dr. Hughes that you've had the baby," said Mr. Barrington quietly.

"Oh no you don't! I'm dead. The baby can be dead as well. There's nothing else here for you to do now, I would say. We died in the fire. Simple. You go back to him with that news, all right? Good day to you, sir."

She picked up the long metal sheet filled with biscuits, standing with a small gasp of pain. I knew she must still be weak from childbirth. I remembered stories I'd heard from old women about the earlier frontier days where a wagon train would only stop for an hour or two for a woman to give birth and then the relentless bumping journey would recommence for mother and newborn, assuming that they had both survived the birth at all. Otherwise they just became yet another one of the countless graves marked along the trail.

After placing the baking sheet into the brick oven, Abigail continued walking away from us and started talking with a man who I couldn't place at first, but that I eventually realized was the bartender from the Heritage Saloon where I'd bought our food scraps just before the fire.

Still sitting, Mr. Barrington turned towards me. "She's one very angry girl," he remarked quietly, shaking his head.

"And she has every right to feel the way she does," I shrugged, keeping my eyes fixed on punching down my own round of dough.

Several children playing tag were shooed away by mothers from our makeshift, hot brick ovens.

"There was also something else that I wanted to speak with you about, Hannah," said Mr. Barrington.

For some reason thoughts of Grady's mutilated body slumped behind our stove flashed momentarily before my eyes. I shuddered inwardly but worked to keep myself steady.

"Along with a couple of other investors, Win's just finished building a small opera house over in Victor. It's set to open within the next couple of months and has been the focus of a lot of his attention up until the fire here. Now that the National Hotel here in Cripple Creek is gone, he mentioned that he also might be considering building a sort of combined complex on that site," said Mr. Barrington. "Well, kind of an attached pavilion to a new hotel, if I understand him. Hard to follow his plans sometimes, you know? New opportunities and all that is what Win Stratton's all about."

I wondered where on earth this information could possibly be leading.

"If the Cripple Creek idea happens, he's envisioning something that a husband would actually take his wife to see. Some of the dance hall girls who came in a few months back from the Dawson and Skagway regions out in Alaska got this idea buzzing around in his brain. He has in mind a kind of stone and concrete pavilion, plans on putting about $100,000 into the opera house alone. The design he's been talking about would have ornately carved pillars, filigree screens and friezes. The works. A gentleman could book a private box with his wife ... or, his lady... to dance and buy her champagne but the stage entertainment would feature legitimate musicians and actresses touring with national shows."

"I can't imagine Cripple Creek wives ever wanting to set foot in anything like that, Mr. Barrington!" I burst out laughing despite myself, my dough a completely forgotten lump on the board in front of me. "Surely he's not serious about trying to include these men's wives?"

"Well, I couldn't exactly see it either, not at first, anyway," he shrugged. "And quite honestly, Win would have to see how his legitimate theater operation in Victor would play out before he would actually invest in such here in Cripple Creek. I mean,

Victor has its bawdy parlors, same as any mining town, but right from the beginning there were a lot more married men and their families that settled over there. That's made a big difference in the kinds of, um, entertainment that has been developed in that town. And it's that opera house, the Victor Grand that he's interested in talking with you about. Of course, Victor is only about five miles away, but, let's face it, still a rather rugged five mountainous miles!" Mr. Barrington smiled and started to a roll marble-sized piece of dough between his fingers.

I just stared at the man and offered no reply. Victor technically shared ownership of several mines along Battle Mountain, including both of Stratton's lucrative Independence and Portland enterprises much to the dismay of the Cripple Creek townspeople.

"But he's betting that good entertainers from Broadway and London will truly help to change their minds. The women in these parts need something other than their husbands and children in their lives, don't you agree? Win thinks he can get Lucy Lovell, she's that breathtaking headliner that Albert and Pearl were so enchanted with while they were in London. Also, Win's talked about bringing in Eddie Foy, Lily Langtree and Lotta Crabtree, if he can finally convince her to actually leave New York City for awhile. And, most importantly, he's interested in having you as one of their regular house singers during weeks when none of the main entertainers can be procured. Starting as soon as possible. They're opening in a few weeks as I think I mentioned before. The pay would be quite good, I might add. I'm sure they'll be in need of your help getting this city back on its feet for the next several weeks, but that won't take all that long in my estimate. And then, you're going to have to figure out how to fend for yourself again."

I ignored most of his details of either performance space, tackling instead his seemingly critical remarks about women's lives and opportunities.

"You say that women need something else in their lives? Yes, Mr. Barrington, I would agree. The women in any small mining town, like most small towns, certainly need something else in their lives. Much better jobs, for one thing. The only decent work for an impoverished unmarried woman is as a laundress or a cook or a teacher. And if she can't make it in any one of those dreary, decent roles? Well, I need not explain further how she undoubtedly then makes her living. She must work constantly to resist the slightest innuendo or blight from her own reputation or it will reflect badly not only on the woman herself, but on her children as well. A man can, of course, do whatever he wishes with his money, his social whims and his reputation, and unless he cheats at cards or salts a mine or kills another man, no one thinks twice about it."

Mr. Barrington studied my face for a few moments, carefully replacing his dough marble on my board then cleared his throat.

"Indeed. Yes, you have a point. And, not to change the subject, but I do wish you would call me John, Hannah. Also, you've just left out an additional accepted line of work, that of a legitimate entertainer who is not a prostitute. They do exist, you know. So will you consider Win's offer?" he said, obviously choosing to ignore my heated protest. "I'm willing to tell Albert that I saw Abigail's name on that wall, if that helps with your decision. Although if Abigail is actually planning to try to raise that little bastard, I suppose Albert might be cajoled to send..."

In spite of myself, I spun viciously and interrupted. "Her name is Alice, Mr. Barrington. She's a beautiful baby girl and her name is Alice," I said tersely.

"I'm sorry. Of course, she is," he replied quickly.

I glowered at him.

"Albert's had a very difficult time dealing with Pearl's death, Hannah. Blames himself in fact. Give him a little understanding.

Please..."

"What else is expected from me with Mr. Stratton's offer," I asked bluntly, floured hands on my hips, ignoring his mention of Pearl DeVere. "Isn't there a good possibility that his only real interest in me is that I seem to remind him of Jenny? I'm not even sure that he's ever been sober enough to hear me sing at all."

"Well, now that I really don't know," Mr. Barrington replied, looking uncomfortable. "But considering your finances you shouldn't ..."

Suddenly Sadie's magpie swooped in from wherever it had been biding its time, landing on my shoulder then jumping up onto my head, its sticky little feet pattering about in my hair. "Hello, Sucker! Go to hell! Allez vous-en! Au revoir blagueur!"

I had no idea about anything the bird was saying in what now definitely sounded like French, but the English expressions were certainly perfectly timed. I laughed at the irony of the bird's appearance, picking up the rolling pin to start rolling out the dough. The magpie finished up its monologue with: "buy me a drink, cowboy? Only eight bucks a go! Mon dieu, mon dieu! Quel renard!" and gave a long, low whistle before it flapped off again.

Mr. Barrington shook his head as the bird flew away. "That damned bird's going to get itself in a lot of trouble one of these days," he muttered. "Stratton and a few others as well have taken a pot shot at it on more than one occasion. Lucky for Monsieur Saint-Jacques Win's a bad shot."

Monsieur Saint-Jacques, I thought! What a perfect name for this marvelously entertaining creature!

Mr. Barrington then made a slight theatrical bow and said he would tell Stratton that I was interested in talking with him about his job offer even though I hadn't actually agreed to such. He said that Stratton would send a wagon over for me in the next couple of weeks so that we could meet at his home to discuss everything.

***

Stratton continued to send food, clothing and construction supplies to Cripple Creek during the next month. The town was rebuilt quickly by the miners themselves. Once the National Hotel was rebuilt, all the women and children were relocated there, while the rest of the men continued living in the tents. Stratton, wise to the ways of his sex, sent no money however, knowing that it would be squandered on less important tasks than the one facing the entire town. He also only shipped in very limited cases of alcohol, yet another means of making sure the important construction jobs were tackled quickly. Once several major structures, including a new Town Hall, Midland Terminal, water works, small electric grid, telephone building, *Cripple Creek Crusher* newspaper, two new dry goods and grocery stores, a druggist, and a couple of hotels had been almost completed, the married men began receiving supplies to begin working together to rebuild their families' homes. Women, both single and married, were finally beginning to receive bolts of fabric, thread and other notions, and began scrambling to construct desperately-needed new clothes for themselves and their families. Meanwhile, the single men tackled the new specifications for the many saloons, parlor homes, cribs and Mr. Stratton's Elite Theatre, which unfortunately, ended up being placed only a block from the newly rebuilt and already up-and-running, sturdy brick edifice the Old Homestead. Whatever grandeur Stratton might have aspired to attain with his Elite Theatre was never realized unfortunately. The edifice was basically just a larger, equally raucous and definitely more expensive version of the entertainments at saloons like Crapper Jack's and the Heritage, establishments that no decent woman would have ever dared be seen much less perform within.

Meals continued to be served en masse by all of the women in a burned out field behind the National Hotel, supplied by Stratton's daily trains, with more than adequate supplies of meat, potatoes and both vine and good root vegetables. The owner and bartender of the Heritage Saloon, Jack Fairfield, started eating with Abigail and me at both midday and evening meals. He seemed to love bouncing little Alice on his knees, careful to hold her head steady in his big hands, while Alice cooed back at him. He said that he loved babies and she was certainly the cutest one he'd ever seen. And her mother was right cute, too. Within less than a week, whatever fantasies Abigail may have still harbored about her lost love Jim Lawson were now displaced by the smooth-talking Jack Fairfield. Something didn't sit quite right with me about this relationship. It just seemed to be much too intense far too quickly. But then, what did I know about the growth of a loving relationship between a man and a woman? Absolutely nothing of course. Abigail was truly glowing with Fairfield's amorous attentions and I concealed any of my suspicions. She and Alice accompanied him daily to observe the construction taking place at the Heritage Saloon. It would be several months before the replacement smoked glass mirrors, monolithic oil paintings, hand-painted Mexican tiles, fancy new glass fixtures and glassware would be arriving, but Jack was poised to open any day now despite lacking those items he had told Abigail. The National Bank was now back in operation and handing out loans like candy, especially to big money saloon owners like Jack (according to Jack). He'd recently brought over an upright piano from Victor. His girls – who were very unhappy to have been housed in the tents down with those nasty Poverty Gulch whores all this time -- were more than ready to move back into the saloon and start entertaining again he proudly boasted one hot summer evening.

XIV. Little Fuss 'n Feathers

A small wagon sent from Win Stratton arrived for me late one afternoon a few weeks after Mr. Barrington's appearance. At first, I tried to make some small conversation with the driver on the way to the Independence mine where Mr. Stratton's ranch house was built, but the driver answered me in vague grunts. After several attempts to engage him, I simply gave in to silence and enjoyed the breeze from the quick, beautifully matched pair of golden-brown trotters that effortlessly seemed to skim along with the light wagon over the rocky terrain.

I had absolutely no idea what to expect when I arrived at Stratton's home. His housekeeper, a very quiet, older Polish or possibly Russian, woman who introduced herself as Anna, opened the front door with a small pair of banded silk slippers in hand. 'Mr. Stratton allow no dirty shoes, no dirty boots inside house' she stated firmly, gesturing to a chair just inside the small parlor where I could exchange my footwear. Glancing around I saw a couple of sturdy beautifully dark-stained wood side tables and padded chairs, all with perfectly turned legs, undoubtedly fashioned by the master carpenter himself. There were also several very large, ornately painted Carcel lamps and surprisingly, what I thought were probably Impressionist oil paintings based on Jenny's mention of Stratton's art collection. Although I had seen few works by these new European artists, I certainly had heard a lot about them in Colorado Springs. I wondered if these might possibly be originals by these masters who Mrs. Hughes utterly despised, ranting about such artistic decadence during her afternoon tea parties. As I stared in awe at one breathtaking painting of a mother bathing her very young daughter's feet, Mr. Stratton quietly entered the room.

"Mary Cassatt, 1893, 'The Child's Bath'," said Stratton. "Are you familiar with Miss Cassatt's work? Over on that wall that's another of her masterpieces, 'Children Playing on the Beach' which she painted back in 1884. I love that little girl's fist on the shovel and the endless blue water and sailboats. Even though, personally, I absolutely despise boats," he added.

Spellbound, I shook my head, continuing to stare, perhaps rudely, at both paintings rather than looking over at my host. He walked over and stood just behind me.

"Mary Cassatt was the only American invited to showcase her work at the Paris Exhibition in 1893 which, apparently, was comprised only of male French painters. She's considered one of 'les trois grandes dames of Impressionism' along with Marie Bracquemond and Berthe Morisot. I'm hoping to acquire more of Cassatt's amazing work." He paused for a moment then continued speaking, realizing I was totally enraptured by these paintings and their backgrounds.

"I'm also most fortunate to have one of Berthe Morisot's last oils, 'Julie Daydreaming' in my library, which I'll show you. She painted it just before she died a couple of years ago. And I have a liaison in Paris attempting to procure one of Marie Bracquemond's magnificent 'plein air' paintings, done in the style of Degas and Monet. However, since the woman's ridiculously jealous husband refuses to let any of her works be exhibited in Paris anymore the fool woman has completely stopped painting, I've been informed. Talk about killing off the golden goose, although ultimately it will probably drive up the value of her work."

I just looked at him, undoubtedly a confused expression on my face. His snow-white hair seemed to sparkle in the soft lamplight, his blue eyes clear without a hint of alcoholic interference. Here was a man about whom I had only assumed the crudest of behaviors, based on firsthand observance in several cases, collecting the newest art by female artists. Not merely for its financial value like most collectors, although certainly that was probably involved as well, but as a man who genuinely loved these works and the artists themselves. I was quite astounded.

"Who," I cleared my throat slightly, "actually ever gets to see your collection, Mr. Stratton?"

"Well, you today, Miss Hannah," he smiled, with a slight gesture. "A few other close friends, but never any dull business people. Jenny, of course, our dearest late Pearl, Albert Hughes, and Barrington, obviously. A sprinkling of other names you probably wouldn't recognize. Or maybe you would, actually. At any rate, I almost never entertain here other than a very occasional dinner with a friend. My housekeeper Anna is most appreciative of that fact. She's an excellent cook but absolutely detests cooking for a crowd -- which actually works quite fine for me since I detest eating in a crowd."

I smiled meeting his gaze for a moment, then looked away.

"When I die, I would love for all of these paintings to be kept together as a small collection to be added to either the Denver or Colorado Springs Art Museums. But all will undoubtedly be squandered among a lot of petty thieves who claim monies from my estate," he stated bluntly. "I try not to dwell on that."

"Ah," I replied. "Well, hopefully you're wrong, Mr. Stratton, and they will all be kept together."

He put his hand gently under my chin, lifting it slightly. "Win," he said quietly, looking for a moment into my eyes.

"Win," I nodded with a self-conscious smile. Then, rather daringly, I added, "yes, of course. Always a 'winner', I suppose. No one ever had a nickname for you?"

He brought his hand back down to his side, an amused look

sparkling in his eyes.

"Well, growing up I had four older sisters. They always called me 'little fuss 'n feathers' when I was a kid. Guess I had a lot of tantrums 'cause I never got my way or something," he laughed. "Hard to believe in a house full of women, isn't it, huh? But luckily very few people know about that!"

I burst out laughing as much at the nickname itself as his willingness to share such information with someone like me.

"That's much better than my nickname!" I mused.

"Which was?"

"Bitsy Butter Toes," I stated, surprisingly managing a straight face.

"Bitsy Butter Toes? What the hell does that mean?" Stratton guffawed.

"I guess when I was little I would dip my feet into the butter churn when no one was looking and squish it between my toes."

"Bitsy Butter Toes," he said again, shaking his head. "Well, you probably don't want to use that one professionally."

"Er, no," I replied, trying not to let him realize that the remark had upset me slightly. I wasn't entirely sure to just what profession exactly he was referring. "Could I see the other art works in your library?"

In addition to the beautiful 'Julie Daydreaming' oil painting, Stratton had several smaller oil paintings in his library, as well as a number of charcoal, pencil and watercolor sketches from various artists. I hadn't heard of most of them. He showed me a Degas pencil sketch which, I confess, just looked like a scribble of wobbly lines to me. He told me that his favorite work was an oil by a local artist from Colorado Springs named William Bancroft called 'The Miner's Last Dollar' which hung over his library fireplace.

"That one always reminds me to remain humble in all my financial extensions," he stated.

He opened the ornate cut glass door to a small cabinet and brought out two wine glasses and a bottle of a dark red wine, gesturing for me to have a seat in one of the large leather armchairs that sat in front of his desk as he uncorked the wine. "I'm really more of a whiskey or bourbon drinker, but thought a glass of wine before dinner would be rather nice," he said. "Anna's preparing one of my favorite meals, stuffed quail, which I'm sure you'll enjoy after all these weeks of cooking up those dreary bland beef and yellow onion stews for the hungry hordes of Cripple Creek."

Taking the glass, I made a small toast with him and took a sip, but then set it down on the desk. Stratton continued holding his glass at first, looking at the light refracting through it, then also placed it on his desk as he sat in the opposite arm chair.

"So Hannah," he began, lightly stroking his silky mustache which I was to learn was one of his habits when in deep thought. "How old are you now?"

"Sixteen," I said evenly, despite feeling very uncomfortable about this being his first question.

"Have you ever heard of the term *abonné*?"

This question completely caught me off guard. Did this have something to do with my age, I wondered?

"*Abonné*?" I repeated slowly, frowning slightly. "No, I'm afraid not. Is that some new painting style, or maybe a kind of music hall?"

"No," he smiled. "The term *abonné* really just means an arts' subscriber. But in reality it's how actresses, dancers and most singers in Europe become um, how to explain this ... let's say, how they become 'favorably elevated' from the *corps des filles*."

I wasn't quite certain what the term *corps des filles* meant and simply replied, "I always assumed that they were talented enough so that it was fairly obvious to their directors they should be promoted. Wouldn't that make the most sense?"

Stratton smiled, again stroking his mustache, not with any malice, and took another small sip of his wine. "Well, not exactly," he replied. "A subscriber or *abonné*, in say, Paris or London, is going to pay for premium box seating for all of the performances of the young lady whose work he is encouraging, when she is seen in a starring or even slightly less-than-starring role. That's paid-in-advance box seating for an entire season you must understand. A windfall for an opera house when you multiply that times many girls, as I'm sure you can see. He will also pay for expensive costuming, jewelry, tiaras and such, sometimes even specially designed scenery, new music and dramatic lighting for her, as well as top notch individual instruction so that everyone else will also be made fully aware of the extraordinary talents of his particular *protégé*. You do know the term *protégé*, yes?"

I nodded and then spoke guardedly.

"So it has very little to do with any actual capability and more to do with just…lining the pockets of the opera house owners, yes? Sounds like the ideal business arrangement for them. However, it's rather like a monkey cavorting to the hurdy gurdy player in a carnival, wouldn't you say?" I stated, taking another sip of wine to keep myself from saying anything more damaging. The wine was delicious and very heady; I would need to be careful not to anger this man with my opinions. If he would just be willing to get in some kind of good word with one of the opera houses that Mr. St. Charles had mentioned, maybe I could find my way to be hired for some of the lesser chorus performances. Perhaps mending costumes or helping with laundry, I thought, while I was learning. I was certain that I could make myself useful if just given something of a chance.

"No, no. These girls actually have to be extremely talented, Hannah. They train very hard to be accepted by an opera house. And since many of them are coming from extreme poverty, often the entire family has paid dearly, fully committed to the girl's training."

I nodded. Poverty was certainly something I'd seen staring me in the face for most of my life.

"But there are hundreds of them every year," Stratton continued, "all waiting to be pushed to the top of the cast list. If they weren't already very talented they would be laughed right off the stage. Remember, this is not Cracker Jack's pitiful exhibitions that we're discussing here! But these opera houses, and there are at least two or three large ones even in the smallest European cities, each hire well over a hundred girls every season for the very purpose of grooming the best of them."

"Is that how Jenny Lind got her start?" I asked suddenly, certain that was not the case.

"Funny how everyone over here has heard of the lovely Swedish Nightingale, Jenny Lind!" replied Stratton with a laugh, pouring a bit more wine into his glass.

"Why, did you see her and not like her?" I countered.

"Well, of course, she played in almost a hundred towns here in the U.S., but I'm not quite as ancient as you must think me. I was only two years old at the time of her American tour, so, needless to say, I wasn't in the audience. Actually, a lot of people didn't know that she had already left the opera stage in Europe just prior to her appearances over here. The man who sponsored her trip here, P.T. Barnum, if that name sounds familiar, may have been concerned that if it was known her opera days were over it would have undoubtedly dimmed her appeal, so he kept that information to himself. Definitely a smart business move, I must say."

"Or perhaps her *abonné* just wasn't dumping enough jewelry around her head!" I said, lightly mocking.

"You know, she abruptly left the opera circuit for the concert stage when she was only in her early 20s, Hannah. I don't think anyone actually knows why she didn't want to continue. She did have some very serious problems with her voice apparently and thought that many of the operatic roles were overtaxing it. And, you might be right that she became at odds with some of her patrons, perhaps with different political or economic views to hers. That happens when these young ladies become really famous; sadly they often become very outspoken as well. I would have loved to have heard one of her concert hall performances, but by the time I made my first trip to London a few years back, she was already dead."

I looked at my hands in my lap and said nothing.

"...which as you might guess would have made it difficult to hear her," he added, with a mock toasting of his glass, then taking another sip.

"That's ..." I began, looking up at him, swallowing something of a smile despite myself.

"Not nice," he finished my sentence with a slight laugh. "You're absolutely right. Sorry."

"I don't know how the reputations of those ... protégés fare, but, any girl I've ever heard about who said she was an actress or a dancer was really just covering up for being, well, being ... just a common prostitute," I blurted out. "I don't think we have the same standards or whatever you want to call it in this country. And I'm assuming that these abonné people aren't just enjoying the company of their young little ladies on the stage, correct? Probably these old lechers are all married and this is just one of their many accepted amusements."

Stratton was silent for a moment, then nodded his head and took a deep breath.

"Hannah, you've the makings of an excellent singer in my opinion. In Pearl's and Albert's far more refined opinions to mine, too, as you know. I would like you to give me the opportunity to see that talent be developed, first up here training at the Victor Opera House and then elsewhere if all goes well. And for which I definitely have the resources to make that happen. Now, your real question is: do I expect more than that from you?"

He looked at me for a few moments and then softly folded his hands around mine.

"Yes, I do expect more than that from you. I can't lie. Yes, you remind me of Jenny. Like her, you're beautiful, very intelligent with a quick and questioning mind and an even quicker eye. I can't lie about that either. But your similarity in looks to Jenny is not the reason I'm interested. Yes, I said several things to you when we first met that I wish I hadn't, but there's nothing that I can do about any of that. You can walk away from this opportunity, but you'll be making a big mistake. Deep down you already know that. Yes, I'm probably the same age as your father, maybe even older for that matter, but I will always treat you with respect. And yes, maybe most importantly for both you and me, our relationship will be kept quiet. You'll never be my whore. And, when the day comes that I stop treating you decently, I intend for you to just leave, no questions asked."

I looked down at our hands, still joined in my lap. He touched my check softly, then leaned forward and very gently kissed my lips.

"Anna probably has our dinner ready by now," he said quietly. "It's almost six."

Our extraordinary dinner, served by Anna and another young maid whose name might have been Katya, was absolutely delicious. Anna planted a lush garden every year with Stratton's favorite vegetables, including mushrooms, cooking herbs, as well as tending several various berry bushes and small apple trees, and methodically put up or dried everything which wasn't served fresh for use during the long winter months. Stratton's dietary requirements weren't outrageous by any means, but they were exceptionally specific. Absolutely nothing went to waste he assured me. All livestock was also scrupulously accounted for various uses on a seasonal basis as well. For example, he told me that he hated roosters and refused to allow them on the property. When they wanted more chicks, some of his men took several plump hens over to a neighbor to "visit" for a day or two then left them in a separate nesting area in the barn so they could simply concentrate on ... "motherhood" Stratton had winked.

When I asked what news he had from Zuma's lawyer down in New Orleans, he showed me a photograph of Zuma in her jail cell that he said he had received in a letter from the lawyer the prior week. She definitely looked thinner, but her hair was obviously clean and nicely piled on her head. There were no dark circles or pouches beneath her eyes and she appeared well dressed. The cell behind her in the photo showed an actual bed as opposed to a cot, a small table and two chairs as well. Tears filled my eyes as I handed the picture back to him. This entire situation still seemed so unfair I whispered to which Stratton agreed. She had only been trying to help her brother obtain a fair trial, I said. He nodded in agreement. He said he had attempted an appeal to have her released earlier, but the judge had convinced the lawyer not to present the matter to the court since it would undoubtedly not be heard, and, might actually increase the amount of time she was being jailed while the matter was being considered. Litigation, like many things in New Orleans, was extremely slow.

Anna had cleared away our dinners and brought in some delicate powdered cookies along with a warm apple and walnut compote. Stratton had taken one look at his dessert and quickly thrust it to one side asking why she put walnuts in the compote when she knew he hated them. She apologized profusely and took the offending dish back to the kitchen, returning a minute later with a nutless dish. "I sorry, Mr. Stratton. Wrong one. Here is right one. I fix walnut for Zane and others. Please forgive."

On the one hand, it seemed that he could have just picked out the offending nuts. But it also occurred to me that his hired men, Zane being one of them, along with the small house staff, were also enjoying the best of Anna's delicious meals. Simply picking out the walnuts and leaving them on his plate would probably have been considered wasteful on Stratton's part. Although, remembering all my days working in Mrs. Hughes' kitchen, I had no doubt whatsoever that someone would have voraciously devoured the offending nuts while clearing the meal from the table.

As we ate our desserts, he mentioned that through another associate, he planned to rent a small house for me just outside of Victor and hire a rig from the nearby livery so that I could easily get to the opera house for lessons, rehearsals and such in inclement weather. When I asked if it would be possible to bring Abigail with me, he gave me a quizzical look.

"And Abigail is ..." he frowned.

"Dr. Hughes daughter," I replied, assuming he had just momentarily forgotten her name.

"His daughter? Last I had heard his daughter was living with Old Margaret the Mauler."

I remembered Dr. Hughes calling his wife something along those lines – did they all refer to her that way, I wondered? "So you honestly don't know anything about Abigail? Or that she was living with me in a place that John Barrington was renting to us for several months? She was also helping me with my laundry service to the Old Homestead before Pearl's death."

Stratton shook his head as I asked all of those questions then just stared at me for a moment. "No offense to you my dear but why would Albert's daughter live in a shack? I'm familiar with that dreadful place John was planning to rent out! And the two of you doing a brothel's laundry? It doesn't make a lot of sense."

I bit my lip, looking down. Stratton was a millionaire many times over. It would be impossible for him to understand my needing to take on mending for whatever pennies I could negotiate. Dr. Hughes and Stratton had been good friends at one time. Rumors of their recent conflicts were still the subject of many conversations. How to talk about the serious financial shortcomings the doctor had imposed on his estranged wife and only daughter? I phrased myself carefully.

"Apparently when Mrs. Hughes refused to sign the divorce papers, Dr. Hughes was only obligated, as I understand it, that is, to pay a very small amount to her each month. He had already moved them to a place on Pike Street because he had sold their other house. I had heard," I swallowed here, "to maybe finance the Old Homestead. Zuma and I, um, left there to come up to Cripple Creek shortly after that move, because Mrs. Hughes didn't need as large a house staff. Zuma and I were taking in laundry, mending and working in the kitchen at the Old Homestead. Dr. Hughes got us those jobs. That's how I ended up singing there for the gold conference that night. Simply because I was just well … there."

Stratton stroked his mustache, sitting back in his chair. "Indeed. Yes. A stroke of luck for all of us. Yes, go on, go on, Hannah," he urged. "Please."

"So, after we left Pike Street, Mrs. Hughes had to start taking in boarders to make ends meet apparently," I continued, grateful that he hadn't questioned further the reasons surrounding my exit from the Hughes' employ.

"Old Mauler Margaret a landlady," snorted Stratton, "now that's a whale of a tall one!"

I smiled in spite of myself. "Yes, I was rather surprised when I heard about that, I must admit. She was very particular about all of her furniture and books and everything. Anyway, one of the boarders that she took in was a young man who Abigail fell in love with."

Stratton shrugged, again stroking his mustache. "That seems normal. That girl is what, seventeen or eighteen now?"

"I think she's seventeen. But anyway, she realized that ... she was with child and when she told this fellow, he skipped out on her and also without paying the rest of his rent."

"Hmmm, decent chap," sighed Stratton.

"Mrs. Hughes threw her out when she told her she was pregnant and Dr. Hughes refused to let her live at his hotel in Cripple Creek. Jenny brought me over to where Abigail was staying in that shack, as you called it."

"And why did you want to live in a drafty shack with a spoiled pregnant girl doing small laundry for a parlor house for heaven's sake?" Stratton continued, realistically confused.

"That night after I sang at the Old Homestead for the gold conference," I said slowly, trying not to envision my encounter with Stratton while he watched Jenny in that horrible viewing room, "my father and brother found me and insisted that I come back to live with them. They were working a small mine they'd grubstaked. Some other things happened shortly after that ... and I ... ran away from a very ugly situation."

"And did you get your 'ugly' situation resolved with your father and brother?"

"Not exactly." When there was no response from Stratton I hastily continued. "Jenny helped me and agreed to keep everything quiet," I finished simply. "Well, John Barrington and Dr. Hughes knew about Abigail of course."

"True to Jenny's integrity," nodded Stratton, "she never said a word about any of this to me. For the other two, it was just a business arrangement; they would have no particular reason to mention it."

"Abigail had her baby, a beautiful little girl she named Alice, just a few days before the fires destroyed everything. As you probably know, all of the women had been living at the Town Hall and then the National Hotel while all the men are building homes for their families and friends. I actually didn't know what we were going to do next, although, she's rather quickly taken up with another man, who owns the Heritage Saloon, in fact. So, I'm hoping something will be happening for the two or them." Why was I telling him this? I really wasn't at all certain of their relationship, but like Abigail, I was certainly hoping for the best for her. I plunged on speaking. "And he seems to adore Alice as well. So I think she's assuming they'll get married and he'll be willing to adopt the infant."

"That would be Jack Fairfield, correct?"

I nodded. "You know of him, I suppose."

"Yes, well, more than just a trickle of a reputation on that fellow, but then, knowing some of the outrageous stories circulating out there about me, probably the bulk of it is just hearsay and wildly flagrant rumor," Stratton replied with a shrug, and then abruptly changed the subject. "The vocal instructor at the Victor Opera House would like to begin working with you by the beginning of next week. He mentioned wanting to give you a few new songs that are all the rage in Paris these days. Do you speak any French?"

"Um, no. None at all," I replied. "I tried to learn one tune for my second program at the Old Homestead, but I made such an absolutely dreadful mess of it. Luckily, no one was really listening at that concert. You seem to know a lot of French though," I stated. "Maybe you can help me with that."

His loud laughter genuinely surprised me. "My French? *Ma foi*, indeed! Yes, well most of my French is bits of fluff learned from the laborers when I was in New Orleans building several houses for the elites. Our dear friend Albert Hughes rooked me into those contracts to pay off debts to him during my wild early prospecting years. Ah yes, and I mustn't forget Monsieur Saint-

Jacques, of course! An education in and of itself."

"That bird?" I laughed. I truly hadn't expected that!

"Indeed! That miserable magpie turns up everywhere. I don't know which of them, Pearl or Albert, brought that thing up here. But it did have some usefulness down there, I'll admit. First words it taught me were *merde* and *veux-tu couché avec moi?*"

"Which means?" I inquired, well aware that the words probably weren't very nice.

"*Merde* means shit and *veux-tu couché avec moi*, means, do you want to sleep with me?" he replied with a small flourish.

"Oh," I replied, biting my lip.

He quietly picked up my hand and gently kissed it, then held it up to his cheek. "But for tonight, I'm sending you back to your castle, my little princess. It's been a wonderful evening, but you're tired and so am I. Zane should have the wagon waiting at the front door already. He'll also get you moved over to Victor in a few days. Look for him the day that I send in the next supplies train. You probably have very little to move since everything was destroyed in the fire more than likely."

I gave a small shrug and nodded in agreement.

"And for a number of reasons, I would prefer that Hughes' daughter and her baby continue living in Cripple Creek. I can easily find a place and pay for them as well without Hughes knowing anything about it. I'm also good at keeping secrets."

Exhausted, I nodded my head. "Yes … Win," I agreed.

XV. The Victor Grande Opera House

Many of the townspeople had gathered at the newly rebuilt railway depot when, what was purported to be the last of Mr. Stratton's delivery trains, arrived less than a week later. In a shockingly short period of time, the town of Cripple Creek had rebuilt and easily surpassed itself without question. Most of the houses now had electricity, still unheard of in most of the rest of the state except for big cities such as Denver or Colorado Springs, along with telephones, running water, multiple fireplaces and stoves for better heating, among many other comforts and amenities. As Stratton had indicated, coinciding with the train's arrival was Zane's arrival with the wagon to take me to Victor. The young girl Katya, whom I had met at Stratton's dinner that evening, was also in the wagon and had been hired as my housekeeper and cook apparently. Not a soul noticed my getting into the wagon or subsequent departure, except for Abigail. However, Abigail had already assured me that a marriage proposal was coming very soon from Mr. Fairfield – in fact, she and Alice were moving into the rooms next to his over the saloon in a day or so. I was both happy and concerned for her, but certainly not in a position to pass any kind of judgment. What I had more than tacitly agreed to with Stratton was far more damaging without question and I had no intention of discussing anything about it with Abigail or anyone else. I had told her that I had found a temporary position taking care of a family and was moving to that house outside of Victor.

My first day of working with the vocal teacher was positively terrifying. I'm certain the man was fully apprised of the nature of

Stratton's support and planned to make me suffer for every moment he had to endure working with someone as feebly educated as myself. During a very brief tour of the stunningly beautiful opera house, Monsieur Delacroix volunteered surprising information that not only had Monsieur Stratton generously contributed as a benefactor, but he had also done much of the interior acoustic design. In fact, the acoustics were on par with many of the major houses in Europe, he declared.

As Stratton had forewarned, there was a French piece but also a German one that Monsieur Delacroix immediately pushed on me, apparently wanting them performed by the end of the month, along with several other English songs, two of which, thankfully, I knew from those Colorado Springs' lessons of Abigail's so long ago. He also had me work on an Italian piece called *"Se Tu M'ami"* which I really liked, but that Monsieur Delacroix said I was as limp and useless as a threadbare washrag singing it. The French piece, however, *"Dans le Jardin"* which apparently had to do with dreaming and something magical happening in a garden, was by Debussy and truly impossible for me to figure out. The melodies were very odd and there were all of these places where notes just went drifting through space without any kind of time or rhythm. I was overwhelmed and beyond being confused. Delacroix stamped, screamed and called me a lot of very ugly sounding names in French. I felt fortunate that I was completely in the dark with respect to his meaning. At the end of my lesson he declared very slowly and painfully in English that he was grateful that he wouldn't have to deal with me again for two days.

The sun was low in the sky but even though completely exhausted I opted to walk back through the dusty streets of Victor rather than sending for the carriage. A delicious aroma drifted out from the kitchen of the charming little cottage that I now so appreciatively called home making me realize how hungry I was and also how grateful for Stratton's gift of Katya as my caregiver. If she hadn't been there, I know I would have simply dissolved in hot tears. If there had been no food available, I would have just cried myself to sleep, too tired to care.

Katya had a hot bath waiting for me, while "meat finish miss", she explained. Her English was about the same as Anna's, but we managed to communicate without any problem. I slipped out of my one good dress and gratefully sank down into the large bathtub filled to the brim with almost scalding water, feeling Delacroix's endless criticisms temporarily soak out of my body. A sweet lavender soap and some other relaxing scent further removed the man from my thoughts. I washed out my hair as well as I lingered in the water.

Katya had laid out a rich peach-colored kimono on a chair. For several minutes I sat staring at it, my hair and body each wrapped in plush Turkish towels, before I set the kimono aside and changed into one of the shapeless woolen tied jumpers which most of the women had made for themselves after the fire. Threading my fingers through my hair, trying to pull through the many badly tangled sections, I walked out into the small dining room and saw that Stratton was standing next to the fireplace. Candles were lit on the small table and two glasses of wine had been poured and were awaiting us. Although I was ashamed to appear with my hair dripping over my shoulders, I was far more ashamed of my utter failure as a singer. I managed to walk over to him, my head bowed.

"Oh Win," I somehow choked out, surprised that I was even able to utter his name. Tears once again spilled unrestrained from my reddened eyes. "I was dreadful today. Monsieur Delacroix knows that I'm a talentless bore, in fact, worse than a talentless bore. I don't know what to tell you, but I'm not the singer you thought. Not in any way. You have every right to withdraw your support. I will clear out of here tonight so I don't embarrass you any further. I'm so sorry. You've gone to a lot of trouble and I know that and please understand that I appreciate it. But this is all just too embarrassing..." my voice just dropped off.

Without saying a word, he smiled slightly and gently put his hand under my chin to make me look at him. "Dinner, Hannah. Let's enjoy our dinner and celebrate your hard work today."

I shook my head. "No, no! I'm absolutely serious," I sobbed, pulling back from him, and self-consciously tightening the ill-fitting woolen dress in front of me. "I was horrible. You've bet on the wrong horse or something. I can't possibly live up to whatever it is that you thought. Please. I don't want to embarrass you any further."

Putting his fingers to his lips indicating that he didn't expect me to say anything else for the moment, he guided me gently over to my chair as Katya entered with a dinner tray. I was embarrassed by how ravenously I attacked the tender roast beef, garlic potatoes and a spicy green bean, chive and tomato medley, along with two healthy glasses of the same delicious dark red wine that we had drunk at Stratton's a week ago.

We ate in silence until Stratton finally spoke. "So, tell me about your lesson, Hannah."

"He started me on this absolutely beautiful piece by Bach called *"Bist du bei Mir"* but I'm murdering all those treacherous German words. Every time! At least the other main piece is in English, *"Entreat Me Not to Leave Thee"* by someone named Gounod, I think. That one went a little better. And I really liked the Italian piece, but Monsieur said I was singing like a wet mop. And, then he tried me with this French piece by Debussy where all of the phrases seemed to go up the scale, but also had to get softer and the notes just kept spreading farther and farther apart with no rhythm that I could ever figure out. And what's worse, there's no place to breathe! I mean no place! Maybe French singers don't need to breathe. All of this music is all so incredible, but I just can't possibly manage it," I said, shaking my head.

"Hannah," smiled Stratton, "to go back to your 'wrong horse' analogy, this was your first time running around the track – that is, first time reading through any of this material. There's no way that it could have gone without problems. These are extremely difficult vocal works he's thrown on you and in a lot of languages to boot! But that's why Delacroix is who he is, my little one. You're working with him again in what, two days?"

I nodded slowly, still feeling very defeated. "He said that he's grateful he has two days off before our next lesson. And he said that very slowly in plain English, so I wouldn't misunderstand."

Stratton stood up and walked over behind my chair, his hands on my shoulders, his chin resting lightly on the top of my hair. "Here's what needs to happen. During this interval you review the music, Hannah. You hear his corrections in your head and work hard to realize those corrections. Trust me. There will be plenty more of them thrown your way. That's why he is who he is, my dear. I don't know of any singer around these parts, male or female for that matter, who hasn't been exasperated to tears under his harsh instruction. But, you know what? They've all emerged, like butterflies from a cocoon, with their gifts developed beyond what anyone, including they themselves, might have possibly imaged. That's where you will be. But, it's a long, very tedious process you have to be willing to fight to achieve."

His hands then moved through my loose hair as he kissed me, slowly and gently along the back of my neck. I was vaguely aware that Katya had slightly opened the door from the kitchen and asked tentatively about dessert to which Stratton had murmured no. He untied the sash which made the dress open slightly, part way down my back, slowly kissing the back of my neck. I held my breath and swallowed. His fingers began to trace along one of the long slightly-raised welts which still crisscrossed up into the middle of my back from Mrs. Hughes' belt. He then came around in front of my chair, pulling his own chair up very close and took my face in both of his hands.

"What scoundrel beat you, my little one," he said quietly, but sternly. "What happened? Is this why you ran away from your father?"

It would, of course, have been so easy to have answered yes to that question, but I shook my head. Somehow, I felt I needed to reveal the truth to this man.

"I was beaten by Mrs. Hughes because she thought I was trying to steal some money," I replied slowly. "It probably looked like that, but I was not trying to steal anything. That's the real reason why Zuma and I had to leave Pike Street. But there's more than that." I took a deep breath. "There are still other marks around my ribs ... and probably elsewhere ... as well, I'm sure, even though it's been several months. I was ... raped by a man working with my father and they planned to ... my," my voice suddenly became very bitter as I recalled those weeks of agony. "They had plans to use me as a prostitute with these men they owed money to grubstake a mine ...to pay off some of those debts," I confessed in a strangled voice. "That's why I ran off. And that's why Jenny agreed to hide me."

Stratton was very quiet for several moments.

"Who was the man?" he asked coolly.

"His name was Jared Grady," I answered, looking up through my tears at Stratton. "But he's dead now, actually. Abigail accidentally shot him, but no one knows that she did it. I mean, we had a gun but she didn't know it was loaded when he broke in and..."

"And good riddance," interrupted Stratton. "I hope he suffered. A lot. The bastard."

He kissed the tears on my face, then handed me his

handkerchief and sat further back in his chair looking at me for several minutes again.

"I don't ever want you to be afraid of me. You've probably heard people say that I have a temper. And, those people are right. I'll be honest with you about that. And as I told you before, you need to pick up and leave when that time comes that I'm not treating you well or if you become afraid of me for any reason. But just so you know, I've never forced myself on a woman, even some who were pretty rough around the edges, if you follow."

"You always seemed very sweet with Jenny ... and Pearl DeVere as well," I said, remembering Pearl kissing Stratton's fingers while watching the end of my concert after Dr. Hughes had left the room.

He crossed his arms, a look of mirth on his face. "All for show, all completely for show, my dear!" he laughed slightly. "As the madam of the most expensive brothel in the business, Pearl had to make it look as though she was flirting with some of her wealthier customers. She was always Albert's, though. Make no mistake. Most everything I did at that place was actually just for show, helping to keep the other millionaires willing to pay her exorbitant entry fees, poker stakes and liquor prices! Like paying for a permanent room I never used and of course, footing the bill for many of her goddamned parties that I despised attending."

"And Jenny in the viewing room that night of the gold conference?" I heard myself inquire before I could stop the question.

"Ah, yes, well, that was indeed for Jenny and me, I must confess. She and I did spend a lot of time together, as you know. And, although you may not believe it, she actually liked doing that kind of er, shall we say, tantalizing scenario. Needless to say I was always an appreciative audience," he added with another slight laugh.

"Were you in love with her?" I asked boldly. "Pearl said that many of the girls could eventually find husbands and leave that life behind. Would you have married her?"

"Was I in love with Jenny?" he replied, slightly stroking his mustache. "Well, probably a little bit. Hard not to love such a beautiful, wildly and magnificently intelligent, free spirit as Jenny Hays, actually. But, Jenny never had any interest in getting married. Not to me or any man. Pearl had no interest either, even though Albert thought she would eventually change her mind."

"Well, they seemed to enjoy a lot of the same things. Theatre, traveling in Europe, music, art, parties … money." I added that last item tentatively at the end.

"You see, Hannah, all men tend to think that women want to wait on them, catering to a man's every little whim and physical neediness all the time. Absolute hooey if you ask me. And all those innocent, unsuspecting women out there, primed by respectable society and the fear of the gospel, well, they all fall for it. Again and again. First thing you know they're giving birth to one kid after another, year after year until they finally die in childbirth themselves. Then, their husband just finds some other poor innocent lamb to take to slaughter," he said darkly.

I stared at him, completely speechless.

"I'll bet your folks pushed all that religious hocus pocus on you, too, right?"

"Actually, my father was a psalm-singer," I replied, looking down.

"What the hell is a psalm-singer? Ain't regular hymns bad enough?" snorted Stratton.

"Someone who wails psalms all day and expects supreme salvation in the kingdom of heaven. Although, considering he more or less attempted to sell me out to Mr. Grady and those other men, I'm hoping that God has permanently stopped His ears," I replied sharply.

"Someone told me once that God listened to the problems of

mankind with strange ears. Never knew if that extended to womankind as well. Some of the nicest prostitutes I've met were ones who ran away from abusive marriages. Sometimes they left little ones at home with the grandparents as well, which, of course, was really sad. But they just desired to have control over their own destinies."

"And you believe that a woman of the demimonde has control of her own destiny?" I said bitterly, anger edging into my voice. What had pushed both Jenny Hays and Pearl DeVere into 'the profession' hardly seemed to be a destiny they would have chosen given different circumstances I scowled within myself.

"No. I didn't actually say that, Hannah," replied Stratton gently, adding a little more wine to his glass and taking a sip before continuing. "Women are denied anything resembling higher education except in very extreme circumstances. How many women doctors or scientists or lawyers have you ever heard about? Even composers or writers? Or if they do make any actual forays into any of those professions, they're almost always overshadowed by a man, usually their husband, who in many instances, actually steals the woman's discoveries or creative endeavors and passes it off as his own."

"Is that what makes you interested in collecting women impressionist's art?"

"Partly, I suppose," he answered. "But truth to tell, the stuff is absolutely gorgeous and so different from the dreck that so many men throw out as art these days!"

I sighed, rubbing my forehead and trying to understand exactly what Stratton was saying to me. My mind was like a tangled squirrel's nest, much like my hair, which was still matted, drying around my shoulders. "You seem to be very bitter about the choices for women, which is very unusual for a man, Win," I said quietly. "Why? What was your mother like? Were you very close to her?"

"Ah, well. My mother," he sighed, pouring more wine into my glass. "My mother, who everyone called Mary, was a quadroon. You're familiar with that term?"

I nodded. This was not at all what I thought he might say.

"No one ever knew anything about her family and I suspect that her name really wasn't Mary. Maybe the name Mary was like the epidemic of Sadies we have in Cripple Creek."

"Ah," I said, barely audible.

"She died at the age of 45 after having given birth to twelve children and burying all but four of us in infancy. Then my oldest sister died in her 20s, and my mother, by then just a shell of a woman, just basically gave up on life and passed shortly after. She was probably about your age when she married my father and he was only about eight or nine years older, so a reasonably normal difference. She was actually quite dark and never allowed any pictures to be taken. Also, I suspect, since we lived right on the Ohio River in southern Indiana, that she and maybe some of her darker friends who were also passing for white, were part of the Underground Railroad prior to the Civil War. In fact she may have actually arrived in Indiana by that means. You've heard of the Underground?"

I nodded again, taking a small sip of my wine.

"All my mother knew was constantly being pregnant, tending to all of those fragile, desperately ill infants and then burying so many of them. She merely exchanged one form of slavery for another. None of us ever really knew who she was at all. I've always hoped that she was part of the Underground and that she was at least able to help others of her race."

"My mother took chloral while pregnant with my youngest sister and was condemned by my father when the baby was stillborn," I stated quietly, staring into the fireplace as several twigs snapped, sending up a very small shower of sparks. "He never forgave her for that sin and she never forgave herself either." I took a couple sips of my wine. "But, there are women out there in solid marriages. Zuma told me that her marriage was very happy until she lost her husband."

"There probably are happy marriages out there," admitted Stratton, "or at least, there are claims to that state. A year after my mother's death, my father married a very young, pretty white woman. She was only a few years older than I was at that time and I was very bitter about it. He said he was lonely and that he missed my mother's company! Hah! As though my mother had ever really meant anything to him, I argued with him. And of course, she never refused him. That was the most important thing to him which was pretty obvious. We actually got into a messy fist fight over it."

"And what happened then?"

"My father gave me $300 to get the hell out of his house and start a carpenter's apprenticeship with my brother-in-law out in Iowa. I'd been working as a carpenter with my father for a number of years. I took the money but came out west to start prospecting. Never told any of them my whereabouts. By now, they all know, of course, and sooner or later they'll come trottin' out here begging for some coin. Money has always had a big mouth."

Finding out about Win's background was truly surprising. Like most people, I had assumed he had been born with entitlement, at least some money, and that the mantle of becoming a millionaire had just settled easily upon his shoulders. We both sat quietly while listening to the low hiss of the fire's glowing embers.

XVI. John Barrington

How we ended up in my bedroom I never really knew, but my anxieties surrounding our intimacy slowly dissolved. For the first time in my life I felt very calm and oddly steady, a small boat drifting on a darkly shimmering lake, catching glimpses of an eyelash moon winking through faint wisps of clouds. I was very much ready to be quietly pulled into the slow, tantalizing current of this man's life for whatever time that we might have together. His power was that mesmerizing, that tender. The brutal markings snaking over my lower back and my discolored ribs and hips were forgotten as they yielded under Stratton's gentle caresses and warm mouth. His many years of driving a pickaxe into granite and shoveling heavy muddy detritus from mine shafts had left his thin body very muscular and strong against mine. As I looked into his light blue eyes, the slow rhythm of our lovemaking brought me to a new place, warm and oblivious to everything surrounding us.

Threads of sunlight were dazzling across my quilt when I awoke. Stratton had left quietly sometime very late into the night. I smiled thinking of how neatly he had placed our garments over the chair as he had carefully undressed each of us. Now only my jumper, under dress and slip were folded there. I wrapped a large blanket around myself and walked out, glancing into the kitchen and parlor. Katya was nowhere to be seen, but she had left a carafe with hot coffee over a modified spirit lamp, as well as a small loaf of bread and two hardboiled eggs. I wasn't used to anyone leaving me a fresh warm breakfast or the prospect of a day with no washing, mending, scrubbing floors or cooking. I just couldn't face working on any of my music yet, however, and decided to get dressed quickly and see if I could catch the next Florence & Cripple Creek train to pay a short visit to Abigail and Alice in Cripple Creek. As I walked past the little writing desk near my window, I saw a small white card. On it was scrawled:

Meeting in Denver

gone ? days ~

WSS

I smiled looking at the swirl of his scribbled initials. The fact that the hastily written note contained no endearments only faintly crossed my mind as I started out on my walk to the depot. The morning air was slightly chilly, despite the fact that it was already midsummer.

I was amazed how many more buildings had been completed in just the very short time since I had left Cripple Creek. Many of the businesses, with the new district requirements to be built of stone, brick or concrete, now had glass windows twinkling in the morning sunshine. Telephone poles strung with several lines now dotted all along Bennett Avenue as I walked along the sparkling new Portland cement sidewalks, which stretched from the rebuilt Midland Terminal about halfway towards the Heritage Saloon, with footings in place for the walk's continuance. Commerce and continuing construction noisily surrounded me on all sides.

The double doors were held open by a pair of enormous cast iron lions as I stepped out of the bright sunshine into the rather dimly lit saloon. It took a few moments for my eyes to adjust, but then I spotted a man and woman talking quietly at a table near the far wall. No one was behind the bar. As I walked over to them the man turned his head towards me.

"Yeah? Help ya?" he said, obviously irritated by my intrusion on his conversation.

"I'm looking for Abigail Hughes or Jack Fairfield," I replied.

"Sorry to disturb you."

"Check upstairs," he stated with a jerk of his chin. "Ask one of the girls. Don't know nobody named Abigail an' Jack ain't around now." The man turned his attention back to his companion.

"Thanks."

As I started towards the back of the saloon I realized that a baby was crying close by. I had probably heard it while I was walking up to the building but hadn't realized that the squalling might actually be in the saloon until that moment. I ran up the stairs encountering only one woman, who was sound asleep, snoring loudly in the middle of the hallway, her wrapper flung wide open to reveal a body badly in need of a metal scrub brush.

Finding the room where the baby was screaming was easy, obviously. I knocked several times and when no one came to the door, I cautiously opened it, called out Abigail's name. The stench from Alice's diaper was overpowering. It was obvious that the poor thing hadn't been attended to in many hours. She was lying in a dresser drawer which had been pulled out onto the floor, with shredded newspapers as a mattress of sorts. Alice, her clothing, and the bedding, such as it was, were completely sopped. Finding a pitcher of water on the dresser, I carefully picked up the infant, discarded all of her clothing into the newspapers, and attempted to bathe her by dipping out the cold water over her. Her little bottom and legs were raw with a hideously ugly red rash. I pulled the thin, filthy blanket off the bed and wound it around her. As I picked her up she was sucking the backs of her hands and then sucking my collarbone once I had her over my shoulder. I walked out of the bedroom with her either screaming or loudly sucking on my shoulder, and headed quickly back down the stairs.

"Jesus, woman, now what?" grumbled the man in the saloon when I walked back in.

"Oh God, not that damned baby again," moaned the woman, rolling her eyes and exasperatingly slumping down in her chair, thrusting her legs out in front of herself in mock disgust.

"I need a new dishrag from behind the bar," I said curtly, no attempt to hide the anger in my voice. "And where would I find a market close by with a milk cow?" I was hoping that by continually dipping the rag in a jug of fresh milk that Alice would be able to suck out the liquid. Older babies could manage this, I knew, but an infant? I had absolutely no idea.

Eager for me to leave, the man quickly found a boiled dishrag, probably as clean as anything available, and gave directions to a market.

When I arrived at the market, only a few minutes' walk from the saloon, I couldn't believe my good fortune. The shopkeeper's wife was a large woman, surrounded by several small children, who was just finishing nursing her young baby. I begged her to please feed Alice. The woman, who spoke little English, nodded with a big smile, and as I handed the famished baby to her I knew that, at least momentarily, things were going to be all right. Alice latched onto the woman's large breast immediately and nursed in greedy, noisy gulps. Finally sated, and thoroughly exhausted, the infant fell into a deep sleep. The woman, who introduced herself as something like Baleen – she had a very heavy accent, completely different from Katya's or Anna's and far more difficult for me to understand – told me where on the shelves to find glass bottles with leather nipples, which thankfully weren't smelly like those awful rubber ones, soothing jelly for the diaper rash, and several yards of fabric to make a dozen diapers and swaddling blankets. She also lent me a clean milk pail and let me milk her cow, which was tied up just behind the store.

When I returned to the Heritage Saloon, the couple at the table had disappeared, and, although a barkeeper was getting set up for the afternoon trade, Abigail still hadn't returned. I laid

Alice down on a blanket on Abigail's bedroom floor, then threw out all of the disgusting newspapers and encrusted baby wrappings. Recklessly I searched through the bedroom for any hint of Abigail's whereabouts but only discovered several discarded women's undergarments, which could have belonged to anybody. Borrowing a slip of paper and pencil from the barkeeper, I wrote a quick note to Abigail that I had taken Alice with me to Victor, leaving my address on the bottom of the note.

Two days later when I left for my next lesson at the Victor Opera House, with obviously no time to work through any music, Abigail still hadn't shown up. Without Katya's help attending to Alice's horrible, stinging rash, soaking and pegging up diapers, finding fresh cow's milk and helping me bottle feed her, not to mention helping me rock the fidgety little one at all hours of the day and night, I know I would have thoroughly failed and the child would have died. I was desperately counting on Abigail's reappearance soon since I couldn't expect Katya to continue to care for an infant along with all her regular work for me as well as at Stratton's household, where she still assisted Stratton's housekeeper. When Abigail reappeared I would somehow have to convince Stratton to let her live with me or beg him to rent another place for her. The saloon was no longer an option.

My second voice lesson with Monsieur Delacroix was easily as disastrous as the first and was probably even worse. He now knew up front that both my training and my talent were completely non-existent. After a full two hours of his shrieking at me in at least three (possibly four) discernible languages, he abruptly got up from the piano and walked over to a side table. He then loudly shuffled through several papers and thrust an announcement into my hands.

I assumed this was a document in which he was dismissing me as a student, understandably refusing to waste another minute of his time. When I looked at the document, however, it was about a concert that he had mentioned previously. According to the announcement this program was now going to be a competition. Young women singers who were training at the Tabor Opera in Leadville, the Colorado Springs and Denver Opera Houses as well as the Victor were being encouraged to compete for a five-week period of exclusive instruction with Viennese instructor Johannes Ress, who was Selma Kurz's original vocal teacher. This opportunity was being offered by the new conductor, a supposedly brilliant composer named Gustav Mahler, at the Vienna Opera House in Vienna, Austria. According to Monsieur D, as I had learned he preferred to be addressed, the winner would also acquire the opportunity to excellent seats for all of Miss Kurz's extraordinary coloratura soprano performances of the season in Vienna.

There was absolutely no hope of my winning the competition asserted Monsieur D with a dismissive wrinkling of his nose and hand flourish, but it would be a good experience for me nonetheless. By my next lesson he expected me to have selected two pieces and actually have made time to rehearse the works on my own, since today's experience had been even more exasperating than the last. There was an entry fee, of course, but he assumed that Mr. Stratton would make good on that. Also, he now intended to work with me for several hours on Mondays, Wednesdays and Fridays until the competition.

Of course, I didn't dare let on that I had positively no idea who Selma Kurz, her original teacher Johannes Ress or this new conductor, Gustav Mahler were. I had heard of the magnificent Vienna Opera House, however, so I knew it would indeed be a wonderful chance for some deserving young woman. We continued working through several more hours that afternoon and then, although Monsieur D once again stomped off in a rage, the rage seemed slightly less intense, if that were at all possible.

I raced home praying that Abigail had somehow reappeared during my absence, but found Katya patiently rocking and patting Alice gently on the back. "She no bohba. She no bohba." I took the baby from her and began to move about the room with her, gently rocking her up and down, until she finally fell asleep in my arms. She looked very pale and listless. She was just so tiny to have nothing but cow's milk and I was certain that it was making her ill. I shuddered. I set her carefully down in a large basket lined in lamb fleece that Katya had brought over from Stratton's. She apologized that she had not been able to start anything for dinner, so it would be very small, which I assured her was perfectly fine. I was now becoming increasingly worried about Abigail and had very little appetite. We both hastily worked to fix some food and I assumed that Katya would be joining me as she had the last two evenings. However, she indicated that Anna needed her at Stratton's house for the next several hours.

Exhausted after eating, I lay down on the sofa in front of the fire and drifted asleep for several hours, with Alice in her basket a few feet away. Faintly I thought that I heard a carriage stopping, then the slight creak of the front door and the voices of two women which startled me awake. Abigail! I thought excitedly and moved quickly to the parlor. But it was only Katya and another quite attractive young woman who nodded and surprisingly curtsied slightly.

"Anna want send for," began Katya, gesturing to the other woman. "Here Vanya. Help?"

I nodded and gave a tired smile, my shoulders drooping. "Very nice to meet you," I said, certain the disappointment of not finding Abigail at my door was more than evident.

"Vanya, live …" Katya gestured with her arm, "road there? Yes?"

Again I nodded. "Very nice," I replied.

"Vanya ..." began Katya, and was obviously stumped with any further explanation at that point and just looked blankly at the other woman finally saying something to her in Polish. Then Vanya pulled down her blouse and cupping her right breast, pointed at Alice.

"You're a wet nurse?" I cried. Women who worked as wet nurses were almost impossible to find any more except those who were retained well in advance and only for the wealthiest of families.

"Ya, ya, ya!" said Vanya, nodding her head eagerly, pointing again to her breast and then pulling her blouse back up. "Baby," she added, nodding again.

"Mr. Stratton, he yell. Anna want you there, Miss Hannah. Vanya, me, here. Alice good here," stated Katya, gesturing in Alice's direction. "You go. Anna want you there."

I heard a horse snorting and pawing the ground and realized that the carriage that Katya and Vanya had arrived in must still be outside. I grabbed my wool shawl, thanking both women, and left. Most likely they would be able to care for Alice far better than I could have done for the next several hours.

When the driver pulled up to Stratton's home, every lamp seemed to be lit throughout the entire place. I realized that I had absolutely no idea of the time; my long nap had definitely thrown off all perception. As soon as Anna opened the door I threw my arms around her in a huge hug, which surprised her slightly, but she gave a small, tired smile, hugging me lightly back.

"Anna, where did you and Katya find Vanya? Does her family live near me in Victor?" I asked quietly.

Anna nodded her head. "I not tell Mr. Stratton over baby. Not good time now. Mr. Barrington, he say he pay Vanya so is good."

It made perfect sense for John Barrington to be involved, of course, and I was extremely grateful. But I was also slightly worried about that development for some strange reason. I decided that I would need to contact John tomorrow to find out exactly what Vanya's job duties would be and also if he might know how to trace Abigail's whereabouts.

"I don't know what's happened to the baby's mother, Anna. I can't believe she would just walk away and leave her newborn baby!"

"No. No mama jes go way," Anna concurred, shaking her head sternly, her arms crossed. "Away new baby? No!"

She asked me to wait in the parlor, her brow furrowing with concern. "Mr. Ramsey here," she whispered. "Never good talk when Mr. Ramsey here. He not here for three months. Now back. And Mr. Stratton? Much, much whiskey and very, very bad words. When start in whiskey, go for days. Then, Mr. Stratton? Always get very sick, very bad."

I suddenly heard a muffled crash, then slightly escalating voices confirming something of a confrontation between Stratton's secretary, William Ramsey, and Stratton. Even though I was two rooms away from Win's library, every word was audible. I wondered how long the two men had been involved in this heated conversation, and more than likely, assuming Anna was to be believed, excessive drinking.

"I still contend that you're completely out of your mind, Win," said a gravelly voice that I speculated must be Ramsey's. "Why you would even entertain the idea of an option to sell the Independence with a notoriously slippery fellow like Verner Reed defies any logic you've ever shown in the six years that I've been working for you! Why now? Why on earth do you want to sell that mine now? God knows how many more millions lie just waiting to be tapped from those ripe sylvanite veins right beneath the surface! I honestly can't comprehend what's going on with you. Was it another letter from that money-grubbing nephew of yours? Or did your damn son Henry show up yet again with empty pockets and the usual bountiful accusations regarding your neglect?"

Stratton coughed slightly and cleared his throat before replying, sidestepping the family references. "William, you're supposed to be my secretary, not my goddamn psychiatrist. That mine's been my bank since it produced its first amazing assay and you know that, dammit. When I've needed money, I've just gone in and extracted it. Plain and simple. And that's been great. But I don't do so well just sittin' still, as you well know. I have plans. Yessir, I have plans and it's time to start moving along on 'em."

"Yes, Win, and that's what I've been trying to wheedle out of you now for the last hour! Just what plans?" Ramsey's hoarse voice demanded. "When did you come up with some kind of hair brained scheme that needs that kind of money and necessitates selling off the Independence? That's like, oh God, I can't even think of a decent analogy…like shooting off your foot so you can go out and buy a wooden leg."

Despite myself I smiled. Both men were silent for several moments. Then I heard Stratton's voice again, this time much quieter, but definitely still audible. I envisioned the two men sitting in the leather chairs in front of Stratton's desk, each with a large glass of whiskey, the almost empty bottle perched on the desk between them.

"William, as you've guessed, part of it is a series of real estate plans, yes. Developments in Colorado Springs, possibly Cripple Creek and Victor, as well."

"You've already got several prime ongoing concerns in Colorado Springs and Cripple Creek, Win, without selling the Independence," growled Mr. Ramsey, sharply emphasizing each of those last four words.

"And, I'm not ready to go into detail about those other developments with anyone just yet, so hold off. But, an equally large piece of it is that I'm completely fed up. What with the miners' attitudes, the continuing crush of their unions and the whole *laissez faire* of the court systems, running this business has become worse than my absolute worst nightmare. Little did I know way back that the actual prospecting for gold is really the easiest part of it! And, don't even ask me about the constant stream of folks, both kin and complete strangers, with their grimy little paws extended, expecting successive handouts and then grumbling when they feel they've been slighted and haven't received their just due. And the mine thefts! An utter travesty."

"I thought all of you owners had worked out several methods dealing with the thefts," said Ramsey. "What happened with that?"

I heard Stratton give a snort of a laugh. "Hah! Yes, well the newest game in town is that a number of the saloon owners in Cripple Creek are now dealing with dishonest assayists. These assayists are extremely crafty at crushing and reducing in small quantities the "picture rock" they call it, to pure gold, and pay the saloon owner half, then he turns around and gives half of that back to the miner. We're talking losses that yield like $40 per pound and amounts upwards of 70 pounds from just one mine every stinking day!"

"That's unbelievable!" growled Ramsey, with a low whistle. "I had no idea the problem was that widespread."

"The saloon owners even give the miners canvas-pocketed belts or armpit pockets to wear under their clothing so that they can hide pieces of high-grade ore without any detection. A lot of the mines' guards now make the workers empty out their lunch pails at the end of their shifts and many of them also demand that the men change out of all their work gear and I mean all, even their underclothes, into other clothing right smack in front of the guards."

I heard Ramsey give another low whistle. "Bet the men love

that! Is that your policy?"

"Not commenting. But the real travesty," Stratton continued, "just last week a Cripple Creek judge ruled on one case that stealing ore was not considered larceny. Judge claimed that you can't steal real estate! Hah!"

"What?" bellowed Ramsey. "That's preposterous! Stealing is stealing for God's sake!"

"No objection there, Bill," snorted Stratton. "More?" I assumed Stratton was refilling both of their glasses.

"Sounds like the saloon owners have the sweetest deal of all actually. Just act as middleman for the deal and then trot away with a sweet 'n easy 25 per cent," Ramsey allowed. "Nice piece of the take."

"Well, it gets even uglier than that. See, right now, a lot of the current miners are scabs because the regular miners, since most of them are union men, are on strike, if you remember. So the saloon owners are actually now working with the scabs and this has caused unbelievable tension. Not only are they cheating on the mine owners themselves, but they're also cheating the original miners who were handing over the stolen gold to them in the first place. You probably didn't hear that a bunch of those saloon bums as well as a couple of mine owners were barricaded into the Strong Mine shaft the other night when it was blown up by the strikers. They probably won't ever be able to identify all of those bodies."

I froze. Was Jack Fairfield one of those saloon owners? Without question I could very easily picture him involved in that kind of dealing. But even if he happened to be there, why would Abigail have been with him? That still wouldn't explain her disappearance I resolutely told myself.

"And, quite simply, that could just as easily have been me being dynamited inside the Independence shaft, Ramsey," continued Stratton in a somewhat subdued voice. "These union men hate every one of us owners in the mining business and don't even think twice before blowing up our equipment or one of our trains loaded with ore heading down to a smelter."

"We'll assume you have a lot more militia helping guard a mine as valuable as the Independence than they have out at that measly Strong Mine, Win," Ramsey stated emphatically. "Nothing but excess water and a load of unexplained accidents in that miserable plot of ground."

A few moments of silence passed and I heard one of the men clear his throat.

"So explain to me one last time about this South African mine problem and your possible deal with London," sighed Ramsey. "Then, I'm going. All of this whiskey's making my head explode. I can't believe you had already gone through half that other bottle before I got here. You sure as hell hide it well, Win."

I heard Stratton give a slight chuckle. "Well, as I explained before, Verner Reed, who I see as being far less slippery than you surmise, William, opened an office in London to sell Cripple Creek mining stocks to European investors several years ago," Stratton began.

"Yeah, yeah, I know that part. Go on," replied Ramsey, attempting to stifle a yawn. "You're not going to change my mind one bit about your offering the option to Reed, but give me all the pertinent facts again."

"So, at that time, the Transvaal Mines in South Africa were the biggest draw without any question for all of the English stockholders and their European investors. Reed worked with John Hammond, who in my opinion is the greatest American mining genius of our time, and they became close friends. So now, when things are very politically unstable for Great Britain in South Africa, which easily translates to -- very difficult to extract and transport more gold to England because of political tensions -- Reed convinces John Hammond that he should buy the Independence Mine here in America because that's a far less risky option for maintaining European investments," explained Stratton. "And he's also convinced them that the yield will be a smooth walk down easy street."

"Interesting, but there are certainly other U.S. mines. Lots of them in fact. Why the Independence? Go on," repeated Ramsey, his voice sounding even more wearied.

"Reed has now joined up with Hammond in a new London company called the Venture Corporation and they've made me an incredible offer," replied Stratton. "This Venture Corporation is sending a mining engineer to furnish a report detailing the gold left to be mined in the stopes and tunnels of the Independence. My own engineer has estimated a value of at least $7 million and we're only down about 700 feet so far. The estimates from my engineers run to about a 3,000 foot depth of ore, so that would mean clearing untold millions more for potential investors in Europe. And, as I always have said, it's worth a lot more in the ground than the effort of hauling the damn stuff out of the ground. But also, Bill, understand that I'm not just selling them the mine. I'm optioning them the ability to sell shares at $100 a piece until we've reached my sale price, at which point they become the owners. There's no way they would be able to cough up the capital needed for this transaction."

"And the price this Venture Corporation has extended so far?" said Ramsey. "You haven't been willing to mention the amount so far, Win."

There was a pause as Stratton, undoubtedly stroking his mustache, tried to decide if he should relay that information.

"This needs to be kept completely quiet, William, understand? I can't have anyone catch a whiff of this deal or the whole thing might blow up in our faces if other American competitors show up at the table willing to underbid equally productive mines."

"Well?" Ramsey's gravelly voice inquired.

"Eleven million, including Reed's million for negotiating the sale," Stratton stated in low voice, but loud enough that I heard him.

Their conversation lasted a few more minutes but I was not at all conscious of anything else that either man conveyed. Eleven million dollars. I couldn't imagine that kind of money. No one could. I was convinced that I must have heard Stratton incorrectly. This man was living in a humble ranch house at the base of one of his mines on the outskirts of a rugged mining camp called Victor, thousands of feet up in the Rockies, not in a mammoth mansion surrounded by acres of pristine foliage and classically inspired statuary in fashionable Colorado Springs. I stepped quickly away from the entrance so that I wouldn't have to meet Mr. Ramsey as he left Stratton's house. Anna helped him out to his carriage and after he had left, shut the door and turned to me, nodding with concern that I should join Stratton in the library.

When I walked in, he was still sitting in the leather chair, staring out the window into the night, absentmindedly stroking his mustache. Moving in front of him, I placed my hand lightly on his shoulder as he looked up wearily.

"Ah, my little sparrow," he smiled, pulling me gently towards him and kissing my hand lightly. He seemed older and far more fragile than the last time I had seen him. "I didn't know you had flitted by. It's been several ugly days of meetings, misunderstandings and general mayhem mashed together with utter hogwash," he continued wearily. "Tell me that you've made friends finally with Monsieur D and that he has miraculously cast you as his next Carmen at the Denver Opera's new production next season."

"My second lesson was slightly better than my first," I replied, "but no "Carmen," in my future, now or ever, I'm afraid."

He tried to pull me gently down into his lap, but I stepped over to the chair that Mr. Ramsey had just vacated which was, not at all surprisingly, still quite warm.

"I heard a lot of your conversation," I said quietly, still holding his hands for a few moments. "You've decided to sell the Independence. I guess I thought that it was sort of your most relished prize from all I'd heard. I'm very surprised. But it sounds as though you've given all of it a great deal of thought," I added quickly when his face suddenly seemed quite distant and oddly disinterested.

He shrugged. "Would you like a glass of wine?"

A glass of wine sounded wonderful but thinking back on Anna's remarks kept me from immediately replying. Before I could answer, however, he was already in his cut glass liquor cabinet uncorking another bottle of the dark red wine that I had found so remarkable and pouring out two well-rounded glasses for us. I told myself that at least wine wasn't whiskey which seemed to be Anna's main concern.

"I'm talked out about mining after four days of nothing but utter mining folderol. Tell me about your songs and any other doings at the Victor," said Stratton, nodding as he lifted his glass as a toast. I had already learned that if he didn't want to discuss a subject, he simply couldn't be persuaded to do so.

"Actually," I replied, "there is some rather interesting news. There's a competition which is going to be at the Victor, including young women singers studying there as well as the Colorado Springs, Denver and Leadville operas houses for a chance to study at the Vienna Opera House in Austria for several weeks this summer with an opera soloist's teacher. I can't remember her name or the name of her teacher, I'm sorry to say. Monsieur D wants me to work on pieces to compete and has indicated it should be a good experience even though he's certain I won't win. I'm very much looking forward to hearing all of these other singers," I nodded.

"Hmmm," said Stratton, lightly stroking his mustache, seemingly amused. "They would have to hold it at the Victor, actually. Way too competitive and unfair to have it at either Colorado Springs or Denver, and Leadville's opera house simply isn't large enough. Hard to believe that there's actually anything like classical opera out here in our merry little hinterland of merry little morphine whores, isn't it? And I suppose there's an entry fee for this competition?"

"Oh, yes, there is," I said, looking down, blushing more than slightly. Was that remark aimed towards those of us, myself certainly included, attempting to cling to some form of the art? I swallowed my shame. "I guess he assumes that you'll be willing to pay that. I'm sorry. I had actually forgotten that he had mentioned an entry fee."

Stratton gave a slight snort and took a long swallow of the wine. Then he gently wiped the back of his hand along his mustache, his head cocked slightly sideways, looking at me with a smile.

"No more talking. Your looks have changed somewhat, my little sparrow, since I left you a few days back," he said gently. He reached forward and twisted a few loose strands of my hair around his finger. The electricity of his touch radiated through me immediately. I brought his hand to my mouth and gently kissed it, twining his fingers through my own. It now surprisingly seemed like such a natural gesture.

The mesmerizing rhythms that I had experienced with this man on our first night together were repeated, the clear skies now boasting a huge, bright golden-white moon that reflected over our naked bodies slowly intertwining on his bed. With something of a sad smile he kissed my forehead and then lay back, gently brushing my hair over the pillow.

"When you were speaking with Mr. Ramsey earlier, he mentioned something about your son, Win," I said softly, then continuing cautiously, "and I just wondered if you're still married."

Stratton exhaled slightly then moved back a bit from me. I felt a shocking rush of the chilly night air immediately which was unsettling. "No, no, I'm not married, but I was for several months about twenty years back," he finally replied. "Surely with all of the rumor and frivolous innuendo flowing freely about this place you've heard about my blighted marriage?"

I did very vaguely remember having heard something about his marriage, from Jenny in fact. But I shook my head no, my hair rustling over his silk pillowcase. Why silk? That must have been Jenny's influence I suddenly realized with a slight pang. There were undoubtedly countless women who had been a part of shaping Stratton's life, I realized. Strangely, instead of feeling discouraged by this fact, I wondered what on earth I could bring to him outside of my naiveté and youth, which I humbly realized were my only attractions.

"Well," he began, his tired voice continuing slowly, "the young lady's name was Zeurah Stewart. This was back in Jeffersonville. That's in Indiana, where I'm from originally. Now I knew when Miss Stewart and I got engaged that I wasn't her first fella, but that really didn't bother me none. I'm not into that virgin-on-your-wedding-night nonsense. Never was, even back then. But once we were married, I figured she would stay true. She was already at least a couple of months pregnant when we got married, actually. That shock you?"

He looked over at me, slightly raising an eyebrow. I shook my head.

"Then, I went out to the San Juans prospecting for a couple months, trying to bring in better money than I was earning as a carpenter, which turned out to be a bust, unfortunately. Anyway, when I got back home, I heard from more than one source that my wife had been seeing several other men, even though she was already pregnant. She denied it all of course, said it was a lot of nosy busybodies interfering, but I didn't believe her. So, I left her. Filed for divorce a year or so later and claimed that the kid wasn't mine. Course, I was pretty sure that he was, despite that."

"Then, why ..." but I stopped myself. I wanted to hear the rest of what he had to say and I knew if I asked any questions that he would probably just shut up completely. "And...?"

"And whenever you meet him, 'cause even though he lives out in California he's always prowling around here every few months or so looking for more money, you'll remark at the resemblance. No way could I ever prove he weren't mine, even I have to admit."

"Did Miss Stewart ever get married again?"

"Not that I'm aware of," Stratton replied, lying flat on his back looking up at the ceiling. I was now very cold, shivering, and nestled close in towards him, pulling his arm around me. "And far as I know, Henry is her only kid. Or 'I' Henry as he calls himself."

"I. Henry?" I questioned, laughing slightly.

"His first name is Isaac and for some ridiculous reason he calls himself 'I' Henry. I've paid a hundred per cent for this kid's education, both high school and college, every last penny of his school and boarding expenses at the University of Illinois, Hannah. Also paid for several apprenticeships for him. The kid's very smart, but just goddamned lazy. Lazy as the day is long as the saying goes. Story after story of my abusing his mother, ruining her reputation, ruining his life because I never acknowledged him as my son and more blather and total nonsense along those lines. A man has to stand up on his own two feet in my book. My own father never did anything at all like that for me. And it ain't my fault if his mother ruined all of that in him," Stratton replied, a very hard edge creeping into his voice that frightened me.

"Win, what happens if I get pregnant?" I suddenly blurted out. "That could easily happen. I don't know how to keep..." my voice trailed off.

Stratton propped himself up on his elbow, looking at me and suddenly started laughing heartily, shaking his head. "Ah, my little sparrow! You're actually worried about that possibility? For me those days fathering children are long, long gone. I'm an old, sick man! Have no fear!" He pulled me into his arms with a fierce hug, kissing my neck, biting me tenderly, his warmth surrounding me all over again.

Our night together then continued without any more conversation. The only difference from our first evening was that this time I needed to leave him in the early morning mist, despite his reassurance that no one would find us nestled there in this quiet little part of his world.

Katya was asleep in her room just off the kitchen, but neither Alice nor Vanya were anywhere in the house when Stratton's driver Zane dropped me off as dawn's frosting of vibrant pinks and oranges glistened low in the sky. Vanya had probably taken Alice to her house so that she could tend her overnight as well as her own child, I assumed. My last thought before falling into a deep sleep was that I needed to locate John Barrington early in the morning.

When Alice's cries awakened me it was already close to noon I was embarrassed to discover. I hurried out to the parlor to see Katya changing Alice, and apologized, very embarrassed that I had slept so late. Katya nodded and indicated that Alice's red-blistered bottom was almost completely healed, thank goodness. I picked up the little girl and started dancing around with her and singing softly, enjoying the weight of her little body so warm in my arms. She was still the most beautiful child, her little grey eyes staring at me. I also realized that I had a wicked headache from the wine last night. I would have to be more prudent; imagine trying to sing with a head like this, I thought, annoyed by my lack of discretion not only in my drinking too much but arriving back home at sunup like a common...I did not want to finish that thought. But, there it was, blatantly in front of me of course.

Katya said that she needed to go to Stratton's house to help Anna and that Vanya would be back shortly to feed Alice again. I asked her if she knew where John Barrington could be found. He was staying at the Victor Hotel, she said somewhat cautiously, which I knew was not even a half mile away from me, actually very close to the opera house.

Vanya, along with her little one, Dannie, a darling little tyke who looked to be close to a year old, arrived just a few moments after Katya's departure. He was willing to sit and play quietly with his toys. She banked him with pillows and blankets, so he could amuse himself while she fed Alice. I told her that I needed to find John or leave him a note and she gave a thin smile and very slight nod, looking quickly away from me. I wasn't certain if she understood me and thought that maybe she was concerned that I was going to be gone for a long time leaving her with both children. I would need to find out from John exactly what his payments were supposed to cover obviously.

Although I had expected to just leave Barrington a note asking that he contact me as soon as possible, I found him eating lunch in the hotel's small café just off the entrance.

"Why, Hannah!" he remarked, standing as soon as I walked in the door. "What a wonderful surprise! I'm assuming I'm not out of line in asking that you join me for some lunch? Surely you must be hungry!" He pulled another chair over to his table and gestured to one of the waiters to bring over additional table service.

I was ravenous, I realized, having completely forgotten

about eating anything this morning. "That would be most kind," I replied, sitting as he moved my chair in towards the table. "And to what do I owe this wonderful, unplanned visit, Miss Hannah?" he asked, once I had looked over the menu and ordered. "No problems at the opera house, I assume? Is Monsieur D driving you utterly insane yet?"

"He's difficult, you're quite correct about that, but I'm learning a lot, thank you. But, there are a couple of other very important things, actually," I replied, taking a much needed drink of water. "Specifically to do with Abigail, as I'm sure you're aware."

The waiter brought two small bowls of soup and John waited to speak again until he had moved away.

"Ah, yes, I know that she's been missing and abandoned her child. That's why I suggested that Vanya help out with her since, well, I knew something would need to be done rather quickly or the kid probably wouldn't make it," he stated, blowing onto a spoonful of his soup.

Barrington's matter-of-fact tone definitely irritated me. I still could not fathom Abigail willingly leaving Alice for one thing and his assertion that the baby 'just wouldn't make it' sounded so frighteningly coldhearted to me. I stared at him for a long moment before replying. His dark hair and eyes as well as his physique were indeed quite handsome. But I realized that, rather like my impression of Jack Fairfield, something about John Barrington had always just seemed arrogant, pretentious and largely untrustworthy to me. Was Win like this as well but I just wasn't picking up on it? I pushed that comparison away as I replied to Barrington's statement.

"You can't possibly believe that Abigail willingly abandoned her baby, Mr. Barring...John," I began. "She adores that child! She had gotten rather quickly involved with a fellow named Jack Fairfield, who owns the Heritage Saloon in Cripple Creek. You may know of him. Win does at any rate. When I left to come to Victor, she said she would be moving in with him and said that they were planning on getting married soon. She said that he adored Alice and wanted to adopt her."

Barrington spooned up a couple more spoonfuls of his soup. I did the same, looking over my spoon at him, waiting for his reply.

"Well, Hannah, I'm not sure what to tell you about any of this," he began slowly. "First of all, it's highly unlikely that Jack Fairfield is even alive after that dynamiting of the Strong Mine several days ago that you may or may not have heard about. His operation was one of the largest and most brazen, definitely one that really angered those union miners. I'd be willing to bet a cool thousand that he was the first one they threw down into that mine shaft before they lit the dynamite."

"I did hear about the dynamiting," I replied. "But what about Abigail? She had nothing to do with his business dealings!" Unintentionally, I dropped my spoon with an audible clatter.

"You're right, she didn't, of course. Women rarely are of any importance whatsoever in business...well, other than prostitution, of course! But, my guess is she was grabbed at the same time and, well..." he finished with a shrug, finishing off his soup. "But, there's something else that would keep authorities from even bothering to look for her that you've apparently forgotten, madam detective."

"And, that would be?" I replied curtly.

"She was quite adamant that I not challenge her desire to be listed as dead, if you recall. Wanted her name on that list of the missing and presumed dead after the fires in Cripple Creek," he asserted, looking up at me.

I had no reply. He was absolutely correct.

"And what's more, the baby's birth was never recorded because of the fire, and even if it had been, all of that newer paperwork was destroyed anyway," he added. "Why would anyone even look for a dead woman and her unborn child?"

"True," I said quietly, but then anger crept into my voice again. "She was trying to keep all of it from her father, as you know. Because she was shocked to discover that Dr. Hughes was determined to simply dump that child in some kind of slum orphanage hoping for a quick death. Something like only two babies out of a hundred actually live past infancy in those vile places as I'm sure you know. But, most importantly, no blot left on the Hughes or Claytor family honor and all that nonsense."

Barrington gave a slight shrug, waiting for the waiter to finish clearing off our empty soup bowls.

"You may not like it, Hannah, but that's the way of our world and I very seriously doubt that it will change any time in the near future – certainly not in our lifetime, I guarantee. And what's more, society will only give an unmarried Negro woman the liberty to raise a child without shame. That's because we've accepted it as a way of life since back in the slave days. I'm sure I don't need to go into the explanation surrounding that issue for you."

I wasn't ready to accept Barrington's shallow explanation without some small protest and decided to change directions. "People would have seen Abigail while all of us were working in the tents after the fire, John," I implored. "She was helping baking bread, making stews, sewing clothing, tending to her child. There were hundreds of women."

"That's exactly right, Hannah," whispered John, nodding, his dark brown eyes wide looking into mine. "There were a couple of thousand of you, actually. All clad in that dreadful blue-grey prison garb type fabric you made your dresses out of because that's all that was available in the short term. Working shoulder to shoulder, day by day, wherever your services were needed that day. How many of those women's names do you remember? Any of them?" he asked.

He was right. I remembered none of them. Not one single face. Not one single name.

"And, if you also recall, almost no one even knew that she was in Cripple Creek at all. Albert had me put her up in that shack of mine when Margaret threw her out of their home in Colorado Springs."

"But what about the women from the Heritage Saloon?" I said emphatically, grasping onto one last attempt for his help. "Wouldn't they have known that Abigail was Jack Fairfield's fiancée when they moved to the new building after the fire?"

"Fiancée?" snorted Barrington. "All those women were registered prostitutes and forced to live over in Poverty Gulch with the rest of the demimonde while the Heritage was being rebuilt. Maybe they all considered themselves Fairfield's fiancées!"

"So, in your opinion, you think that Abigail was murdered," I said bitterly. "But there's no way for anyone to look into it. I suppose Dr. Hughes wouldn't care either, would he?"

"Hannah ..." he began, then sighed and shook his head.

In my own mind, I refused to give in to this theory of Abigail's demise. She was out there, somewhere, trying to get back to her beautiful child. I was absolutely certain. Our meals were served. As we ate, I tried to manufacture other possible scenarios for Abigail's absence, but came up short every time. Finally, I realized that I hadn't yet asked about Vanya's responsibilities.

"It was most fortunate that you knew about Vanya," I admitted. "The cow's milk we were feeding Alice was causing her to decline. It was evident hour by the hour and very frightening. I do want you to know that I sincerely thank you."

"Indeed, I'm sure that was true," Barrington replied rather shortly, giving me an almost curt nod.

"What exactly are her duties supposed to be, other than the obvious," I asked, knowing I needed to be gracious despite his rude dismissal of Abigail's situation. "I have a bit of difficulty talking with either Katya or Vanya so I'm not sure we always understand each other very well. Also, how did you locate her so quickly?" I added.

Barrington shrugged. "Have you met Dannie yet?" he asked, looking at me with a lopsided smile.

I nodded. "He seems like a very sweet little boy," I replied.

"Well," added Barrington, "Dannie's my son."

That possibility had not even crossed my mind. I was way more naïve than I realized!

"So you and Vanya are married or planning to get married?" I inquired, somehow doubting the question as the words tumbled out of my mouth.

"No, we're not married and she certainly knows that's never going to happen," Barrington answered with a hearty laugh. "But, I've agreed to give a monthly contribution to him until he's a year old, as well as house them, which is far more than most men would ever do for a prostitute's child. After that she'll be able to find a place for him to stay when she goes back on the line."

"But he's also your child ..." I began slowly, frowning.

"And you'll notice that I'm willing to acknowledge that better than most men, Hannah," he added rather curtly, "even though I basically rescued the girl from working in one of those filthy, godforsaken cribs she was sold into by her supposed boyfriend a couple years back."

"That had to be a rather daring thing, John," I replied, trying my best to envision him in a better light despite his hardhearted words. "Not many men would go to that kind of trouble, I suppose."

"I won her in a poker game," he chuckled, sitting back in his chair and crossing his arms. "She begged me originally to give her enough money to go back home to her family in Poland. Now with that kid she really can't go back anyway. They sure as hell wouldn't want her either."

XVII. Se Tu M'Ami

My life now became a blur of lessons with Delacroix, whom I firmly believed truly hated the very sight of me, much less the sound of my voice, rehearsing at the theater with the pianist for the competition, as well as fiercely rehearsing on my own, Baby Alice, madly coordinating Katya's, Vanya's and my schedules to be with Alice, and of course, Stratton, without whose financial support, love and encouragement, none of this would have been possible. I had originally looked at these lessons, in fact this entire singing venture, as a childlike manifestation somehow. I still had no actual confidence in my work, but I now realized that I needed to push as hard as possible before Stratton completely lost interest in sponsoring me. And I didn't entertain any aspirations that he wouldn't soon lose interest if my performance was substandard. We had to choose a work in German and one in Italian for the event. My selections of *"Bist Du Bei Mir"* and *"Se Tu M'ami"* seemed to enrage Delacroix further with every rehearsal since my emotional involvement with either work was ridiculously nonexistent in his opinion. How could I be so displaced, so frigid, so hideously and utterly vapid in my presentation, he roared? And at every rehearsal I simply became worse and worse! How was this even possible, he bellowed? I knew it was my constantly reevaluating whether my pronunciations were correct, as well as maintaining true note values, not slowing down enough or picking up the tempo too much in certain sections, reserving enough vocal power when needed in phrasing, but letting go when essential, crescendos, decrescendos, and so many other criticisms he hurled my direction that there was truly no space for any emotional involvement. Every note that came out of my mouth was 'grossly pregnant with inexhaustible errors in music technique' according to the man. And I had every reason to believe him. I now utterly detested my singing as well.

There was also the matter of my needing to have a new dress made for the contest evening. How I longed for Pearl's beautifully fashioned gown that Jenny had lent me! If there was one item I so wished I could have rescued from the fire it was that amazing dress! I tried to describe its shimmering light green material, with its generously puffed sleeves and contrasting trim, as well as the general cut to the seamstress, but her creation sadly left much wanting. I made several alterations on the fit of the bodice, adding darts and some additional trim, which helped only slightly. Win of course paid for the dress and I desperately wanted him to be pleased at least with how I looked.

Several days before the competition, there was a dress rehearsal at the theater. All of the girls from the Colorado Springs Opera House as well as those of us at the Victor had a chance to hear one another sing since we supplied the audience for one other. Without question, this was the most revealing detail in terms of my own confidence. Quite a few of the girls were singing one of my same pieces. Also, I was rather surprised to discover that many of them were quite a bit younger than me, yet presented themselves far more professionally. Listening to some of them blunder through the same passages with problems in pronunciation, vocal miscalculations, tempo miscues and pitch problems made me realize that I was far from alone with my insecurities. However, none of their insecurities registered in their faces while singing I noticed. They just smoothly continued. Was this what actually infuriated Delacroix about my own errors I wondered?

One young woman was flawless in my opinion, however.

Her rendition of *"Se tu m'ami"* showed exactly the coy, lightly flirtatious, yet at times, wonderfully dramatic, interpretation that the piece demanded, her face a true joy to watch throughout. After listening to her performance I felt very clearheaded where to direct my own work for the next two days. Obviously there would be many more girls coming from the Tabor Opera House in Leadville and the Denver Opera House. The competition would be divided into two long sets, or acts, and we would be allowed to sit in the back balcony seats during the set in which we weren't singing. The order was alphabetical and, "Owens" obviously being in the second half of the alphabet, put me in the second half of the program, meaning I would be able to observe the first half.

During the last week's preparation for the concert, John Barrington showed up briefly one evening with news that Jack Fairfield had definitely been one of the saloon owners herded down into the Strong Mine's shaft before the dynamiting. A witness, who refused to give his name since he was terrified for his own life, thought that there might have been a woman thrown down there with him, but he had no idea who she was, or actually, if it was really a woman at all since she was wearing men's clothing. However, her body looked more female than male, according to this witness.

John also told me that Win had fired William Ramsey and that he was now Win's personal secretary. This definitely took me by surprise since I had thought that Mr. Ramsey was probably the most trusted man in Win's extremely small circle of confidants. I asked if he knew where Win had been all of this week and John simply shrugged it off. "Ah, probably in his library reading up on religious cults, spiritualism and fanaticism all night, fretting over the conditions of sale of the Independence with all of his lawyers, and spending far too much time in the presence of his one true favorite mistress, Mlle. Whiskey," he relayed with a nonchalant shrug. Also, speaking of lawyers, he mentioned that Win had received a note from the lawyer handling Zuma's situation and that her prison sentence would now be up within the next couple of months. At that time she would be sent back to Colorado according to the note. I thanked John for all of the information and feeling obligated asked if he would like to stay for dinner, but confess I was very grateful when he begged off.

My mind swirled around John's information about Abigail. For the last couple of weeks I had somehow known this had to be what had happened to her. Also, I knew that Abigail's last thoughts undoubtedly must have been a prayer for her little Alice. And the depth of that prayer had undoubtedly led me to find Alice at the saloon that day, probably the morning after the dynamiting. In my own opinion, Abigail's involvement with this man Jack Fairfield, whom she really scarcely knew, had been her attempt to grasp his lukewarm promise of marriage in order to give her child a respectable name – a respectable future. I wanted to somehow be able to offer respectability for this beautiful little girl as well. But given my own muddied path, that route was far from clear. For right now, though, it was keeping up with Alice's feedings, diaper changing, constantly shifting sleep cycles and general care. And the last few days, her smiles, giggles and singing whenever I held her in my arms absolutely broke my heart knowing that her mother would never get to experience those indescribable joys.

The day of the competition I awoke very early, a hard rain drumming on the roof. I now hadn't seen Win in slightly over a week, and perhaps naively assumed that he was giving me time to adequately rest for the program, for which I was grateful, but I was also very concerned based on what John Barrington had told me regarding Stratton's excessive drinking. I heard Vanya and Katya speaking in low voices and assumed that Vanya had just brought Alice over from her house. We were now starting to give the baby some cow's milk again mixed in with a little oatmeal at night and Vanya said that within another week we would be able to keep her at my place all night since she wouldn't have to be nursing her at night. I would have to figure this out with Win, I realized, but just hadn't had time to assemble all of the pieces in my mind yet. I had finally told Win that Alice was living with me and that Abigail had mysteriously, and possibly violently, disappeared. His reaction seemed rather odd, but I now wondered if he wasn't so deep into his own problems that in reality Abigail's disappearance just hadn't registered with him at all.

Katya helped me to get dressed and pinned up a few curls of my hair in ribbons while Alice lay giggling in her basket, her little legs pinwheeling in the cool morning air. I gave her a big hug, asking her to be patient with me. There was no way that I could win this contest, but I needed to do well enough to keep moving the two of us forward. I was only sixteen years old, but somehow, I felt as though I was already forty.

With the downpour, the opera house was already mired in a sea of mud that everyone was trying to circumnavigate. After my arrival, I did the vocal warm-ups in the great room where one of the Denver teachers was directing, then found out from a rather snooty soprano from Colorado Springs that there would be another vocal warm-up during the intermission for those who were singing in the second set. Many of the girls had received beautiful large bouquets of rare hothouse flowers, extremely lavish gifts and notes from their admirers, family or sponsors, but nothing appeared for me at my dressing room space. I wondered if Win had been informed by Delacroix that I was such an embarrassingly hopeless subject for Stratton to sponsor that he had already abandoned his support.

The balcony was extremely hot and humid as the late

summer afternoon wore on. Everyone tried to fan themselves as quietly as possible so as not to distract from the performers, but the air became increasingly saturated and uncomfortable. All the performers began to blend together to me. Their voices, their gowns, their upswept hair, their gestures, their youth, in fact, everything after awhile became the same, one girl after another in my mind. And the judges still had an entire second act of us to listen to I thought despairingly, feeling large damp wads of the ill-fashioned sleeve fabric grinding under my arms. I tried to locate Stratton in one of the boxes. He had at one time indicated that he had bought one for the program, but I was unable to see into many of them from my aerie, since most of the boxes were directly underneath me.

When I finally walked out on stage, I was just ready for this whole program to be over. Waiting to perform I realized was every bit as much a torture as the performance itself. As I stood center stage and nodded for the pianist to begin, I spotted Win in the box just to the left, center back. He was sitting with his arm around a well-known, very notorious and disgustingly wealthy society divorcée from Colorado Springs, who was glistening in diamonds so brilliant, nestled low between her scarcely concealed breasts, the jewels were practically blinding from the stage. Suddenly, all of the coy, sometimes sultry passages, alternating with the sweeter developments in *"Se tu m'ami"* became startlingly alive for me. The lyrics' pronunciation, the phrasings, the passion behind all of those phrasings, cycled into a power I had no idea I possessed. Although I had never been directed to move anywhere on stage, I found that I couldn't help but do so as the music within me paced itself through tempo changes that had never been suggested, let alone rehearsed.

"Bist du bei mir," suddenly became dedicated to Abigail, I realized. A part of the translation was "and at the end will your warm and loving hand reach to gently close my eyes, until my

death and unto my rest." When I started singing, I realized that I was deliberately slowing down the accompanist from the brief piano introduction, an almost ethereal calm taking over my voice. The harsh guttural German that had seemed so impossible to pronounce correctly yet instill with any soft emotion seemed effortless. The last several measures of the piece ended themselves shockingly almost in a whisper, tears glistening in my eyes.

I only glanced in Stratton's direction a couple of times. Although his arm was still draped around his companion for the evening, his blue eyes were fixed on my face. With his other hand, he stroked his mustache, that familiar gesture I so adored. At the end of my performance, I gave a low curtsy, as instructed, not even remotely aware of the audience's reaction. It no longer mattered. As I walked offstage, I glanced at Monsieur D sitting to the right in the dress circle. Eyebrows lowered, he seemed to be glowering at me, shaking his head slowly, his arms crossed. The winner, or winners, since there was the possibility of a tie it was feared, would be announced in several days after the judges had finished their discussions and evaluations. I no longer even cared which of these young women would be selected. In fact, I no longer even cared about ever singing again.

I walked back to the dressing room, gathered up my shawl and a few other items and left, eager to just walk home in the cooling, light rain and hoped to have a chance to rock Alice to sleep. I pushed my performance in the concert, Stratton, his disgusting companion, my dripping wet hair and soggy, muddied dress out of my thoughts. I had done my best. And, rather surprisingly, I realized that whatever caustic reaction that Delacroix would have regarding my departure from his months of strict instruction, he certainly couldn't find fault for the raw passion I had experienced in my performance this evening. It all cut very deep.

When I walked in my door the house was empty. Alice was probably at Vanya's and Katya undoubtedly had been helping again at Stratton's house. Katya had left a large pot of her delicious, thick vegetable soup on the modified spirit lamp, along with a small loaf of brown bread, a dish of blackberries and wedge of cheese. I changed out of the dress, making a half-hearted attempt to scrub the mud out of the hem before just throwing it in the tub to soak, and then dished up a large bowl of the tantalizing soup. I had almost finished when there was a gentle knock at the door and I heard the unmistakable sound of Stratton's familiar soft leather boots in the parlor.

I continued to sit at the table, concentrating on buttering a piece of bread, as he entered the small dining area. He stopped in the doorway, looking at me for several moments, then quietly pulled up the other chair and sat opposite me. Despite myself, when I finally made an attempt to look up there were tears in my eyes.

"You were absolutely stunning, my little sparrow," he said in a hoarse voice. "Even more exquisite, more passionate, more alive, than I could have ever imagined."

"Why?" I choked out, his face now completely blurred through my tears. "Why would you attend with that … that dreadful Mrs. Wilson? She's one of the most notorious divorcées in the state, Win! All of the other girls had beautiful flowers, gifts and notes of encouragement from their sponsors. But I just sat in my little dressing room space awaiting the ceiling dust to drift down and bury me in obscurity. I don't understand! I really just don't understand!"

"Hannah," he said softly, putting his hand under my chin. "That's how you wanted everything, if you recall."

I jerked roughly away from him, dropping the half-eaten piece of bread on the table.

"You didn't want anyone to know of my relationship with

you, which was very wise and quite understandable," he continued tenderly, but still hoarsely, "and I've worked very hard to keep that an unknown, my sweet little sparrow. Most people have deduced that I'm sponsoring your training with Delacroix and providing your room and board here. It would be almost impossible to hide those facts as I'm sure you're well aware. But beyond that? They know absolutely nothing. I've made certain that I've been seen all over town with women such as Mrs. Wilson, or even worse if I must confess, to deflect any gossip about you, my dear. If I had sent you flowers or gifts this evening or greeted you before or after the program that gesture would undoubtedly have lent itself to extensive tongue-wagging, gossip and conjecture."

"And you're just seen all over town with these women? That's all? You don't expect me to believe that," I replied, still looking away. "I have no claims to you, I know that. But up until tonight, seeing you ... completely ... wrapped around that hideous woman, I guess that I really thought that I was in love with you. And even more foolishly, I guess I thought that you were with me as well."

A few moments of silence spread out between us.

"In my own way, my sweet little sparrow, I do love you. Believe me. Love is so much more than just uttering those flabby, hollow words themselves, or just a long rainy afternoon spent together getting to know one another on a soft leather couch. There's respect, devotion, commitment and a desire to place the other person's respectability above your own no matter what. One day I hope that you'll be able to understand that. But right now, you're too young. And I'm far too old and too tired to explain it very well."

I wiped the tears away with the back of my hand and faced him. He looked awful. His coloring was a grayish yellow and he looked horribly gaunt, almost as though he had aged a decade since I'd last seen him. I slowly brought his hand to my cheek, somehow also managing a small smile. He took my face in his hands and we kissed softly, then just sat back looking into one another's eyes for several minutes.

"You look as though you haven't had any rest for weeks, Win," I whispered, as I stroked his silky mustache. "Both Anna and John Barrington have mentioned…"

"Mentioned what?" he sighed, his voice very tired.

"That they've been concerned for your health," I replied.

"When have you been talking with John?"

"He stopped by sometime last week to tell me that Abigail may well have been in that mine explosion along with Jack Fairfield. He also said that you had fired Mr. Ramsey and hired him as your new secretary. I'm hoping that the mine sale is finally going a little more…smoothly," I continued.

Stratton shook his head, an exhausted shadow passing over his face. "No, it's not going smoothly at all, actually," he replied. "But I'm determined as ever to make it happen. That's why I had to fire Ramsey and hire on Barrington as my secretary. John and Verner Reed should be able to push in unison to get this deal finalized. Ramsey was against the whole transaction from the start and was really dredging up every possible legal loophole imaginable since Noah threw all of those animals up on the ark."

I couldn't help smiling at the reference.

"I'm going to have to leave for London sometime in the next few days to crank out the many details and I'm thoroughly dreading the trip itself: a week on the train to New York and then another week on that steamship to Southampton, the meetings with this Venture group, none of whom trust Americans one whit – not that I blame them -- that horrid English food where they conspire to bury peas in everything rolling about on one's plate, the lack of privacy everywhere, the London filth. All of it."

He pulled me into his arms, whispering. "But before I have

to face all of that, there's absolutely nothing wrong with that one long rainy evening spent together getting to know one another on a soft leather couch, or wherever, my little sparrow."

Indeed.

XVIII. The Independence Mine

That evening was the last time I saw Win before he left for England. Without trying to sound too interfering, I urged him to at least try to drink less whiskey since he readily admitted that it was making him ill. He mentioned that he really had no appetite whatsoever and wasn't eating much of anything, as I had suspected. And in fact, he also acknowledged that Dr. Hughes had severely admonished him that his liver was failing and that he was drinking himself into complete oblivion. The problem, Win admitted, was that he never felt drunk. He could continue to drink all afternoon, evening and well into the night, and still function as though he were completely sober. The only difference, he admitted rather coyly, was that he felt his lovemaking was far more enjoyable for his lady when he had already consumed several drinks. And he really didn't consider wine as alcohol.

John Barrington was of course traveling with him since he was now Win's secretary, so John would undoubtedly try to keep him in line Win had admitted with something of a rather insincere wink. I received a brief note from him mailed just before they boarded the Hamburg-America line to England out of New York. He grumbled about the numerous railroad detours and mishaps that had occurred that week, but was quite intrigued with the ship's dual engines and mammoth dual boilers, large watertight, private sleeper compartments and the three wide promenade decks surrounding the boat, and was hoping that this second leg of the trip would be less objectionable. The note was signed with his flourishing WSS and contained no endearments or personal asides other than addressing it, quite sweetly, "my dear little sparrow". I now understood why and smiled. In the time that it had taken his letter to find me, he would now have arrived in London. I prayed that the meetings were going well and that he was eating, disgusting peas or no peas, and making at least a small attempt to be more moderate about his whiskey.

While awaiting the opera judges' final decision, Monsieur D was taking an extended time off from instruction and I was ecstatic to be able to spend so much time with Alice. Katya and Vanya had each contributed so much extra time to the baby's care during the two weeks prior to the competition that I tried to now give them some time away. Although it was only early September, the weather had turned very cold and long undulating veils of snow had rushed down from the higher elevations on more than one occasion. I had almost no warm clothing myself and little Alice had nothing whatsoever. After shopping at the couple of dry goods shops in Victor and Cripple Creek and constructing fairly crude patterns, I started cutting out and stitching together several basic medium-weight wool dresses, under dresses, stockings, aprons, as well as winter cloaks, scarves, mittens and hats for myself, and lambs' wool-lined sleepers, new blankets and knitted hats for Alice. Vanya also gave me several long, warm outfits that Dannie had outgrown. I wondered what she would do when her son was a year old and Barrington cut off his funding. But I also worried about what I would do if Win cut off his funding to me. Abandoning Alice, even though she wasn't my own child, loomed as a dismal threat. I vowed to work harder for Delacroix.

The same day that Win's note arrived, I had also received a brief notice from Monsieur D asking me to meet him the following day in our usual rehearsal room. He actually stood up from the piano, exuberantly walked over and kissed my hand, then guided me to a chair. You could have knocked me over with a feather! I had fully expected to be greeted with hot iron tongs! I hadn't won either of the placements, of course, but of the fifty-one girls who competed, I was actually ranked number five Monsieur told me, a huge smile, the first I'd certainly ever seen, broadening over his face. And, most importantly, except for another of his students from the Victor who ranked number eighteen, the Denver and Colorado Springs entrants took all of the first thirty positions he stated, making my ranking even that more amazing. Delacroix handed the evaluation sheet to me:

"After listening to so many dreary representations of the same tunes, with the same contrived gestures, meaningless banal, facial expressions, and attempts to bring vocal flourishes to languages in which most of these girls can just barely grasp the nuances of the language itself much less add any musical ornamentation, Miss Owens' stunning performances of "Se tu m'ami" and "Bist du bei mir" radiated both a fresh vocal purity and yet the extraordinary passionate delivery one seldom experiences from a novice. We urge her to continue her studies, preferably abroad, if her family can possibly afford this. For one so new to this experience, as is shown by her record of such a startlingly short time of serious vocal study, she possesses that exceedingly rare, innate, enormous gift. As a committee we thoroughly look forward to hearing her on the professional stage in the very near future. ~ Miss Hannah Owens, ranking #5." It was signed by the three judges.

This was far from anything I might have expected. I just blankly attempted to hand the notice back to him, but he said it was mine to keep. Early on, Mrs. Hughes had occasionally included me when she had taken Abigail to small house concerts and musical gatherings in Colorado Springs, but I had never seen an actual opera, of course. I really wasn't even sure that I wanted to be an opera singer if they had to learn hours upon hours of songs in Italian or German! We talked about my resuming lessons in the next week as well as his encouragement that I ask Stratton to pay for a couple of months' instruction at either the

Vienna Opera House or Hamburg State Opera. I asked about London and he shook his head emphatically stating that the Alhambra Theatre in London, which had just been rebuilt a couple of years ago, was basically now a music hall that catered to "loud, very provocative popular music these days" in his opinion. If I was going to be serious about my studies I should avoid such dreadful, lackluster places, in Europe or in America, he cautioned. He again kissed my hand as I departed saying that he was honored to continue to work with me. I scarcely felt the sharp, howling winds buffeting about me on my way home. I couldn't wait to share the notice with Win when he got back in town in the next couple of weeks.

My excitement was short-lived, however. When I walked in my door Katya handed me a telegram from John Barrington: "Stratton collapsed. Independence sold. Spa, Aix-au-Bains. Need you here." It was signed John B. There was also a message from Dr. Hughes that had been delivered within the last hour. He needed to talk with me immediately about Stratton's treatment at this particular spa and furnished his telephone number at his hotel in Cripple Creek. Anna was trying to deflect Stratton's son Isaac and only nephew, Carl Chamberlin, from rampaging Stratton's home, Katya managed to convey to me. The two men had already made off with several of Win's prized paintings – brazenly stolen them right off the walls – along with several first edition books from his rare Americana literature collection. She feared that they had also broken into his private safe, looting gold and who knew what else, and stolen numerous cases of Stratton's favorite whiskies from his cellar. Needless to say, I wasn't concerned about the missing whiskey and doubted that Anna was either. The outright theft of the paintings, gold and Americana was outrageous, but Win would have to deal with his family when he returned home. I responded first by telephone, although I still felt quite intimidated by the machine, to Dr.

Hughes' urgent letter regarding Win's treatment.

"Hello?" Dr. Hughes voice barked into my ear once we had been connected through.

"Dr. Hughes, hello. Hannah Owens."

"What's going on?" he demanded, coughing. "Why on earth did Barrington have Stratton taken to that ghastly spa at Aix-au-Bains and not to Baden-Baden for real treatment?"

"I have no idea, sir. I only just found out about all of this myself in the last hour. Mr. Barrington has asked me to get there and I'm going to try to book passages immediately. What's wrong with the spa at Aix-au-Bains?"

"Oh, my lord, girl! It's an utter joke!" He continued in a hoarse, singsong voice: "Serenading by a band, then a light breakfast, a cool bath followed by a light lunch, sightseeing and concert attendance, more theatrical nonsense after the evening meal. The only thing even moderately curative is the fact that certain foods are not allowed and only moderate drinking is allowed. Ha! Stratton and moderate drinking? Now *that's* a tall one! In bed by 9 p.m., up by 6 a.m. for another day of this nursery school nonsense!" He lapsed into a congested coughing fit.

"What do you suggest then? Where should Mr. Barrington take him?"

"Baden-Baden, of course," barked Dr. Hughes, finally catching his breath. "And immediately! I've left messages with Barrington but haven't heard back from the scoundrel. We need to get Stratton some real care immediately, do you understand?"

"What do they offer..."I started to say, but Dr. Hughes' rasping voice overpowered mine.

"Baden-Baden has both hot air and hot water showers, vapor baths, massages, water fountains and pavilions with *Trinkhallen* – those are drinking water halls – as well as an inhalatorium to inhale the vapors and relaxing '*sprudel*' room sand pools. Very strict dietary requirements and most importantly, absolutely no hard liquor! The man's liver is a horrible mess, Hannah. He has sugar diabetes and serious stomach issues. He's going to die within the next several months if he doesn't curtail this non-stop drinking! I don't think he realizes how deathly ill he is! And I don't seem able to get that point across to him no matter how hard I press." Although luckily our connection was surprisingly clear, Dr. Hughes sounded as though he could benefit from that spa as well – his voice sounded horrible. I remembered Abigail telling me about his lung issues so long ago. I vowed to do what I could and hung up.

I then made a quick trip over to Stratton's ranch home, telling Anna that she needed to begin to pack up all of his belongings since the property had just been sold to the Venture Corporation over in England. Win still owned a very small home on Weber Street in Colorado Springs and another telegram from Barrington had instructed me to have Win's possessions moved there since all the outbuildings on the Independence property needed to be vacated immediately.

At Dr. Hughes' insistence, Win was transferred to the spa at Baden-Baden. When I arrived there two weeks later, after a lengthy rail delay which caused me to miss my original sailing connection, he was still limp, a ghastly greenish yellow-grey color, and any attempt to speak was such an effort that he just lay on his back, sometimes gasping for breath for hours, staring up at the ceiling while holding my hand and never even uttering a word. The spa itself was indeed quite beautiful with luxurious mosaic floors, marble walls, classical statuary all offset with beautifully detailed arched openings, domed ceilings and Corinthian columns which would have ordinarily intrigued an architect's eye such as Stratton's. But he was completely unaware of his surroundings it appeared. On several occasions John Barrington urged me to accompany him and attend one of the operas at the Hamburg Opera House, but I had absolutely no desire to do so. I simply wanted to stay with Win.

A couple of expensive trunk calls from Dr. Hughes to John and me relayed several other messages. When Dr. Hughes had spoken to Stratton's doctors, he had demanded that they forgo giving him calomel treatments which so many doctors were now prescribing to treat every ailment under the sun. In his experience, calomel was actually causing many extended horrors, such as neuropathy and brain damage, while treating other illnesses. Did I remember his warning to Zuma about the quicksilver that she had been sprinkling so liberally trying to kill bedbugs many years back? Well, quicksilver was just a form of metallic mercury, Hughes argued, the same horrible poison as calomel. Great for killing bugs but for curing liver ailments? Utter nonsense! Also, Zuma had now been released from prison in New Orleans and had just arrived at my house, helping with these two babies who apparently belonged to Katya and Vanya as he understood it. Since neither woman seemed to have very good command of English, it was difficult for him to find out exactly what their relationship was to the children. I knew that Zuma would embrace having to help care for those two little ones, as well as help with the move of Stratton's belongings over to Colorado Springs.

And there was also another baby who would soon be needing Zuma's help I had come to realize in the last few weeks. My own.

XIX. Emma Winfield Jackson

After Baden-Baden we visited a spa in southern France. Although still extremely weak, Win finally became stable enough that we booked our passage back to the States. Our return trip was reasonably calm and Win, exhausted, slept for practically the entire excursion. With three men positioned in rooms adjacent to his, attending to every possible need, I found myself in John Barrington's company after an early dinner each evening. Although I still found his pretentious views objectionable, I confess that having someone to talk with during the voyage relieved some of the tedium.

Since it was far too cold to wander about the deck in the evenings, we sat in the small café listening to various entertainments. John spoke to the pianist and I ended up singing a few songs one evening. I hadn't uttered one note since those days at the Victor so many months ago and was surprised how good it felt. Hot tea and a few baking soda biscuits brought up to my cabin, along with a short, brisk walk on the frigid deck each morning helped immensely with my ever present nausea, thankfully.

When we arrived back in Colorado, Win was taken to the hospital in Colorado Springs while Anna, Zuma and I worked to get Stratton's new home on Weber Street ready. Katya stayed at my house in Victor to take care of Alice. Zuma looked thin, a bit older, rarely speaking to any of us, but was still an incredibly strong, tireless worker. She deflected my questions about her ordeal in New Orleans and had quietly gotten to work in Stratton's household. Oddly, I noticed that she typically vacated a room any time John Barrington walked in.

We found that Win's belongings had been recklessly slammed into ancient trunks, his beloved Americana editions shoved in wooden crates, his beautiful handcrafted furnishings dented and horribly scratched when everything was thrown into rugged open wagons during a wet snowstorm and roughly transported to the new address. Anna had screamed at the swarm of inebriated workmen as they desecrated her employer's home in Victor, but they had roared with laughter, gagging her with a dish towel, and then chained her to a post out in the barn for several hours.

Like the ugly slag refuse creeping down the once pristine mountains, the jumble of Stratton's belongings had been dumped in his living room almost the entire time we had been in Europe. When we began opening all of the crates we discovered that Win's collection of Impressionist paintings, imported china, and his several dozen pair of expensive Swiss-made soft leather boots had vanished, just as Anna had feared, doubtless courtesy of his son "I" Henry and nephew Carl Chamberlin.

John Barrington had made sure the three women, all of whom had been living at my home, received their wages and had also kept up payments on my other bills. He had also informed Delacroix that my return to the opera house would have to be decided at a later date. I appreciated yet simultaneously resented John's attention to these details pertinent to keeping some manner of order in my life. He was Win's secretary, I thought. Not mine.

As I expected, Alice was sitting quite sturdily, scooting about after her toys and was at first very shy of me. Now that she had cut several teeth she was thriving well on oatmeal and mashed foods with cow's milk. Vanya had left Victor a couple of weeks ago, heading out to Missouri where Mr. Barrington had written and found a good job for her Katya told me. I realized that John's support for Dannie must now have ended as well and was glad that he was at least compassionate enough to secure decent employment for Vanya.

We began sifting through Win's furniture, transporting much of the badly damaged pieces to an outbuilding until Win was healthy enough to make the needed repairs. We managed to get his bed put together, night table and dresser drawers filled correctly. Anna said he was very strict about the placement of his personal items inside and on top of all his furniture. Zuma moved several larger rugs to a back fence and began beating as much of the dust and debris from them as possible, snowflakes swirling down about her in the cold late afternoon. Anna had gone back into the kitchen to get a start on Stratton's favorite thick bean soup, with plans to take a bowl over to the hospital hoping to tempt his sluggish appetite. Since our return, Win had insisted that only Anna attend to him and refused medicines or any other care by the hospital nurses or myself.

I was pulling the contents of Win's writing desk out of one of the battered trunks, when suddenly I felt a strong wave of nausea pass over me, the first reoccurrence in several weeks, and immediately sat down. For close to four months now as I had held Win's hand while he fitfully slept or tried to coax him to eat a few bites of soft food or cradled him during his frequent bouts of delirium or manic hallucinations, I wondered when I should tell him. Obviously he had been wrong that he could no longer father children. However, would he even believe that this baby was his? And even if he did, what happened then? Absolutely nothing would change in his life, but my entire world was about to be thrown upside down I feared.

During many of his rages he had shrieked about all the filthy whores who had scorned him, screaming hoarsely for hours on end, listing a long series of names in which occasionally I was shocked to hear mine included as well. I remembered his admission that twenty years ago he had refused to acknowledge his wife's son even though he was fairly certain that the child was actually his. And, like Abigail, giving the child to any kind of orphanage was not an option for me. I already loved this tiny feather of life nestled so deeply within me. I could only hope that Win would realize how fortunate we were to bring this little one into the world.

I realized that I was still holding a small bundle of very lightly perfumed letters from the desk, tied together with a narrow burgundy leather string. Glancing at them I realized that they all had the same handwriting and were postmarked from The Yukon – Skagway – District of Alaska. I willed myself to just place the bundle into the desk drawer and not look at any of them. But I knew I lacked that courage. According to the cancel stamp date, Win would probably have received that top letter very early this summer. Surely these letters simply represented a general correspondence between two longtime friends I reasoned, even though each envelope looked to contain several pages. My hand shook slightly as I opened the top one.

My Ever Dearest Win ~

Your last letter was truly delightful! I can't begin to tell you how happy I am to hear that your plans to sell the Independence are finally on track after all these months of delays! What a horrific slog it's been for you, my dear. Also, I'm so glad to hear that you're considering my idea to replace 'Ole Ramblin' Ramsey' with 'The John B' as well. Do it, do it, my darling!! John is so much younger and more forward (and less froward!) thinking – important elements as we blindly stumble into this new Century. He's sure to serve all your interests well I firmly believe.

You wanted to know about everything going on up here and I honestly don't know where to begin! Three of the girls (Muriel, Lana and "the" Sadie – sans M. St. J, thank goodness -- I think that damn bird would freeze to death flitting about) from Pearl's place are now working for me. And believe it or not, I've actually hired a dozen other girls that even Pearl with her exacting standards would have approved of along with several others who are at least adequate in the trade. I passed along your excellent suggestions to those woefully inefficient workmen about how to rework the ceilings to better connect with the roof joists on the "New Homestead" as I now refer to it, and it was a miracle! I wish you could find time to get up here a little sooner than you indicated to see your money so well spent!

I dropped the letter to my lap. I really didn't want to read any more, but for some reason looked through to the last page and spotted my name in the last few sentences.

About Hannah, I urge you to please go very slowly with her. (I terribly miss those deliciously sweet long afternoons of our lovemaking, dearest!) She lacks that hard crust so many young women of today just naturally seem to develop -- she reminds me of a very fragile little fawn and I worry that her naïve spirit will get horribly trampled in this ugly life.

I need to get everyone organized for this evening – entertaining big *money in town this weekend -- so I must end here. I assume that you'll be heading over to London in the next month or so to meet with the Venture people so am sending buckets of love that all goes well. And just remember to tell those silly waiters up front: 'no peas!'*

~ as always,

your loving Jenny

ps ~enjoy the enclosed picture – I just had them done! Not too *naughty, but just enough!*

I could hear her lilting, carefree voice, never malicious or condescending, within every word she had written. That he had advanced her money and rendered the architectural design to build her own place was not surprising. After all, he was an excellent architect. He had obviously also gone into great length about his business decisions with her, which I could also understand, even though I was slightly hurt that he had always refused to speak to me about his work. They had been good friends, and lovers, for a very long time I reasoned. The picture was no longer enclosed. When Dr. Hughes and Pearl DeVere had traveled to Europe together many years ago, very likely Win and Jenny had traveled with them. That would explain the constant joke everyone seemed to share about the detestable London peas. But when had he been planning to visit her? Immediately after his London trip? That trip was originally scheduled to last less than a month. How long would he have been out in Alaska, I wondered. He could have just told me that he was considering gold mining investments out there and I wouldn't have doubted him for a second. But worse, learning that Jenny had coached Win on how to steer past my sexual naivety or detailing her longing for their deliciously sweet, long afternoons of lovemaking, word for word almost identical to those he had said to me, cut very deep. Had he written her back before he had left on his trip, before he had become so violently ill? What might have been in his letter? What descriptions about our lovemaking? When his hands sweetly caressed my face or fingered curls in my hair pulling me towards him, or his mouth playfully bit my breasts, or his fingers softly explored me deep inside, knowing instinctively just when to alter his tantalizing rhythms ... was it me lying there with him or Jenny?

I carefully refolded the letter and tied the leather string around the bundle, placing it in his bottom desk drawer. For several minutes I just sat shivering, eclipsed in the darkening, cold room. Jenny was certainly right about my being naïve. Win had adroitly avoided the word 'love' with me, affirming that love was just a meaningless, hollow declaration, and honoring the other person's respectability was the true measure of one's love. Which when you thought about it, those words were also a meaningless, hollow declaration as well. Similar to the experience of countless other young women made pregnant by their lover, Win's interpretation of our relationship obviously differed completely from my own.

With serious misgivings, Win's doctors released him from the hospital only five days after we had arrived in Colorado Springs. His greenish-grey color was only slightly improved and his appetite still non-existent. When he was awake he was often incoherent, and when he was asleep he mumbled constantly, suffering even in his deepest dreams unless he had been given sufficient morphine to deaden the pain.

We had gotten the house fairly well organized, but as soon as John and two other men helped Win in the door, Stratton's piercing blue eyes, the whites still badly yellowed with jaundice, widened in horror. He began hoarsely yelling at Anna and Zuma to move various pieces of furniture, lamps and rugs around (and then invariably had them moved back to where we had originally placed them). He demanded that John get all of the books out of those piles and organized on the bookshelves, alphabetically and by subject, and was enraged to discover that most of his prized Americana selections had now undoubtedly been sold by his bastard son to pay off gambling debts. I had hung the only remaining original painting, "The Miner's Last Dollar" over Win's sofa in his library. He began shrieking that he never wanted to see that worthless piece of garbage again and I hastily removed it – even though the next day, he demanded to know why I had removed it from the wall. Goddamn it woman that was his favorite painting, he'd bellowed! Didn't I know that?

Anna finally got a few doses of his various medicines, including morphine, and a little food into him, and she and John managed to ease him into his bed late in the afternoon. I felt completely useless and frighteningly forgotten by him. He had lost so much ground since we had left Europe, but I attempted to remain optimistic. Now that he was back among his own belongings, once they were organized as he demanded, everything would undoubtedly improve. Anna stayed in the room until Win was completely asleep, but John came out closing the door and motioned for me to join him in the library.

He gave me a firm hug, lightly kissing the top of my head, then moved over and sat in one of Win's favorite leather chairs that were once again positioned in front of his desk. I sat in the opposite chair.

"He's dying, Hannah," John began bluntly. "Whether you're willing to believe that or not, there's no hope with a liver that badly poisoned. And as you can undoubtedly see for yourself, it's now spread hideously affecting his brain. Albert looked in on him a few times and concurred with the hospital doctors."

"He does seem to have gotten so much worse since we left France," I reluctantly agreed, my shoulders slumping. "At least he was trying to eat a bit more and just seemed more, well, 'alive' I guess, during that last spa's treatments. Or so I thought, anyway. Then on the ship and the trains he just slept constantly which you and I both assumed was a good thing. At least he wasn't suffering any longer from those horrible hallucinations."

"He did have that one brief respite, you're quite correct, Hannah. He was surprisingly coherent, even though extremely weak, for a couple days if you recall. In fact, I was able to meet with Stratton and his lawyers and we managed to make certain revisions to his will, as well as re-issue several very important Independence mining stock certificates that he still held for the Venture group's deal. I don't know if you were aware that he had agreed to take the stock certificates in lieu of cash at the Independence sale so that the corporation could actually afford the transaction."

I thought somewhat bitterly again about Jenny's letter. Having no idea what reissuing a stock certificate meant I simply nodded my head and smiled slightly praying my ignorance wasn't visible.

"I persuaded him to issue you 2,500 in stocks in the

transaction which he signed for," said John, looking up at me for some kind of reaction. "At a rough minimum value of $100 per stock, that's at least $250,000 at sale, Hannah. There's so much buyer interest right now we may easily be looking at closer to double that amount. And I plan to make them available for sale to European investors very soon."

I didn't miss the plural pronoun but said nothing.

"That's for your additional vocal studies in Europe and a large deposit to get you started on your career that I urged Win to establish for you." Then he gave a snorting laugh that I've never forgotten and continued by saying, "I would have tried to get him to grant me an advance like that, but I'm sure the courts would have hung me out to dry in no time flat, yelling coercion, blackmail or fraud from here to Wall Street!"

I stared at John for several moments and then looked down in my lap, folding my hands and taking a deep breath before speaking again.

"I can't accept it," I said quietly.

"There's really nothing to accept. These stocks are in your name and I plan to get them on the market for you within the next month or so. Let the investor frenzy continue to build for a time before actually selling. I saw to it well before we left the Continent."

'No, you don't understand," I continued, still looking down in my lap. "I can't accept his generosity funding a career that I won't be able to even begin."

"Hannah," said John softly. "I know."

I stared at him. "You know what," I replied evenly.

"That you're pregnant."

I couldn't help asking the next question, although at the time, I actually wasn't exactly certain why I asked it. "And did you know that before or after you persuaded Win to have these stocks put in my name?"

"What possible difference does that make?" he laughed lightly. "It's yours to use to continue the advancement of your career or use as you see fit actually."

I sat further back in the soft leather chair. So often when Win and I had been in these same chairs back in Victor we had been enjoying a bottle of his delicious dark, red wine, after one of Anna's simple, yet wonderful dinners, laughing about Monsieur D's antics or comparing our unrealistically demanding fathers and frighteningly spectral mothers. Remembering those nights hung so sensually, so painfully, all around me right now.

"He intends for you to use it as you need it, Hannah," John repeated, using a different approach to his words. "If your vocal training has to take a small hiatus, well, so be it."

"A small hiatus?" I blurted out, laughing. "Well, that's certainly one way to put it, I suppose!"

He leaned forward and took both of my hands. "Hannah," he said quietly, peering directly into my eyes, "I would like to see you move up in the world. You're a beautiful, very gifted young woman. Anyone can see that. And secretly, I've been in love with you for a very long time," he continued, with a smile that played about his mouth but never reached his cold eyes. "If you'll be my wife we can make all of these problems disappear in an instant. I can easily pay Win's lawyers to quietly backdate a wedding license for us, along with a birth certificate for Alice as our first child, filed just before that Cripple Creek fire, and consequently claim both items lost in the blaze. Sorry to say that the two documents can only be dated about a week or so apart without arousing any kind of suspicion. Copies would have been filed in the state otherwise, of course," he winked. "Then when this little one is born, he or she is already ours. I certainly won't stand in your way to continue your training and find work in a local concert hall or opera house. You've maintained your respectability, kept your children and been allowed a career as well."

I stared at him. Yes, and most importantly, then you would have control over all that money, John, I thought suspiciously. This man was no more in love with me than he was with a wobbly footstool. Thoughts of Jenny's letter and Win's recent maniacal behavior faded. This was Win's and my child. These doctors could very easily be wrong. It happened all of the time that a diagnosis, especially involving liver issues, was completely incorrect. Hadn't some of those European doctors attested to that? Who was to say that Win wasn't going to pull out of this delirium and be fine within the next few days or weeks? Miraculous recoveries had certainly happened before I had been assured at all three spa resorts! And deep within I was still convinced that Win would want our child.

"I'm very flattered, John," I began, pulling my hands slowly out of his. "You're most kind to make this extraordinary offer. But I've decided that I need to speak with Win about his child and hope that he's..."

"What, willing to marry you? To make an honest woman out of you as they say?" scoffed John, leaning back in his chair. "Hannah, listen to me. Winfield Scott Stratton was married for maybe four months over 20 years ago now. He cheated on her and by golly she just retaliated and cheated back, plain and simple. And he just couldn't accept that any woman would have the gall to do that to him! When he dies there will be at least three dozen women lined up in court with their hands out, either claiming to be his wife or that their kiddies are his bastards and deserve part of his fortune. It will probably take at least a decade for the courts to settle all of that nonsense, if they actually ever can!"

His words sliced deeply into me but I simply took another slow breath.

"As I said, I need to speak to him first," I reiterated, standing, although the effort was a shaky one. "He should know about the baby and...decide...something," I managed to say before my voice simply trailed off.

"Well, my offer still stands, Miss Owens," replied John, as he stood and rather dramatically kissed my hand. "It's been an exhaustingly long day for us all. Let's see what hangs on the morrow."

***

Stratton did get slightly stronger, but Anna told us that he was now staying up all night reading some kind of fanatical religious theory in his library, yelling at her to re-stoke the fireplace every hour, going through an entire bottle of his favorite whiskey every night, night after night. For several days Anna said whenever he was awake he would periodically begin a seething chant of "Slag everywhere! Mountains oozing with slag! An' for what, dammit? Where's God's beauty now?" She assumed he still thought he was at his house in Victor. Often she would put him to bed at daybreak, drunk yet still in pain, demanding morphine, where he would stay until he'd awake the following night. Dr. Hughes had dropped by to see him late one evening and told John Barrington that he doubted the man would live another two months at the rate he was going downhill. Even if he were to stop drinking at this point it was far too late to save him from self-destruction.

Katya, Zuma and I stayed in my house in Victor, often drifted in for many days with the harsh winter snows, playing with Alice, whose giggles and love of life kept me sane during those dark months. The trains from Victor to Colorado Springs were often delayed for days at a time while the tracks were cleared from one blizzard after another. My inability to visit Win was actually for the best since he rarely seemed to know me at all. My faith in Win's return to normal had now dimmed to a small heap of barely glowing ashes. Thankfully, my morning nausea had passed long ago, but the small swelling in my abdomen was becoming more obvious with each passing day. When I finally broke down and told Zuma, who like John, had already guessed, we both cried and silently held each other close for a long time, late into the night.

On one of my visits to see Win, John insisted that I let Dr. Hughes examine me to which I reluctantly agreed. I had seen Dr. Hughes for a few brief moments only once recently and still had a difficult time accepting the man's complete lack of empathy for his own daughter.

"Well, everything seems to be going at a good pace," said Dr. Hughes, packing up his stethoscope and other instruments. I had been lying on the couch in Win's library. "My best guess is you have about another month or so. Does that seem to line up?"

"Yes, I suppose," I answered, as I elbowed my way back to a sitting position with his help.

"What did Stratton have to say about this by the way?"

"I never really had a chance to say anything to him about it. His illness..."

Dr. Hughes scoffed. "Yes, his illness! More like his inability to actually see through that damned mine's sale without the constant reassurance from a bottle of whiskey. Big man, but has absolutely no confidence in himself and refuses to listen to anyone else. And the craziest part is that none of us really understand why in the hell he wanted to sell off that mine in the first place. He's ranted for months about all of these plans and investments he intended to make, but even before he'd gotten so bad no one had any idea what those plans entailed. Ramsey talked to him 'til he was blue in the face, but Stratton wouldn't budge on anything. It's just such a horrible waste of a good mind. Horrible, horrible waste."

"Maybe Jenny knows something," I offered quietly. "They still seemed to be keeping up a correspondence even after she had moved to Alaska."

Dr. Hughes snorted, shaking his head. "I highly doubt that. Win has always been willing to discuss the day-to-day with any of us close to him, but he's always highly secretive of any long-range plans. I've caught him talking to that painting hanging up there right over your head on more than one occasion! Too bad it can't speak!"

Yes, 'discuss the day-to-day with any of us close to him' except me, I thought, fighting back unwarranted bitterness. "Other than Henry, do you know if he has any other children, Dr. Hughes? He seemed to think that he wasn't able to father a child…"

"Oh, they're out there somewhere, mark my words! I seriously doubt he believed he couldn't manage that! Remember Methuselah in the Bible? According to Genesis he lived to be something like 900 and was still siring kid after kid, woman after woman! I'm kind of surprised you believed him, Hannah. There are the ones who probably really are his, along with all of the ones who'll be doing their damnedest to whittle off a chunk of that multi-million dollar inheritance for themselves," laughed Hughes.

I slowly exhaled, looking down at my hands folded over my swollen belly. Yes, indeed. Why had I believed him? Because I had wanted to. Because I loved him. It was that simple.

"Anyway, first babies are notoriously pretty balky, but send word as soon as your pains start and I should be able to get here in plenty of time. It would be easiest for you to just have the baby down here in Colorado Springs. Zuma and that other girl -- what's her name, Katya? -- can certainly be here with you. Anna's more than got her hands full with Stratton these days, obviously. In fact, you should have Barrington just look for a place for you to stay here in the Springs for a couple of months after the kid is born until you're back on your feet."

"Well, there's also Alice," I replied, not thinking.

"Who's Alice?" he asked.

"Katya's niece," I quickly lied, looking at him steadily. I refused to betray Abigail's secret to this man. Not now, not ever. "Both of the child's parents died recently and she's been living with us."

"Sounds like she needs to figure out other living arrangements then," replied Dr. Hughes.

There was an occasional gust of warmer air that finally heralded spring when Zuma and I moved temporarily to Stratton's home a few weeks later. Anna had fixed up a small bedroom for me, the window looking out over an extraordinary view of the mountains. Zuma stayed in Anna's room, although typically Anna slept in a chair in Stratton's room most nights attending to Stratton who was now completely bedridden. How Anna managed to stay calm as he endlessly shrieked obscenities, spit out medicine in her face or threw plates of food at her astounded me. A huge egg-shaped swollen bruise on her cheek showed where a full bowl of soup had made contact at close range.

With each day I also remembered Abigail's last several weeks of her pregnancy -- scrubbing and pegging up all of that often heavy laundry, shooting Jared Grady, then helping me strap his corpse onto the sledge and dragging him up to that dugout, and then, of course, her giving birth to Alice. I truthfully had never considered how exhausted she must have been throughout that entire time. No wonder that even as a tiny infant her daughter had always possessed such a fierce fighting spirit!

As the countdown to my own child's birth narrowed with each day, I tried to convince myself that my plans were at least somewhat better defined than Abigail's had been. Accepting Stratton's money was now a given. My intention was to then head to Europe, with both my own child and Alice, claiming to be a widow, hoping to find a permanent engagement in one of the many smaller opera houses. I knew I would have enough money to make the journey, find us a home and get settled in. And I was fairly certain that the notice from the competition attesting to my career possibilities would help me find employment. I had mentioned all of this to Zuma hoping she would want to accompany us, but she had no interest in going anywhere except back to rural Louisiana. Even though she had so many ugly memories, including the deaths of her husband, child and murder of her brother, as well as her time spent in jail, that was still her home she declared. She had always felt as though she had been dragged up to Colorado by the Hughes' family against her will. John Barrington's intervening statements to the New Orleans courts had resulted in her early release from jail but that action was based on the caveat that she return to Colorado for the short term. After a brief period working for Mr. Barrington, she had been assured that she would finally be released to find work elsewhere.

Several stabbing jolts woke me from a deep sleep. I must have shouted out as well since Zuma was at my side quickly. We waited until just after dawn and then contacted Dr. Hughes. By the time he arrived I was already exhausted. Knives were surging up in waves, their sharp blades twisting relentlessly within me for several long minutes at a time. Then, a sudden release and I would fall back into a blissful unconscious euphoria. Yet only a few minutes later, the next knife would begin its relentless gutting along the same path. Drenched in sweat, I was swimming in blood, either real or imagined, I had no idea.

"She ain' doin' so good," I heard Zuma's voice.

"No, she's not. But the labor is moving along, even though it's going too slowly, so that's always a good sign," was Dr. Hughes' terse answer. "I'm giving her a stiff dose of laudanum to help deaden the pain. She'll still know more or less what's going on. I'm going to have to cut into her to enlarge the opening for the baby. Otherwise...don't worry, Zuma. Morphine works wonders."

After several sips of morphine, the pain gradually wore down to a low drone that seemed miles below me. But in that distance also loomed a blackening pit of raw fear. Dr. Hughes and Zuma moved around me in my sleepy haze although occasionally the knife's slashings broke through the veil. All sense of time vanished. Somewhere in the fog I heard the doctor's voice saying, 'all right, all right, that's good, Hannah ... ah, yes, yes ... here we are ... yes ...' Then I passed out.

Hours later, as I came up from the depths of the drug, I thought I heard Stratton shrieking and Anna's calm voice trying to quiet him. As I came closer to the surface though, I realized that I had been dreaming of their voices. Everything was very quiet. At first I didn't even remember that I had actually had the baby, but as soon as I moved even slightly, paralyzing pain echoed through me. The bedroom shades were pulled, but looking through the cracks, it was dark past them, the mountains lit only by a sprinkling of a few early stars. I probably fell asleep and then awoke several times, then sensed that Zuma was sitting next to me on the bed in the darkness.

"How you doin' chil'?" she asked quietly. "You had quite a time. You sit up here an' have a sip of this hot tea 'n honey. Gotta be might parched."

"The baby," I said, managing a smile after taking a few sips. "Is it a boy or a girl?"

"A girl," Zuma nodded, with something like reluctance in her voice. "A big one. She's sleepin' right now. Mebbe you wanna wait jes' a bit ..."

"No. Now. I want to see her now. Please!"

Zuma returned far too slowly with my child, swaddled in one of Alice's old soft thermal blankets. She seemed reluctant to hand her over to me, however. I wasn't able to sit up very well in the bed. Even though my arms were still shaking from a combination of the drug and birth, I eagerly guided Zuma's hands to bring the baby alongside me. As I pulled the blanket back, turning her slightly to reveal her face, her eyes sleepily opened, and I caught my breath. Staring up at me with Win's piercing light blue eyes, visible even in the dark room, was a beautiful black infant, framed by fluffy tufts of light hair like spun gold.

"She's gorgeous," I said softly, tears coursing down my face, dripping onto her blanket.

"Yeah, she gorgeous, you right 'bout dat," replied Zuma, smiling, smoothing my hair from my face. Several minutes went by before she spoke again. "But honey, you and I both know you can' raise no color'd chil', Miss Hannah," she continued gently.

I started to make some kind of protest, but Zuma just shook her head.

"Lissen tuh me, please, honey, this your Zuma talkin' to ya," she went on. "Any white woman tryin' to raise a black chil' won' be accepted nowhere, honey. An' I mean absolutely nowhere. Not here, not California, not Paris, not nowhere. An' you knows dat same as me. I doubt you could even whore down in dem nasty cribs back in Cripple Creek, dat's how bad it would be. Dem white trash whores would run you outta town an' dem black ones soon as knife ya as give up any der trade to ya."

I started to speak but Zuma shook her head again, putting out her hand to stop me.

"An' the chil'? She won't be accepted nowhere eithuh. No fam'ly, no friends. Nothin' 'cept tryin' to sell herself intuh da trade when she still young 'til her looks long gone. Distance herself from her white mama soon's she can fo' dat. An' if you thinkin' Mistuh Stratton's people gonna believe dat this baby's his chil,' you got fuzz up where yo' brain used to be, Miss

Hannah."

I finally found my voice.

"He told me that his mother was a quadroon, Zuma. And that there are no pictures of her because she... was ashamed that she was...so dark." I curled my daughter close in by my side. "Of course, Win isn't normally dark either, just kind of ... weathered ... except now with the jaundice he's that ... ghastly yellow."

"Well, if Mistuh Stratton's mama was a quadroon, that'd be mighty hard fo' you to prove now, Miss Hannah. An' no pictures of her? Yeah, well good luck wid dat! I seen a light skin color'd woman havin' a very dark baby an' a dark-skinned woman havin' a lighter baby. But dat's accepted, y'see. All dem white slaveowners havin' babies by their slaves all dem years down in Louisiana? Nobody knew who belong'd to who lotta times. My mama was half white too but dat's all I knew 'bout her. It wasn't right, but it jes got accepted. A child was a child. But a white woman havin' a black baby and tryin' tuh raise tha' baby? No ma'am. Never. I have tuh tell you. It can' be done. No way."

Several minutes went by while Zuma just sat on the bed, stroking my hair again. She asked if I was hungry and I said no.

"Well, Mistuh Barrington is here an' wants tuh talk wid you."

She reached to take the baby from me but I shook my head, pulling the infant as close as possible.

"I want her to be with me when I speak to him," I replied. "And, please could you bring in a lamp?"

Zuma left and several minutes later John walked in with the lamp. He set it down on the dresser and opened the blinds slightly. More stars now appeared in the evening sky. Then he quickly kissed my cheek, still wet with tears, and sat down on the bed.

"I spoke with Albert a few hours ago. He said you went through quite an ordeal. But he feels certain that you'll be able to have other children in the future."

"I'm not giving her up," I stated stubbornly. I felt the childish recklessness in my voice despite my determination.

John completely changed the subject on me.

"Win's been in a coma now for the last two days, Hannah. I don't know if anyone has told you that. His son Henry is expected to come by within the hour to pay his last respects. If you ever wanted to meet Henry, this will probably be the only good time."

"A coma? That ... can't be ..." I stammered. "What?"

"There's several documents that I need for you to sign right now, Hannah," he continued curtly, cutting into my question. "First are the ones we discussed before to obtain our backdated marriage license and a birth certificate for Alice from Cripple Creek."

I had blocked any consideration of this idea completely since my plan had been to leave with both children and go to Europe as soon as I was able.

"And then, you need to sign off on those stock certificates on the Independence so that I can telegraph Verner Reed to sell them immediately to the highest bidders in Europe. The Venture group is sending their own engineer in to assess the mine's potential yield because they've heard a number of vicious rumors that it's already tapped out. Do you know what that means?" he demanded.

I shook my head slowly. Why was this important now, I wondered. My head was still fuzzy from the morphine and the most important problem was what to do about my baby anyway not potential mine yield.

"What it means," John continued, "is that your stock certificates could easily become null and voided out if the Venture group challenges the worth of that mine, Hannah. They could easily sue Stratton, or more likely, Stratton's estate, at this point. Kiss that $250,000 goodbye if you will. Or, we sell immediately before any possible discovery."

"So I marry you, at least on paper it seems, and you sell the stock and invest it somewhere I assume. Just like that." I replied blankly. "And the mine may not be worth anything at all anymore. That seems completely dishonest."

"No," he said emphatically. "No, it's not dishonest. It's just doing business. And if I don't get the transaction moving before Win's death, there will also be serious delays, possibly for years if his will is contested in any way, even if the stock values remain constant after the mine's reassessed by Venture's engineer."

"And what about Win's and my baby?" I asked pointblank.

"Look, Hannah, none of this is on if you ever admit to being identified as the mother of this...," he stated coldly. "And I'm sure I don't need to tell you that your life and the child's will be completely destroyed if you attempt that on your own. What I've proposed to Zuma is that she stay on with us as a domestic, listed as the child's mother. That way you are at least around it."

"Her!" I cried, summoning up what little voice I possessed. "Our baby is a girl!" Suddenly I remembered this exact conversation that Abigail had suffered through with this self-centered animal after Alice's birth.

"Hannah, you should be aware that there's a lot more to Zuma's involvement with that uprising and jailbreak of her brother's down in New Orleans that I managed to keep out of the courtroom for her. I'm quite sure she doesn't want that case reopened with newly discovered evidence. She's agreed to state that she had a relationship with one of her white jailers down in New Orleans and was pregnant when she returned up here."

"You would actually do that to her?" I stammered in disbelief. "You're a bastard!"

He shrugged. "I'm a businessman, Hannah. Plain and simple. Plain and simple. I've gotten involved with purchasing some excellent real estate and also made headway into some political involvement out in Kansas City, Missouri. Once Stratton is gone he certainly won't need me as his secretary! And, you'll be excited to know that I've spoken with the management at the Coates Opera House in Kansas City. They're very interested in your joining their resident theatre ensemble based on your work with Delacroix at the Victor. So that's some very excellent news to your benefit. Yes? I won't stand in the way of your embarking on something of a small singing career right near our home, Hannah. That's far more than many husbands would allow."

"You certainly have all this very well worked out I must say," I replied bitterly. "And you're right. How can you stand in the way of someone who has no place to turn anyway, John? You've got Zuma, my baby and myself completely trapped."

He ignored both my words and my tone and pulled a large envelope out of his coat pocket. "I need your signature on these documents immediately. And Zuma's."

I signed the backdated marriage registration, then entered on Alice's birth certificate: Name: Alice Elizabeth Barrington; Mother: Hannah Owens Barrington; Father: John Daniel Barrington. I then signed the paperwork designating John Daniel Barrington, now my husband, to sell the shares of Independence stock that had been held in my maiden name.

I had to help Zuma sign my child's birth certificate, although I was ashamed to admit that I had never known Zuma's last name. Name: Emma Winfield Jackson; John had balked at the middle name, but I held firm on that. Mother: Zoraide (Zuma) Jackson; Father: unknown.

Zuma then helped me get dressed in a wrapped flannel housedress and she and John guided me to the parlor into a well-padded armchair. Henry had arrived and had been in Win's bedroom for the last half hour. I had to ask Zuma for a small dose of laudanum in order to sit even for a few minutes.

When he emerged from Win's room, John introduced me as his wife to the young man. He was the spitting image of his father, Win had certainly been right. Henry Stratton was a tall, thin, somewhat pale man, with curly dark hair, a well-trimmed brown mustache, and brown eyes set into a very handsome, expressive face, a mirror of his father's probably 25 years ago. He wore one of Win's unstructured cloth coats, a freshly starched white shirt and a pair of Win's soft leather boots, I noticed as well. During our brief conversation he stroked his mustache several times, his eyes and face crinkling up into that same innocent smile I had so adored on his father. I was grateful that our meeting only lasted a few minutes.

Win died two days later. I was told that he had realized one brief hour of lucidity and spoken to those in the room with him at the time, but I never spoke with him again. He lay in state at the beautiful brand new Mining Exchange, one of the many buildings he had designed and paid for right in the heart of Colorado Springs. It was estimated that over 9,000 people came by to pay their last respects. His service in the Presbyterian Church was held by invitation only. Even though I had been issued an invitation, I declined, although of course, John attended.

The residents of Colorado Springs, Denver, Cripple Creek and Victor waited anxiously to hear what each of their towns would be receiving from the multi-millionaire's will. Despite Stratton's many large monetary gifts to these towns during his lifetime, he was still reputed to be worth at least $15 million and probably far more it was rumored. However, when the will, which his lawyers readily admitted had recently been revised while Stratton had been ill in Europe, was read in court, an angry outcry arose. Other than some funding to complete a new interurban railway in Cripple Creek and Victor, those towns received practically nothing. A couple of new hotels and some small upgrading of utilities for Colorado Springs and Denver marked their only monies. His only son, I. Henry Stratton received $30,000, his sister Ida Chamberlin (who had died just after the will had been revised) had been awarded $20,000 and her son, Carl, $20,000. So by law, Carl now also would be receiving his mother's share, thus receiving more than Henry. Anna was to receive $50,000 which seemed fitting, but William Ramsey was to receive $25,000 which surprised everyone, including Ramsey himself. John's name was not mentioned and thankfully, neither was mine. In reality, I had already received my inheritance, of course, given to me in a way that Win had undoubtedly assumed could never be challenged.

But the biggest mystery contained in the will was the endowment for the Myron Stratton Home in Colorado Springs. Stratton stipulated in the will that it was to be *"a free home for poor persons who are without means of support and who are physically unable by reason of old age, youth, sickness or other infirmity to earn a livelihood."* The site for the home had been purchased, the architectural plans completely drawn up by Stratton himself and included in the will, and the strategies strictly outlined for the home to financially maintain itself into perpetuity.

The uproar created by this outrageously unexpected direction of Stratton's estate enraged so many men on the various town councils that they, along with sixteen women claiming they had either been married to Stratton or borne his children, Henry, and several other long term employees on Stratton's staff, demanded an analysis into the sanity of the man when he had made this ridiculous revision to his will. No one could understand how Win's father, Myron Stratton, with whom Win hadn't had any contact for at least 20 years before Myron's death, and had only spoken about in the most disparaging of terms, should be the recipient, even in name, for such a huge piece of the Stratton pie! It would seem more likely that he would have left something to the memory of his mother, Mary Stratton, who had died when he was fairly young. But no mention was made of any remembrance of Mary Stratton. Various cases brought to the courts, seriously depleting the estate's worth, delayed the start of the home for many years, but it was finally built according to Win's exact specifications.

XX. Dannie Barrington

John, Zuma, Alice, Emma and I left for Kansas City about a month after Win's death. I never joined the Coates Opera House ensemble in Kansas City, however. Like countless other small theaters, in countless other small towns all over the U.S., it had burned to the ground early in the new century only a few months after our arrival. All of the major Coates' performances were moved to the Standard Theatre, a 2,400-seat house, and renamed the Century, but the ensemble was considered nonessential and permanently disbanded. I became pregnant with John's child about six months after we were married, but that child and another, a year later, both boys, were stillborn. Our third son, Johnnie, was an extremely fragile infant, but seemed to be finally thriving as he neared his first birthday.

The sale of my Independence mining stock had brought to our family one of the largest, most lavish homes in that part of Missouri. In fact, it reminded me of the beautiful McAllister house that Win had built back in Colorado Springs, complete with sprawling marble fireplaces in both the living room and library. Zuma and Emma had their own spacious apartment within the home, and, for several months until John's politically motivated private dinners completely took over our lives, all five of us typically ate dinner together, often tantalized by Zuma's pie wheels for dessert.

But less than a year into the marriage, John became intensely involved with an Irish tavern owner named James Pendergast. Along with Pendergast's younger brother Tom, the trio networked with other local business leaders to build a powerful faction for the Democratic Party in our county, bought the Ready-Mixed Concrete Company and enjoyed substantial kickbacks from all of the endless turn-of-the-century downtown building projects. Prosperity rang out seemingly from every northwest Missouri street corner. The Kansas side of the sister cities as they were known, was steeped in a paralyzing adherence to prohibition, but the Missouri side was well-oiled by the big money of these corrupt officials and close proximity to the influence of hardened criminals. Many a private late night meeting took place in our library, thick expensive cigars smoldering in a dozen cut glass ashtrays, long streaks of ashes smudged into my sofas' light damask upholstery. "Big Jim" as James Pendergast was known, who had become an alderman a decade earlier, appealed to all of the Irish and other immigrants by providing thousands of jobs and expansive free food programs for the poor in return for their support, often illegally obtained, on election days. He illegally handpicked his own mayor and staffed every other important office within City Hall, achieving his extraordinary political power by granting favors with the caveat that the favor might necessitate a return, often with a rather murky explanation.

The Pendergast brothers and John used that influence to sway any conservative-leaning, local town council to build country clubs, taverns, gambling dens, men's clubs and brothels. Even though Tom Pendergast was a non-drinker and strict Catholic family man, he was a notorious big stakes gambler. Men would travel from all over the world to play against him at one of the well-known lavish saloons owned by "Big Jim's" machine.

I closed myself off from the wagging tongues of the town as best I was able, embarrassed by my husband's unscrupulous entanglements. My life plodded from one day into the next, one season to another, revolving around a decision I so wished I'd never been forced to make, married to a man who was now a ruthless financial mogul and political tyrant – a man who I now thoroughly despised.

I watched my beautiful daughter Emma, so lovingly raised by Zuma, singing, laughing, acting out her amusing little stories, reciting her little poems, her light blue eyes ablaze in that sweet milk chocolate face framed by that uncontrollably fluffy deep golden hair that seemed to drift everywhere. There were no black schools so I had quietly started educating her as best I was able, without John's knowledge, and was immensely grateful for that opportunity. There was talk of opening the white schools to include black children since there weren't very many black families in our district, but so far, it was just that – all talk. Grammar schools had been segregated in the state for many years and if there weren't enough black children to make it worth offering a separate school for them, the community simply went without. I was very bitter to learn that as a newly elected State Senator, John had been one of the representatives to consistently rally against bothering to provide public education for these children.

Alice was also a beautiful and extremely intelligent little girl, seemingly aglow with a sunny head of long, spiraling blonde curls, surrounding a pale porcelain complexion, those steely-grey eyes widely focused on her world. She had developed a frighteningly quick tongue when only a toddler and each year seemed to become less and less tolerant of anyone less capable in her midst. She possessed a certain cunning, sly, almost devious look at times, which John fully adored and encouraged, but which very uncomfortably reminded me of Mrs. Hughes, her grandmother.

And then one summer evening, all of our lives changed in an instant. An eight-year-old boy, who stated that his name was Dannie Barrington, calmly walked out of his mother's place of business at the Cat-L Corral, a brothel in Jefferson City, following

State Senator John Barrington who had just emerged from said brothel, and pointing a large pistol at the senator's chest shot him point blank, killing him instantly. The boy stated that he didn't know the gun was loaded and was only playing a game.

***

The nightmarish image of that bloodied pulp I had identified as my husband just three days beforehand continued to haunt me at his funeral. I had hoped that somehow John's infatuation with the Pendergast brothers' schemes would end, that we could move elsewhere and start anew. Never had I considered any ending this twisted and brutal, however. I had never even remotely loved this man but now tortured myself over that very fact as I dealt with the finality of his death. Hundreds of Big Jim's and Tom Pendergast's constituents snaked past the closed coffin to pay their last respects as John lay in state at the mortuary. Alice, scowling, standing next to me beside the casket, scratched at several mosquito bites on her legs. Men tipped their hats and several women tentatively clasped my hands, murmuring what I perceived as hollow condolences such as "so sorry ma'am," or "he was way too young," or "such a sad end to a fine young family man."

The following hot afternoon, as we stood at the cemetery listening to the pastor's lengthy drone and final blessings about God's promises to all of us in the afterlife, my thoughts aimlessly wandered. I glanced momentarily over at Zuma who was holding little Johnnie on her hip, our girls clinging to her skirts, then overhead at the puffs of clouds limply hanging in the humidity. As the small crowd began to disperse and move to the surrounding carriages, another of the City Hall officials whose name I couldn't recall came up to me.

"Mrs. Barrington, again, my deepest condolences," he murmured, touching the brim of his tall silk hat, bowing his head slightly. "I just wanted to inform you that your husband's will is scheduled to be read next Monday in my offices over on Harrington Street. Andrew Reedy and Associates. Uh, that would be me, Andrew Reedy, of course. I can send a carriage over to assist you if you would prefer ma'am."

"No thank you," I answered with a slight smile, shaking my head. "I can manage, I'm quite certain. Perhaps you could give my driver your exact address before you leave today."

"Of course, ma'am, of course. I had fully expected to do so. Also, rather irregularly, my office has received a note from the mother of the young boy who shot your husband, requesting to meet with you."

"That's most kind of her, but I really have no interest in speaking with her," I replied wearily.

"Well, actually she has formally requested a meeting with you this Friday down in Jefferson City. She indicated that there is a 10 a.m. train which arrives there around 11. Apparently she is unable to travel here, hence her asking you to go to her, ma'am."

"Who is this woman, anyway? How did she sign the letter, Mr. Reedy?"

"The letter appears to be signed by a solicitor, ma'am. I have it right here, in fact."

He handed me the letter sent to his office which had originally been stamped and sealed from a law firm in Jefferson City. His client requested a meeting with me at 11:30 a.m. this Friday at the Driscoll Café to discuss the recent passing of John Barrington. There would be a carriage at the station to take me to the café for this meeting. Due to the nature of the private information to be discussed, the letter went further to suggest that I would mostly likely want to attend this meeting alone.

Heat shimmered relentlessly above the sidewalks two days later as I walked from the train to the carriage; the short trip to the Driscoll at least provided some moving air around the open barouche, thank goodness. It took several moments for my eyes to adjust as I walked into the densely smoky, yet practically empty and oppressively dark café. A small dark-haired boy appeared beside me, motioning for me to follow him over to the far corner of the room. As I followed him, a woman with blond hair came gradually into focus. She was sitting in a wheelchair at a table, smoking a thin black cigarette, her head turned away from me. I swallowed hard. My first impulse was that it was Abigail. But then the woman turned slightly as we neared her, methodically stabbing out her cigarette in her plate of scarcely eaten breakfast.

"You pardon me I not up an' greet," the woman said curtly, gesturing to the opposite chair. "Please, sit. Dannie, you go now." He kissed his mother on her cheek, glanced suspiciously at me, and then left the room.

"You know me, yes?"

. "Of course," I replied, trying faintly to smile. "It's so good to see you again, Vanya."

"Bah!" she snorted. "Good see me again! Ja, like hell! Sure it is. You not give me thought since I go! Sit."

I bit my lip. She was right, of course. I hadn't. Not once. I carefully sat down in the chair next to her.

"So it was your son Dannie who shot John," I somehow managed to state. "I actually hadn't made that connection, I confess." Then I added quickly, "but, of course, I realize it was just an accident."

"Accident?" Vanya scoffed, giving a low laugh, shaking her head. "Good story for police, but no accident." Her hands trembled as she lit another cigarette, blowing the bluish smoke over her shoulder. I noticed she wore numerous large diamond rings as well as several sparkling diamond and gold bracelets. Although she was still an attractive woman despite almost clownish makeup, these last several years had padded her with the spongy flesh which often eerily crept up on an invalid.

"And you?" I asked quietly. "Did you also have an accident?"

She took another couple of puffs from her cigarette, her face now inside a swirling blue haze.

"Have argument with man. He throw me down steps at brothel. Broke my back, so legs no work now," she finally replied.

"Oh God, Vanya! How long ago was this?"

Vanya settled further back in her wheelchair, which creaked slightly, both elbows on the chair arms, her cigarette's smoke slowly curling upwards towards the discolored ceiling. "Look in leather folder. There. On table."

She leaned slightly forward and pushed the folder over to me. I took out two documents. The first was an embossed, official marriage certificate for John Daniel Barrington to Vanya O. Zygmunt, from Denver, Colorado dated more than two years before the date on John's and my marriage license. The other was Dannie's birth certificate stating that his parents were Vanya Zygmunt Barrington and her husband, John Daniel Barrington.

"I don't understand," I said, carefully replacing the documents in their leather sleeve.

"I don' understand," Vanya mimicked me in a singsong voice, blowing another stream of smoke over her shoulder. "John Barrington marry me. Not you."

"He told me…"

"He tell you win me at poker game, yes?"

I nodded yes, frowning. "He said that you were working as a prostitute for your boyfriend and you ended up with him after that game."

"No, no. John lie. He the boyfriend and then husband I whore for!"

In many ways this actually did not surprise me at all given the increasingly brazen public forays into prostitution my late husband had found acceptable during our marriage.

"All right, so he lied to me about how you met. But you mean that you *were* married to him, correct?" I questioned. "You were divorced and then he married me."

"Your license backdate," she scoffed. "Our lawyer do that. You never the real wife!"

"What are you talking about? You're not making any sense, Vanya!" I replied, now nervous. How did she know about all of that? Had John confided in her about backdating the certificates? And if so, why on earth had he done something as unbelievably reckless as confiding in her?

"John was Mr. Stratton's secretary, yes?"

I nodded my head slightly, continuing to stare at her.

"John tell Stratton give you mining shares when sell gold mine, yes? Then John marry you, get your money, split part of money each month to Vanya. I no divorce John an' he pay me so mouth stay shut up, yes? I need money for food, place to live, many doctors, many medicines, for hospitals, for Dannie. No man wants fuck lame whore! Bah!"

"Well," I replied uncomfortably, now that all of this was becoming clearer to me, "it would seem that your son has gone and murdered the golden goose then, doesn't it? Is that what you wanted to discuss with me today? Continuing my husband's payments to you each month? And if you're going to say now that he was never my husband anyway, then you still don't necessarily manage to get anything. Those shares were issued by Win Stratton to me, not John. If John was never my husband than he had no rights to any of that money and therefore, neither do you. I don't know what you're expecting from me."

Vanya shook her head, took another long drag from her cigarette then viciously twisted it out, looking sideways at me.

"John get tired of pay dear Vanya. Want stop. Say now no money. Bah! But I have plan, you see. Good plan. Talk to Dannie on good plan."

I held my breath waiting for her to continue.

"See, you forget," said Vanya, staring at me, an irritating smirk seeping over her ghoulish red mouth.

"Forget what?" I replied, frightened, but still irritated. I wondered when the next train back to Kansas City was scheduled to depart. This unreasonable half-crazy whore was completely different from the meek young woman who had once so graciously worked with me back in Victor.

"Two 'whats'. Alice and Emma."

"What about Alice and Emma?" I replied, my temper rising.

"They how old now? Five? Six? Seven? Alice a year younger than my Dannie, yes?"

"Yes," I agreed coldly. Leave my children out of this, I seethed inwardly.

"I breastfeed Alice, ja? She no your child. She your friend child. Your friend no come back. And I work with Zuma when she come back, yes? After jail. You in Europe then, yes?"

I nodded warily, sinking inside. Where was this going?

"See, I know Zuma no pregnant she come back. She have her monthlies. But you pregnant then, yes? Ah, ha! Stratton's kid maybe, maybe not. Don't matter. So, how you daughter be when she find her momma no want dat black baby, eh? That you want show off friend white baby, but not keep black baby, eh? Make black baby go be with black momma?" she snorted. "How you daughter feel 'bout dat, eh?"

I felt sick inside. Dannie hadn't killed the golden goose at all. He had just delivered an entire basket brimming up with more than enough golden eggs to ensure both his and his mother's survival.

"You look down me," Vanya sneered, giving the table an angry resounding slap, then pointing at me. "You look down me as bad whore. I know dis. But you know what? You even bigger whore, yes? You Stratton's whore, yes?"

"No!" I exploded, jumping angrily to my feet. "I wasn't Win's whore! He insisted that wasn't how it should be! He never wanted it to be like that!"

"Be like what?" laughed Vanya raucously. "You his damn whore! You his fuck! You his woman! What else you think? Anna know, Katya know, John know, that doctor know, even dat big time fancy whore Jenny know. Everybody know! You think first time we do this? Bah! Many times! Many girls! That why we all there, help keep Mr. Stratton whore – you! He pay good all us help his whore," she spat out.

I was on the brink of shrieking at her, but somehow managed to calm myself, even though I was still shaking violently, and sat back down.

"All right, Vanya. All right. What is it that you want from me exactly? How do I buy you out of blackmailing not only my name but completely devastating the lives of two sweet innocent little girls as well?"

"Easy. I want all. You fancy big house, fancy furniture, clothes, land, saloons, brothels, all investments. Everything." she replied coolly, folding her hands together almost reverently. "For Dannie."

"And how do Zuma and our girls live then, Vanya? If you demand everything that I own, how do we support ourselves?"

A gravelly cough shook Vanya momentarily, after which she uttered, "You find one small house, take things need for dat. Any other problem not my concern. My lawyer be at your lawyer for John's will next Monday. He show papers that John bigamist, that married still me. Never legal you. You be surprise, of course! You not know! But, too bad that," she shrugged, coughing again.

"And if I contest anything you'll bring out Alice's and Emma's backgrounds, and that I knew John had illegally backdated our marriage license when we got married," I stated as evenly as possible.

"Ah, yes. Now you smart woman!" nodded Vanya, her blood red lips breaking into another fake smile. "An' you start over. Easy for you. Me? Life over. Money needs keep Dannie when I die. Poison in blood say doctors. I die maybe soon."

She waved her arm overhead beckoning to Dannie and a short heavily bearded man who had been standing near the entrance during our entire conversation I now realized. As I stood up, more than ready for our conversation to conclude, Vanya winked at me, roughly grabbing my elbow and whispering loudly, "See you in hell, sister."

As promised, at the reading of John's will, Vanya's lawyer promptly produced the incriminating documents regarding the status of John's legal marriage followed by my signing an agreement to the uncontested passing of his entire estate to his legal heir, Dannie Barrington. Dannie's mother, Vanya Barrington, would act on his behalf until he turned age 16. Or, if she were unable to provide such service for any reason, the solicitor in attendance was named as a temporary guardian.

When I had returned home that afternoon from my meeting with Vanya, I had immediately petitioned the Kansas City town council that I wished to open a new school at the recently vacated post office building exclusively for the education of black children. To get the school started I agreed to be the only teacher, asking only a very small wage along with free use of the entire building. The council agreed unanimously, I'm sure assuming that this was my way of dealing with my grief and that I would just let the whole experiment go by the wayside after a short period of time. After the reading of the will they soberly realized however that this was not a frivolous experiment and, most graciously, actually granted me a much appreciated increase in my salary.

I put our house and most of the furnishings up for sale,

taking only the barest of kitchen, bedding and basic living essentials with us as we moved into a small but reasonably clean house over on a street very close to town. Zuma quickly found work as a cook for a new wealthy family, the Dawsons, who had recently moved into a mansion near our old home. The job paid well but the hours typically ran incredibly late most evenings with the entertaining expectations of Mrs. Dawson's lavish, intimate dinner parties.

In the unbearable heat that summer Johnnie was covered with prickly heat rashes, causing him to spike high fevers and vomit constantly. Many times it seemed as though his eyes were deeply burning holes in his skull. But somehow, he was still with us thankfully. Alice pouted constantly, complaining about one ailment or another, only superficially helping out with cleaning and organizing the house. Little Emma made up tunes about her chores and happily sang while working most days until Alice screamed at her to stop being so annoying! Her headache was getting even worse with all that awful singing! Then Emma would apologize and just hum quietly until she forgot and started singing once again.

I set to scrubbing the floors and walls to prepare the old post office space to open the school. Small whiskey barrels and crates donated from several nearby saloons would have to serve as chairs and desks. I purchased three small chalkboards which all of the students would need to pass around for handwriting practice; paper and pencils were far too expensive. Alice would now be attending a brand new school that had been built over the summer with all new textbooks as required by the state. There were no such restrictions for my school, however, and I was most fortunate to latch on to multiple copies of the older texts for each grade level before they were destroyed or sent elsewhere. We were just about finished as the cooler autumn breezes thankfully began softly drifting into town.

On the first day that the district grade schools opened, Zuma made the long trek with Alice to her new school building on the north end of town and then trudged over to the Dawsons to begin her workday. Only Emma and a small handful of children who lived nearby were in attendance at my post office school that day. Johnnie sat quietly on a blanket on the floor, playing with his toys near my desk, a battered relic fortunately left behind when the post office had moved out. But word about the school spread quickly and by the end of two weeks, my classroom had surprisingly grown to twenty-one young faces of many varied hues, eager to learn at the Mary Stratton Elementary School for Colored Children.

The Myron Stratton Home in Colorado Springs remains in operation to this day as an assisted living facility for senior citizens in extreme poverty. Winfield Scott Stratton's amazing financial wizardry has indeed kept his legacy solvent now for well over a century.

An excerpt from "Muskrat Ramble"

~ a novel by Mim Eichmann

One's life is not at all like a book I reasoned.
Things are never fully resolved, never fully wrapped up in
nice, tidy little stacks
and neatly placed in the corner awaiting our leisurely
perusal and analysis.
We simply do our best to glue together the often shredded
pages of our fragmented chapters
and arrange them in some kind of meaningful sequence.
~ Hannah Owens Barrington

Chapter 1: Kansas City, Missouri - 1913

The splintering explosion of glass jolted me from a deep sleep followed by the inevitable screams of my neighbor's newborn child penetrating the paper-thin walls that separated our apartments. A large rock, shrouded in brown paper and loosely tied with coarse string, was nestled within the shards that had been my tiny front window. I called out to my daughter Alice that everything was all right and then methodically began sweeping the glass into my dustpan, the full moon glistening over the shattered remains. I knew what the message undoubtedly stated although I did not know which group had resorted to so violent a nocturnal delivery.

As I carefully unwound the hemp from the note Alice appeared, tightly wrapping her faded blue flannel robe around herself against the chilled night air that now invaded the room. Exhaling loudly, she propped herself against the fireplace. "Now what? My God it's cold in here!" My neighbors had succeeded in cajoling their little one back to sleep I realized. Other than a trio of dogs still faintly barking in the distance, the night was finally quiet once again. As I had expected the note was almost illegible, scrawled in thick pencil by a scarcely literate hand. I read it aloud to Alice. *Lady techer: if you don stop tech them nig—s youll be varie varie sorry.* Well, for what it was worth, I now knew which group had most likely delivered the note. The grown men from the town certainly wouldn't have felt a need to abridge the word and without question it was one they would have known how to spell.

My thoughts drifted momentarily back to this morning's exceedingly monotonous sermon. "A man needs to put down deep roots, yes, deep, deep roots, in his community. And with those deep roots, he needs to work hard to flourish my good friends. Send his branches out far and wide, regardless of where and in what capacity, whether he's a rich man or a poor man. For we can all flourish in whatever place God has chosen for us to send down those deep roots. God always has a plan for our place both in this life and for the one beyond," the pastor had droned. An older, exceptionally well-dressed woman wearing an immense, slightly out-of-style, dark green velvet Edwardian hat, complete with sprouting feathers, yards of bunched tulle and topped by a fluffy yellow bird, who was sitting in the pew in front of me, had remarked quite audibly to no one in particular: "Pfft. Roots indeed. Utter poppycock."

"Well," yawned Alice, then continuing with a smirk, "obviously they'll be delighted to know that you've already been fired and that Thursday is your last day at that awful place."

"I wasn't fired, Alice," I replied, glancing at her. "I wish you wouldn't say that."

I had started carefully stuffing newspaper into the hole, trying to avoid dislodging any of the few larger pieces that still held fast to the window frame. I would have to find a board to nail over it in the morning and then look into having it replaced as inexpensively as possible.

"Three old paunchy men from the town council show up at our door last Friday telling you that your services are no longer required for this 'school' you've been trying to make work for the last five years and that they are closing it down. I would consider that fired, Mother," she retorted, twirling one of her long blond curls around her finger.

"I'm sorry that you see it that way, Alice. It's only been within the last year or so … so much suspicion, unclear rules, parents afraid … I just don't …"

"And besides, now that your little pet student Emma has moved away you really didn't have much interest in teaching there anyway, did you? I notice she sent you another letter. She's written what, at least three times since they had to move down there. So that's almost a letter a month. I'm surprised the ink didn't melt right off the envelope from all that heat she constantly chatters on about."

"I think the window should hold until I can board it over in the morning," I said, clearing my throat in an effort to sidestep any unnecessary confrontation with Alice. "We should try to get some sleep now. You have a full day of classes tomorrow. And a mathematics exam. I almost forgot."

Alice took a few steps into the narrow hallway and then stopped, turning back towards me, her head slightly tilted.

"Did I tell you there was a new boy in my class on Friday? His mother just died over in Jefferson City and now he's living with his solicitor's family here. He bragged that he'll be going to a very fancy boarding school out in Massachusetts next term so he won't be around much. He told me that he's the one who shot

Father and that he's actually some kind of brother to Johnnie and me. I told him he certainly didn't know very much because Johnnie had died a couple years ago. His name is Dannie Barrington. Same as ours."

I swallowed. I felt as though another rock had just shattered the fragile crystal prism I had so cautiously grown around myself almost since Alice's birth. Her grey blue eyes unwavering, Alice stared at me, arms rigidly folded. Even as a toddler she had always chosen her moments. Usually I attempted freely and pleasantly to give in to these dark questioning tempers of my daughter, for she was well-rehearsed in said overly dramatic style. But this time I needed distance. My roots were simply not deep enough. The woman with the yellow bird hat had been right.

"It's too much to discuss now. We'll go into it tomorrow when you get home from school, Alice," I stated, knowing full well that she would not budge from where planted in the hallway. Indeed she maintained the same pose glowering at me. Brushing against the wall I squeezed past her, ignoring her stare.

"I'm going to bed," I added tersely. "I'm exhausted. If you want to stand here shivering in the cold until morning, have it as you wish. Good night."

I arrived the following morning at the pitifully-maintained former post office building that had served as my teaching establishment only to find it padlocked, windows newly boarded over, with a hastily scribbled sign nailed to the door stating simply "School Closed until Further Notice." There would of course be no further notice. The few remaining colored children in this district whose parents felt the necessity of any education would have to seek it elsewhere. Most of those families had been less-than-subtly encouraged to leave town. And of the few that remained, typically small business owners who were reluctant to abandon their shops, they were quietly being thinned out as well.

There would be no reason to establish or attempt to maintain such services, schools or restaurants for a group of people who didn't live here anyway in the eyes of the town councilmen. I knew better than to attempt to seek out those few families, to possibly hand over some reading materials for their children until they could once again sit in a classroom. It would be dangerous for them as well as for Alice and me. All this was a part of the high court ruling established well over a decade ago that seemed every year to become an even more malicious, voracious mongrel of a hound, eagerly displaying its huge white fangs throughout Missouri and elsewhere. Sadly, from what little I had read about our new president Woodrow Wilson, scarcely in office a few months, Mr. Wilson was quite eagerly aligning himself towards the justification of this schism having recently installed 'whites only' bathrooms and drinking fountains on the White House grounds.

After finding a thin board and nailing it lightly over my home's window as well as making arrangements for the glass to be replaced mid-week, I continued my walk into town circumventing the worst of the snarl of streetcar tracks, nervous horses hitched to small delivery wagons and the newest unpredictable menace maddeningly raging over the already clogged streets: the motor. The only advantage I could discern about the invasion of the motor, truly a wealthy man's toy if ever there was one, was at least there were slightly fewer horse piles (and accompanying swarms of biting green flies) steaming along one's route.

My destination was Andrew Reedy and Associates, the law firm that had represented my late husband's estate. Or at least, the late John Barrington's estate as it turned out. For I had learned just after my husband's murder that he was in fact still married to Dannie Barrington's mother, Vanya, and therefore a bigamist. I could have contested Vanya Barrington's claim to practically everything we owned but, expertly played like a splendid hand of poker, Vanya held scandalizing proof about me, my daughter Alice, my good friend Zuma, who was a Creole of color, and Zuma's daughter Emma that would have permanently ruined all of our reputations. And without question my interference would have resulted in the retrial of a prison escape and resulting deaths in which Zuma may have been directly involved.

Mr. Reedy was also one of those 'three old paunchy men from the town council' as Alice had less than eloquently referred to them, who had shown up last week to inform me of my school's impending closure. His secretary explained to me that Mr. Reedy was in a meeting with another client but should be available within the next half hour. Perhaps madam would like to find a café down the street and order a coffee rather than sitting in the dismal waiting area, the young man behind the desk so eloquently offered. I elected to just wait.

"Ah, Mrs. Barrington!" exclaimed Mr. Reedy as he walked his other client to the door. "Please, come in, come in. I only have a few moments before I must leave for an appointment at City Hall, I'm so sorry." And to his departing client: "make sure you follow up with them quickly George. He's quite the slippery one as you know."

Once inside his closed office he began hastily apologizing for the recent seemingly severe actions that his committee had been required to take in closing the school.

"We just really had no choice, Hannah. No choice whatsoever. The enrollment had been falling off as you know and we just couldn't continue to pay your salary, admittedly as small a pittance as it was I realize, and the rent, utilities, books, supplies. The whole of it. Well, you understand, I'm sure."

"Yes," I replied quietly. "I know you're only following orders from farther up."

"Exactly," he said with a grateful nod. "I'm so glad you

completely understand."

Well, I didn't completely understand and I never would, but questioning the committee's motives was not even remotely the reason for my visit. Since Mr. Reedy had another pressing appointment I moved quickly forward with my question.

"I'm assuming that you had been made aware that Vanya Barrington has passed away and that her son Dannie is now living here, apparently with his solicitor's family in Kansas City."

A quick, slightly guilty trace of a smile accompanied Mr. Reedy's furrowing brow. "Ah, yes. I had just learned of that, er, change in circumstances, from her lawyer in fact. I had just received a letter quite recently."

Change in circumstances? That was certainly an odd way of expressing the woman's demise I thought.

"But you didn't think it necessary to let me know that he was moving here?" I asked.

"Well, Hannah," Reedy replied, a brief look of amusement quickly passing over his haggard face, "the young man is only here temporarily. He leaves for, um, I believe the name of the school is Sheffield Academy, somewhere in New England, when the next term begins. Since he was only eight years old when the accident happened over in Jefferson City, no one here would even recognize him or really remember the circumstances surrounding the unfortunate incident, I'm quite certain. You'll forgive me if I offend you, but I honestly cannot imagine any reason why he would want to contact you. His mother invested, er, Mr. Barrington's assets quite successfully so I wouldn't be concerned that he would be looking to you for any kind of, well, forgive me if I sound condescending, Hannah, any kind of handout or anything."

"Right. Of course not," I nodded in terse acknowledgement. "He just turned up in my daughter Alice's school last week and mentioned that he was her 'brother or something' which upset her."

"Ah yes, well, children will be children teasing one another, of course, Mrs. Barrington," he laughed. Dannie seemed to have shrunk in stature from a wealthy young man heading off to an expensive boarding school to a silly child rendering nursery rhymes. "I'm sure as a teacher you're more than aware of that fact. Now, if you'll excuse me I really must be collecting myself for my meeting over at the Hall."

"Actually, Mr. Reedy, the reason for my visit, since my teaching post has now been permanently terminated here, is to obtain a letter of introduction and recommendation outlining my teaching skills and personal reliability of character so that I'm able to obtain employment in another state."

"Of course, of course! My legal assistant, Allan James, who you undoubtedly met in my outer office, has all the necessary paperwork and can even affix my signature and stamp to it. Just talk with Allan now before you leave and he'll have all the introductory information you require. And where exactly do you think you might be heading?"

I realized suddenly that our entire conversation had transpired while standing in front of his desk like two wooden actors rehearsing a poorly staged scene from some hideously written play.

"New Orleans," I replied evenly, walking toward the door and then turning briefly to address him face to face. "New Orleans, Mr. Reedy."

***

"New Orleans? What?! You mean as in down in Louisiana? *That* New Orleans?" shrieked my daughter that evening as we ate our meager supper of yet another tasteless, thinned out stew and coarse bread. "Where it's at least one million degrees all year and if the mosquitoes don't completely eat you alive the alligators will finish off the job?"

"Yes," I sighed, settling back in my chair, hopefully resilient enough for what I knew was going to be a nasty confrontation. Not surprisingly, she had apparently been paying attention during her geography lessons. "Exactly that very same New Orleans. Well, even last night you were complaining that you were too cold, so…"

"And just how far is that from this Reserve place?" she countered suspiciously, arms folded on the table. "Isn't that where this plantation is that Zuma and the annoying pet pupil ended up?"

"Yes, you know they're in Reserve. The Dawsons bought a plantation called Godchaux at auction and they wanted to take all of their house staff down with them. And actually, that's where Zuma's from originally. She was hoping many years ago to move there before we all ended up in Kansas City when you and Emma were just babies. It's about 30 miles or so west of New Orleans."

"So why didn't she just go then? I certainly wouldn't have missed the pet pupil all of these years."

I made no reply.

"I honestly can't believe that you're doing this to me! So we have to go trailing after a couple of ni…," she stopped short realizing that she was just on the verge of pushing too far and changed her tactic. "What about my school? We're not even halfway through fall term, Mother! I have excellents in all of my subjects! Do you know how hard I have to work for those grades? Any idea at all?"

Actually, I did know. She was an extremely bright, very pretty and quite popular girl, and really didn't have to put forth much effort whatsoever for her studies, friends or anything else. Alice's wealthier friends even gave her their beautiful clothes after only a couple of wearings. How she managed that I never did discover. But I declined to mention this at present since it would hardly have contributed in any positive fashion.

"Does this have anything to do with this boy Dannie Barrington showing up all of a sudden?" she interjected suspiciously, her eyes narrowing. "Is he really my brother?"

I exhaled then resolutely plodded on.

"When your father died he was apparently still married to Dannie Barrington's mother and not to me, Alice," I said, surprised at how evenly I was able to answer her. "But I wasn't aware of that situation until his death. In fact, I didn't know that they had ever been married at all, although I did know that they… had a child, Dannie, together. Then when Dannie was just a little boy, playing around with a gun, he accidentally shot…"

"So he *is* my brother, then," she interrupted. "Or, half-brother at least. There's another girl in my class who has half brothers and sisters because her mother was actually divorced and then got married again. A nasty, low business to be sure. No one wants to have anything to do with her, of course. That's just terrific for me to find out now."

Alice was far better informed about these kinds of matters at the tender young age of 13 than I certainly had been at that age. I held my breath wondering just how far she might go with this. Despite my husband's duplicity, I had managed to keep my married name and my daughter's and my honor due to the fact that the court proceedings at the time of the reading of John's will had backed up the fact that during the entire time of our marriage I had indeed believed I was his legal wife.

"Why didn't you ever tell me about any of this before? About Dannie Barrington, I mean, not about your stupid idea to move down to the loony land of alligators," she scowled.

"I don't know, Alice," I replied, the exasperation I usually managed to hide from her pushing through. "I can't answer that question. Maybe I just hoped that you would never have to know about any of it. As for moving to New Orleans now it just seems like a good place for us to pick up and sort of start over. I'm hoping maybe to work towards getting a position at the French Opera House."

"Doing what, for heaven's sake? I think you're a little old to suddenly become an *étoile* at the opera even though you and the prize pupil were always dueting about like crazy shrieking magpies," she stated, morosely slumping down even further in her chair.

"I've heard that they're actively looking to hire seamstresses for costume construction and alterations, as well as women to tutor children who are in the casts or minding young children whose parents are in the casts," I replied evenly. "The pay can be erratic at the start, but I hope I can manage to make enough for us to live on if they'll hire me. I think that I'm qualified at any rate." Actually, this information had been in a small article I had seen in a year-old fashion magazine even before Zuma and Emma had left for Reserve. I really had no idea how extensive the need or how overwhelming the qualifications for any of these services might actually be. "And, if that doesn't work out, I should be able to find something else with Zuma's help."

"Well, it's too bad you can't cook like her," Alice sighed. "This stew tastes like old boots."

Look for "Muskrat Ramble" in Spring 2021!

About the Author

A graduate from the Jordan College of Music at Butler University in Indianapolis, IN, Mim Eichmann has found that her creative journey has taken her down many exciting, interwoven pathways. For well over two decades she was primarily known in the Chicago area as the artistic director/choreographer for Midwest Ballet Theatre, bringing full-length professional ballet performances to thousands of dance lovers annually. A desire to become involved again in the folk music world brought about the creation of her acoustic quartet Trillium, now in its 15th year, which performs throughout the Midwest and has released four cds. Among many varied music avenues she's written the lyrics and music for two award-winning original children's cds and occasionally schedules children's music and movement concerts.

Her short story *"Slomp"* won first place in the 2018 Short-Edition/Public Library Association's "Set Stories Free" Competition and she was also a fiction finalist in the 2019 San Francisco Writer's Conference Contest. *"A Sparrow Alone"* is her first novel. Please take a moment to visit her author website at www.mimeichmann.com.

Author photo by Don Box; Don Box Photography

Bibliography

"A Sparrow Alone" deals with the choices, nurturing and support of women for one another, set against the historic background of emerging social ambiguity of the late 19th century. A bibliography of non-fiction books, women's journals and diaries which have influenced this novel includes:

Bird, Isabella L. *"A Lady's Life in the Rocky Mountains"* University of Oklahoma Press, Norman, OK, 1960

Brands, H. W. *"The Reckless Decade – America in the 1890s"* The University of Chicago Press, Chicago, IL, 1995

Brown, Dee *"Wondrous Times on the Frontier"* August House Publishers, Little Rock, Arkansas, 1991

Cunningham, Chet *"Cripple Creek Bonanza"* Wordware Publishing, Inc, Plano TX, 1996

Dorset, Phyllis Flanders *"The New Eldorado – The Story of Colorado's Gold and Silver Rushes"* Simon and Schuster, Inc. New York, 1970

Draper, Fanny McClurg (edited by Arthur Gibbs Draper) *"My Ever Dear Charlie – Letters Home from the Dakota Territory"* The Globe Pequot Press, Guilford, Connecticut, 2006

Enss, Chris *"Pistol Packin' Madams – True Stories of Notorious Women of the Old West"* The Globe Pequot Press, Guilford, Connecticut, 2006

Enss, Chris *"The Doctor Wore Petticoats – Women Physicians of the Old West"* The Globe Pequot Press, Guilford, Connecticut, 2006

Enss, Chris *"The Lady Was a Gambler"* The Globe Pequot Press, Guilford, Connecticut, 2008

Fisk, Elizabeth Chester (edited by Rex C. Myers) *"Lizzie – The Letters of Elizabeth Chester Fisk, 1864-1893"* Mountain Press Publishing Company, Montana, 1989

French, Emily (edited by Janet Lecompte) *"Emily – The Diary of a Hard-worked Woman"* University of Nebraska Press, Lincoln, NE, 1987

Hickman, Katie *"Courtesans – Money, Sex and Fame in the Nineteenth Century"* HarperCollins Publishers, Great Britain, 2003

Jameson, Elizabeth *"All That Glitters – Class, Conflict, and Community in Cripple Creek"* University of Illinois, Urbana, IL, 1998

Lee, Mabel Barbee *"Cripple Creek Days"* Doubleday & Co, Garden City, NY, 1958

304

Lucy, Donna M. *"Archie and Amelie – Love and Madness in the Gilded Age"* Three Rivers Press, New York, 2006

Marcy, Randolph B., Captain, U.S. Army *"The Prairie Traveler – The Bestselling Classic Handbook for America's Pioneers"* Berkley Publishing Group, New York, first published in 1859

Monahan, Sherry *"The Wicked West ~ Boozers, Cruisers, Gamblers, and more"* Rio Nuevo Publishers, Tucson, AZ, 2005

Morgan, Lael *"Good Time Girls of the Alaska-Yukon Gold Rush"* Epicenter Press, Alaska, 1999

Moynihan, Ruth B, Susan Armitage, and Christiane Fischer Dichamp, editors *"So Much to Be Done – Women Settlers on the Mining and Ranching Frontier"* University of Nebraska press, Lincoln, NE, 1990

Murphy, Claire Rudolf and Jane G. Haigh *"Gold Rush Women"* Alaska Northwest Books, Portland, OR, 1997

Peavy, Linda and Ursula Smith *"Pioneer Women – The Lives of Women on the Frontier"* University of Oklahoma Press, Norman, OK, 1998

Pender, Rose *"A Lady's Experiences in the Wild West in 1883"* University of Nebraska Press, Lincoln, NE, 1978 (original printing 1888)

Read, June Willson *"Frontier Madam – The Life of Dell Burke, Lady of Lusk"* The Globe Pequot Press, Guilford, Connecticut, 2008

Reese, Linda Williams *"Women of Oklahoma 1890-1920"* University of Oklahoma Press, Norman, OK, 1997

Rutter, Michael *"Boudoirs to Brothels – The Intimate World of Wild West Women"* Farcountry Press, Helena, MT, 2014

Sanford, Mollie Dorsey (journal) *"Mollie – The Journal of Mollie Dorsey Sanford in Nebraska and Colorado Territories 1857-1866"* University of Nebraska Press, Lincoln NE, 1959

Schlissel, Lillian *"Women's Diaries of the Westward Journey"* Schocken Books, New York, 1982

Schlissel, Lillian, Byrd Gibbens, and Elizabeth Hampsten *"Far from Home – Families of the Westward Journey"* University of Nebraska Press, Lincoln, NE, 1989

Schlissel, Lillian and Catherine Lavender *"The Western Women's Reader – The Remarkable Writings of Women Who Shaped the American West, Spanning 300 Years"* HarperCollins Books, New York, 2000

Seagraves, Anne *"Soiled Doves – Prostitution in the Early West"* Wesanne Publications, Hayden, Idaho, 1994

Stewart, Elinore Pruitt *"Letters of a Woman Homesteader"* University of Nebraska Press, Lincoln, NE, 1961

Stratton, Joanna L. *"Pioneer Women – Voices From the Kansas Frontier"* Simon and Schuster, New York, 1981

Udall, Stewart L. *"The Forgotten Founders – Rethinking the history of the Old West"* Island Press, Washington, D.C., 2002

Waters, Frank *"Midas of the Rockies – Biography of Winfield Scott Stratton, Croesus of Cripple Creek"* Swallow Press/Ohio University Press, Athens, OH, 1937

Wyman, Mark *"Hard Rock Epic – Western Miners and the Industrial Revolution, 1860-1910"* University of California Press, Berkeley, California, 1979

Made in the USA
Monee, IL
23 July 2020